~~~
£7.99
~~~


THE WOODEN QUEEN

SEBASTYEN DUGAS

URBANUM
ÉDITION

GET TWO FREE BOOKS

Get two free short novels by the same author. You will discover two other literary styles of the author by reading the two books offered on Sébastyen's website.

Download them for free by subscribing to Sébastyen's newsletter by clicking on this link: https://link.sebastyendugas.com/abyfrontlibrary

1

A distressed adolescent girl rushes towards Bellerive Street in Longueuil. She passes through Roland-Therrien Boulevard, desperately seeking to get home despite the horrific images running through her mind. The kind of monstrosity a girl her age should never see.

Beyond measure.

Although she's panicking, Marie-Eve Dansereau runs towards the triplex where she lives. Her long brown hair twirls from left to right, following her strides, whipping her face in the process. She bumps into passerby's as she unintentionally pushes them around. Why don't they get out of the way? Couldn't they see what's going on?

She's unaware of their horrified stare at her blood-stained clothes.

Who is she running away from? No one's chasing her. But her bulging eyes reddened by tears don't lie. She's fleeing from something awful. Her face tensed with fear. She runs as though her life depends on it. She wipes vomit stains from her chin as she carries on with her wide, powerful strides that make her schoolgirl skirt twirl.

It feels like she's in a movie. A scary movie. What she saw was unreal. And yet it's not. It's hard to tell right from wrong, but even if she'd rather be wrong, it's all true. She's on autopilot.

Her heart is beating so fast that she's worried it may burst off her chest before she reaches her destination. The warm gentle wind rubs her face, as a bicycle emerges in front of her, forcing her to swerve sharply to her right towards a car braking just in time. She puts both hands on the hood, as if she could stop it. She looks at the driver for a few seconds, then goes off again. She doesn't hear the cyclist asking her if she needs help. She turns left on Bellerive, replaying the horrible images over and over in her head. The loud echo; the sharp blast of air in her hair, the crowd screaming, Ariane lying in a sea of blood, Marie-Eve kneeling to help her up, and the dreadful sight of her shattered head practically ripped off from her body.

Marie-Eve got up, screaming with horror. Vomiting as she took a few steps back, while everyone else was rushing away. Her first instinct was to flee the scene. To get help. She crashes hard on the ground, her feet entangled in a tree branch lying on the pavement. She feels no pain despite her gashed elbow and the scraping on her knee. Adrenaline is pumping through her veins. Marie-Eve gets up and starts running again.

Only a few more meters, and she'll be there. The more she moves closer to her home, the clearer the image of Ariane shows up in her mind. Heartbreaking. They've been insepa-rable since elementary school. Their parents know each other and are close friends. Ariane's mother is like a second mother to Marie-Eve. She has spent so much time with them she knows them better than some in her own family.

Ariane was her exact opposite. So much so that one was envious of the other's strengths. They complemented each other wonderfully. Ariane was the beautiful girl all the boys wanted as a girlfriend, and all the girls wanted as a friend. Average student, her interpersonal skills were undeniable. Extroverted, she was involved in extracurricular activities.

As for Marie-Eve, she was more reserved, pretty but more subtle than Ariane, or at least she wasn't as striking. Top of her class, often nominated for school's awards, she's a two-time winner of the Governor's Award because of her GPA. A self-confessed introvert, she likes libraries more than nightclubs, books more than parties, and boy band posters more than actual boys at her school.

Ariane forced her out of her comfort zone, to mingle with others. Marie-Eve instilled a rigor in her that was unnatural to her. Ariane took notes on how to structure her study, on how Marie-Eve prepared for exams. She gave Ariane tips such as focusing on lessons objectives to figure out which subjects she should concentrate on. But it's all over now.

Marie-Eve left Ariane behind, alone, drenched in her own blood. She feels guilty about it. But it was impossible for her to cope with the horrifying image of her mutilated body. She reacted instinctively. I must alert someone, call an ambulance, the police, someone to take care of her. Even though she knows it's too late. She has no idea that several witnesses have already taken care of that. 9-1-1 has been swarmed by dozens of witnesses pressing for immediate help.

Out of breath, Marie-Eve climbs the main staircase towards Ariane's parents' floor. She stumbled on the last step and crashed against the Légaré's front door. She kneels down and strikes the white wooden door as hard as she can.

"Madeleine, it's Ariane. Quick, it's Ariane."

As Madeleine Légaré opens the door, Marie-Eve collapses, her entire body shaking. Madeleine doesn't understand a word the young girl says. She makes no sense. Then she gets it. The girl screams out her daughter's name again and again.

. . .

Two kilometers from there, the assassin quietly puts a briefcase and a crowbar back in the trunk of his black BMW. He exits the Palladium's rocky parking towards Fernand-Lafontaine Street. He parks a couple of kilometers further behind a convenience store, near a garbage container. He throws his gloves and boots out, puts on sneakers and calmly enters the store to buy a Heineken. Always a Heineken to celebrate the completion of one of his mission's milestone.

He drives on and passes six police cars heading at top speed in the opposite direction, the shrill sound of sirens blasting out in the sky. He watches them in the rearview mirror to make sure they didn't turn back to chase him, then smiles as they disappear at the horizon. The road is empty. As if he were the only person left in the world. As if life was bowing to him, allowing him to leave like some kind of hero in a vintage western movie. The thrill is slowly fading out, and he gets cooler. Everything went exactly as planned. To a tee.

A group of schoolchildren walks on the sidewalk to his right, smiling, unaware of the drama that has just unfolded. He feels nothing particular as he sees young girls wearing the same schoolgirl skirt as his victim. Why would he? He's on a mission, he's at war. He signals to turn left and patiently waits for the streetlight to change. He cranks up the volume on his radio and savor every note from Beethoven's Fur Elise. He closes his eyes for a few seconds and takes a deep breath. Then he slowly exhales. He has rarely felt better.

Felt this close to her.

He opens his eyes and relives what he saw through his rifle scope. Two girls walking side by side, the young blond girl's head blowing off, her body tossed towards the boulevard's central platform. He sees the panic-stricken crowd fleeing in all directions like frantic ants. A masterful shot. A masterpiece.

By tomorrow, media will demonize him. The public will

seek revenge. They'll want to lynch him. But they must agree that it was an incredible shot. The work of an outstanding marksman. He feels tremendous pride as the light turns green.

2

Abygaelle Jensen would have liked to get a good night of sleep the day before her debut as a new detective sergeant at the homicide squad, but she couldn't. As always when she feels worried, her brain was firing at full blast all night long.

Anxious, she envisioned the worst for today. She's now convinced that she wouldn't be proficient for this job. She knows nothing about it other than that she's supposed to put murderers behind bars.

Sitting on the corner of her bed wearing a white tank top and a black thong, she bitterly regrets her decision. What was she thinking when she agreed to this new challenge? What exactly is she trying to prove? And more importantly, to whom?

Like every time she is lost in thought, she distractedly rubs the swollen scars on her forearms, remnants of a troubled and distant past.

She should have stayed in the vice squad. She was in full control of her cases and of her abilities. This is the department she worked for since the beginning of her career.

After over ten years of service, it took one case, one case too many, to be the final straw and for her to apply at this new position on the spur of the moment.

Once the bitterness had subsided, she was less enthusiastic about all this, but since she thought that they would not choose her, she didn't pull back from the process, sucked in by an unrelenting force. Even though the stages of the process of the interview went on and the psychometric tests added up, she carried on, as if her mind was unwillingly deciding to drag her into the unknown.To put her at risk.

Admittedly, as the years rushed by, she felt more and more trapped in a dreadful vicious circle. When she needed to take on another abused child case, she used all her might to put on the strongest evidence, seeing images and elements no one should ever see. Hearing stories that haunted her for days, asking innocent children to point at a doll to show where their father or uncle touched them.

Then the perpetrators would walk away with sentences that are immeasurably lighter to serve in the community or stay in jail for a far too short a period.

She just could not cope with it anymore.

She wanted to be a police officer to work on sexual assaults, especially those involving children. She wanted to make a difference, to help the victims and to put the perpetrators away.

To help those whose souls are deeply scarred, those who are forever disgraced.

You are hurt deep in your soul when you are sexually abused. It rips your innocence in shred as you are dragged into a world entirely different from the one you knew.

A world where men can be bloodthirsty, flesh-eating beasts. Willing to do anything to indulge their worst instincts.

You're no longer a shade of the one you used to be, just a disembodied copy of yourself. Of what you were before.

Before all this.

Abygaelle knows it too well. She knows how the victims

feel. She would like to know how to stop abuse before it happened, instead of after the fact. When it's too late. But that's the nature of the beast. She believed that convicting these sexual predator scum would help her heal her own wounds.

Work therapy.

But while she's content to pin these bastards down, it never quite makes up for the damage that's inside her.

In the past, one would comfort themselves with the idea that prisoners, which are not sympathetic to sexual abusers, would take care of them in their own way. But now it's just folklore. Now, these assholes are isolated from other inmates in separate areas for their protection.

That's what's really pissing her off. All the protection. All the support to help criminals while the victims have to heal themselves on their own.

Abygaelle believes in rehabilitation, but she finds it hard to tolerate the inequality of the means used to rehabilitate criminals versus helping victims.

All the money and effort spent on desperate cases, career criminals, incurable felons who will never rehabilitate.

Sick people who will relapse as soon as they set foot outside, like the scumbag who murdered a young prostitute in a Quebec City hotel.

Deep in her thoughts, Abygaelle enjoys the warm shower water surrounding her slender body. She mechanically combed her hair, using repetitive gestures in the same order as usual. The gigantic dark circles under her emerald eyes do not make her look good. Her eyes have no shine and her features are drawn.

After placing her flat iron back in the dresser drawer, Abygaelle studies her reflection for several seconds, motionless, as if her appearance would improve miraculously.

Since the beginning of her career, she hasn't used too much make-up because she doesn't want her supermodel look to impair her credibility. While she's not deliberately making herself ugly, she goes on as natural as possible, only very subtle improvement here and there. Despite men's interest, she acts like she doesn't have a clue, so that people can focus on her talent and her performance instead of her looks.

Anyway, she's far too complicated and troubled to think about a healthy relationship.

She's been single for three years already, she has had very few lovers. Only inconsequential one-night stands.

She needs to work on herself, reconstruct herself once and for all.

Love herself before she can love someone. It's not a foregone conclusion. There's a long and perilous road ahead.

Abygaelle has been standing there paralyzed at the entrance leading to the homicide squad's office for about three minutes. With her cardboard box containing her belongings in her hands, she has no idea what to do next.

Should she just walk in and sit at the first available desk in the room, or did they already assigned her a place? The other option is to wait until someone notices her and tells her where to go. It's amazing how all the offices look the same in this precinct. Here too, the carpet was probably changed for the last time in 1981. They bought the binders in a batch when they build the place. They look the same as in the vice squad. Just as old and worn out. In addition to the remnants of disconnected fax machines resting on top of binders. The cupboard separators are also the same. She's wondering if it's deliberate. If it made to ease the integration of staff working across departments.

As always when she has insomnia, she feels as if she's not really there, like an out-of-body experience. This is not ideal when you begin a new challenge. She may be nervous to the core, but if she's honest with herself, she knows that at thirty-five; she was up for a new test.

Especially since killers face stiffer prison sentences in homicides. Life sentences. She can soothe herself knowing that. She's likely to be less disappointed than she was in Vice.

Either way, it's too late to back down. She won't run away with her cardboard box in her hands. It would be ridiculous. At some point, you need to let go to your fate. Trust your instincts, which have served you so well in the past.

As a hopeless introvert, Abygaelle has to drag herself to blend with a new group. She only feels comfortable after she has observed people extensively, finding out who holds what rank in the department's social hierarchy, and only then does she take her own place.

She's not the kind of person to show up authoritatively somewhere, gun blazing, faking self-confidence.

She made that mistake early in her career, trying to prove herself as a woman in a man's world, but it sounded so phony that she made a fool of herself. She knows what she's worth; she knows what she is capable of, at least as far as her work is concerned. She doesn't have to climb up on a desk and shout it out to the world.

She's said to be endearing and an excellent teammate, always ready to help. Her colleagues will quickly embrace her, they always did. So why force things?

"Abygaelle? Abygaelle Jensen?"

She's not sure if she really heard her name or if she's delirious, but since everyone is looking at her and a grey-haired man is waving at her across the room, she quickly understands.

"Yes?" she says with a hesitant voice.

"Charles Picard, welcome aboard. Come into my office."

Picard goes back into his office in a nervous pace. His ruffled grey hair and wrinkled shirt suggest he has been sleeping in his office for the last three weeks. Probably a workaholic who has put all his eggs in his career basket.

Abygaelle hates attracting attention. She must be flushed

right now. Only thing missing is a huge luminescent spotlight with a big pink neon arrow pointing at her. No one even noticed her before, but now all eyes are on her. Some look at her selflessly, while others whisper to each other and giggle.

She wants to sink under the old carpet beneath her.

She now has to walk to her new boss's office, doing her best not to look like a complete idiot. Focus on putting one foot in front of the other and looking straight ahead.

Don't drop the box. Don't stumble.

She tries to look as graceful as possible under the circumstances, but she feels like she has the elegance of an ostrich. As if she can't remember how to walk properly. She moves through a silence that is so thick, a knife could cut it. Only the phones rings fill the silence.

Some folks have gone back to what they were doing, but a large contingent of them keeps looking at her, as if they were waiting for disaster to happen. As if it was the first time they had seen an ostrich-liked woman walking so slowly.

Her vision is so blurry that she blinks strongly to regain focus. She looks like she's walking through a muddy pool so much she doesn't feel like she's making any progress. Or maybe it's Picard's office that's moving away from her?

Either way, she's afraid she'll never make it to her destination.

Picard is on the phone as she finally arrives to his office.

She doesn't take offense at his lack of tact. He seems overwhelmed. He signals her to sit down with an energetic hand gesture whilst carrying on with his call.

Abygaelle goes in and puts her box on the chair next to her. She sits in a vacant chair and crosses her legs. She wears her fetish navy blue pants that she keeps for special occasions. She has put on her favourite white shirt, loosening up the top button to display a silver necklace with the effigy of a Madonna which her grandmother gave her shortly before her death.

Her good luck charm.

Charles Picard is one of those people who threaten to die of a heart attack at any moment. Aby can feel his stress from across the desk, and sees his reddish face, a sign of hypertension. He speaks bluntly in short, dry sentences. His non-verbal language is explicit. He reacts to everything the other person says by tensing his face, frowning and pursing his lips. He gestures even if his interlocutor can't see him, and he speaks loudly at a rapid pace.

In a large brown shelf behind are frames with pictures of him with celebrities. They show Picard with what Aby presumes to be his wife. Picard with his children, Picard with Guy Lafleur, Picard in a Formula One car, Picard—

"Sorry, minor emergency," he says after hanging up.

Despite his gruff facade, he seems like a nice guy. Aby feels like he's the type of man who's tough but fair. The kind of person who will be on your side and support you as long as you do your best, and deliver the goods.

Perfect for Aby. She's always bringing her best, anyway.

"So let me officially welcome you among us," Picard says. "I'm sure your experience in vice will help us. Fresh blood, new vision, an outside eye, it can only be beneficial. Also, Roland Michaud had nothing but good things to say about you. I have enormous respect for him and his judgment."

Roland Michaud.

The mention of her ex-boss's name is heartbreaking. More than a boss, he was his mentor. He believed in her from the very first moments so much that it quickly made her feel confident. He supported her in tough times and gave her good advice. A great boss, but also a friend. The father she never had. She had wept so much the night before her announcement about her decision. He was aware of the process, but she was downplaying her interest about the move. Abygaelle said she was only doing it to confirm her credibility within the organization, to validate what people thought of her.

"Of course they'll be interested, Aby, come on. You're an excellent candidate. Stop underestimating yourself like that. You have every right to do something else. I support you."

His voice was soothing and composed. It calmed her down when she was nervous. Roland is her idol, both as a manager and as an individual. She doesn't see any flaws in him. He had reassured her he wasn't going anywhere. He was just on the floor below her. It wasn't like they'd never see each other again.

"I love Mr. Michaud," she said, restraining her tears the best she could. "He has helped me a lot throughout my career."

"So do I," Picard retorted, standing up. "Come, I'll introduce you to the team and show you your desk. You'll see, we're a friendly bunch."

Aby follows him as he introduces her to each of the investigators, but she doesn't catch any names. She can't concentrate. She'd just want to sit at her desk and unpack her box, take the time to digest it all. Let's just get all this formalities over with and move on.

Her office neighbor's is Murielle Bouchard. She graces her with a smile that brings the pressure down. She looks like a sweet little aunt. Small but strong, with short white hair cleverly tousled, mocking eyes that are soft and tough at the same time. They're going to get along well, that's for sure.

Aby relaxes a little as she unpacks her box and settles down. Picard quickly returned to his office when he heard his phone rang. Aby plans to take a few days to settle in, get used to her new role, and learn the basics of the job.

Fate will decide otherwise.

3

Monique Primeau is standing in front of the kitchen pantry as though waiting for a divine revelation that won't come. Short of an idea, she calls out to her husband who is sitting at the kitchen table.

"What do you want for dinner, Raymond? I have no idea."

Focused on his task, he takes a few seconds for him to understand the question at hand, and to ponder a sensible answer. Not only does he have no idea, he doesn't care. He just wants to get back to what he was doing.

"I don't know, a roast beef?" he mumbles, trying to get out of it.

"It takes too much time."

"Well, anything else then, pasta?"

A retired army veteran, Raymond Primeau loves to piece model cars together. Since he can't afford luxury cars in real life, he collects miniature versions of them. For him, working on these miniature cars takes a great deal of precision and concentration, which brings him in his comfort zone. He sees himself as an intellectual. In the army, he was recognized as an accomplished strategist. He was more interested in carrying out plans than a gun.

The red 1968 Maserati Mistral he holds in his hands is a wonderful addition to an already well-stocked vintage car collection. He has a soft spot for Italian cars and is happy to work on the colouring of this dream car.

He keeps his work on display in a large glass shelf in the basement where he can show it to anyone who shows any interest. He is more than happy to display his vast knowledge of each model. He can talk for hours about car history, their technical and aesthetic attributes. Unfortunately for him, few people share his passion other than members of the Facebook group he has created with another fellow car enthusiast. There are almost three hundred of them enjoying discussing, posting photos of their work and congratulating each other on a job well done.

The thrill he gets by showing a new piece of work is intoxicating. So much so that if few people praise his work, he questions himself and sleeps poorly the following days.

Monique boils the water. She's married to Raymond since forty-one years. They had a boy and a girl, but lost them both, so to speak.

William has exiled to London to pursue a prestigious position in finance. Monique never really understood what he does for a living, but he makes a lot of money. She's glad for him. As long as he's happy, that's all that matters. William is close to his mother, but not so much to his father. The two have had many conflicts over the years she doesn't understand. She can't accept that a father and son who've been so close all their lives don't talk to each other anymore. That they can't work through their issues.

She got no answers to her questions. Both remain vague about their dispute. Raymond claims that it's William who doesn't want to talk to him anymore, but she doesn't consider he's trying very hard to work things out. At least William loves her. He calls her several times a week.

As for Nathalie, well, she's dead.

A suicide. A tragic story.

With her son halfway around the world and her daughter gone, her husband is all Monique has left. She's doing everything in her power to preserve it. Although Raymond is physically present, occasionally going out to do God knows what, his mind is less and less so.

Monique would rather deal with that than lose him altogether. She couldn't bear it.

We're getting married for better or worse, they say. She's not trying to change him anymore.

"Meat sauce is all right?" she shouts from the kitchen.

"That's fine."

She takes a jar filled with spaghetti sauce and walks over to the pot of boiling water to put the pasta in. Every winter, Monique cooks an enormous amount of spaghetti sauce, which she then freezes. The jars contain just enough sauce to feed two people. It's convenient when she doesn't know what to cook.

Raymond has mood swings when he's anxious. Especially since Nathalie's death. He always been a hard-working man who liked to be active, a former military officer with high credibility. He has shut himself off, rarely hanging out with his friends now.

Monique, on the other hand, was happy as a stay-at-home mother. Raymond's time away from home for work didn't bother her, she was independent. She's an orderly woman who likes to have it her way, while Raymond has little interest in the household matters and decisions related to the family. She was in charge, and she loved it. They complemented each other well.

Raymond spent his career in the military from his youth until 2001. He's very disciplined. A quality that appealed to Monique from the start. She liked his boy scout persona, but it came with an introversion that she found hard to deal with. Raymond has a perpetual sad look on his face, collateral of the horrible images forever engraved in his brain.

Vietnam, Kosovo and Rwanda missions, would wear anybody down. But they mean nothing compared to the horror he experienced in his own home. You fight battles all over the world, in hopeless conditions. Strangers put their lives in danger to kill you, but it's in your own house that you experience the ultimate atrocity. The Army drills you up for many things, but not for detaching the body of your young daughter hanging from the garage ceiling.

Monique wishes he would talk more about his feelings. But he doesn't, and he refuses to see professionals of any kind.

It's gotten worse since Nathalie died. He shut himself up even more.

They don't have a lot in common either. Raymond enjoys sports while she's more of a movie buff. Without being misanthropic, he doesn't particularly like to be around people, whereas she loves being amongst friends. She likes to laugh, but she can't remember the last time she heard her husband laughing for real.

She loves him so much. Despite all his shortcomings, despite his taciturn personality. He's a good person. He's always been there for her in good times and bad. He's her rock. He's stigmatized by wars and Nathalie's death, but he's still standing, like a majestic oak tree spreading its branches to protect those he loves.

Nathalie's room has remained intact, just as it was when she last left it on a chilly November day. Nobody dared to touch it. Sometimes, when Raymond is away, Monique sits on her daughter's bed, hugging her favourite teddy bear against her belly. She cries quietly for several minutes, then she pulls herself together and puts the plush toy back next to the others. Then she feels better and can go about her business without needing this for several weeks.

This is her therapy.

She has never shared her routine with her husband. He'd be furious. He'd tell her it's not healthy to dwell in the past. He'd blame her for preserving her pain, but for Monique, it's the only way to keep Nathalie alive, close to her, if only for a few moments. Even if it's in her head. Even if she isn't really there.

When she holds the teddy bear against her belly, she can feel her daughter's energy, just like when she was pregnant. She senses her presence. Like she's never been robbed of her presence. Like none of this ever happened.

She would have been thirty-nine years old today. In November it will be exactly twenty years since she left this world. Nathalie will always be nineteen until the end of time. This is the image that Monique keeps of her.

Nineteen years old, frozen in time. Like a wax sculpture.

The news bulletin is on the living room TV set. As usual, Monique listens distractedly. From where she is, she sees Raymond, who cares neither about what's happening on TV, too consumed by his hobby.

When she hears the name of their town from the newscast, Monique stops draining the pasta and reaches out to hear what it is about. There's been a murder.

" ... the victim is fifteen years old, Ariane Légaré. No witnesses saw what happened. The police are amid a mystery."

Monique brings her hand to her mouth. It's awful, she thinks.

"Can you imagine Raymond? Fifteen years old. My God,

imagine her parents. What kind of monster can do this to such a young girl? It's a sick world we live in."

She's watching Raymond, waiting for an answer or a reaction from him, but he's still focused on his miniature car. But he's not moving.

He looks in the void.

4

Abygaelle is gradually relaxing. The stiffness in her neck decreases as time passes. She finds it easier to fit in than she expected. Her desk neighbors have taken care of her. They ask her questions about her background in Vice squad, what brought her to Homicide, where she's from.

She recognizes a few people for having bumped into them around the building in the last few years, or for working with them on mutual cases.

Her two office neighbors are Murielle Bouchard and Jacques Morris. But he prefers to be called Jack. Abygaelle is fascinated by the pure chemistry between the two friendly detectives.

They are about the same age and have been working together for over two decades. They have a familiarity that's typical of friends who've known each other forever. Aby's afraid it'll be difficult for her to enter their inner circle.

Jack seems to have a quick and explosive temperament in the way he talks, but also a charming gullibility in the way he falls for Murielle's antics.

She is more laid back, but she doesn't have a very long fuse if something bothers her. She's the kind of person who will tell you the cold, hard truth very openly.

Jack is on the heavy side, charming at first glance with a bald patch of white hair and a goatee of the same shade. Piercing and striking blue eyes and a swagger that reminds her of an uncle she liked.

What's strike her about Murielle is that she looks like an artist. A silk scarf around her neck, loose-fitting clothes, a little bohemian and colorful. White bush hair skillfully combed as if she had just gotten out of bed. If you didn't know she was a detective sergeant, you would easily confuse her for a painter or sculptor.

Jack was in the middle of a monologue about how to handle a homicide investigation when a deep voice in the distance interrupts him:

"Rookie!"

Jack and Murielle look at Aby who doesn't immediately realize that she's the rookie in question. She stands up timidly. Picard also shouts to Morris and Bouchard to come down also and then goes back in his office. They quickly make their way over there, followed by Abygaelle.

There has been a murder earlier in the afternoon near Jacques-Rousseau High School. A young girl killed in broad daylight under mysterious circumstances. First responders are on site. It's now up to them to solve this case.

Abygaelle thought she misunderstood when Charles Picard appointed her as lead detective on the investigation. So did Jack.

Only Murielle took it with a grain of salt. They'll work as a team anyway, no matter who's in charge. It's only a matter of having an official contact.

"Is there a problem?" the lieutenant asks as he notices Aby and Jack confused gaze.

Abygaelle nods. She hasn't blinked for several minutes,

totally in shock. She couldn't tell if Picard is smiling or if it's a scowl of impatience. But he's had that look all along, so Aby determine it's his natural expression.

Later, Murielle will confirm that although she specifies that he's very competent, Picard is theatrical and teasing. He's the best boss she's ever had, and she's seen one and another, she swears.

As Jack walks to the service car, he breaks the silence with a chuckle:

"Well, sweetheart, for a starter, that's as good as it gets."

Seeing Abygaelle's tormented face, Murielle gently grabs her shoulder.

"Don't worry, we're here to help you. We'll show you the ropes, but it'll cost you a couple of bottles of wine."

Aby smiles timidly, not convinced it's going to be that easy.

In Picard's office, Detective Sergeant Philippe Bélanger is leaning against the edge of the door, with a broad smile on his face.

"What do you want, Philippe?" Picard says still looking at the the document he reads.

"Come on, boss."

Picard takes off his glasses and drops them on his desk with a hint of exasperation.

"Come on, boss, what?"

"The rookie, are you sure this is a good idea? On her first day?"

"You know very well she's in expert hands with Jack and Murielle. She's not out of police academy either, she has experience. I've heard great things about her. About her poise, her intuition, her composure. Murielle and Jack will fill out the blanks as needed. I'm confident she'll succeed. Then, he says, as for himself, there's nothing like diving into action to see exactly what you're made of."

Bélanger whistles with admiration.

"And I thought you made this decision on a whim."

Picard sticks his authoritative gaze into Bélanger's reminding him he leaves nothing to chance.

On the scene, Abygaelle grasp quickly the severity of the situation: a body in laying in the middle of a boulevard covered with yellow canvas, blood on a concrete parapet. Two ambulances are on the scene along with half a dozen police vehicles. Several onlookers are watching from the outside of the security perimeter outlined by yellow ribbons. Further on, police officers divert traffic to secondary roads. Knowing the area, Abygaelle thinks it must be difficult to get around the boulevard. Horn sounds in the distance speak for themselves.

The game plan is for them to split up to gather information. Abygaelle approaches the police officer guarding the corpse. To her right is the high school where she's so often taken statements from young sex-crime victims.

The huge brown swarm building hasn't changed. Leaning against Edouard-Montpetit College, it sits in the middle of nowhere.

Aby spots the apartment block on the Bruges street, the same as the one she grew up in. She doesn't have wonderful memories of her youth. She has lived through so many things that inspired her to become a cop.

One officer on the scene has been watching her for a few seconds with a stunned look on his face.

"Aby?"

Abygaelle recognizes Patrick David's familiar face.

"Hello Pat, how are you?"

"I'm good, but—what are you doing here?"

She tells him about her choice to leave the vice squad, that it's her first day at homicide and she's inherited the investigation, against all odds.

Aby ran into him several times in her career. Often, she had to have a police escort with her to remove children from abusive families. She loved Patrick's calm and sensitivity. He was second to none in defusing stressful situations.

His presence comforted her. She's well aware that he had a crush on her, but she never opened the door. She doesn't trust herself with men; she doesn't like what she becomes. She needs time.

But she's not entirely impervious to the charm of that tall, dark-haired, blue-eyed hunk.

"You've stumbled onto something tricky," Patrick says. "Not a pretty sight. The victim is young, about fifteen years old. She's a high school student. Look at this."

He lifts the canvas up while two cops position themselves so the crowd can't see the body. Abygaelle is struck by violent nausea and takes a few steps back, covering her mouth with her hand.

It's gruesome.

The victim's head is practically torn off. How is it possible that nobody saw anything? Patrick noticed the distress of his co-worker and gives her some time to come to her senses. He goes on a few minutes later.

"Preliminary analysis suggests that a high-caliber projectile blew her head off. Her body ended up on the ledge right there. According to witnesses, there were many people there at the time of the murder and everyone panicked. Total chaos. No one knows what happened, no one saw the shooter. Several witnesses heard a firecracker-like echo seconds after the killer shot the girl."

"A blast from a distance," says Abygaelle.

Patrick David nods.

"We're sweeping the crime scene thoroughly. Hopefully, we'll find more clues by then. Are you sure you're okay?"

Aby who still has her hand over her mouth is nodding yes. She thanks him and takes a few seconds to get some fresh air before talking to the first witness. She's a little dizzy.

At La Belle Province fast-food joint, just across the boulevard, people claim to have seen the incident from the picnic table where they were seated. They confirm what Patrick David pointed out: the sound of a firecracker like a car muffler exploding, then a commotion. One witness said that a teenage girl with bloody clothes ran past them, totally horrified.

Jack Morris walks up to Aby.

"What do you think?" he asks.

"A shot from a distance," she said, looking to her left. The shot probably came from there, given where the body ended. It's hard to tell if she was the intended target or if they shot her at random. Still, there were a lot of teenagers crossing the boulevard at that time. It's hard to imagine anyone intentionally murdering a teenage girl in the middle of the street.

"You think the shooter fired at random into the crowd?"

"That's a possibility," Aby says. "Except that if that's the case, why did he stop? Why didn't he keep shooting?"

"That rules out a terrorist attack, in my opinion," Jack adds. "Terrorists want to maximize casualties, do as much damage as possible. That's not what we're dealing with here. Unless his gun jammed after his first shot."

"You're right," Abygaelle says. "Incredible as it may seem, there's every sign that the shooter was targeting this girl."

She bites her lower lip like she does every time she thinks. Jack says that he saw no one from the family among the onlookers. The girl's name is Ariane Légaré, and they are trying to reach her immediate family from the information found in the victim's wallet.

The three of them meet two hours later to debrief. They all have the same version from the witnesses, but nothing that would put them on an interesting trail.

One shooter from afar, who then disappeared.

Abygaelle, Jack and Murielle will go over the evidence again tomorrow, once the crime scene analysis is complete.

5

Maxime Fauvette is anxious as he usually is every time he's about to go on a trip. Especially since his children are coming this time, and they are a handful. Maxime is proud of him since he's fulfilling a commitment he made to his kids a few years ago: get them to Disneyworld.

His parents made a similar commitment when he was young, but they never delivered. He remembers the bitter disappointment he felt when he realized they would not keep their word. He vowed not to put his own children through this ordeal. And now they are about to leave for the promised land.

It's the first time they've traveled together as a group of five, and it takes a lot of planning. It's not a problem for Maxime, because he's very organized, he leaves nothing to chance. However, he wonders if he will enjoy the trip, or if he will be tense as he is right now. His back muscles are already sore from the stress.

This week off will be good for him, especially since it comes just before tax season. Then, the hellish pace will start for several weeks at work. Having a logical mind, Maxime has always been fond about numbers. Being an accountant was therefore a perfect fit for him. Everything was planned since he was a child. Mathematics was by far his favorite subject at school. He juggled to study actuarial science, but he opted for accounting.

He's proud of how far he's come and how things have turned out for him. Coming from a very modest background, he had to work for all he has. He followed his career plan to a tee and everything went accordingly. The same goes for his personal life. Actually, it didn't. There's one thing that didn't go as planned. Something he had no control over.

He wanted three kids, a house with a garage, a big yard and an in-ground pool. He wanted a wife he loved and golf at least twice a week. He got all that, but not the way he planned. He loves his wife. But things should've worked out differently.

He's filling out the cast of the perfect accountant. He's tall, thin, with round glasses that make him look like Harry Potter. He wears drab clothes and is not athletic. He's an introvert who suffers from mild obsessive-compulsive disorder. Moreover, he's irritated when he sees the utensils drawer not completely closed. He closes it, complaining to himself. He keeps repeating to his children to close cupboards and drawers tightly and to put everything back in its place.

The mess drives him crazy. His wife urges him to relax, saying that just because he's like that doesn't mean that his children should be like him too.

They have two boys, Anthony, the oldest and Patrick the youngest. In the middle is Nathalie, the apple of his eye. As little as he worries about what might happen to his sons, he's just as scared shitless that something might happen to his daughter. Normal under the circumstances, he thinks. Nevertheless, he tries not to overprotect her, not to asphyxiate her, not to be too sheltering. It's proving very difficult for him to let go.

He's checked the contents of his luggage and the children's

fourteen times now. His wife Laurie tells him to chill. She promises that everything will be okay. She has checked and everything is in there. She's been through the list several times, everything's fine.

Just relax.

Laurie's made her peace with time. She's learned to live with her husband's sometimes unbearable flaws. She knows when she needs to leave him alone, to give him space, and when he needs company. She would like him to care about her feelings too, but that is seldom the case.

Maxime is a bit of an egomaniac, maybe even a narcissist. She feels like she's always making all the efforts to make things right between them, that she's the one who's giving up and that they end up doing what he wants. Sometimes it blows up.

She confronts him and pushes him over. In those moments, Maxime realizes that he's suffocating her, that she too has her say. So he becomes more thoughtful, even giving her unexpected gifts, as if he had understood that he could lose her.

He won't lose her. Laurie loves her family unit far too much to break it up over mood swings. Anyway, it probably wouldn't be any better than anywhere else. Might as well work on what she's got instead of dreaming of something better.

Her life suits her. She works in a hospital as a receptionist; she does stuff with her friends. It satisfies her. She's had no big ambitions. She just wants to be happy.

She knows about her husband's dramatic past. She knows that if things had gone as planned, he wouldn't have married her. To be honest, neither was Maxime her first choice, or at least the one she thought she would end up with as an adult. He's not her first love either.

Except that Maxime has never gotten over his, despite what he says. Largely because of the way it ended.

Laurie understands, although she hopes that one day he'll

move on, that he'll stop carrying this resentment with him. She'd want him one hundred percent for herself.

To stop fighting a ghost.

"Kids, stop playing, we're leaving. Has everyone had their pee-pee?"

Maxime's thunderous voice took Laurie out of her thoughts. Nathalie appears in the door frame and smiles at her. Laurie agreed to name her Nathalie instead of Marie-Eve, the name she favoured. Because it was important to Maxime, because she hoped it would help him forget, that it would help him accept the unthinkable.

She was probably naïve.

Today, she doesn't regret having made that concession. She wouldn't see her daughter by any other name.

"What is it, sweetheart?"

The little girl's wiggling her feet.

"I can't find Boubou."

Boubou, her favorite stuffed rabbit that her maternal grandfather gave her before he died.

"He can't be very far. Come on, I'll help you find him."

In the master bedroom, Maxim is going through the list one last time. He has everything. The passports are in a plastic envelope with all the other travel documents. He has enough clothes, his sunglasses are in his jacket pocket and he has his favourite baseball cap on his head.

On the plane, Laurie will sit with the two boys in a three-seat row, while Maxime and Nathalie will be right behind them. This is Patrick and Nathalie's first trip and Anthony's second, but he must not remember the first one, as he was only two years old.

Maxime is concerned to travel with children aged three, five and nine. He's not worried about Anthony, he'll have his tablet and his games, but the other two have trouble sitting still for five minutes under normal circumstances, so imagine spending over three hours on a plane. He's apprehensive about this trip. He hopes for sympathetic and patient cabin neighbors. He hates being judged by people who don't tolerate children who talk too loudly or kick seats.

Since he has double-checked everything several times, he's confident enough that everything is there to close everyone's suitcases. He doesn't want to find out they forgot something once they are at the airport, or worse, in Orlando. Airport shops are too happy to take advantage of the people sloppiness and sell them items two to three times the normal price. Laurie would tell him it's not the end of the world if they forget something, but as an astute accountant, it makes him angry to overpay for stuff he already owns.

The weather's fickle in Florida this time of year. It can be very hot one day and very chilly the next. It can be sunny and suddenly rainy, and then the blue sky reappears an hour later. You need clothing for every occasion. Maxime refuses to pay a surcharge for overweight suitcases, so everything is weighed and reweighed.

Once the luggages are in the car, he curses that nobody has followed him. He goes back inside immediately.

"Come on, everybody, we're going to be late. Hurry," he shouts.

His wife appears slowly in front of him in the hallway.

"Keep your voice down, Max. We're on our way."

"I'll wait in the car," he says as he goes back outside.

He loves his children, but none have inherited his awareness to detail, his precision. This is normal since they are still young, but it seems to him he was already pretty meticulous in their age. They're as messy as their mother, and that irritates him terribly.

That said, he envies Laurie's free and bohemian spirit. More relaxed, less obsessed with small stuff. She deals with things as they arrive.

He would like her to be more organized, less frivolous. The two have a long way to go to meet somewhere in the middle. He's the one who keeps coming back behind everyone to close the doors, turn off lights, and align the shoes in order in the lobby.

He honks at them. His irritation is dangerously close to the level that makes him unpleasant to everyone around. It's not what he wants, but it's visceral.

"What are they doing for the love of God?"

He breathes a sigh of relief at the sight of his three children jumping out of the house, even though Laurie is glaring at him furiously.

They can finally leave.

6

Abygaelle has read Ariane Légaré's autopsy report three times. The images of the teenage girl's mutilated body still haunt her. Murielle Bouchard has read it as well. The sniper theory is gaining ground. The girl's head exploded at the impact of the bullet. The shot came from the left in a downward trajectory. The bullet struck the girl above the left ear.

A perfect shot.

The coroner said the incredible amount of damage caused by the projectile puzzled him. He has seen many victims killed by large caliber projectiles in his career, but rarely has he seen a bullet do so much ravage. Looking at the wounds, Abygaelle is troubled by the sheer violence of the attack. At least the girl didn't suffer, she died instantly. This inexplicable act upset Aby and her two colleagues.

"Are you all right?" Murielle asks.

Aby nods and reads the report over again.

"I can't wait to see the ballistics report," Jack says.

"I've got it."

Charles Picard walks into the room in that very moment, proudly brandishing a dossier. He motioned them to follow him to his office. He reads the document aloud, quickly skipping over the less relevant information.

"The bullet is 7.62 x 54 mm."

It startles Jack.

"That's a Russian bullet, isn't it?"

"Exactly."

The answer comes from a voice behind them. Picard takes care of the introductions. Michel Cloutier is a retired ballistics expert, hired as a consultant when needed. He sits down next to Jack.

"Impressive Mr. Morris. And if you're thinking of a sniper, what would be your hypothesis about what weapon he used?"

Jack rolls his eyes.

"I don't play guessing games, Cloutier," he says to cover up his ignorance.

The expert moves on.

"The 7.62 x 54 mm bullets have been around for more than a hundred years, since the end of the 19th century to be precise. They are still used nowadays, mainly because of their great ballistic performance. It's a heavy bullet that enables accurate shooting from a great distance."

"How far?" Abygaelle asks.

"Up to six hundred meters."

"Perfect," Jack says, "all we need to do now is circumscribe a six hundred meter perimeter, and that's it."

Disregarding the detective's sarcasm, Michel Cloutier carries on.

"Only one sniper's rifle uses this caliber today."

"The Kalashnikov."

Cloutier smiles condescendingly.

"I said a sniper rifle, Mr. Morris, not a machine gun."

Murielle laughs.

"The sniper rifle known to fire this caliber is an SVD, or a Dragunov if you like," Cloutier says. "Even though it's old, this rifle is still being manufactured. It's very easy to service, and it's extremely reliable. On the other hand, it's rather unusual to find them in North America. It's widespread in developing countries, especially to weaponize militias."

Aby is not sure how this applies to the investigation, but no information is dispensable at this stage.

Picard asks Murielle what she thinks about this. The autopsy report, the Russian bullet, the Dragunov.

"From the little that we have, I would guess the killer is someone in the girl's immediate circle. A family member, perhaps. We should dig deeper, find something that could give us a clue. A relative with a background as a sniper or a soldier."

"Very good, Mrs. Bouchard," Cloutier says in an admiring tone.

Murielle looks at Jack with a mocking smile. Picard and him agree. Aby also, but she's not one to jump to conclusions on assumptions. She is cautious by nature, and all this is quite slim.

"So we need to get a record of Dragunov's owners out quickly," Charles Picard says.

"That's fine, provided the killer didn't get the rifle from the black market," Cloutier says.

Jack responds that the gun registry can't be dismissed out of hand, however. Not all criminals are smart. He's seen proof of that more than once. Picard gets up from his desk and strolls towards the window to his right, hands clasped behind his back. He looks out across the park as usual when he needs to think. The heavy silence in his office emphasizes the gravity of the situation. After a few minutes, Picard sighs and turns to face the group.

"We have to quickly figure out what to do next. It's been over forty-eight hours since the murder happened, and we still have no clue of who this lunatic is. Even worse, we don't even know if he acted alone or if there were several killers, or accomplices. Terrorists perhaps? A premeditated crime? Was Ariane's targeted or was she killed randomly? The press is asking more and more questions. The pressure is growing. I'm going to need answers sooner rather than later."

Abygaelle refrains from saying they think exactly the same thing. She just nod in agreement. Michel Cloutier looks at them, happy not to be in their shoes. Picard's urge to find a lead irritates Abygaelle, as if they weren't already doing everything in their might to get one. What does he think, that they are wasting their time?

Charles Picard addresses her directly.

"Aby, it's time to show us what you've got. This is your moment."

She shakes her head, moaning inwardly. She could have done without this unnecessary pressure.

"We'll get to work, Mr. Picard," she says with much less confidence than she would have liked, and walks out of the office.

Everyone follows, except for Murielle who remains seated, lost in her thoughts. Picard sits down as well.

"What do you think, Murielle?"

She pouts and shrugs.

"No idea. Let's do as we always do. Investigate relatives, go through the clues over and over again, see what the crime scene tells us, and go from there."

"Excellent," the lieutenant says. He puts his glasses back on and grabs a document, showing that the conversation is over.

Murielle leaves the office.

7

Stephane Ranger hasn't slept for the last two days. He can't calm down his destructive urges despite many calls to Annie, his sponsor from Narcotics Anonymous.

Usually, he's encouraging her to hold out, not to give in, to stay strong. He tells her to take it "one day at a time" as a word of the gospel. He helps her not to fall into drugs orgies over some guy she fell madly in love with, and who treats her like trash. But this time he needs her to be there for him.

The thing he can't admit to her is that at the very moment he's talking to her, at the same time he's begging her for help, he's standing outside a triplex he knows too well.

This triplex is the root of his suffering. He has walked a thousand times from his car to to his drug dealer's white glass door. Each time, he wished it was the last time he would ever make that trip. And lately, it was the case. Normally, he wouldn't even go down that street for fear that the sight of that building would light an unwanted flame in him.

But today is not a normal time.

His demons will prevail over his will, he can feel it. He

doesn't have the strength to cope with Ariane's death. He's incapable of handling the great pain biting through his heart. This devastating and numbing pain that cripples his limbs and gives him a stabbing headache. He listens to what Annie tells him, tries to find the means to start his car's engine and leave. But he knows he won't.

He lost before it ever began.

The demons destroy everything in their path, leaving behind only devastation and despair. Only regret and suffering.

"Remember the Serenity Prayer," Annie told him. "You must accept what you can't control."

She's no fool, she knows why he's slipping up. She knew it the moment someone killed his niece. There's a limit to willpower. A limit to what you can go through. She would have liked to find the words to persuade him not to go for it, not to go through with it. But it didn't work this time.

The Serenity Prayer was certainly not written by someone who had just lost a loved one, their life cruelly snatched from them by a mad killer. Stephane thought it would have been easier if she had died in a car accident. It would have torn his heart out, of course, but at least he would take comfort in knowing that it was by sheer bad luck, that she was in the wrong place at the wrong time.

Just the opposite of what is happening now. He is convinced that she was deliberately targeted. A fifteen-year-old girl murdered like one kills high-ranking Mafia officers, like one shoots a general in wartime.

It makes little sense.

He looses everything without having the power to do anything about it. His sister Madeleine is in a catatonic state in the hospital. His nephew Marco cries incessantly, and his brother-in-law Jacques has shut himself up in a worse than usual silence. If they find out he has given in to his demons, he's no better than dead. Madeleine has warned him several times that she won't tolerate another lapse in his behavior. She wants him in their lives only with a cool head. No more foolishness.

She has given him several chances, but he has more than once betrayed her trust. For the first time in her life, Madeleine needs her big brother to be there for her. To be strong and up to the task. She needs him at her side, to pull her out of her slump. Not the human wreck he becomes when he's doing heroin.

But he's in so much pain. It's too much suffering. Even though he hasn't seen the corpse, he has heard about what happened, about the shape of his little niece's body. He heard horrible things, like how her skull was shattered, how her eye came out of its socket. And the enormous amount of blood, so much blood everywhere. He saw the pictures in the newspapers.

The blood of his blood. His little princess.

My God, what did she do to deserve such a terrible fate?

He doesn't recall ever getting out of his car and climbing the stairs towards that doomed white door. He's an arm's length away from the doorbell. If he presses on it, it's over.

Like an accident in slow motion. You know it's coming, and you know there's nothing you can do about it. You just hope that the damage will be minimal, that the impact won't kill you.

Except in this case, he's both the accident and the victim. An accident that will cause permanent damage. An accident from which one does not come out unscathed.

His inner demons are gaining ground, inch by inch. It's too late. "I'm sorry Madeleine, thank you for everything. I wish I was stronger. I wished I was there for you. But it's me after all. What did you expect?"

"Stephane Ranger, holy shit, I never thought I would see you again," his dealer said.

He hates this face so much. That horrible twisted head with a demonic grin.

If his demons had a face, it's his.

Stephane sits on his couch, all five bags of heroin lying on the wooden table in front of him. He has been analyzing them for about five minutes now. He doesn't really know what he's waiting for. Maybe divine intervention, providential help, enlightenment. He needs to stop suffering so badly right now. He can't take it anymore. Years of abstinence destroyed in a few minutes.

He looks out at the majestic fir tree outside his window. The partner of his loneliness. How many times had he stared at this conifer, talked to it as if it were an old friend? So beautiful in winter with all the snow on the branches, so beautiful in summer with the sun illuminating through it. He looked at it, imploring his help. He needs help to uproot his demons, to build up his strength, from the power of the soil and the Earth. Until recently, he found his answers through this friend of a different species. He prevented him from acting out, from giving in.

But that was before.

Now even he can't help him. He's a lost cause. The slope is too steep, too hard to climb. The effort is inhuman. No one would go through that, let alone somebody as sick as him. Someone as weak as him.

The phone ringing wakes him up. It's dark, and he's sweating as if he's just come out of a sauna. A look at the table in front of him confirms his worst fears: the bags are empty. He has been lying on the couch for several hours, disoriented in his own apartment.

He picks up the phone after the fourth ring, it's Jacques. He calls him from Madeleine's hospital room to give him some news. Probably under Marco's insistence, because Jacques doesn't care about Stephane's worries.

He tries extremely hard to speak normally and to articulate much more than necessary. Jacques immediately realizes what is going on. He giggles so viciously that it hurts Stephane.

The tone in which he warns him to stay away from his sister leaves no room for discussion.

Madeleine doesn't need that right now. Stephane's mind spirals out of control, as he only hears part of the insults his brother-in-law spews at him. He overhears him, saying he knew that eventually he would relapse. That he was right to be suspicious. But Stephane doesn't catch the rest of what he says, only realizing several minutes later that Jacques had hung up. He drops his cell phone on the hardwood floor and plunges back into the abyss.

He wakes up trembling. What time is it? Standing there, Ariane watches him with compassionate eyes. Stephane cries and apologizes for not being strong enough. He tries to get closer, but his legs refuse to cooperate. He knows deep down that she isn't really there, that he's delirious. But she looks so real, she's so close he could touch her, take her in his arms. Tell her he loves her one last time. Everything turns black again.

He comes back to himself, this time lying on his back, a ray of sunlight burning on his face through the curtains left open. He feels as if a ten-wheel truck has rolled over his body. His aching muscles hurt terribly. He regrets taking all the heroin bags at once. He would need some right now.

That's the problem with drugs, it numbs you for a while, but you're back to square one and you have fixed nothing. Eventually you have to face your pain or drug yourself to death.

Death.

It sounds like such a pleasant way to go. Of course, death. To join her, what's he waiting for? It could happen very quickly. Anyway, Jacques will never let him back into the family. He might even blame him for Ariane's death, who knows?. Anything to keep him away from them. After all, he blamed him for the death of his mother, didn't he?

"She died in a car accident, you moron, I didn't kill her," he told him one day.

And then, out of nowhere, an unexpected adrenaline rush. A burst of energy that urges him to fight. Jacques won't take him away from his sister so easily. He won't allow it. Madeleine needs him and he will be there for her.

The Serenity Prayer says to take it a day at a time. His demons won yesterday, but today is another day. He lost a battle, but the war is far from over. It's just one day, there are many more to come.

He feels confident to get through this day sober. He will move forward headfirst, with a clear mind. He moans as he gets up. He sits on the couch, his scalp hurts terribly. He swallows two aspirin and, after picking up his phone from the floor, calls the hospital.

His speech is so eloquent and assured that Jacques is easier to convince than he thought. No, he didn't do drugs yesterday. What on earth is he talking about? He had an awful headache and went to bed. His call woke him up, that's probably why he sounded so weird. He feels much better this morning, although he's tired. He hasn't done all this work on himself to screw it up in just a few minutes.

Regardless of their vice, addicts all share this unalterable ability to lie masterfully. He fooled Jacques despite his reservations. He calls Annie to tell her he's okay; he doesn't deny he took some drug the past day, but assures her it was only a mistake. He feels better already. She reminds him to take it twenty-four hours at a time. That's exactly what he just said to himself.

He watches his own reflection in the mirror for long

seconds. He looks like someone who slept in a dumpster. It fit with what he told his sister's husband. Feeling content, he puts on his sunglasses, grabs his car keys and leaves his apartment.

8

The assassin is lying in his apartment bedroom, going over the latest events in his head. He's at peace with what he has done. This isn't the first time he has killed someone. The first murder is always the most daunting. Afterwards, it's as if something inside you is broken.

There's no difference between killing once or a hundred times. You are a murderer whether you want it or not. You're part of a small band of humans who took a life. A selective club you don't want to belong to.

Although he may not have much issue and scruples anymore about killing people, murdering an innocent victim is harder. This is the second time it has happened to him. The first time was the most distressing. The inner struggle he had waged before carrying out the task was intense. But once he was at peace with his actions, he did it and never looked back.

Simple as that.

His mission is bigger than him. A mission so grandiose that it's moving. Reading the newspaper articles about the murder, people ask what kind of sadist can do such a thing. They don't understand.

If they knew, they would.

He doesn't have a choice, so he doesn't care what anyone else thinks. He knows he's not the monster they portrayed. He has a big heart. Only, he has a unique task to perform, like a soldier in wartime. Would they dare to say that a soldier fighting for his country is evil? Of course not. They would thank him for his services and give him a damn medal. He doesn't need a medal, he's not looking for glory. He just wants people to know he's not a monster or a bloodthirsty madman.

He's intelligent, methodical and decisive. In perfect control of his movements and emotions. He leaves nothing to chance. Cartesian to the core. The sun shining through his bedroom window warms his body. The temperature is wonderful. No clouds to distort a blue sky so beautiful it would make you weep.

A magnificent time to die.

He had stepped out of his car that day and had halted, swooning at the gorgeous colors of the huge purple oaks across the street. But in autumn, the leaves turn from green to a bright brick red. The oak does not drop its leaves in the winter, facing the terrible weather against winds and tides with strength and courage. He enjoys autumn because of that. For everything that dies with the promise of rebirth in the spring. That mild and cold weather at once.

The last stretch.

Once at his destination, which he had been to several times during his research, he opened the door of his car and pressed the button to open the trunk. He walked quietly along the vehicle, counting his steps in his head. He grabbed the long metal suitcase at the bottom of the trunk of his BMW and the crowbar beside it. He gently closed the trunk and cut across the street with a quick and confident step. The service door on the left side of the UPA building was half-open as usual at that time, held only by an a deteriorated piece of wood. He had about three minutes left before some employees would head out for their cigarette break.

He dressed in a dark tracksuit with the logo of a bogus repair company in case he ran into someone. He had a black toque over his head and was wearing large sunglasses. He was amused that he looked like an Unabomber sketch. He had opened the side door and climbed the stairs two by two, as he had done a few times with the agility of an athlete.

He takes jealous care of his body and eats well. He could have made this trip with his eyes closed since he knew it by heart. He had taken care of blocking the door to the roof with the crowbar, and had walked to his left towards the edge of the roof, the spot with the best view overlooking the high school building. School buses pack the parking lot. He checked his Breitling watch.

Right on time.

Only four minutes left before school ends. He opened his suitcase and put on his black Rudsak leather gloves-always the same ones, used only for this one time. He was wearing military boots with wide soles, a point too large for him, knowing that the police would look for footprints. He didn't wear the same boots he normally wears for reasons that were obvious to him.

He had knelt on the rough tar roof and assembled his sniper rifle while looking distractedly at what he was doing. He could do that too with his eyes closed. He took a deep breath to lower his heart rate as much as possible. He had grabbed his Bushnell 7X50 binoculars and aimed at the school's main door. He was happy with how steady his hands were.

The first students were running out of the school. The assassin watched each girl matching his victim like a leopard lurking in the grass. And that's when he spotted her. She was walking to his left, towards Roland-Therrien Boulevard.

His target was a pretty blond girl that he had watched for

several days, in order to figure out her routine, the pace of her steps, and the people she was walking with. What a pity, he thought, such a beautiful young adolescent. She had nothing to do with any of this. She was simply a victim of circumstances.

Sometimes chance is so cruel.

Upon seeing her, jumping up and down, chatting with another teen, he had put his binoculars back in his suitcase, grabbed his long rifle and stuck the tripod under his weapon on the edge of the wall. He had her in his sights. He would gently adjust the settings according to the favourable wind.

Perfect conditions.

He had the girl's head in his sights, her hair bouncing from side to side in rhythm with her cheerful strides. He had put his finger gently on the trigger following her, regulating his breathing the best he could.

Then time slowed down. Like a soothing lull. The assassin had smiled before pulling the trigger, confident in his shot. He knew even before he fired that he had made it. Snipers have this instinct of their own. An inexplicable feeling for a layman. You feel as if you were in a zone that simplifies an otherwise risky shot.

A small red cloud had formed around the girl's head just before she collapsed to the ground. He had just made a perfect shot. The assassin had not paid attention to the crowd running around. He had stared at Ariane Légaré's inert body lying on the ground. Her friend had first leaned towards her, then quickly got up and fled across the boulevard, making her way through the frantic passers-by.

The assassin had closed his eyes for a moment, breathing deeply. Savoring his accomplishment, like an exhilarating orgasm. He was almighty. He had gotten up, disassembled his weapon in a few seconds, and hurried down to his car. As expected, the side door of the building was closed. The employees' break was over, and he hadn't run into anyone down the service stairs or on his way out of the building.

The brightness in his room was diminishing as the sun was quietly hiding beneath the horizon. He shuts his eyes and falls asleep instantly.

9

The mood is heavy in room 1408 of Pierre-Boucher hospital where Madeleine Légaré is recovering from a severe nervous breakdown. The doctors allowed the family to be on her side as long as they don't talk about Ariane's death, and would change the subject if she did. But since they have given her enough sedatives to put an elephant to sleep, she won't wake up anytime soon.

Sitting back, Stephane Ranger is pondering while he bites his nails. He watches his sister, who is sleeping soundly. She looks so peaceful; he thinks. Better to sleep than living in this nightmare. He sits in an old green leather armchair that gives him aches and pains, forcing him to constantly change position.

His nephew Marco is dozing on a wooden chair, his torso lying on his mother's bed. He has been holding her hand for two hours. He has cried so much that he has no energy left in his body. In the distance, Jacques Légaré paces around, trying to look in control. He doesn't allow himself to grieve. Someone has to be strong, and it's his job to look in control. He hides his pain the best he can.

He would like to escape, away from all this, but his son and his wife need him. Sometimes he feels like he's downplaying what's going on. His daughter is dead, murdered in the street, and he's here, standing guard as if it were an unfortunate fall from a staircase. Life can change in a snap of the fingers and, like a tsunami, destroy anything in its path. Everything you believed in, your beacons, all the values you stood for, this life you built by working like a slave.

It's all gone.

A new reality takes its place. A reality without Ariane. Her daughter's face flashes in his mind like a lightning bolt. His eyes fog up instantly. He turns to the window to hide his watery eyes. Stephane Ranger doesn't hide his tears. He lives his grief loud and clear, which deeply irritates his brother-in-law, feeding the aversion he already has for him. How weak and selfish he is! But Stephane considers crying to be healthy. A sign that he will live out his sorrow instead of numbing it.

He hopes that every teardrop will drown his demons.

No matter how he looks at it, it doesn't make sense. Who would target a harmless teenage girl? A young girl who meant well for everyone? A young girl so generous that she volunteered to help the homeless. Stephane doesn't have nearly half of her kindness, and he's still alive. No, life makes no sense. He would trade his life for hers in a heartbeat. Society would benefit from the trade.

It was a mistake, there's no other explanation. No one had any reason to kill her. It must have been a random choice. He watches Jacques walking around in circles and wonders if he had something to do with it. Does he have any enemies? Does he owe anyone money? Stephane never believed in Saint Jacques, a perfect man from the outside. He's definitely hiding something. There's something disturbing in his gaze, but now is not the time to talk about that. First, let's take care of Madeleine.

Stephane's brain has been constantly racing since the tragedy. It's spinning so fast that his neurons are overheating. His need to find a logic to an inconceivable drama prevents him from mourning. He thanks God for his understanding boss, who arranged for him to take an early vacation. His boss, a recovering alcoholic, has been instrumental in his rehabilitation. He was unimaginably blessed to get that job despite his criminal record. Not all is bad.

What is he saying? Of course it's all bad. Ariane is dead. How can he still find a silver lining in this? My God, Ariane. His sunshine. The one he loved like his own daughter. The only one who never judged him. The only one who loved him unconditionally. A sharp pain knots his stomach, as he brings his knees closer to his chest and wraps his arms around his shins. He cries again quietly, rocking gently on his chair. Everything is dark.

Opaque.

The nurse says that visiting hours are over, Stephane kisses his sleeping sister on the forehead, and returns home. Jacques barely shook his hand as he left. It's time to stick together, to show solidarity, but he can't even do that.

"It's not that he doesn't love you, Steph," Madeleine once told him. "He's shy. He doesn't know you. He's an artist."

An artist, my ass. He's a sales manager for a frozen food supplier. Hard to be less of an artist than that.

Once in his apartment's parking, he realizes he doesn't have any memory of driving home. He has no recollection of what happened since he left the hospital. He looks in his rearview mirror at his tear-soaked face and his reddened eyes. Fatigue wrinkles dig into his face like gullies.

He remains in his car for several minutes, staring into the void. He has such an urge to go back to his drug dealer that he panics for a while. Where is his unwavering motivation from earlier? Yesterday was supposed to be just a mistake, he sincerely believed it. But now, an insidious evil grabs him by the throat and he senses that his good intentions are slipping through his fingers. Why isn't he stronger? Because he doesn't handle suffering very well. It has always been his problem as long as he can remember.

Even as a child, he couldn't handle suffering, whether physical or emotional. That's what his demons represent. His visceral inability to cope with pain. His urge to eradicate all forms of suffering. Fate is biting him hard. He doesn't have the best of karmas. He pays for his past mistakes, it's the only rational explanation he can find, but why does he have to pay such a high price? A price that seems greater to him than others. He could not have thought of a worse torment in his life than the death of the being he loved most in the world. The person he loved more than himself. If he makes it through this, the world will be his. Life is testing him, he must rise to the challenge.

It's a matter of life and death.

He takes a deep breath, gets the key out of the ignition and sticks it into his jacket pocket. He closes his eyes, takes another deep breath, and recites the Serenity Prayer aloud. He knows it by heart.

"My God.

Give me the serenity to accept things I cannot change.

The courage to change things I can

And the wisdom to know the difference."

About twenty minutes later, when he finally made his way from his car to his apartment, he checks the mail he picked up from the floor behind the small slot at the bottom of his front door. His cat Oscar rubs himself on his pants. Stephane picks him up after placing his correspondence on the counter. Oscar's purr and his snout close to his lips make him smile for the first time in several days. The cat is so lucky to ignore the suffering of humans. His life consists of following the sun rays streaming in through the living room window to gild his belly as he lies down on his back.

Stephane should have been a cat.

He pats the Oscar's head while he purrs louder and louder. Stephane attention is drawn to a red envelope different from the rest. He puts Oscar back on the floor and opens the envelope. He unfolds the only paper inside. A huge shiver runs down his spine as he reads the tiny quote printed in the middle of the note.

"Now I know.

This world, as it is made, is not bearable.

I need something crazy maybe, something out of this world.

- Caligula"

He inspected the enigmatic quote a dozen times before it hit him hard. He remembers a similar message he received a few years ago. An e-mail he kept while he was still in prison. He rushes to his room to turn on his laptop. After a few unsuccessful searches, he finally finds what he was looking for. An e-mail he received shortly after his mother's death. He double-clicks on the message and it appears as he remembered it, almost word for word.

"From: Bundy <Tedbundy@m0198747387.com>

Date: 2016-04-14 11:05 a.m. GMT-04: 00

Topic: Quote

At: stephranger@hotmail.com

Are you asking me what a killer feels when he stalks his prey?

It's hard to say.

How can I explain the taste of certain things?

How do you describe what a quiche tastes like? Or what the juice of a bouillabaisse is like or why it tastes the way it does?

- Ted Bundy"

An email, a letter. One after the death of his mother and

one a few days after the death of his niece. He doesn't understand. Actually, he doesn't like the link he makes between these two notes. The e-mail meant nothing to him at first. But this letter written from a typewriter obviously comes from someone who knows him, or at least knows how to reach him. Is this a bad joke? Stephane's mother died in an accident. She wasn't murdered.

Stephane attempted to trace the sender by looking at the e-mail header with the help of a friend who works in computer security, but without success. The sender's IP address belonged to an obscure anonymous server in Bulgaria. Now, this letter. Why switch to paper? He understands nothing anymore. Is it a coincidence? Although he would like to believe it, the more he thinks about it, the more he's convinced that someone is messing with him.

10

All the big cheeses from London's financial world came together on this beautiful starry evening in the superb Gibson Hall Gardens. It hosts the Women's Rescue Foundation fundraiser, chaired by William Primeau, a prominent investor in his late thirties who was featured in Forbes magazine's "top 40 before 40".

Formerly Vice President of Investments at Jones, Brown and Davies Financial, Primeau has just launched his private fund management practice with two partners and the help of angel investors. All of them have invested a significant amount in the company, but especially in William, who holds an impressive reputation in the field.

His responsible investment philosophy attracted investors, and they believe in the firm's potential to succeed in this highly competitive market. Big names close to his former firm have already entrusted him with their portfolios. Having signed a five-year non-compete agreement, William can't sign former clients, but he has made so many connections that he doesn't need to solicit clients, referrals are pouring in. He has far too much respect for his former bosses to test the limits of ethics.

He's known as a workaholic and for his great discipline. He's not the one to seek quick profits. You can damage a career by taking shortcuts, by not respecting those who helped you get where you are. William feels like he's on cloud nine. The event is going great. Everyone is excited, which shows how much they value the moment. Even the weather is on board. The sky is strewn with stars, which is quite unusual in London at this time of the year.

A meal was served earlier, cooked by one of the region's leading chefs. William likes to give the nation's young talent a chance in all fields. A string quartet is sitting between two of the majestic white pillars on the balcony next to the garden. They are emerging soloists from the London Philharmonic Orchestra.

Heather Ramsay, William's wife, has once again outdone herself. The party is flawless. Although he's the chairman of the foundation, Heather is the real boss. She's in charge of the organization and runs the day-to-day operations. She is aware of her husband's fondness for the Gibson Hall. Its rounded shrubs remind him of his first days in the United Kingdom. William hugs her with his powerful arms, a gigantic smile on his face. The foundation is in its sixth year of existence, and it really took off this year. The success of the event is a testament to that. This is no small feat. The foundation's latest fundraising efforts, besides this benefit evening, have raised over one million pounds sterling.

"Very nice Will, congratulations."

Sir Thomas Smith, William's mentor, is a world authority on portfolio management. He who took him under his wing and taught him the intricacies of the financial sector, skills you don't learn in university. Smith looks at his protégé with great pride. His tuxedo makes Sir Smith look like an aristocrat he takes great pleasure in maintaining.

William has a reservation about wealth that comes from his

Quebec Judeo-Christian upbringing. He's dressed modestly in a dark grey tuxedo and wears his favourite watch given to him by his uncle Maurice. Aside from his estate on the London plains, the only luxury he has allowed himself is a gleaming silver Bentley bought on a whim. He had just posted the best results two years in a row at the Jones, Brown and Davies.

"Thanks, Tom, but the credit goes to Heather. I did absolutely nothing."

"By the way, where is your delightful wife?" he says, with a mischievous sparkle in his eyes.

"She must be out charming everyone, making sure that no one needs anything."

William scans the surroundings but doesn't see her. He doesn't tell her enough, but he admires her deeply. She's one of the smartest people he knows. Heather looks like a supermodel, tall, slender, her hair ashy and curly to the middle of her back, carefully pulled back to the right side of her neck. She is wearing an ochre pearl necklace that William gave her as a wedding gift. She glows in the Gibson Hall garden.

After shaking hands with most of the guests, William is lulled by the string quartet's sweet melody. He greeted them by raising his glass. He wishes his mother could be there to share this with him, but she cancelled her trip at the last minute. Travelling extensively around the world for business, William has earned enough miles to fly his mother in business class a few times a year. The benefits of being a VIP customer.

Towards the end of the night, he addresses the crowd on a small white podium set back to the right of the Gibson Hall entrance. He praises the guests for their tremendous generosity. He speaks about his commitment to the Foundation before handing it over to Heather. She's second to none for selling the organization and its ambitions, and describing the initiatives that the donations will support.

The charity intends to open another shelter for victims of

domestic abuse and sexual assault. Her speech was so inspiring that she received a long standing ovation, which deeply moved her husband. All these ruthless business folks, hardly impressed and supremely intelligent, are blown away by Heather's verve and poise. Her composure is undeniable and the progress the foundation has made in such a short period speaks for itself. William knows that she has won them easily with her personality and incredible charisma. He's as proud as he is blessed to share his life with her, and they are finally considering having another child.

Heather is her greatest pride and joy along with their son Edward. It's not about his fortune or his career. Not about being recognized as one of the world's great fund managers. His family is his pride and joy.

Nothing means more to him than that.

11

Jack Morris looks north, standing right where Ariane Légaré was at the time of her death. He points to a three-story brick building in front of him.

"The first option is a shot from the top of the physiotherapy clinic right there, in front of La Belle Province restaurant."

Abygaelle and Murielle listen carefully to Jack's theory. He told them to look for buildings of three or more storeys in the area and identify which ones could've used likely to have a support to shoot from. The veteran investigator scratched his head while scanning the building, which was about eighty meters from the target.

"I don't think that's it," Abygaelle says.

"I agree," Jack says. "But let's not rule out any possibilities at this point. If he had fired from there, he would have hit his target from the front rather than from the side, and the girl wouldn't have landed against the cement structure, but backwards into the street."

"Unless we use the same esoteric physics as with your JFK theory," Murielle chuckles.

Jack sighs as Aby tries to make sense of this. Seeing her

colleague's confused face, Murielle asks Jack to explain his grand theory.

"The shot threw JFK's head to his left and back. Lee Harvey Oswald did it from behind him."

Aby frowns.

"Didn't the shot come from the grassy knoll, behind the palisade?"

"Clearly," Murielle says, arms folded, looking at Jack with an amused look on her face.

Jack doesn't budge.

"Tests have shown that Kennedy's head was first thrown forward and then recoiled from the whiplash."

"Of course, and I could prove you can fly like a bird jumping from the Eiffel Tower in scuba gear through experiments. That means nothing," Murielle says.

After some childish arguments between the two, Aby calls everyone to order.

"OK kids, let's go back to business," she says with a smile.

Murielle was still laughing as Jack carried on:

"The killer could have used other spots. Like the shoe store on the left, the old restaurant where we used to go, about a hundred meters away; and the building at the corner of the industrial boulevard, over there."

"There seems to be a lot of trees though," Murielle says,

"I have been told that there is a visual from the roof, and it's far enough not to be seen."

"Is that where you think he was shooting from?" Aby asks.

"No," he answers with a contented smile, "there's another location."

After browsing the surroundings, Abygaelle points to an imposing building in the distance.

"I assume that's your last option?"

"Good eye. The UPA building, my favorite. Several floors, totally unobstructed view, a place of choice. The only downside is that it's four hundred meters away. But it's a bit far to hit a moving target through a crowd. Not to mention it was a perfect shot, right to the little girl's temple. Boom," Jack says, pointing to the left side of his head.

"Cloutier told us that under five hundred meters, there was an eighty percent chance of hitting our target. It's quite possible that an experienced shooter could have made that shot," Murielle says.

Morris nods, but points out that a shorter distance would have given him a better shot success rate.

"All we have to do is ask around to find out if anyone saw anything," Aby says.

The three officers split the job of interviewing people around. They hoped that video footage has picked up some clues. But Aby doubts it. Not only are the cameras too low to record any activity on the surrounding rooftops, but most of the businesses only keep a 24-hour history.

Jack spoke with the UPA security service, but the manager told him that there is no way to climb onto the roof without walking past the gatehouse, and in front of all the cameras without being noticed. It's impossible to go anywhere without an access card. He asked for a log of all employees and visitors in the office that day. He went through the list of names and did criminal background checks.

Murielle was not more successful with the stores she visited. No one saw a thing except for one individual who remembered hearing a huge firecracker sound around that time, but didn't bother. The video footage no longer exists, replaced by more recent images.

Morris and Jensen go to the pet store across the street from the UPA. The manager greets them as if he was waiting for them. He saw nothing at that time, but he made a copy of the videotape when he found out about the murder. He then analyzed the footage taken late in the afternoon to check for any interesting details. And that's when he spotted something odd. He told them to follow him into the back room. The manager starts the video clip of a camera pointing at the parking lot on the left side of the screen. On the other side, there is the front door of the UPA building.

At the beginning, it shows the side door open and a person exiting the building for a few seconds and then re-entering. On closer inspection, the investigators note that the side door remained slightly open. However, it's difficult to confirm this, considering the average quality of the image. A few minutes later, they notice a silhouette cutting across the street from the parking lot to the left and approaching the side door. It stops for a few moments and enters the building.

"He went in," says Jack. "Looks like he's carrying something, doesn't he?"

The two women didn't notice at first, so they request to see it again. On closer inspection, they confirm that the silhouette in the shadow is carrying something long and wide.

"It looks like a bag," Murielle says.

"Or a suitcase," the manager adds.

Jack also believes it's a long bag.

"Nothing out of the ordinary so far," Murielle says. "Probably an employee."

"It's possible," the manager says, "but there's one other thing that caught my attention."

He's far too happy playing detective for Murielle's taste. He's getting on her nerves.

"See? Someone enters the building at 3:46 p.m.," the manager says, pointing to the time shown in the lower left-hand corner of the screen.

He forwards the sequence until several people are exiting through the same door, meeting within a few meters for several minutes before going back inside one after the other. The door closes completely shut this time.

"These are the employees of the facility," he says. "I see them every day at the same time there. They're taking their cigarette break."

"So what?" Jack asks, trying to figure out what he was getting at.

"Wait... and here it is."

A silhouette comes out of the side door, still carrying something long and wide, and moves away to the left of the screen. He then disappears from the camera's sight.

"So this guy comes out at 4:18 p.m. If it is the same individual who walked in at about 3:46 p.m., then he spent exactly thirty minutes in the building."

"You are a math genius," Murielle says, smirking.

Jack gives her a disapproving look.

"4:18 p.m. is five minutes after the supposed time of death," Jensen whispers.

"Can you do a copy?" Jack asks.

The man grabs a laminated DVD sleeve looking triumphant and hands it to the investigator.

"Efficient," Jack says, looking at his colleagues with a grin on his face.

The three detectives gather on the sidewalk in the front to stare at the UPA building. After a few minutes, Abygaelle breaks the silence.

"Well, we must talk to the security staff again. Either they are hiding something from us, or they are not as foolproof as they think they are."

"You assume it's our killer we saw on the video?" Murielle says.

"It's the best lead we have so far," Aby answers. "Let's start with that."

They have to start somewhere indeed.

12

Ste-Hélène-de-Bagot, October 7, 1999

IN A VERY DEAFENING turmoil for a weekday, patrons at Truck Stop 152 were having a great time. A man coming from the washroom was loudly belching to entertain his friends drinking from a pitcher of tepid beer. They were all laughing like fools.

"Bob, bring us some nachos," the man shouted.

François Lavoie sat at the table with his trucker friends. The thirty-three-year-old man was morbidly obese, with little concern for personal hygiene, and was plagued with a bald patch that he was cleverly trying to conceal. He chain-smoked and considered himself to be a socialite. He loved women and food. Of course, a drink now and then was part of his ritual. He sometimes drove his ten-wheeled behemoth with limited faculties, but he had always been lucky despite his recklessness.

Lavoie wasn't working that evening, but he had met up with three friends who weren't as lucky. The group of four was noisy, like everyone else in the bar. No one noticed them except for a man dressed in black, sitting at the bar who was also eating a plate of chicken nachos and drinking a beer. He had sat there and watch the four truckers through the mirror.

The assassin was especially looking at François Lavoie. He was wearing a red and blue hunting shirt that was two size too tight for him, and a green John Deere cap. The assassin appreciated the effort that he put into complying with the perfect trucker stereotype.

"Another beer, sir?"

The bartender waited for the assassin's answer with both hands on the counter. He thought his client looked rather odd from the moment he first got in about ninety minutes ago

"No, make that a mineral water, please."

"Coming right up."

After another hour of heated conversation, François Lavoie got up to shake his friend's hands as they were about to go back to work. Lavoie didn't feel like leaving, so he sat next to the assassin who was sipping another Perrier while nibbling salted peanuts. The bartender had smiled:

"Busy night, Frank?"

"Always Bob, always."

Lavoie looked at the man to his left, he wanted to chitchat.

"You're not from around here."

The assassin had smiled politely and nodded.

"Where are you from?"

He had lied:

"Montreal."

"The big city."

"Hmm."

The assassin waved at the barman to get his attention.

"Give my friend what he wants, and another one for me," he said, pointing at his empty Perrier bottle.

Lavoie was caught off guard.

"Well, thanks, man."

"You're welcome."

The assassin had taken another handful of peanuts.

"What are you doing around here then?"

The man was expecting this question from Lavoie. He had an answer already made.

"Business."

"You do business in Sainte-Hélène?"

"No, Drummondville, actually."

"And you figured why not eat at this wonderful third-rate restaurant here in Sainte-Hélène, right?" Lavoie sneered.

The assassin had forced a smile.

"You have good intuition."

Both men had talked about their respective lives for another hour, during which Lavoie claimed to have been a truck driver for ten years, that it had always been his dream job. He had made some misogynistic comments about three young women sitting at a table behind them, which had greatly irritated the assassin, but he had said nothing. With no children, Lavoie described himself as an immature adult. He had no problem with that.

By contrast, the assassin provided few details about himself other than that he worked as a salesman for an eyeglass frame company, had four children and was living by himself in Montreal.

All of which were lies. When Lavoie asked for his name, the assassin could not resist.

"Eric Gagné, he had said as he extended his hand."

Lavoie was momentarily shocked, but then shook his hand.

"Funny coincidence, that's one of my best friends' name."

"It's a small world."

"Maybe you're related."

"I doubt it," the assassin answered laconically.

"Oh yeah? Why is that?"

"I don't know any other Eric Gagné, except for the Dodgers' pitcher. And I'm not related to him either."

He had gotten up after he finished his last Perrier.

"Well, I have to go, it's been a pleasure, Francois."

Disappointed, Lavoie got up too.

"Well, it was a pleasure, Eric."

It took the assassin a second to remember his fake name. He had left and Lavoie sat back down at the bar.

Outside, the assassin was looking at his watch. 7:13 pm. He had walked to his used car he had paid cash earlier in the day under his fake name. He circled around it for five minutes, staring at the entrance door. He walked back to the restaurant in a hurry and stormed in.

"Fucking piece of shit car, do you have a phone in here?" he asked the bartender.

He pointed at the pay phone.

"What's going on, Eric?" Lavoie asked as the man walked past him.

"My fucking car is broken again, and my cell phone battery is dead," he said as he walked towards the phone.

The assassin called the number of a business he knew was closed. After three rings, he hung up, swearing out of his lungs. He headed towards Lavoie.

"Do you know anything about cars?"

"A little bit."

"Can you come over and see what's going on?"

"Yeah, sure. No sweat."

On his way back to his car, the assassin had complained about his bad luck. His acting skills moved him.

"This is it."

He pointed towards an old 1989 Cutlass Sierra that once was grey. The doors were not the same color as the rest of the body, which really gave it an image of a trash can on four wheels.

"Oh boy, that's old as fuck," Lavoie said as he took off his cap to rub his bald head. "You're a sales rep in that garbage car? That shouldn't impress your clients."

The assassin didn't expect that and had to improvise quickly.

"Actually, my actual car is at the garage. Ironic, huh?"

"Not lucky," said Lavoie, chuckling.

Lavoie had to concede he didn't know how to fix the issue at hand, exactly as the assassin had predicted. He had altered the motor in a way only an experienced mechanic could fix. Lavoie offered to drive him to the nearest garage, even though everything was closed.

Bingo.

The assassin was satisfied with his plan unfolding the way he had planned.

Following Lavoie to his vehicle, the assassin replayed the rest of his master plan in his head.

He got into the passenger side. Evidently there was a photograph of a naked woman hanging from the rearview mirror.

"That's about fifteen minutes from here."

After about five minutes of silence observing the road, the assassin spoke out.

"It's bugging me since I saw you," he had said for himself.

"Excuse me?"

"Your face, it looks familiar."

"Does it? I don't know where we would have met before. I'm pretty sure I don't know you."

"Yeah, I think we know each other."

Lavoie looked at the man who seemed lost in thought, with an impassive stare. No matter how much he tried, he couldn't remember ever knowing him.

Another long silence.

"I have a question for you," the assassin said.

"Go ahead."

"At what point in your life, looking at yourself in the mirror, do you say: Yeah, maybe I'm too much of a fat piece of shit?"

"The fuck you just said?"

" What's it gonna take for you to stop eating like a fucking pig?"

The effect had been satisfying. Seeing that Lavoie was furious filled the assassin with immeasurable joy.

"Hey asshole, what's you're fucking problem? I help you and you find nothing better to do than to insult me?"

He pulled over to the side of the road, sputtering with rage.

"Get out of my fucking truck before I rip your head off." Lavoie yelled, his face a few centimeters away from the assassin's head.

He felt a painful pressure on the side of his stomach.

"Keep driving," the man ordered in an icy voice, "and do as I tell you. But above all, shut the fuck up, you fat fuck. You smell like shit."

Lavoie was assessing the situation. He had a handgun pointed at his ribs.

"You fucking asshole.

"Go straight ahead."

"The fuck you want from me?"

Lavoie's tone was more interrogative than aggressive.

"I want you to go straight ahead and follow my instructions."

Seeing Lavoie panic like that was a delight.

"Who the fuck are you?"

"I told you, I'm a salesman."

"Bullshit."

The assassin chuckled. He was enjoying himself.

Lavoie didn't think it was funny. Not one bit.

The assassin had armed the hammer of his gun and ordered the trucker to stay quiet. Lavoie obeyed, but not without grumbling.

After a moment of silence, the assassin carried on.

"You like to party, don't you?"

Lavoie squeezed the steering wheel so hard that his knuckles turned white. The assassin repeated his question, getting more persistent.

"You're a crazy son of a bitch, you know that?" Lavoie said.

The assassin pushed his weapon even harder against Lavoie's ribs. He screeched in pain as he deviated slightly from his path.

"Answer my question. You like to party, yes or no?"

"Like everyone else, yes. Why do you care?"

"No, not like everyone else. Not like everyone else," the assassin mumbled.

Another silence.

"With your friends, huh? Eric Gagné you said? Who else?"

"Pretty much him. Sometimes he brought people along," Lavoie said, answering questions while thinking about how to regain control of the situation.

"Turn right."

Realizing he was heading towards a wooded area, Lavoie became agitated.

"Why are you doing this, what did I ever do to you?"

"Turn here."

Lavoie had contemplated smashing his truck into a tree, but the gun could fire from the impact, so he complied. How could he overpower the man, even though he was bulky and taller than him?

"Are you on drugs? Do you drink?"

"Yeah, like everybody else. Sometimes a joint, sometimes a beer."

"Not like everybody else. Not like everybody else."

All of Lavoie's senses were on high alert. His sluggish legs made driving tedious. He wished he hadn't left his Smith &

Wesson in the glove compartment clogged by the assassin's knees.

"Pull over."

They had stopped in a small clearing near the still smoldering ashes of a recent campfire.

"Get off the truck."

The assassin had noticed Lavoie's furtive glances towards the glove compartment. When he got out, he opened it and found the revolver. He got out of the truck after he grabbed it.

"Go there," he ordered, pointing to the front of the truck.

Lavoie concurred. His body was trembling, full of adrenaline.

"I guess you wish you'd been more careful, huh?" said the assassin in a mocking tone as he showed him the Smith & Wesson. He took it apart and threw it deep into the woods.

Lavoie was screaming:

"WHAT DO YOU WANT FROM ME? WHY ARE YOU DOING THIS?"

The assassin pointed his gun at Lavoie and ordered him to shut up.

Lavoie was breathing as if he had just run a marathon.

"You sick fuck, you don't know who you're dealing with." Lavoie said.

"That's what I'm trying to remember," said the assassin, pretending to think. "Let's see, where could I've met you?"

"I don't know you, man, I swear I've never seen you before in my life. You got the wrong guy, I've done nothing to you."

The man had a disappointed pout.

"Oh François, come on. Have you already forgotten me? After all we've been through? I'm terribly disappointed in you."

Lavoie didn't get it, but if he knew one thing, it was that he'd never seen that man before in his life.

"I don't know you."

"Let's recap. You told me you were from the Montreal south

shore, that you knew a guy named Eric Gagné, that you used drugs…"

The assassin was scrolling through the information as if he was trying to put all the pieces of the puzzle together, even though he knew exactly who François Lavoie was and how he knew him. He was having fun tormenting him.

A slow and painful torture.

"Oh, but maybe you know her?"

The assassin had taken a photo out of the inside pocket of his jacket. Lavoie couldn't see because of his nearsightedness, but insisted he didn't know her anyway.

"You don't? Maybe I was wrong then."

Lavoie was regaining some hope. Perhaps he would free him after all.

Stay calm, don't argue with him.

Buy some time.

"Excuse me, buddy, I really thought you knew her."

"It's okay," Lavoie responded, still gasping for his breath.

He was walking quietly towards the driver's side door when a bullet shattered the truck's windshield.

Lavoie had jumped to the side.

"What the fuck?"

The assassin had lowered his weapon.

"I didn't tell you to leave."

"But we don't know each other."

The assassin had fired again, this time just inches from Lavoie's feet.

"Are you fucking crazy?"

The assassin shook his head.

"No, I'm not crazy, he whispered. Do you want to die?"

"No, I don't want to die."

"Louder."

"NO I DON'T WANT TO DIE"

"How can you be sure? What do you know about death?

What makes you think it's worse than life? Look at you, look at your miserable life. A fat, stinking, debt-ridden man. A fat pig that no woman wants to sleep with unless he pays them. Unless he forces them. How do you know you don't want to die? Maybe I'd be doing you a goddamn favor."

Lavoie wasn't saying a thing.

"Get back in front of the truck."

The assassin's voice was low and deep. Lavoie couldn't take it anymore.

"I told you I didn't know the girl. Let me go, you goddamn jerk."

The assassin was pointing his gun at the trucker's head as he approached.

"The next one won't miss. Look at the picture again."

The assassin had moved the photo closer to the trucker's face, and Lavoie collapsed to his knees.

It was a nightmare.

How did he track him down? After all this time? Lavoie clasped his hands behind his head and looked at the assassin. He wanted to lie, to tell him he didn't know her, but what was the point? He's going to kill him, anyway. All this time, he knew who he was. He was playing with him like a cat with a mouse before he stuck his fangs down his throat.

"Yeah, I know who she is."

"Good."

He only hoped that by telling the truth, his tormentor would show mercy.

The assassin put the photo back in his jacket, then moved closer to his prey.

Lavoie was praying in silence.

The assassin was about to kill him, but Lavoie had raised his hands, begging him to wait.

"I know who you are, and if I were you, I would do exactly the same thing. I understand your rage and I know I'm going to die. I deserve to die for what I've done, and others deserve to die too. I hope you will find the strength within you to move on, to get rid of all your hatred, to get rid of all the hate that is poisoning your life. You see, I'm not the same man anymore, and I'm not telling you this so you would spare me, but because I want you to know. I'm not the same man anymore, and I'm at peace with myself. But you got to move on, man. You can't spend the rest of your life fighting some ghost."

The killer didn't flinch. His gun still pointed at Lavoie.

"That's it?"

Lavoie shrugged, closed his eyes and took a deep breath.

"Yes, that's it."

"Touching."

The assassin had pulled the trigger, and a bullet had passed through François Lavoie's skull, splattering the hood of his truck with his brain. His inert body slid quietly to his right.

The assassin was still aiming straight ahead as he closed his eyes.

He didn't feel the expected thrill he thought he would when he came up with his plan. He felt disillusioned. He would have wanted Lavoie to beg and cry to spare him. Instead, he resigned to his fate, acting like a fucking philosopher before his death.

"You asshole, you took it away from me."

He had spat on the corpse.

It made no difference; he had to complete his mission. He had fired another bullet into the corpse's heart, pulled a switchblade knife out of his inner jacket pocket, and leaned over his inanimate victim, who was still oozing beer and urine.

As soon as he had finished with him, the assassin had gone through the woods and, after walking three kilometers, had opened the door of another car parked in a private area and quietly left the area.

13

Jack Morris looks at the tower housing the UPA offices, hoping to find meaning in what he saw in the clip earlier. One thing's for sure, it supports his sniper theory, shooting from this roof, especially since the timing matches. Staring at the building will not help his investigation. He needs to show the video to the security team. Once in the lobby, Morris stops.

"The video, Jack. You forgot the video."

He sighs and goes back to his car. Then, he notices several people coming out the side door. A worn wooden plank holds it in place so it won't close. He recalls the video images. The shadow entered through this door that seemed to be ajar. Jack approaches three men talking in next to the door.

"Hello gentlemen."

They stop talking. The one directly in front of Jack greets him, wondering what the hell he wants. After he introduces himself, Morris asks some questions about their work there. The three are on the same team in the accounting department.

"Are you always taking your break here?"

"Yes, the smallest of the bunch says. Feels good to get some fresh air."

Jack smiles and nods.

"Do you usually go out around this time?"

They confirm at the same time. Jack points to the plank holding the door open.

"Did you put that there?"

"Yes, otherwise we can't get back in, we have to walk all the way to the main entrance."

After moving away from the group, he walks to the security gate, and waits for the supervisor impatiently. When he arrives and sees him from afar, he has a suspicious look.

"You again?"

"Thanks for the warm welcome," Jack says with a mocking grin, "I want to show you something. Do you have a DVD player?"

Jack follows him to a room secured with a heavy metal door.

The supervisor is captivated by what he sees on the video clip. He too believes that the silhouette is carrying something.

"To your knowledge, is there any reason someone would go through the side door instead of the main door? Construction work perhaps?"

Keeping his eyes on the screen, the supervisor says that everyone must go through the main door, register and be escorted by a staff member. No one may walk alone in the building if they are not a company employee.

He asks a co-worker to pull out the logbook for the day of the murder, but none of the visitors were there for construction work, or had a reason for accessing the roof.

"Can anyone get to the roof without an access card?"

"It's impossible, I've already told you. You must first go through one of the entrance doors and you either need an access card or you have to register at the gate."

Jack thinks for a second.

"Okay, but what if someone had gotten in? For example, if an employee had let him in or if another door was open? From there, could one get in without an access card?"

"Possibly, but someone would have seen him. Especially the person who let him in. We constantly reinforce to our staff that they shouldn't keep the door open for anyone without making sure they have an access card. Doors are always closed."

"That's not quite true," the investigator says.

"I beg your pardon?"

"The door aren't always closed."

"I don't understand what you're getting at."

Jack shows his phone screen to the supervisor

"This picture was taken about twenty minutes ago. This is the door overlooking Fernand-Lafontaine street."

The supervisor looks closer. He bursts out of anger.

"Who put that board there?"

"I have no idea. It was there when I arrived. You don't have an alarm to warn you when a door is open?"

The supervisor signal no, as he looks down.

"So, let me repeat the question, is it possible for someone entering through this door to get to the roof without an access card?"

The security manager looks at his employee, who shrugs. He confesses that he does not know.

"So let's see shall we?"

A few minutes later, out of breath, Jack joins the supervisor as he opens the rooftop door. No access card needed.

The supervisor explains something he can't understand, too busy catching his breath putting his hands on his slightly bent knees. Once he recovers, he moves to his left and walks to the point with the best view to the school.

The perfect spot for an experienced sniper.

Jack is positive the killer was exactly positioned there when he killed the young girl. He came in through the side door, climbed up the steps to the roof and waited patiently for his target to show up, looking through his rifle scope. Patiently, methodically, ready to strike at the right moment.

The detective pictures him stowing his weapon and leaving the scene calmly. Few people can make this shot.

A killing machine, deprived of any emotion.

"Strange," the supervisor says to himself.

"What?"

The man crouches down to pick something from the ground.

"What is this doing here?"

He was about to grab the item, but Jack stopped him.

"Touch nothing, it might be evidence."

He gets closer and pulls a handkerchief out of his pocket. There is a tipped beige wooden chess piece at their feet.

A queen.

He slips it into his coat pocket to further investigate the scene. Maybe there is a cartridge somewhere. But there is not. The only thing of interest is this wooden queen. Upon his return to the police station, Jack sends officers to interview the UPA employees working that day. Maybe someone had seen something out of the ordinary. But the next day, the verdict is clear: no one saw anything suspicious.

Jack doesn't get how the killer could get to the roof with the gear he was carrying, stand there for almost thirty minutes without being bothered, shoot his victim and then come down again without being seen.

Either he is lucky as a four-leaf clover, or he is a calculating, cold-blooded killer.

14

The assassin logs in to his Onion browser in order to access the illicit weapons website he usually goes to. The Tor network allows him to surf anonymously in the marginal section of the Internet, making it very difficult for anyone to discover his identity. He doesn't use Windows, the Swiss cheese of computer security. He only trusts the Linux operating system, which gives him all the versatility he needs.

He has more trust in open source software developed by IT specialists with a romantic view of the Internet free of any constraints, these people draping themselves in their anti-capitalist values. It makes him laugh. All these anti-capitalists with iPhones and other devices. However, if behaving like a poor man's Che Guevara helps them sleep at night, then why not? As long as they don't hold him from carrying out his mission, he couldn't care less. He types in his information on the Russian website. He can place his orders in English, he has done so more than once.

Thanks to the translation software he uses, most of the site's menus are more or less correctly displayed in English on his screen. He needs to buy more of these explosive bullets. He has only recently started using them, and they perform beyond his expectations. Not only do they perform like normal bullets, but they do incredible damage on impact. Even the human body's spongy tissue can't resist them. It's even better on solid substances like a human skull. This is where they cause maximum damage.

The Provincial Police are already investigating his latest murder, but he doubts that they have connected it with any of the others. The longer they take to solve this, the more time he'll have to finish the job. He seeks neither glory nor recognition. That is not the purpose of his mission. On the contrary, he cherishes anonymity. He reads the news on major Quebec media websites. So he can track the progress of law enforcement—or rather the lack of it. He laughs at the wacky theories he reads on social media. Chemtrails, the government's work to control the population, a big deep state conspiracy. These morons really believe the debilitating stories they tell. Not to mention all the racist theories spewed out by colossal morons.

On his way to his apartment, he reflects about the girl. His most recent victim. He has thought about the question several times. Did he cross a line by killing her? Were the children and teenagers untouchable, or were they target like any other? His mission is more important than any moral concerns he may have. When he took action, his composure and lack of remorse pleasantly surprised him, even when he saw the girl's head explode looking through his scope. This is war. And in wartime, the end justifies the means. You are at the service of the cause. The poor girl was only collateral damage to something bigger than herself.

Bigger than him.

He places an order for a package of twenty explosive bullets. The image of the shopping cart in the screen right-hand corner makes him smile. He clicks on a button labeled

"Send to Shopping Cart" in Russian, like when one order an iPad. Except this time, he's buying death.

Send death to the shopping cart.

The current Bitcoin value has not fluctuated. He's relieved. Because Bitcoin is a highly volatile currency, you can make a big buck one day and lose your bet the next. He doesn't particularly like Bitcoin; it's too complicated to buy. Fluctuations make it insecure. Especially since you are dealing with shady Eastern European characters. He wonders if a small mobster will one day try to hack into his system and steal his money, even though he has great confidence in its security. One of his contact computer engineer implemented it.

"It's the Cadillac of the mafia," he told him, puffing out his chest. He didn't query about his need for anonymity. So much the better. It saved him the inconvenience of having to make up a story. The engineer learned to mind his own business.

Bitcoins have the undeniable quality of being untraceable. This is even truer if you don't pay with a credit card. This was obviously his case. He's not stupid. He refills his electronic wallet with cash, via two brokers who act on his behalf using anonymous encrypted communications. He then simply uses the money in his Bitcoin wallet to complete his transactions. His name does not appear anywhere. It's impossible to trace it back to him. No one has seen him in the flesh, none of them could find him.

Even his contact with the Montreal Russian Mafia has never met him. He drops off the goods he ordered in a vacant lot, and a courier sent by another contact drops it all off in the trunk of a car. Another guy drives the car into an underground parking lot, and finally the assassin gets to the car after making sure he's alone. All these precautions are expensive. Bribe a few people along the way, but peace of mind is priceless. Only he knows that as more bodies pile up, the chances of linking up and tracing them back to him increase. That's why it's important to act quickly. Do what he has to do and disappear. Prudence is his greatest ally.

His ego, his worst enemy.

If they trace it back to him, he will quickly end it. He won't rot in jail. He's not fearful of death. All he has to do is stick the barrel of his gun in his mouth and that's it. Eventually, the thrill-seeking media will suggest that he's a potential serial killer. In a purely semantic matter, that's true. He murdered more than one person. On the other hand, can one really compare him to a killer who picks his victims at random, driven by a murderous madness? These monsters are crazy. Plain and simple.

Not him.

He targets his kills, calculated to the millimeter, and he's much smarter than the average Joe. He has nothing in common with a David Berkowitz, for example, or that asshole Ted Bundy, even though they say he was highly intelligent. God did not send him a message from the Afterlife ordering him to kill someone. Especially not through the neighbor's black labrador.

He's sane and rational.

He's not done. He will keep going until he gets what he wants. Until now, he has experienced nothing but disappointment and disenchantment, but this time he believes he has found the right pattern. Once his order is complete, he writes an email to his contact saying "We need to talk". He received a reply a few minutes later, simply stating "Chat". He opens up his secure instant messaging application. His contact is already there.

Guest2: Gustav?

Guest1 : Yes

It's probably a pseudonym, but it doesn't matter. He doesn't give out his actual name either.

Guest2: I ordered some stuff on the website. I paid with my Bitcoins. Do the usual.

Guest1 : Yes, I will stop the package before it's processed at the port of Montreal as soon as I get my commission.

Guest2: Yes, twenty percent, I'll send it to you immediately.

Guest1 : I'm waiting.

The assassin transfers Bitcoins from his wallet to his contact's wallet.

Guest2: It's done.

A few seconds elapse before an answer emerges.

Guest1 : I've got it. All right, I'm on it. You can pick up your shit in the same place as usual.

Guest2: Spasiba, I need to get the information of all the last names on the list. Quickly this time.

Guest1 : You know I like to keep you waiting. I'll get back to you with the information, but you must make a wire transfer before I send it to you.

The remark offends the assassin.

Guest2: Yes, I know how it works, thank you. Give me your price. I want the rest of the list and then I want you to destroy everything.

Several seconds go by. The assassin stares at the blinking cursor as if his life depended on it.

Guest1: There are three names left besides the ones you've already got. It's won't be easy, I have to be careful, especially since my crew is putting a lot of pressure on me. They don't like the attention.

The murderer sighs.

Guest2: HOW MUCH?

Guest1: $30,000, $10,000 per name.

Guest2: But that's a lot more than I normally pay.

Guest1 : You want all three names, I'll have to expose myself. It's $30,000 or else we'll do it the conventional way.

The murderer hates to be duped, but he has no other option. He can't waste too much time. If he knew who this Gustav was, he would add him to his list for good measure.

Guest2: Okay, $30,000.

Guest1 : Excellent. Give me a few days, I'll get back to you.

Guest2: Okay.

Guest1 : As soon as I get your payment, of course. I don't work for nothing.

Asshole.

Guest2: I have always paid you well, Gustav. And that won't change. You'll get the money soon. I've got to replenish my wallet first.

Marko Gusarov is shutting down his computer, and for the first time since the beginning of this matter, he can't wait to get rid of this man. He's more and more obnoxious. Marko didn't like the fact that he uses his bullets to kill the teenage girl. His organization's top leadership isn't yet aware of this business relationship. He knows that they will be happy about the money he brings. But this mudak has killed a child. He should have gotten out of this mess when he had the chance. Now it's too late.

He knows that his contact is not using his name, and he doesn't care. He pays three times the market price, requiring complete discretion. So he can call himself Dumbo the Elephant if he wants to. As long as he keeps paying it well, he's fine with it.

Gusarov is small, but very massive because of his experience as a weightlifter. He sits on the chair at his desk that squeaks because of his weight. Originally from Magnitogorsk, Russia, he has been living in Montreal for over fifteen years. He quickly rose through the ranks in the Russian mafia.

He clicks on the red X in the top right corner of the mailbox window and decides to see Darya.

He feels like fucking her.

. . .

After logging out of the Tor network, the assassin connects to the La Presse newspaper's website. An article catches his attention. "Murder of Ariane Légaré: The police are still in full mystery." An insane grin appears on his face. After reading the article, he bursts out laughing in his study.

"It's perfect, simply perfect."

That's what he thought. It will take these useless police officers an enormous amount of time to gather evidence. He will be long gone by then. It will give Gustav time to collect information on the latest targets. The assassin closes the lid of his laptop and goes downstairs to fix himself a sandwich.

15

Customers have a hard time hearing themselves talk at the Western Brewery Pub on this Tuesday evening. It's packed with softball players like every week during the summer. Each one tells their story, embellishes their game prowess, and makes excuses for their mistakes. The damn lights blinded us, that's why we couldn't catch a ball in the field in the third inning.

In a world where most players are in less than passable physical condition, softball is the only sport they play. Then they annihilate all the benefits from this exercise by gorging themselves with beer and cigarette. Marc-André Davison is no exception. This obese forty-year-old only plays for beer at the end of the game and the all-you-can-eat end of the year party where succulent T-bones and endless chicken wings are served.

He's certainly not part of the team because of his ballplayer skills. Like most overweight player, he plays at first base and a faster runner takes his place when he hits a single. He doesn't have many friends and rarely mingles with his family. He used to be close to his brother with whom he did petty crime, but they've grown apart over the last few years. These softball games provide him with a minimum of social life. He fools around with his teammates while drinking several beers, bringing him close to the legal limit for driving.

He knows his limits. He will switch to carbonated water in the final hour, which will give him enough awareness to drive properly. His doctor advised him to stop drinking, that it would worsen his diabetes, but he's not listening to him. Davison doesn't have an enjoyable life anyway, he's never had a woman in his life and some prostitutes even refuse to sleep with him because of his weight. Why would he do anything in his power to lengthen his misery? Might as well have some fun on the way down. Everyone is going to die one day, he says to justify it to himself.

Marc-André Davison knows that he's not educated and he wasn't gifted with high intelligence. But he has a good sense of humour that his friends and teammates enjoy. Even though he's not rich, he often pays for drinks. Anything for the boys. He sees their looks when he voices his strong opinions about immigration and ethnicity. He doesn't paint everyone with the same brush, but he tells anyone who will listen that he no longer knows his country. All these immigrants make him feel like a minority.

"Cut the crap, Davison," one of his close friend, Paul Demers says. "Look around you, there are ninety-eight percent of whites. What are you talking about?"

"Maybe here, but have you visited downtown Montreal lately?"

"I did," Demers says, "and of course, there is multiculturalism out there, but to say that we are a minority is wrong."

"Whatever."

Davison uses this word when he doesn't know what to say.

At about 11:30 p.m., several of the team's players left the pub, and got on their respective cars.

"Don't forget, no game next week," Demers says to Davison.

"I know," Davidson says. "Thank you."

"Are you okay to drive, Marc?" another teammate asks.

"Yes, I'm good."

He was more drunk than he would admit, despite the extensive amount of water he drank in the past hour. But he's been worse. He often drove his car a lot more intoxicated than that. Besides, he's only a few blocks away from home. He sits behind the wheel of his old blue Pontiac Sunfire, which has been barely hanging on for years.The exit from the parking lot leads to a street with a median between the two lanes, forcing a right turn. Davison's apartment is towards his left. He will have to make a U-turn at the traffic light and then go back. He drives up to the exit of the parking lot and then brakes so two cars can pass.

Paul Demers is following, patiently waiting for him to make his turn. He jumps when he sees the rear window of Davison's vehicle shatter into pieces. He couldn't understand what was happening. Davison doesn't seem to be overly agitated, his head is motionless. His car drifts, but instead of turning right, it crawls to the median strip ahead of him. His car comes to a stop and then nothing happens. Demers waits a few seconds before honking.

"What is he doing?"

A car arriving from the left brakes and blows its horn for a long time. Still nothing, Davison doesn't budge. Demers gets out of his car and approaches carefully to see what it is all about. Obviously, there is a problem. Has he fallen asleep? Did he lose consciousness? Or worse, has he had a heart attack? Judging by his waistline and his reddened face from the high pressure, this is very plausible. He feels the broken glass crumbling under his feet.

He signals the other driver to calm down as he moves around Davison's car. He knocks on the window, but there is no response. He can't see well inside the car because of the reflection of the streetlights on the car windows. He puts his face against the window and then he sees it.

He backs away abruptly, screaming. He immediately runs towards the pub.

"What's he doing, for God's sake?" the driver asks. Demers enters the pub, pale like a ghost.

"Call 9-1-1," he yells before going back out. He hasn't thought about using his own cell phone.

He races back to Davison's car and sees the other gentleman standing next to it. Demers tells him an ambulance is on its way.

"He's dead, buddy," the man says while looking in the car.

Even if it was obvious from the horrifying image he saw, Demers was still hoping he was wrong. As if not making his friend's death official left a slight chance that this nightmare isn't real.

"How can you say that? Maybe he just had a stroke," he said unconvincingly.

"No, buddy. I looked inside. Half of his face is gone."

Demers sits on the floor. His head is spinning so much that he thinks he might faint. He's seen nothing like this. He's trapped in a horror movie. Only after getting up several minutes later did he notice the blood in the shards of glass still clinging to the outline of the rear window.

No one notices the assassin dressed in black, quietly walking towards an old black Nissan Altima parked a little further away.

16

Abygaelle Jensen is livid. She just learned about Marc-André Davison's death. Another victim killed like the first victim. It's the kind of news she was worried about, because if it's the same killer, then it means we're dealing with a serial killer. The shock was so bad that she had to sit down for a few minutes. As with Ariane, no one saw what took place, no one saw the killer. Davison spent the evening in a pub and witnesses say that it all happened quickly.

The rear window of the car shattered, but whoever was following him didn't get hit. The damage to the victim's head was as severe as Ariane's. The face was ripped off three-quarters of the way; the head wasn't holding on by much. As if someone shot him in the face with a bazooka. If we find out that the bullet is the same, and it's the same killer, the media will go nuts, and that will make Aby's job much harder. The population will panic and politicians will seek answers quickly. The pressure is already intense because Ariane was a pretty innocent teenager. Comments about their incompetence on social media will take up steam.

Thinking about it makes her dizzy.

Despite Jack and Murielle's support, she knows in her heart that it's the same guy. When they arrive on the scene, Abygaelle's colleagues feel the same. Analysts at the crime scene comb through the place thoroughly. They need to find that damn bullet. And hope it wasn't fired from the same gun as the previous murder. A glance around the area shows that there was nowhere the killer could have climbed up without being visible to the people living in this residential neighborhood. The roofs did not provide the discretion necessary for a killer to get away with murder. Abygaelle believes he fired standing from the ground. Based on the entry wound, the killer would have been directly in front of his target, probably standing in the yard across the parking lot. It's a small brown bungalow with a flat roof, hidden by large mature trees, including an immense fir tree.

Jack turns on his flashlight and walks up to the cedar hedge. He leans over and lights up the ground near the tree. There are traces of soles near the trunk.

Abygaelle joins him.

"Look," Jack tells her, lighting up the ground.

"Do you think they are the killer's?" Aby asks.

"They're fresh. It rained and the ground is muddy. As you can see, there's not much grass, probably because of the lack of sunshine. It's full of mud."

Jack lights up the sidewalk near his feet and then further but there are no muddy footsteps that would show the direction the killer was heading. The rain washed away everything in its path.

"We need to mould the imprint."

"I'll take care of it," Jack says as he walks back to his car.

Abygaelle inspects the footprint which looks like a boot. She turns and looks toward the brewery parking lot.

The perfect spot.

The shooter must have been standing there, close to the

tree where he fired from. He used the rain and darkness to blend in. There are no lights in the house, meaning the owners are away. The first witness, Paul Demers, did not hear any gunshots, the volume from his radio was loud. Everything was going well until the back window shattered, as if it had disintegrated from a shock coming from the inside. Then Davison drifted slowly to the median. At first, he thought Davison had a heart attack or something like that, except that the broken window dumbfounded him. He saw his teammate's inert body, his head tilted forward. He didn't linger and rushed over to the pub to ask them to call 9-1-1.

The other driver, Serge Francoeur, saw nothing either. He almost ran into the car which was blocking his way. He honked, thinking he was dealing with a drunk, but when he saw Demers running towards the pub, he realized there was a problem. He opened the driver's side door and saw blood all over the cabin. The back of Davison's skull showed a gaping wound, and the blood was still leaking with a fairly large flow. He closed the door. As a paramedic, he sees dead bodies all the time, but he has seen nothing like this. He knows that he should not touch the corpse until the police arrive. There was nothing more he could do for this poor guy.

The patron at the pub didn't see nothing either, nor did the employees. Nobody saw anything apart from Demers, white as a ghost, who stormed into the place. Jack tells Aby that technicians will do a print mold of the sole footprint. They will then compare the print with all the shoes and boots of the house's residents to see if there is a match. Abygaelle is freezing from the rain. Jack and Murielle agree to meet early the next day.

"Hopefully we'll find something useful," Abygaelle sighs.

"There must be something, somewhere," Jack answers, but he doesn't put too much hope into it.

A policeman holds a plastic bag in his hands. Abygaelle

asks him what it is. It's something the technicians just found near the cedars as they were casting the footprint.

Jack approaches.

"You have got to be kidding me."

"What?" Abygaelle asks.

Jack rips the bag out of the officer's hands, then lights it with his flashlight.

"I found exactly the same thing on the UPA rooftop."

"What do you mean?"

"On that roof, there was the exact same piece of a chess set. A beige wooden queen."

Abygaelle is dizzy. Her fears are coming true.

It's the same killer.

"This son of a bitch is signing his murders," Jack says.

"Somebody has to have seen something. It's a residential neighborhood, for Christ's sake," Aby says.

Except that the zone visit the next day yielded nothing tangible. No one saw anything. Of course, with the rain at that time, it would have been hard to see much. All that remains is the footprint as a glimpse of hope for progress. At least they confirm that the footprint does not match any of the shoes belonging to the residents of the house. There's at least that out of the way.

Later in the day, an anonymous caller reported that he saw a black Nissan Altima slowly leaving the crime scene with its headlights off. The caller saw parts of the licence plate. The first characters were H6N or something like that. Murielle immediately called the car registry office to get more information about the vehicle, if, of course, it was the killer's car.

Abygaelle closes her eyes. Although she is not religious, she silently prays that the car will lead them on the trail of this madman.

17

There are days when the job of a police officer is difficult. For officers Malboeuf and Lamontagne, this is one of those days. Working at a roadblock to catch drunk drivers, on a Friday night when it's raining, is enough to discourage you from this job. But since there are plenty of good things about it, it's just a hard time to pass. All professions have less enticing sides to them.

The evening has been rewarding so far. Already a dozen drivers have been arrested for impaired driving, and it's only been ninety minutes since they set the checkpoint up. That's almost a record. It was predictable considering it's a long weekend. It's often like that at times like this. Knowing that they'll have several days to recover, the partygoers take advantage of it. Except that sometimes it makes them lose their minds, and they get behind the wheel, putting their lives at risk and worse, the lives of others. On top of having a criminal record and all the inconveniences that come with it.

Pascal Lamontagne has seen the crushed look in the eyes of those he picks exceeding the blood alcohol limit more often than not. Especially once the effect of the drink has worn off. That moment when these men and women understand that they have just thrown away part of their lives for a moment of bewilderment, for bad judgment call. Because they took the risk of driving, believing that the chances of getting caught were slim.

Wrong call.

The last driver that Lamontagne questioned looked sober, but he was belligerent. He obviously didn't enjoy getting stuck in a traffic jam on a Friday night. Fortunately, the individual in the next car is much more calm.

"Good evening, sir, how are you?"

"Very well and you?"

According to Officer Lamontagne, the man wasn't intoxicated. He doesn't have red eyes or dilated pupils. His speech is clear and steady. However, he feels shivers running down the back of his neck. His instincts tell him that this guy is off, or at the very least, that he should question him further.

"Where are you coming from?" he says, trying to act cool.

"I was at a restaurant. I'm on my way home."

"Did you go with friends?"

"No, I was by myself."

Lamontagne doesn't like the way he feels. He asks him to move his vehicle to the side, which he does willingly.

"Is there a problem, officer?" the driver asks.

"No problem, just a routine check-up," the officer retorts. "Is this your car?"

"Yes, it is."

"Driver's license, insurance papers and registration, please."

The man looks at him puzzled, but he complies.

This damn storm isn't helping with the conversation. Drivers are annoyed by raindrops getting into their cars, and it's difficult to read the papers without ruining them.

"How come you went to a restaurant by yourself on a Friday evening, Mr. Béliveau?"

"Is it forbidden?"

"No, but it's surprising," the policeman says.

"Well, I do this very often. My wife is out of town right now and with this terrible weather, I figured I'd buy myself a nice meal and then go to bed. Not really a good time for an evening with friends, anyway."

"Wait here."

Officer Lamontagne turns on his flashlight and steps back to get a better view of the vehicle. Richard Béliveau's BMW is in good condition, approximately ten years old. Béliveau is quiet and waits patiently as he looks forward.

With no good reason, Pascal Lamontagne feels that he's not acting genuinely, as if he's trying to hide something.

Too calm, too laid back. Something is fishy.

Agent Malboeuf approaches.

"Is there a problem?" he asks.

"No, nothing unusual," Lamontagne says, "but this guy gives me the creeps."

"What do you mean? Is he drunk?"

"No, he's sober. But I don't like what he exudes. His vibe."

Malboeuf bends over to look in the car, pointing his flashlight at the driver. Béliveau squints and turns his head slightly down. He's getting closer to the car while Lamontagne goes around the vehicle. Back in the police car, he checks the license plate, but everything is in order. Béliveau is the owner of the car, as he mentioned. He hasn't lied until now. Lamontagne has nothing to blame him for, and yet he senses that there is trouble. He gets out and heads for the BMW.

"Everything is in order," he says before backing up and pointing his flashlight at the back seat. "Can you roll down the back window for me, please?"

Béliveau complies, and Lamontagne bends over to scan the bench and the rear floor with his flashlight. Nothing.

"You can roll up the glass. Now, open the trunk."

"Officer, am I suspected of anything?" Béliveau asks, with an irritated voice.

"Open the trunk."

The trunk opens, activated by the electronic mechanism from inside the vehicle. Lamontagne goes through it from top to bottom, but finds nothing special except for a pair of leather gloves and empty reusable grocery bags.

He closes the trunk and goes back to Malboeuf.

"What do you think?"

"That you're paranoid. This guy's clean. Let him go and let's get this over with."

After driving around for a few minutes, the assassin finally relaxes. The policeman was acting weird. Yet he didn't drink, he was polite. Why did he feel the need to search his vehicle? It made him nervous, even though there was nothing incriminating to find. His discipline saved him once again. He took his sniper rifle back to his apartment shortly before heading to his favourite restaurant downtown. Even if it would have taken less time to go directly there, he still followed his protocol, and he's happy he did.

The police officer will never know, but he came close to seize the most wanted weapon in the country. The assassin smiles at the close call. Everything is going his way at the moment, but this is no time to relax. He needs to stay focused on his mission and plan his next move.

Luck can turn at any moment.

18

Abygaelle's face is drawn.

She has slept little these last few days. Her brain is constantly struggling to figure out how to get a hold of the killer. She took two espressos in a few minutes to get some energy.

Jack is on his way to the dealership where the suspect car in Davison's murder was purchased. Murielle is making another round in the neighborhood near the crime scene. Abygaelle is afraid that the population will panic. A serial killer means that everyone is a potential victim. Nothing to make people feel safe. Already there is some grumbling about the lack of results concerning Ariane's killing. Things have to progress, and fast.

"Abygaelle, line two."

Aby picks up the phone.

"Hi, I think I have some relevant information regarding the murder we saw on the news yesterday."

"Which murder are you referring to?" Aby asks to make sure we are talking about the same thing.

"The gentleman who was killed in his car. In front of the pub."

"Marc-André Davison."

"That's it."

"When can we meet?"

"At lunchtime. I'm a teacher at the Gentilly school in Longueuil."

"I'll be there."

That's perfect, Abygaelle needs to get some fresh air, anyway. She puts on her coat and sets off.

She waits on a wooden chair at the reception desk. She immerses herself in the typical atmosphere of an elementary school. She is surprised to feel nostalgic. As a child, it was her safe haven. She felt protected here, unlike at home. We were so carefree; she reflects. I was, too.

A lady introduces herself as Marie-Michelle Grégoire. She is a bit of a dork and wears a flowery summer dress. She has short hair common to women of her age.

"What I'm about to tell you may not be connected, but I think it might help you. I told myself, Marie, if you don't talk about it, you'll always wonder if you made a mistake. I don't like to interfere in other people's business, you know?"

Abygaelle smiles and lets her go on.

"I was Arianne Légaré's fifth grade teacher, you know the girl who died last week?"

Aby notes she said died instead of was killed. She assumes it helps her accept the awfulness of the situation more easily.

"Yes, I know who Ariane is," Aby replies without giving more details.

"One day, as I was getting ready to go home, I saw her sitting on the stairs in front of the main entrance. I asked her what she was doing, and she said she was waiting for her uncles to come and get her. I suggested she call them, but she told me that everything was okay."

The teacher pauses, as if to put her thoughts in order.

"Since I didn't wish to leave a child alone without supervision, I waited with her to give a piece of my mind to her uncles, because it had been over an hour since school was done. I found it inconceivable to make a child wait that long by herself. When they showed up, Ariane thanked me and ran to the car. I followed in her footsteps."

There were two men in the vehicle. The one who was driving apologized for being late, but he didn't seem really sorry, and above all his eyes were reddish. I looked at his passenger but didn't speak to him. I never saw these men again, except—

She remains silent, as if she was afraid to tell more.

"Except?"

"Except last night on the TV news. The person who was killed, I'm sure it was one of Ariane's uncles."

Abygaelle feels her legs go limp.

"Are you sure about that?"

Marie-Michelle stares at the floor.

"Not a hundred percent, but it hit me. I told my husband, "It's the little girl's uncle. The one who died last week. It's Ariane's uncle". Then I realized how ironic it was. Two family members killed a few days apart. It gave me the creeps."

Abygaelle is stunned. Not because she doesn't believe the story, but because she expected anything but that Davison is related to Ariane. It's a complete game-changer. She doesn't know what to think about this anymore.

Aby needs to know for sure. She thanks the lady and asks for her contact information in case she needs more information. Meanwhile, lying on his couch, Stephane Ranger was once again unconscious from drug abuse. There are several empty heroin packets on the living room table. On the screen of his computer, an e-mail :

"After the fear and panic caused by what I had done had disappeared, I started again.

From then on, it was like a desire, a hunger, I don't know

how to describe it, a compulsion, and I continued to do it, and do it again, and again, whenever the opportunity presented itself.

- Jeffrey Dahmer"

A neighbor worried by disturbances coming from Stephane's apartment earlier in the day called 9-1-1 to report a potentially distressed person. The phone kept ringing in the apartment across the hall and no one answered. She knows he's at home because she heard him come in earlier, and he hasn't come out since.

Initially reluctant, she thinks it's best to call for help, even if she doesn't know if there's something wrong, rather than not to call for help when there is a problem. She knocked on Stephane Ranger's door several times but didn't get an answer. She heard noises of laments, like someone sobbing. Something is wrong, she feels it, and it upsets her.

The police forced the door when they couldn't get an answer from the tenant. The neighbor looks in from her half-open door. Seconds after breaking down the door, the officers called for an ambulance.

"We have a 621."

She doesn't know what the code means, but the worried look on the cops' faces tells her she did the right thing.

Happy to have trusted her instincts, she slowly closes her apartment door.

19

Abygaelle drives on the wet pavement on her way to the office. It's been raining for three days, the weather is getting more and more dreary as the days go by. She sees it as a metaphor for her investigation. Grey and depressing. It's ridiculous, of course. But she can't wait for the sun to come out in all aspects of her life.

She reflects on the call she received about a burnt-out car found on a vacant lot. The report came from hikers who were passing by. The flames caused extensive damage to the car, leaving only a metal skeleton abandoned by its owner. The grass around is completely charred. An abandoned and burned car: the bikers' modus operandi.

One hiker, fan of crime TV shows, assumed that it was a vehicle used in a crime, as if someone wanted to destroy all potential evidences. The car was in such a poor condition that the witnesses could not pinpoint the model or manufacturer. Fortunately, the license plate wasn't completely destroyed. On location, Abygaelle realizes they won't get anything useful out of this car. Not much is remaining. They won't find any DNA or fingerprints. She looks around and sees only endless fields as far as the eye can see. Either the perpetrator had an accomplice, or he had another car waiting for him there. Or he walked for hours to get back to town.

“I'm thinking we're talking about a criminal organization,” Jack says. The mafia or the Hells, but I doubt it's just one guy. I can't believe he acted alone, let alone walked that distance.

“It's a long walk, I'd say at least two hours. But it's doable,” Abygaelle says. “That said, you're right. Probably he didn't act alone. He got help, but from whom? And above all, why?”

The forensic analysis team is combing through the scene, hoping to find tire or tread marks, anything that might point them in the right direction.

“Burnt cars are the organized crime's trademark, aren't they?” Aby asks.

“Yes, Jack replies. Especially bikers. But anyone with a basic IQ can set a car on fire. If I'm the killer and I don't want to leave a trail, I figure that if burning a car is good enough for criminals, it is for me too.

Jack is right. One can't draw a conclusion on this simple fact.

“The question remains,” he adds. “Why would organized crime murder a teenage girl next to her high school? Her parents aren't in shady business for what we know. But I don't think criminal organization are involved. Remember, in the nineties, when bikers blew up a jeep and killed a young boy by mistake?”

“Yes, it made headlines for months.”

“That's right. But more importantly, it resulted in their demise, and gave the judicial authorities the legitimacy to set up a law on gangsterism.” Jack says. “Once the population is pissed and asks for justice, the judicial system will do everything it can to dismantle such organizations. No taxpayer will challenge the use of additional public funds. The mafia, bikers and street gangs know it. They know that the public doesn't care if they kill each other, but civilians, even prison guards and police officers, they won't go away with it."

Sitting in the car driven by Jack, Abygaelle contemplates the golden fields of the Montérégie countryside. These golden valleys soothe her. Nature calms her. She should go over there way more often. Jack drives slowly as he delves into the surroundings, while Aby is lost in her thoughts.

She still feels an enormous lump in her stomach, close to despair. She feels like she is just a spectator of a dreadful drama unfolding before her eyes, and she can't do anything to prevent it. Like an avalanche heading towards her at full speed, uprooting a forest of evergreens along the way. Crushing everything in its path. There are no links. Each path leads nowhere, as if the killer splits the trails into several small pieces, preventing them from tracing anything back to him. Aby feels like she's fighting a ghost. Up against an evil spirit.

The return to the city is brutal. The cracked pavement jumps the Impala suspension. There are buildings as far as the eye can see, where the city rubs shoulders with nature so closely. It's quite peculiar to feel so far from the wheat fields she was pondering less than an hour ago. This cold and anonymous city, grey and dull, magnifies the terror in the killer's gestures and the screams of despair in her head. She has a nascent migraine.

Abygaelle sinks into the police station, which suddenly seems darker than before. The colours of the walls and floors all have a shade of grey that gradually darkens as the days go by with no convincing result. She's not foolish. She catches the furtive glances from her colleagues, probably wondering in what world it made sense for her to be leading such a complex investigation. It's far too big for a newbie. What did Charles Picard thought? At least that's what Aby gets from their interrogative stares. At the same time, she senses their relief that they are not in her shoes. No matter how much they judge her, she bets none of them would open this can of worms.

Two days later, Jeff Biron, nicknamed Dexter because of his crazy serial killer look, informs her that they found nothing noteworthy at the scene. The arsonist left nothing behind. He probably used a plastic gas container he tossed into the burning car. It melted from the heat, since they found fine traces of a plastic-like material. Abygaelle is increasingly frustrated to see evidences vanishing, just like the killer.

For the first time in her career, she feels completely helpless.

20

Brossard, July 21st 2006

ERIC GAGNÉ HAD JUST COME BACK from an evening with friends in a sports bar near Montreal. He went straight to the bathroom to relieve his urge to urinate.

"Honey?", he yelled from there.

No answer. With all the lights off in the apartment, his girlfriend was probably absent. He couldn't turn the lights on from the switches. Weird.

"Annie?"

Gagné was walking along the wall towards the living room. There was a smell of cologne. Strange, since he never used it. The smell became more intense as he moved closer.

Around the corner of the living room, he sees two shadows in the half-light. He heard a muffled moan, like when one cries with one's face buried in a pillow.

"Annie?"

A male voice answered.

"Sit down."

Gagné was stunned, but quickly came to his senses.

"Who are you?" he asked as he stepped forward.

"Sit down or I'll cut her throat."

He saw a silhouette of a man in the dark. Next to him, his girlfriend of the last three years. A bright reflection illuminated Annie's face. He figured it was the exterior light reflecting off the blade of a knife.

"Motherfucker."

"I said sit down."

Gagné reluctantly gave in. It was the first time he had ever faced a situation where he wasn't in control. As an alpha man, he was the one who terrorized people normally. He was a tough guy, the product of years of weight training and steroid abuse. He had his share of shenanigans throughout his life. He had a long criminal record. No one dared disobeying him, and he would become extremely violent, especially if he had had a few too many drinks. Aggravated assault, assault with a weapon, theft, drugs. He had done everything in the book except kill someone.

And it wasn't for lack of trying.

He'd settled down in recent years. He had had health problems induced by his alcohol and drug abuse. Steroid use had damaged his ligaments and joints. His back was his weakness, despite several chiropractic procedures that he could no longer afford. He enjoyed his quiet, boring life with Annie, the woman who had changed his life for the better.

"What do you want from us?" he asked.

"From both of you?" the assassin sneered. "I don't give a rat's ass about her."

"Then let her go."

"You're not in a position to request anything, buddy. If I want to gut her just for fun, I will."

"You sick fuck."

"Yes, maybe I am. But never as sick as you are."

Eric Gagné didn't know how to deal with his feeling of powerlessness. He wished that Annie wasn't stuck in the middle of this. In the middle of what, exactly? What was the reason of all this? Who was this lunatic and what did he want from them? He suspected it had something to do with his past antics, but there had been so many of them to point one out.

He wasn't a choirboy; he knew that one day or another someone would have the audacity to stand up to him. Although he struggled to find a way to challenge the man who held them captive, he commended his balls. No one had ever dared to challenge him like that.

Gagné studied the individual's shape, which gradually became more defined as his vision accustomed to the darkness. He was of average size, not very massive, but that wasn't relevant. You didn't have to be a giant when you had a deadly weapon.

Gagné was thinking of a way to get them out of that mess. Of course, he was curious to know who this madman was, but that was incidental. He needed to gain back control.

"Sweetheart, how well do you know your boyfriend?" the assassin asked after a few minutes of silence.

She was too petrified to respond. After a few seconds, she felt the man's hand grab her hair from behind, as he instructed her to answer. She was afraid he would break her neck. She was crying, even though she was doing everything in her power to stay calm.

"I don't know," she said in a weak voice.

"You don't know how well you know him? That's a drag, sweetheart."

Annie didn't answer.

"But you're right. We don't always know all about our partner. I mean, we all have our own little dirty secrets, don't we?"

The tip of his knife pressed against her larynx was hurting

her. Visibly, the blade was very sharp. The assassin could cut her carotid artery with a sharp twist of the wrist. He spoke again in a neutral voice.

"You know he's a bully, don't you?"

Annie nodded.

"That's what drew you to him, right? You like bad boys? Good, then let me tell you a story."

21

Jack Morris enters the office like a gust of wind.

"Aby, I'm back from the used car dealership. I have more information about the black Nissan."

Abygaelle spins on her chair to face him and listens carefully.

"We already know that the burned car owner is Leo Dion. The surveillance camera behind the counter took he his picture. He paid cash. No credit card."

"What does he look like?"

"I'd say mid-20s, blond, chubby."

Abygaelle types the name to search in the computer. Some Leo Dion, but they're all too old. She then searches for all L Dion born between 1985 and 1995. Nothing conclusive. Many Loïc, Luc, Laurent, Louis, etc., but no Leo.

Later in the afternoon, they moved the picture around the Provincial Police officers and detectives, but no one recognizes him.

"Let's share it with the media. We will seek the help of the public," Murielle suggests.

Abygaelle agrees. She notices the strange look Murielle had

earlier when she heard the young man's name. Murielle admits that it may be just a coincidence, but it's still curious.

"And why?" Abygaelle asks.

"Leo Dion. Someone remotely cynical could see this as a subterfuge. That someone's messing with us. Any conspiracy theorists might think it's a reference to Leopold Dion."

Abygaelle doesn't get it. Jack sits down and wipes the sweat from his forehead. He sneers as he gets what Murielle is talking about.

"Leopold Dion," he says. "The Pont-Rouge monster. The most prolific serial killer in Quebec history."

Then it hits Abygaelle in the face. Of course, Leopold Dion. She read about him in criminology class.

"It's a fake name," she says.

"We don't know that yet, maybe it's just a a fluke," Murielle says.

"No, it's fake," Aby insists. "I'm convinced it's an alias. I don't believe in coincidences. Someone has a fixation on serial killers."

Jack and Murielle know she's right.

So far, the killer has left nothing to chance. No clues to track him down except for the wooden queens, and the few seconds on the video from the pet store. He's not stupid enough to purchase a car with his actual name and show up on a surveillance camera.

"It may not even be him on that video," Jack says.

Total silence.

Abygaelle finally breaks the tension.

"Probably not, but we still need to talk to that guy. Let's run the picture around, just in case."

Picard waited for the discussion to end and asked Abygaelle to follow him to his office. He felt that she was shaken earlier in the day, and he wants to see how she feels. She ensures that she is putting all her energies on this case and is confident that they will soon make some progress.

She won't let a serial killer wander around for long.

Picard is not duped by her fake confidence. She's overdoing it to hide her blatant lack of self-confidence. He admires her willingness to fight, but the doubt he perceives in her face does not lie. He's thinking about taking the investigation away from her. Things have changed. What started out as a simple murder case has turned into a serial killer case. If he had known, he would never have assigned the investigation to someone on her first day as a homicide detective.

He waits until she leaves the office to speak with Jack and Murielle alone. He puts his cards on the table about his thought process and wants to hear what they have to say about it before he decides. After all, they are the two best able to paint a realistic picture of the situation. He has full confidence in them, so he needs their insights. Jack is the first to speak out.

"Listen Chuck, the kid is a tad inexperienced, but you put her in that position, with all due respect."

He's walking on eggshells, but he feels that his lieutenant has an open mind.

"Having said that," he continues, "she's a good detective sergeant. It's not an obvious case and quite honestly, I don't think we'd do better than her with what we have. You asked us to help her, and that's what we do. I don't know what Murielle thinks, but I don't believe we would be better off if we were in her shoes."

Murielle agrees.

"We're astonished too. I doubt we need a change."

Despite Picard's disapproving pout, she continues:

"Chuck, if you pull her off the investigation, there will be no benefit other than alleviating some pressure off her shoulders. On the other hand, it will be like a slap in the face for her. She may never recover. Not to mention the damage to her credibility, not only with the public, but most importantly, with her colleagues. Aby has huge potential. She's bright, she has strong intuition. She has the right instincts, and she asks the right questions."

Picard watches Jack.

"That's right, boss. Murielle makes a good point. Abygaelle is great for a rookie who started a few days ago. Let's be real. She's learning at an amazing pace. And she's an excellent leader, a great teammate. She listens to everyone's advice, she has good judgment. The last thing we need is to take her off the case, Chuck, believe me."

"Unless she requests it," Picard says.

"Unless she asks for it. Then it will be another story," Murielle concurs.

After a pause that seems to last forever, Picard drops against the back of his black captain's chair and sighs heavily.

"I respect your judgment. I won't do anything for the moment, but I want results. Abygaelle told me about the used car, and Leopold Dion, but it's thin."

As they leave the meeting, Murielle and Jack see that Abygaelle is back at her desk. She asks about what Picard wanted.

"To talk about the car lead, but you weren't there. Everything's under control," Jack says reassuringly.

Satisfied, Aby returns to her computer screen while her two colleagues shared a worried look. They feel accountable for her success. They will have to work even harder to help her.

They didn't like Charles Picard's innuendoes. They need to roll up their sleeves and support her. The three detective sergeants know they can't afford more slip-ups.

They really can't.

22

June 12, 1999

The weather is superb. Twenty-five degrees Celsius with plenty of sunshine. Nathalie Primeau had just finished her last week in college. This psychology student had received the good news about her acceptance at the University of Montreal. This was her first choice. All the efforts she had put were paying off. She was getting ready for her first girls' night out in a long time. She loved the way she looked in the mirror. Her long brown hair was drooping on her shoulders as she wanted, the subtle streaks of colour that her hairdresser had advised illuminated her bright blue eyes. Her body was slender and muscular, the result of her training for fitness competitions. This former gymnast needed to work out in the gym.

Content by the way she looked, she had descended to the first floor of the family home to grab an apple before joining her friends. Her mother asked her about the evening. The two had a great relationship, and she had detailed what they planned. Dinner with friends at Janie's favourite restaurant for her friend's bachelorette party. Nathalie didn't approve of her getting married so young, but it was her choice.

They would then tour the city's bars to raise money for her. Justine, one guest, had made a sign for Janie to wear throughout the evening.

"You should see this, Mom," Nathalie said, "It's so funny. She's going to look so ridiculous."

They both chuckled.

Nathalie knew she was lucky to have such a close-knit family. Her mother was adorable, her father, falsely gruff, was the best dad a girl could hope for, and her older brother was her best friend. As protective as their father. Raymond Primeau escorted her outside to give her his usual speech.

"You know sweetie, no matter what time it is—"

"I know Daddy, I can call you anytime. That I don't need to be afraid, you'll never judge me. I'm going out with my friends, you know nothing will happen. I promise."

She had kissed him on the forehead, told him she loved him, and headed to the car waiting for her. Raymond looked at his daughter walking away, philosophizing about time going by too fast. Soon his two kids would be gone, and then what? What was he going to do? He smiled as he saw Nathalie getting into the car, heading towards what was going to change their lives forever.

After a nice dinner and a tour of some local bars, the quintet headed to Le Bleu est noir, a pub on Rachel Street. The girls had raised a surprising amount of money. Clearly, five beautiful girls could do great things, especially when surrounded by males full of testosterone. They were on unstoppable, their motivation at its peak. Nathalie led them and with her charm and endearing personality, persuaded most of them to " give generously ". She thinks that her telethon host approach is very amusing. It worked very well.

She was having a great time, but Michelle and Maria didn't feel that great. Both had eaten chicken at the restaurant, and obviously there was a problem. It took a lot to convince them to hit one last bar before going dancing. They had already picked up money from many young men when Nathalie, Justine and Janie reached the table of three men who appeared already intoxicated.

"Hello, gentlemen, take a look," Nathalie said, pointing to Janie's sign.

The boys had stopped talking.

"I represent the bride-to-be, Janie, over here, and I'd like to ask you guys to give generously for this young woman who will ruin her life soon."

The tallest of the group had a disappointed pout.

"What a shame. Such a beautiful girl. It's a waste."

Janie hadn't responded. After the three men handed out some cash, the largest guy among them made the presentations.

"I'm Eric, he's François, and this is Stephane."

Nathalie had returned the favour.

"I'm Nathalie," she said bowing out, "Janie and Justine. Over there, there are our two other friends Nathalie and Michelle, who are too embarrassed to fool around with us."

"You're staying here all evening?" Eric Gagné asked.

"Certainly not," Janie replied in a sharp tone. "Let's go, Nath, we have other tables to do."

"Bye guys," Nathalie said, humming.

Turning to Janie.

"He's cute, isn't he?"

"Nath, I'm getting married. I don't give a damn. And you too have a boyfriend."

Nathalie had glanced at her other friend.

"Ju?"

"He's not really my type."

"I think he's handsome, Nathalie said, "the tall one, Eric."

"What about Maxime?"

Nathalie had rolled her eyes.

"Come on, just because I think one guy is cute doesn't mean I'm unfaithful."

By the end of the evening, the two sick pals wanted to go home. The dancing project was falling apart. Nathalie was disappointed because she had been waiting for this party for a long time. She deserved it with all the effort she had put on for her final exams. She didn't want to go home immediately, but no one wanted to go with her and continue with the party. It was too late to work out something with other people. Outside, the girls had run into the three young men also leaving.

"Hey, girls, already done?" François Lavoie asked.

"Yes," Nathalie said. "Some of them aren't feeling too good."

"Too bad," Eric Gagné said.

"I know, I felt like dancing or something."

Eric smiled.

"Would you want to come with us?"

"Where to?" Nathalie asked, intrigued.

"There's an open house party hosted by one of our friends. There will be many people. He lives not very far."

Nathalie was tempted, but uncertain. It was not her style to leave with strangers, especially not to an unknown destination. What would Maxime think?

"So, what do you say?"

Nathalie distractedly twirled her fingers, as usual, when she weighed the pros and cons of a situation.

"OK, I'm game," she answered.

Janie had intervened quickly.

"Hold on, young girl. Come here."

She had dragged Nathalie aside.

"Darling," she said, taking her friend by the shoulders and looking her straight in the eyes, "it's a bad idea, you don't know these guys."

"That's okay, Janie, they are going to a party. You heard them, there's going to be many people there."

"Yes, but you don't know where it is, you'll be alone with three guys and honestly, the fatty, François? He freaks me out a bit. And Eric looks like a player. What do you think Maxime would say?"

"I will just dance. Nothing more."

"I know that, but some of them may have a long criminal record, we don't know. I don't like it."

"Janie, you're scaring me right now."

"That's exactly what I want. Come on, let's get out of here."

Nathalie had backed off abruptly.

"Listen, I've been busting my ass for weeks in school, I haven't been out on weekends to make sure I get everything done. I've been waiting for this for weeks, and you're letting me done. Can I at least have some fun?"

Hurt, Janie's face had stiffened.

"Alright then. Go for it. But if something goes bad, I'll be the one saying I told you so."

"Nothing will happen. You saw their faces, you know who they are."

Janie wasn't listening, she was heading towards the guys.

"Hey, what's the address where you're going?"

Eric and Stephane looked at François as he read the paper where the address was written. It was a North Shore property. Janie had noted the address. She had then looked to the three guys with attention. She moved closer to them, her eye falsely threatening.

"If you people don't take good care of my friend, I'll be pissed. I have a good memory," she had threatened, half-seriously.

Janie pointed two fingers at her eyes and then at them to signify that she had them in her sight.

"Don't worry, we're good guys. We just want to have fun," Eric Gagné replied.

Janie walked back to Nathalie.

"Nath, please come back with us. You know it will piss your father off if you go with them."

"I'm nineteen years old, I'm an adult, he has nothing to say."

It stunned Janie. Nathalie normally worshipped her father. She never thought she would say such things. She had mistakenly thought that by alluding to her father, Nathalie would come back to her senses, but she was obviously wrong. She had let go. She had kissed her twice on the cheeks and join the other girls.

Nathalie had hopped over towards the guys. Eric had put his arm around her shoulders and smiled.

"We will have fun, you'll see."

"I hope so."

The group headed towards François Lavoie's car, parked in the shadows while Janie Labonté looked on in concern.

"Let's go, Janie, I'm going to be sick," Michelle said.

The bride-to-be got into the car.

23

Madeleine Légaré has the defeated face of someone who survived a shipwreck. Released from the hospital only a few days ago, she still can't come to terms with her daughter's death.

Far from it.

Abygaelle is worried about her. Despite the explosive cocktail the psychiatrist has prescribed for her, it's like Madeleine is standing on a wire ten thousand feet in the air and, depending on where the wind comes from, she can sway in the void at any moment. She has slept little since her discharge from the hospital. She's as exhausted as ever in her life, but she can't get to sleep. She lies down and daydreams, but she really never slumbers. She doesn't know why, but in the back of her mind, she still hopes Ariane will come home, looking at her with her big blue eyes.

Murielle and Abygaelle drink the coffee Jacques Légaré brought them, hesitant to get to the core. They are afraid to talk about Ariane. After all, what is there to say that has not been said? They want to know more about Stephane. They think there's something wrong about him.

Madeleine confirms that Marc-André Davison is her brother. They have the same mother, but not the same father. After answering laconically to a few questions about Stephane, Madeleine wishes to clarify something.

"I have cut the ties with my brother, I have taken him out of my life. So everything he can do or have done is of no interest to me. If Ariane's death has taught me one thing, it's that I have to straighten out my life, starting with him. He's responsible for her death and that of my brother."

"Why do you think it has something to do with him?" Murielle asks.

"Because he's a bum. No one in my family has had any trouble with the law. Neither me, nor my husband, nor my mother, nor—"

Madeleine choked with a sob.

"Nor my daughter."

Abygaelle and Murielle maintain a respectful silence. Madeleine carries on.

"Stephane is the only reason someone would target my family."

"But why you and not him directly?"

"I don't know. There are so many sick people out there, you know, you deal with them every day, don't you?"

Abygaelle nods, clenching her lips.

"It's the only logical reason," Madeleine says in a muted voice.

"Fate can sometimes be cruel," Murielle replies. "It can indeed be an unfortunate coincidence. There have already been two victims from the same family."

"Three."

"I beg your pardon?"

"Three victims," Madeleine says. "Including my mother."

"Your mother died in a car accident, didn't she?"

Madeleine is perplexed by Murielle's comment

“Didn’t you read the file about her death?”

Murielle admits that she hasn’t.

“If you had read it, you would have made the connection.”

“Your brother mentioned no suspicions about your mother’s death,” Aby says. “He said she died in a car accident.”

“Stephane doesn’t know the truth.”

Abygaelle is becoming increasingly impatient.

“What truth, Mrs. Ranger? What are you talking about?”

“She indeed died in her car. She crashed in a cliff by the roadside, that’s true too. But she was dead before the accident.”

Abygaelle looks at her, urging her to elaborate. Madeleine sighs.

“A bullet in the chest killed her.”

Aby is speechless. Murielle is as baffled as she is.

“I said nothing to him, for fear that it would jeopardize his recovery from his drug problems. I didn’t want him to relapse. So I pretended that she had had an unfortunate car accident, like so many others. Even Marc-André didn’t know. He wasn’t very discreet, so I didn’t want to take any chances. What was the point? I kept it a secret until today. Only my husband knows.”

“Have they found the killer?” Abygaelle asks.

“No, they never found him. It’s a huge mystery. The police don’t know how she could have died that way. All we know is that a large-calibre projectile killed her. And that the killer fired from a distance, several meters in front of her. Sound familiar?”

There are no coincidences in life, Abygaelle thought.

“Where did it happen?”

“Sainte-Anne-des-Plaines.”

Abygaelle scribbles “Sainte-Anne-des-Plaines, file of Ranger mother’s death.” Madeleine informs them that her mother’s name was Louise Laflèche. She had taken back her maiden name after their father’s death.

“I want people to know that we no longer associate with Stephane. I want my family to be protected. My son and my husband will leave for a while, take a long trip together, until things settle down."

"What about you?"

Madeleine shrugs.

"I don't care."

"What do you mean?"

Madeleine ponders for a few seconds.

"Would it be terrible if I die? I would like it to be otherwise, but I no longer have any reason to live. I wouldn't want my son to hear this, but it is true."

Abygaelle tries to entice her to go with her husband and son, but she quickly gives up, realizing that she won't change her mind. Madeleine is resolute, she has no intention of hiding. Everyone dies someday anyway.

"I don't mean to pry," says Aby, changing topic, "but do you think it's a good thing to write your brother out of your life? Don't you think he needs you more than ever? He's still in a coma, you know?"

Jacques Légaré has a mean laugh and turns his head away. Madeleine's gaze hardens.

"I told him if he ever did drugs again, if he drank even an ounce of alcohol, he'd be out of our lives. He would no longer see the children, nor my husband or me. He ducked into that shit when we needed him the most, to be there for us. I picked him up so many times over and over because his demons, as he calls them, had gotten the best of him once again. At some point I got tired of pretending to be a mother to my older brother. I gave him an ultimatum after mom died, and he didn't honour it. It's over now. I don't want to hear about him anymore."

"And now what?" Murielle asks.

"What do you mean, now what?"

"If he comes out of his coma, what do we do?"

Madeleine's eyes are full of disgust.

"I don't give a damn. I hope he never will."

She starts to cry. Her husband wraps his arm around her shoulders.

The detectives feel a deep discomfort with the violence of Madeleine Légaré's words. Aby has goose bumps. She does not insist.

"Where are you going?" Murielle asks Jacques Légaré.

"It's been years since I promised myself to go on a trip with my son, just us guys. Anyway, he won't go back to school. The school year is almost over and he cries all the time. We will live this together, we will go to the sea, go around New England, see where the wind will take us next. We will leave right after my hunting trip with my friends."

Abygaelle asks them to call them if they come back, and the killer is still at large. They will provide them with protection. Légaré nods and smiles timidly. Madeleine hasn't stopped crying since her acrimonious statements about her brother.

Abygaelle is taken aback by her pain. A guttural, animal pain. She has only seen this kind of distress in people at the end of their rope. She won't survive another tragedy. Abygaelle will do everything to prevent it. But one thing is clear: Madeleine holds her brother responsible for her daughter's murder. The logic is dubious, but it is undeniable.

All that's left to do is wish he wakes up.

24

Eric Gagné loathed feeling vulnerable. He looked for Annie's expression in the dark, but there was a limit to his eye's ability to see in the night. He wanted to gauge her level of panic, to figure out exactly how she was feeling after the story the madman had just revealed. Once he had told her about the terror he had forced Nathalie Primeau to go through on that fateful evening. How he acted like a monster not only at that moment but also afterwards at the trial, in front of the media, with all the outrage of his twenties!

So that was it. All this time, he wondered what chunk of his troubled past had caught up with him. His darkest secret. Which he would never have disclosed, even through torture. Who was this scumbag? What was his connection to all this? Clearly he knew all about it. He had described what had happened with such precision that even he was shaken to his core. His brain was boiling, his senses were on alert. How could he take control of the situation?

"Let her go, she has nothing to do with it," he had said in a tone he would have liked to be more assertive.

"Is it true, Eric?" Annie asked in a composed voice.

"Shut up, Annie, this is really not the time."

"Is it true?"

"I said shut the fuck up. Can't you see I'm trying to get us out of this?"

The assassin applauded sarcastically and laughed.

"What a gentleman! That's how he treats women," he said to the girl. "It's pathological. These sons of bitches will never change."

Annie didn't know what to think anymore. She was swaying between fear, surprise, hatred, and dismay. Her world was collapsing in front of her eyes. She was just starting to live a normal life. She thought she had finally found the love of her life. But if what this crazy asshole was saying is true, she could never get over it. She had a job she loved, and she volunteered to help drug addicts.

But tonight, none of that mattered. Tonight, her world was falling apart. She no longer recognized the man she loved. She had never seen him like this, his fangs protruding, foaming at the mouth, like a bloodthirsty monster ready to kill. He was breathing like a hunted animal, as if an evil spirit had taken possession of his body. She didn't want to believe this madman's account.

But the more he disclosed details about this horrifying story, the more Gagné metamorphosed. And the more it was plausible. She had never seen that look from him, those predatory eyes. It tore her heart out. For a brief moment, she forgot the cold knife blade on her throat. Instantly, the thought of dying was insignificant.

"I'm sorry," Gagné mumbled.

The assassin was dumbfounded.

"What did you say?"

"I said I'm sorry."

"You'll feel even more sorry in a few minutes," the assassin answered, pressing the blade a little more on the young woman's throat.

"Asshole."

Gagné's eyes were bulging with rage.

"Say that again, and I'll slit her throat."

"Fight me like a man, you coward."

"Like a man? How dare you say that you're a man? You're the last one who should refer himself as a man, you filthy coward."

"What I'd give to be alone on a street with you, you dirty bastard," Gagné shouted.

"You feel helpless and trapped? You wonder how to change the situation, how to turn it to your advantage? Great. That's exactly where I wanted you. That's exactly how she felt."

Gagné didn't know any other way to defend than to attack.

"Yes, I fucked her like a whore, she had a goddamn fine ass. I would do it again if I could."

The assassin sneered softly. A laughter that gave Annie chills.

"Yeah, like a whore," Gagné whispered, resigned.

The more Gagné spoke, the more the assassin's laughter intensified.

Annie cried silently. She was about to faint, trapped between two beasts, ready to jump at each other's throats. She was just an innocent victim of an unhealthy game between two sick minds.

The assassin had put his face close to hers and whispered something in her ear. It took ten seconds before she had gathered enough energy in her sluggish legs to move. She got up and ran for the door. The assassin jumped out after her.

"Come back here, bitch."

Seeing Gagné standing up, the assassin had made a sharp turn and jumped on him like a beast. Gagné hadn't had time to react, nor to parry the blow to his throat. He tried to retaliate, but his breath suddenly shut off, as he felt a warm, thick liquid flowing down his chest. With his hand at his neck, his index finger slipped through the wide slit in his throat. He realized that the thick, warm liquid was his blood, pouring out at a rapid pace. He could see Annie lying on the ground in front of the doorway, staring fearfully at him.

Gagné had collapsed on the couch behind him. The assassin looked at him impassively. Gagné saw his eyes for the first time. Despite his demonic gaze and distorted face full of malice, Eric Gagné had recognized his killer.

"And now let's have some fun," the assassin had said in a neutral voice.

Gagné's legs were soft as a rag and the man's voice lost its intensity. He had had time to hear Annie begging for mercy before he sank into eternal darkness.

25

"The file you requested."

Abygaelle was surprised to hear Maryse Beaudoin's voice coming from behind. She was focused on her reading. She thanks her while trying to regain her senses. Finally, the dossier on Stephane Ranger's mother's death. She refuses a dinner invitation from her colleagues and opens the file quickly. Ranger said that his mother died in a car accident on the way to the prison.

"A great tragedy. It took me years to come to terms with my guilt, and still today, there' s a part of me that hasn't made peace with it all," he told her.

He blamed himself for hurting her. What he has put her through all these years. He seemed really sorry. Abygaelle was sympathetic. She scrolls diagonally across the pages, looking for the information she is looking for. Dead in her car found in a ditch. Face smashed against the steering wheel because she wasn't wearing her seat belt. Car in flames after impact, body charred. Coroner's report.

And there it is. Cause of death: Homicide.

"Are you all right, Abygaelle?"

She jumps again.

“For God’s sake, stop coming around my blind spot.”

She blushes as she sees Charles Picard.

“My God, Mr. Picard, I’m sorry, I didn’t know—”

“Are you nervous?” he says. “What’s going on?”

Abygaelle takes a deep breath to calm down.

“It’s Ranger’s mother’s record,” she replies, pointing to the file. “Stephane Ranger thinks she died in a car accident, but his sister and the coroner say it was a homicide.”

“Do we know who killed her?”

“That’s what I’m trying to find out. I haven’t finished reading it yet, but it would be the third victim from this family.”

“Talk about bad luck,” Picard chuckles.

Abygaelle thinks the joke is dubious, but goes on :

“All three were shot dead.”

Picard pauses for a moment.

“Do you think it’s the same killer?”

“I don’t know if there is a connection, but I don’t believe in coincidence either.”

“Neither do I,” Picard says. “Who would have done this?”

She shrugs.

“No one’s ever been convicted for this, tough.”

“And neither for her brother’s and her niece’s,” the lieutenant says.

“We’re working on that.”

Abygaelle answered back with a bang, which made Charles Picard smile.

“Can I take a look?”

Picard grabs the file before Aby can answer. The autopsy report is concise: A thorough analysis of the body. Chest perforated by what is in all points consistent with a high calibre projectile entry. Bullet hole in the windshield, in the driver’s seat. Bullet fired, coming from the front in a downward trajectory. Picard, pondering, gives Abygaelle back her file.

"The mother too, then."

Abygaelle doesn't understand.

"What do you mean?"

Picard stares at her as if it were obvious.

"Come on, Aby, a sniper also killed her mother."

Abygaelle wonders how he came to that so quickly.

"Simple. If someone killed her in that place where, as far as we can see, there were no residences around, no high-rise buildings, only a road. Then the shooter knew she would use that way. He shot her with a sniper rifle from that spot. It's the only logical explanation. Otherwise, he would have had to wait for her to crash exactly where he was, approach a potentially exploding vehicle, and shoot her point-blank through the windshield."

Abygaelle agrees. It's the only logical explanation.

"But it's been two years between this murder and Ariane's. Why wait so long?" he asks.

Abygaelle shrugs. She's thinking out loud.

"If it's the same killer, then why is he going all-in now? Why the sudden rush? By rushing in, he'll be more likely to make a mistake. He thinks he's invincible. The wooden queens are proof of that. He challenges us to catch him."

Picard frowns.

"We don't have time to wait for him to slip up and do more victims in the meantime. We need to do something fast."

Abygaelle smiles.

"I have an idea to get him to react."

26

Abygaelle is nervous. Not only is this her first TV interview ever, but the bluff she's about to pull is far-fetched. Even though Picard told her it was a good idea, she is doubtful. Will the killer take the bait? All questions to which she has no answers.

She wears her red polar fleece sweater and her grandmother's lucky necklace, as she does every time she needs some luck. She nervously fiddles with a strand of her long brown hair. It amazes her at how much smaller the studio is than she thought it would be. It looks bigger on TV.

Set technicians are swarming around like bees in a swarm. People are in such a hurry these days, she thinks. In her line of work, she's expected to be calm and meticulous. It's hard to be Zen when bodies are piling up and there's no solid lead to catch the culprit. The closer the moment of her interview approaches, the more nervous she gets. The mere idea of being on television makes her dizzy. She is an assumed introvert. She needs to approach this just like any other conversation.

"Two minutes."

The voice of the stage manager startled her.

"OK, thanks."

Aby would like to look in control, but she knows everyone can see her legs shaking.

Just a conversation like any other. She closes her eyes and takes a deep breath, moving her arms on either side of her body to get the blood flowing, as if she was about to swim the one hundred meter breaststroke at the Olympics. Host Jean Lajeunesse informs his audience that after the break, he will meet with the detective in charge of the investigation about the most recent murders. Lajeunesse is a popular TV host that Abygaelle doesn't particularly cherish. But he has the advantage of reaching a large audience. Maybe the murderer is one of them. Abygaelle only hopes to chat, ignoring Lajeunesse's false toupee. He waves to her as the stage manager puts her hand in the middle of her back to lead the way. She needs all her strength not to collapse after two steps.

Calm down, for God's sake. Abygaelle is annoyed to be so edgy. She used to see dead bodies without flinching, children torn apart while keeping her cool, but talking to a wigged-out host traumatized her to the utmost.

"Good morning, my name is Jean Lajeunesse."

The host lends her a sweaty handshake while some woman hooks a lavalier microphone to her shirt.

"Don't worry, everything will be fine. Just think of it as a casual conversation between two friends."

Abygaelle couldn't suppress a laugh.

"I'm sorry," she said smiling, "thank you, but I'm not nervous."

Lajeunesse's dubious look is not reassuring.

After the customary greetings, the TV host gets to the heart of the matter.

Abygaelle quickly gets comfortable. She says that the investigation is progressing well. The population has no reason to panic; they have singled out potential suspects and things should get better soon. She mentions that according to what they know; the killer is not targeting his victims at random. Back at the police station, Murielle and Jack listen carefully to the interview. Further behind, Charles Picard bites his left thumbnail.

Abygaelle waits for the discussion to shift to where she wants it to go.

"Are you saying that the same killer perpetrated all two murders?"

"That's what we believe."

"What kind of person could do this?"

The moment she's been waiting for. She's taking a pause to mark the moment.

"I'd say he's a coward."

Lajeunesse is speechless, a rare feat in her case.

"What... what do you mean?" he asks after a few seconds.

"Someone who kills people from afar is not very brave, to say the least. Killing unaware people already shows a certain form of cowardice, probably coupled with a definite mental disability. Moreover, he kills them from a distance. In fact, such cowardice is quite phenomenal."

Lajeunesse can hardly conceal his excitement, since he is used to interviewing drab politicians. He is looking at a photogenic detective with a fluid delivery and sparkling eyes, and she insults some serial killer on his show, live, in prime time.

What a dream.

"Go on," he adds, crossing his arms, a slight smirk on his face.

"Clearly, this individual is a pussy. Not the kind of individual you want fighting beside you in the trenches. Some theorists would say the killer suffers from erectile dysfunction. That he compensates for it with a very long rifle, a macho phallic representation to counterbalance his sexual impotence."

Abygaelle's heart beats quick. She has delivered her speech so eloquently that she surprises herself. Picard chuckles while Jack has his mouth wide open. The interview continued for about ten minutes, during which the TV host relished every word Abygaelle said. This woman is a wonder. Once the interview was over, Lajeunesse thanked her, saying she was fantastic. Abygaelle smiled, but she didn't care about the praise. She just hopes her plan works.

Several miles away, Raymond Primeau watched the entire interview, standing motionless in the middle of the room. He fled from his home a few days after Ariane Légaré's murder, bringing with him the bare minimum. He rented an apartment under a false name while he thought about what he should do. Monique is not aware of his motives. He left a vague note scrawled by hand on the kitchen table. He needs to be alone; the moment is serious. He comes out of the shower with a white terry cloth towel tied around his waist and smiles as he remembers the detective sergeant's harsh words.

27

Annie St. Onge is shocked to see her unconscious friend, plugged to ventilators breathing for him. The heart monitor beeps regularly. She hears them even when she is no longer there. They are imprinted in her brain. She hears them in her dreams.

There will be no more silence.

It's strange, though, that no one would ask for her opinion about Stephane's faith. No doctor or nurse inquired about a vital detail: if Stephane had his say, would he rather die than being artificially kept alive? After all, isn't what he tried to do by using all this drug at once? Stephane is a savvy heroin addict. Hardly a beginner. He knows very well how much he can inject to get a buzz, and how much puts him at risk of an overdose. He didn't take all that crap by accident. No one will convince her of it.

Yet, he looks so peaceful, at peace for the first time since she met him. And she feels guilty and useless. Her job was to say the right stuff so he wouldn't do anything stupid. She's done it so many times before. Why did she fail this time? She's his last line of defence, the one preventing him from falling into the void. Without her, he breaks down. If he should die, she would never forgive herself. It's a shame since he was doing so well lately. This guy never had a chance in life. As soon as he gets his head out of the water, something crushes him and pulls him back to the bottom. It'll kill him one day. Maybe that day has come. Maybe this time he won't wake up. Even if you're a lifelong addict, you can control the disease enough to live a normal life.

It's probably because of her guilt that she's here, in this gloomy hospital room every night. Each time she hopes he wakes up. He has been in this vegetative state for two weeks now, and doctors decline to offer an opinion about his future. Is he going to make it? It depends, they say. Every person is different, it's too early to tell. It will depend on him. No one can predict whether he will have after-effects if he survives. So many years of study and residency to come up with vague answers like that, she thinks. Sometimes he moves. Sometimes he grunts, but most of the time he's inert, with his eyes closed. As if he were sleeping peacefully. Maybe it's better that way.

No more pain.

Annie too has been recovering. Without Stephane's support, she would never have been successful. Her family also means a lot to her. She recently broke up with her former boyfriend to get out of the vicious circle of toxic relationships she has wallowed in since her youth. She can't stand bad boys who treat her like shit anymore. She deserves better; she knows that now. She looks at Stephane and smiles. They have grown so close through their misery. If asked, a few years ago, Annie would have said that she didn't believe in a platonic relationship between a man and a woman.

But it is. These two have no desire for each other beyond a great affection. There has never been the slightest doubt about it. Neither expressed a wish to be intimate. They have each suffered through disappointment in their relationships, like two lonely souls cursed with an unhappiness gene. Like failed romantics who can't grasp the rules of the game, how it's supposed to work. So they are the eternal losers in this grim jousting of the heart.

She shifts position on the uncomfortable chair she's sitting on next to the bed. Sometimes sitting with her legs crossed, sometimes sitting on her side, or as in this moment, with her head lying on Stephane's bed. She reflects on her own existence. She hasn't had it easy either. So much drama and experiences that no human should live through. She's slowly reconstructing herself. She forces herself to enjoy the little things in life. Her apartment, which she decorated to her liking, is her little peaceful haven.

Where nothing bad can happen to her.

This is the first time she has ever lived alone. She has never endured solitude. Even if it's still sometimes difficult, she rediscovers who she is; she learns to love herself. Her therapist tells her she needs to first enjoy her own life, to live by herself, before she can expect to live in a harmonious relationship with someone else. Otherwise, she is doomed to make the same mistakes again and again, to make the same poor decisions. Even if at first Annie thought it sounded like esoteric theories. She realizes that it's true. And it gets easier as time goes on. She believes in her chances of success, she's optimistic.

A shadow to her right makes her startle. Someone is standing in the hallway leading into the room. She lifts her head and her blood flushes to her feet. A pair of eyes stare at her, as surprised as she is. Then the man's gaze hardens, and he stares threateningly at her, like a struggle over who will dominate the other. With a wicked grin, he puts his finger in front of his mouth as a warning to remain silent. He has a bunch of flowers in his left hand. Annie is sick to her stomach as she smells the scent of the man's cologne. The same as last time.

Crippled by fear, it blurs her vision. Her hands dance in a frightened tremor on the chair's armrests.

After a few seconds, the man slips away like that, without saying a word, bringing his flowers with him. She feels a warm fluid running down her thighs as she realizes that she has pissed herself. She looks at Stephane and wonders if he knows him. Is he close to this monster? Of course he is, otherwise why would the man visit him? Why would he bring him flowers? Has Stephane been lying to her all this time? Does he have something to do with Eric's murder? Watching her world collapse, Annie holds back vomit with her hand in front of her mouth, just long enough to get to the small bathroom in the corner. She pukes up her gut, tears of incomprehension moistening her cheeks. She can no longer stay next to him any longer. He will owe her explanations if he recovers. What was this sick man doing in his room?

Nothing makes sense anymore.

Annie grabs her belongings and rushes out of the room. As she walks past the nursing station, a woman asks her if she's okay, but she doesn't answer. Her only ambition is to leave this place as quickly as possible without running into the assassin.

She goes down the twelve floors by the service stairs instead of using the elevator. She is anxious at every new door she opens. What if he is there? What if he's waiting for her? She feels the warm evening breeze sweeping over her face as she walks out the door. She weeps, but stays focused. The bus stop is only a few meters away. She would rather hail a cab to escape as quickly as possible, but she doesn't have enough money. Fortunately, the bus turns the corner as soon as she walks next to the bus stop. At least something in her favour.

The bus driver looks at her strangely when she gets in. Once she sits down, she grabs the little mirror in her purse to look at her face. She has reddish eyes and diluted mascara under her eyes. Even though other passengers glance at her, no one is asking her if she needs help. She muffles a scream at the sight of a man dressed in black in the back of the bus, but it's not him. She doesn't understand what she has done to dive back into this nightmare from which she thought she had escaped forever.

Back at the hospital, a maintenance worker notices some flowers on her cart. She smiles, assuming they come from the young intern she has been charming for weeks. She is heart-rending as she reads the card.

"Killing is like changing a tire. The first time, you're careful, but after the thirtieth time, you don't even know where you put the jack.

-Ted Bundy."

28

Abygaelle looks at the restaurant's menu while waiting for Roland Michaud to arrive. She can't decide what to eat. Even though she goes through the menu repeatedly, she can't memorize a thing of what she reads. The waiter approaches her and asks if she would like an appetizer while she waits, but she says no. He turns away, looking irritated, but Abygaelle doesn't mind. She's eager to chat with her former boss about what's going on.

She looks forward to to see how their relationship will develop now that she left the vice department. She's worried that they won't be as close as they used to be. She's worried that they might be distant from each other. She has so much to tell him. She needs her guidance so badly. Her soft, reassuring voice that will guarantee that everything is going to be okay, that everything is going to work out. Even if she suspects he'd say that just to calm her down, and that deep down, he doesn't really know. She still enjoys these empty phrases which give her a tiny glimmer of hope.

After waiting for several minutes, she asks the waiter to get her a glass of white wine. She wishes it would cool her down a little. She rarely drinks alcohol when she's on duty, but she needs it. The sight of Roland's figure in the restaurant lobby fills her with joy. She feels she's overreacting, it will freak him out. He approaches her with a smile, dressed in a blue-grey suit that makes him look like an English dandy. He's elegant and exudes class. People naturally respect him the moment he walks into a room. You immediately admire this man. He has an innate charisma. An undeniable presence.

Roland is like a father to Aby. She has no sexual feelings for him. She loves him very much, of course, but as one cherishes a parent. Nothing more. Michaud himself considers her as his own daughter, his protégé. She and her actual daughter get along very well, even though she is a few years younger than she is. He sits down and, looking back at the waiter, asks for a Perrier with lemon before he even asks him if he wants something to drink.

"Are you all right, Aby?"

She smiles stupidly, then she feels a surge of emotion. Her eyes fog up and, feeling deeply discouraged, she begins to cry, putting her hands in front of her face.

"My God, what's happening for crying out loud?"

Abygaelle can't stop crying. She's more emotional than she thought she'd be. As if her mentor's presence confronts her with her drawbacks. Homicide squad is too much for her. She can't cope with all these people getting killed because she can't stop the killer. She misses Michaud; she misses being in control. She feels totally incompetent. She used to be a superstar in vice, she's an abysmal loser in homicides. Roland comes closer and hugs her tightly, until she calms down. He doesn't care about to other clients staring at them; they are alone in the world.

He disputes all of Abygaelle's arguments. Of course, she's good, she just needs to be patient and to trust herself. She's only been there a few weeks, it's far too early to judge. She'll be fine, she should give herself the chance. Many murders are never cracked. You must learn to live with this reality like you do with rapists and pedophiles freely roaming the streets.

Aby shrugs and keeps on crying, unable to utter a single intelligible word. Roland keeps consoling her with his soothing voice. After a few minutes, she calms down and wipes away her tears. She takes a long sip of wine. The waiter brings the bottle of Perrier ordered earlier and walks away in hushed steps. Roland Michaud is back in his seat in front of Abygaelle, and pours himself a glass of carbonated water, looking at her worriedly.

"Why don't you tell me what's going on?"

Abygaelle smiles and exhales. She describes for Ariane; that she inherited the investigation, although it was her first day at her new position; that she wishes she hadn't had this burden on her shoulders to start with. She can't figure out why Charles Picard insisted so much on putting her in this role. Then, there were other victims, probably killed by the same murderer, and she has just learned that the last victim is Ariane's uncle. Her mother is in shock and her other uncle had overdosed. This is probably a serial killer. Her first case and it had to be a goddamn serial killer. She didn't even think it existed anymore. Roland Michaud lets her vent, and when she's done, he suggests that she take this opportunity to show what she's made of. See it as a challenge, an opportunity instead of a hurdle.

"Abygaelle, you are an extremely intelligent woman. You lack self-esteem. You are hesitant. You're not the Abygaelle Jensen I know. You have what it takes to succeed. You have the ability and the character to do it. Own it. It's your case, make it yours. You won't fix it by crying. Go for it. It's not a problem, it's a chance to shine. Picard put you in charge because he did his homework, he knows what kind of girl you are. He spoke to me, he checked with your former colleagues. He knows very well what he's doing. Okay, he probably didn't know that you were after a serial killer, but he trusts you. So you have a decision to make: either you crash and roll under the table, or you grab the bull by the horns and fight. The Abygaelle I know would never roll down and hide. Am I right?"

Abygaelle nods.

"Then let's go. It's your turn to shine. I know you can do it. This psychopath has no chance."

Abygaelle smiles. He'd never shaken her like this before, and that's exactly what she needed. She feels rejuvenated, empowered with a whole fresh energy. The black mist that has surrounded her since joining Homicide has slightly dissipated. If this is what their new relationship is going to be like, she's thrilled. After having received their dish, a salmon tartar for Roland Michaud and a Nicoise salad for Aby, he asks her a little more about this killer everyone is talking about.

Abygaelle realizes at that moment that she knows all the details at once, she comprehends her case completely. There are no grey areas, no hesitation. She knows it from top to bottom. Roland is right, she will succeed. She can do it, nothing will stop her. She's Abygaelle Jensen, former star of the vice squad and future star for the homicide department. She'll catch this son of a bitch, she's confident now. Roland looks at her with a kind smile. He asks her if he can help. Abygaelle appreciates his offer, even though there's not much he can do.

His motivational speech was sufficient.

29

It took Stephane Ranger a few minutes before he grasped what was going on. He lies on his back in a hospital bed, a tube of serum stuck in his right arm, an old, yellowed, switched off TV hanging on the wall in front of him. The room is empty. The curtain on his right separates him from the other bed, but he can't hear any sound coming from that side. It's obvious that his sister Madeleine knows about his overdose since she isn't at his bedside. The fuzzy memory of his carcass squashed on his apartment rug gradually recurs to him. As the fog dissipates, guilt grips him by the throat.

"I'm a moron," he thinks, closing his eyes.

He sighs as he looks out the window. The weather is gloomy, it's probably late afternoon. It puzzles him that Annie St. Onge is not around. She will probably arrive later. She vowed to be there for him, even if he relapses. He doesn't know how long he has been unconscious; it doesn't matter. His entire body is hurting terribly. It's unbearable. He pushes the button to ask for help. A few seconds later, a nurse springs into his room. Noticing he's conscious, she backs up, then comes back several minutes later alongside a tall doctor carrying a chart in his hand and a stethoscope around his neck.

"Mr. Ranger, I'm Dr. Miller, can you hear me?"

Ranger nods. He doesn't have enough strength to speak.

"Please stay calm, you've been in a coma for three weeks. Your muscles haven't functioned for a long time. Be careful of sudden movements."

Three weeks? How is that possible? How one can be in a coma for three weeks from an overdose?

"How do you feel?"

The doctor looks at him nervously.

"Good," Stephane answers with discomfort. His jaw is stiff.

Dr. Miller writes a note in the file. He looks at him for a few seconds and then smiles.

"Let's say good, given the circumstances."

Ranger would have smiled if the muscles in his face had permitted it. He just shrugs off an inch.

"You were very lucky, you know?"

The doctor describes the condition he was in when he arrived, and the actions required to save his life. His heart stopped beating three times while he was in intensive care, but fortunately his condition stabilized afterwards.

"The least we can say is that you're a fighter."

Alone again, Stephane stares at his room's beige ceiling.

He has failed again.

His demons have won. He's all by himself. His sister will never forgive him. He knows. His brother-in-law will do anything to get him out of their lives. This is the worst-case scenario. His brother and niece are dead, and now the abandonment. He's alone. Alone like the loser he is. Alone like the loser he's always been. He has done nothing good in his entire life. Everything he touches turns to shit. Why didn't they just let him die?

A little later in the evening, he asks a nurse if there have been any visitors by writing his question on a notepad.

"A young woman used to come to visit you every night, but nobody saw her lately."

"A young woman?" he mumbles.

"Yes, a little blonde, a bit skinny. Pretty."

Annie.

He has to call her. He's not physically capable at the moment, but as soon as he can string complete sentences together, he will. She hasn't given up on him. She will be his anchor from now on. In the middle of the night, he had a masterful idea to win back his family. Of course, it makes sense. A spark of hope ignited in him. There's no way he's giving up. Not only will he regain Madeleine's respect, but he will give a new meaning to his life. He's invested of a new mission, that of finding Ariane's killer. If he succeeds, Madeleine will forgive him. And he will have honoured his niece's memory. He will never give up until he has found this motherfucker.

Even if it takes years.

For once, he will use his shady past to do something positive. The underworld has a lot of tentacles. No one would stand by child killers. Not even the most psychopathic of criminals. He closes his eyes and smiles. All that's left is to plan for redemption. Redemption for his family.

But mainly redemption from himself.

30

The assassin enjoys the warm wind blowing on his skin. His thoroughness has been undermined by his ego, the damn ego that drove him to Ranger's hospital room. He didn't need to do that. What exactly was he trying to prove? He must control his impulses or else he'll never carry out his mission. He takes a deep, invigorating breath.

He followed the girl home. After a thirty-minute bus ride, she walked for six blocks before reaching her place. She didn't notice the black BMW following behind. Nor did she see the assassin walking behind like a shadow, so close that he could have reached her shoulder. He crossed the street when she veered off towards the entrance of a gloomy apartment block. A chicken cage would be a more appropriate term.

From the adjacent sidewalk, he studies each window of the apartment building to find out where she lives. After a few minutes, two apartments light up almost simultaneously. So it's one of the two. But which one? After looking for hideouts in the surrounding area, he decides that one building directly in front of his target's appears to be the best option. The two buildings are similar in height.

Perfect.

He heads to the parking lot behind and climbs the spiral stairs two by two to the top floor. With his powerful arms, he propels himself onto the roof with ease. Crouching down and moving forward with muffled steps, he hides behind a balustrade providing an excellent view of the units across the street. It breathes deeply several times to relax. He puts down his backpack and grabs his binoculars to scrutinize the interior of the rooms, stalking his prey like a thorough and calculating hunter.

A shadow suddenly appears in front of the right apartment window. A satisfied grin emerges on the assassin's face as he sees Annie St. Onge light up a cigarette.

"There you are, sweetheart."

Annie's legs are still shaking. She thought this nightmare was just a dark memory, but she plunged back into it at the least expected moment. She left a phone message for the detective working on Stephane's case, the one who is working on finding his niece's killer. Although she doubts the individual in the hospital is the actual killer, the fact remains that he has killed someone and has never been prosecuted for it. Therefore, no rocks should be left unturned. One can never be too careful.

She fears for her life. But the man ran from the scene without coming after her, as if he was more afraid than she was. He doesn't know where she lives, so as long as she's holed up in her apartment, she's safe. She checks for the tenth time if she locked her door. There is something wrong with all of this. What was that monster doing standing there with flowers near Stephane's room? Was his faithful friend hiding things from her? If he knows this man, does that mean he played a role in Eric's murder? She herself almost died. She related the story to him several times, and he didn't even flinch. He seemed to be completely unaware of what had happened. He pretended to be Eric's friend. How could he have been involved in something so horrible?

But why? Why would he lie to her? Why keep things from her? She would understand if he explained. This betrayal is intolerable. She helped him so much, and he returned the favor as well. She told herself that finally a man could love her without trying to get in her pants. A pure and innocent friendship that she treasured. She doesn't want to jump to conclusions until she talks to him, but she doesn't see how the assassin could have shown up at the hospital without them knowing each other. How did he find out about his mishaps? How did he know which hospital he was in? And why did he bring flowers?

To take her mind off things, Annie turns the television on. Her head is spinning, the craziest theories are jostling around in her brain. Nothing makes sense anymore. She won't be back at the hospital as long as Stephane is unconscious. Then he'll owe her an explanation. If he doesn't die before.

She curses the lack of variety on television. Always the same boring soap operas, the same actors returning from one series to another. As if there were only five actors in the book. She rests her head on the back of her couch as she looks out the ceiling lamp. She dust it regularly, but there are constantly damn cobwebs knotting up on it. She notices that she has again forgotten to close the curtains of the large living room window. The pervert in the apartment across the street must salivate at her at the moment. Dirty old man.

The reflection from the window doesn't do her justice. She looks as skinny as when she was shooting crystal meth. She didn't see the spark coming from the roof of the building across the street, it's all happening too fast. Fortunately, she doesn't feel the powerful bullet going through her chest. She does not suffer.

She dies instantly.

31

Maxime Fauvette has been walking in the snow for several hours. At least that's how it feels like. It's freezing cold, and the wind is lashing at his face. The pain is unbearable. By squinting his eyes, he still manages to see where he's going. He's head in the right direction. The blizzard is so intense that he can barely see two meters in front of him. He must be careful not to fall into a crevasse or a ravine.

His steps are heavy, and the trek is difficult. Each stride is extremely strenuous. He won't be able to keep going like this for long. If only he knew where he was going. Is he getting closer? He couldn't say. Why is he standing in the middle of a snowstorm ignoring how he got there? He can't remember what he's doing here, alone and at his wit's end. There is nothing around. No trees, no houses, just an endless white desert. An icy and depressing wasteland. He's totally disoriented. He's not even sure if he's moving forward, even though he puts one foot in front of the other. What if he's hovering? His body goes numb, his limbs are frozen.

The more he progresses, the deeper he sinks. He has snow up to his knees. He looks behind. Maybe he should go back?

His instinct, however, urges him to keep moving forward. Ahead, ever further. He lowers his head and keeps pushing. One step at a time, that's all he can do. Then a distant child laughs. Through the fog, he sees a little girl running around in her nightgown. Amidst this cold? Impossible. Is he crazy or is he hallucinating?

"Hello?" he says in an off voice.

Nothing. Only the kid's snickers. His mind is playing tricks on him. Kind of like seeing an oasis in the desert. His subconscious is in survival mode. But why a little girl? If he is to dream up something useful, it should be a house, or an outdoor fireplace. He disregards the child's squeals. He puts his head down and carries on. He will eventually get somewhere or he will die frozen, like Jack Torrance in The Shinning.

Then, about half an hour later, he sees it, his oasis. Ahead of him, in the shape of a house from afar, lights gush out through the wind. Even though he's convinced that it is the product of his imagination, he has nothing else to hold on to. What if it's real? He has to find out for sure. He rushes towards the house. At this pace, he'll get there in about forty-five minutes. Like a trooper, headlong rush towards his target. He's dipping into whatever energy he has left deep down. The girl's laughter lingers behind him, but he doesn't care. He has only one goal in mind. He has to reach this house.

For Laurie. For his children.

The closer he gets, the more the house emerges from the fog. Holy crap, it's happening. There really is a home out there. He pauses to catch his breath, to look at the house. That's when it hits him hard. He recognizes it. He has been examining it for so long that he knows every nook and cranny of it. It's definitely it. Scanning the surroundings, he sees no trees, no frozen lake. It doesn't fit with his memory. This house wasn't in a desert or a wasteland. He looks at the huge, illuminated windows to see if there is anyone inside. A sign of life.

He wonders who lives there now. He keeps on walking, stuck in the snow up to the middle of his thighs. Every step is a threat to end him. He grows comfortable with the idea that he won't make it out alive. The child's laughter has stopped. The little girl stands behind him, motionless. She watches him quietly. She doesn't say a word; she doesn't smile. He feels like he knows her, but his memory is as blurred as the surrounding moment.

He moves forward with pain and misery, but halts at the sight of a shape moving in front of him. He can't perceive what it is with the goddamned blizzard. The creature is slowly approaching. There is snow up to his hips. If it doesn't move, it will turn into a block of ice in seconds. He's not claustrophobic, but it feels like his throat tightens and his vision gets narrower. He's breathless. Frightened by what is coming. Every fiber in his body urges him to flee. But he can't. The snow traps him like a clenched screw. He can barely move.

Two prominent blue marbles emerge from the haze. Maxime stops moving, obsessed by these shiny orbits. Just underneath are huge, sharp fangs. He panics as he watches a white wolf coming towards him, its protruding fangs, its threatening eyes. He tries to break free from the snow the best he can, but he fails. The wolf's blue eyes are striking. If Maxime wasn't so afraid of dying, he would swoon over this splendid animal. The wolf grunts as he moves softly up towards him, as if he were gauging the extent of his prey's strength.

Maxime howls at the house. But no one could hear him with the strong wind. He himself has trouble hearing the sounds coming out of his mouth. Maxime makes big sharp gestures at the animal in an attempt to scare it. Blood drips under the animal's belly. It's hurt. Does it think that Maxime means him harm? Or worse, that he's responsible for its wounds? Maxime stops waving his arms and looks into the wolf's eyes. His eyes have gone from topaz blue to black.

Opaque black. Scary black.

Maxime is petrified. The wolf advances slowly, leaving a thin trail of blood in his path. The predator's growls cause Maxime's ears to buzz. He's just a few meters from him now. That's where it will play out.

"What do you want from me?"

Maxime feels ridiculous to ask, yet should the wolf answer back, it wouldn't be the most strange thing right now, given the circumstances. The wounded creature is still exhibiting its fangs. An exhilarating growl in the background. Maxime doesn't see how this could end other than by his demise. He casts an ultimate glance towards the house in case he sees someone, but still nothing. Only smoke coming out of the chimney. The house looks so warm and cozy. It must smell like burning wood inside. Never again will he smell that sweet perfume.

The wolf hardly walks towards him, it's only two meters away. Maxime is hypnotized by his gaze. Then he recognizes it, clear as daylight. The wound, the blood. Its look both terrifying and desperate. How is this possible? He thought it was all over. Now he understands why the wolf wants him dead. He knows he'll perish. In an ultimate act of bravery, Maxime raises his fists. If he's going to die, it will go out swinging. The wolf bows down, ready to jump at his throat, his tail making an unsettling sideways motion, his drool dripping from his deadly mouth. Then it leaps towards him.

Maxime sits up straight in his bed, covered in sweat. He takes several seconds to realize what's going on, that he's safe in his room, at home. That there is no bloody white wolf. That he won't die. That it's just another damn nightmare. His heart is racing, and he's shivering. What does that mean? He dreams regularly about this wolf and this house. He knows the house, and he remembers the wolf. He has trouble stretching out his fingers because he has clenched his fists so tightly.

"Are you all right, Max?"

Laurie woke up just as Maxime rose abruptly.

"Yes, darling. Nothing to worry about. I had a nightmare. Go back to sleep."

"You worry me, it's not the first time this happens. What are you dreaming about?"

"I can't remember."

He never told her about the house, or the wolf, or the little girl.

And he never will.

32

Murielle Bouchard stands next to Stephane Ranger's bed. She has been staring at him for several minutes with her hands clasped in front of her. She feels a mix of pity and disgust for him. He has been through a lot of hardship lately, but somehow he's to blame for his own misery.

Of course, he didn't kill his niece, but Murielle abhors those damn junkies who only sow suffering with their filthy weakness. She looks at the solute bag connected to his arm, full of scars from unskilled stings, typical of drug addicts. This guy is just a little boy suffocating in an adult body.

The tiny drop that runs through his veins at a regular rhythm put a wicked grin on her face.

"You'd rather it be other stuff going through your vein, wouldn't you?" she says, whispering.

She immediately regrets her scornful comment. Since he doesn't seem he will wake up anytime soon, she goes back to the office. She stopped by the hospital because she was in the neighborhood. She took a chance. Maybe he would have been awake. But he wasn't. She has no business being here anymore.

She chats for a few minutes with the nurse on duty. Asking

if anyone's been visiting lately? Suspicious-looking individuals? She says a young woman used to come every evening, but she hasn't seen her in a while.

"I think she was his girlfriend or something. Or, at the very least, someone close to him," she adds.

"What's her name?" Murielle asks.

"She said her name is Annie."

She describes her summarily: pretty blonde with pale eyes. A warm smile.

"Now that you mention it, she looked weird the last time I saw her. She walked past my unit unseeing me, she looked scared. I asked her if she was OK, but she didn't respond."

Back at the office, Murielle hears that one Annie St. Onge has left a message for Abygaelle. Could it be the same Annie from the hospital? That would be quite a coincidence, admittedly. Murielle calls Annie St. Onge and hears a cheerful woman's voice uttering the usual voicemail formula. Murielle leaves a message and searches for what she can find out about her in the police systems. The driver's license photo depicts a good-looking, long-haired blonde with a straight face. She has the sad look typical of those who have been scorched by life.

A few days later, with no news, Murielle goes to her apartment with Jack. They knock on the door and although they hear the television, no one answers. Murielle calls up Annie from the hallway, identifying herself as a detective sergeant.

"What do we do?" Jack asks. "Smash the door?"

"Take it easy, buddy."

Murielle ponders for a few moments, then turns the doorknob. It's unlocked. The two investigators look at each other as if they were waiting for the other's permission to enter. She opens the door and walks into the apartment. She takes three steps and stops short. A strong smell stinks the room, and they realize exactly what is going on.

Annie St. Onge will bring her secrets to her grave.

They find her slightly putrefied corpse sitting on the couch, as if she was still watching television. She still holds the remote control in her right hand. Covering her nose, Murielle moves closer to the corpse. No apparent sign of violence. A huge stain of dried blood covers almost the victim's entire white shirt. Looking more closely, Murielle spots a cavity in her chest. Jack steps forward near the living room window.

"Murielle, look at this."

He shows a hole in the glass.

"You have to be kidding me?" Murielle says.

She looks through the window at the other side. An apartment building stands in front, providing a perfect angle on the apartment. Once back outside, Jack suddenly has a flash. He picks up the walkie-talkie of a police officer standing next to him and speaks to two officers near the building across the street.

"Climb up on the roof and scour it thoroughly. See what you can find," he says.

Several minutes go by as a crackle of waves clouds Jack's mind. He hopes it's not what he thinks. After getting the confirmation, he gives the device back to the policeman, swearing. He walks furiously towards his colleague.

"So?" she asks.

He just looks at her, clenches his jaw and nods.

No need to say more.

A wooden queen.

33

William can relax at last. The last few days have been challenging. He's had a lot of work. It's good to be back home, in his stuff, with Heather and Edward. Nothing beats being with family and friends to recharge your batteries. William is a superstar at work. He deals with some of the best financial brains on the planet; he rubs shoulders with some of the richest men in the world. Sometimes he gets carried away. But it all becomes meaningless once he sits down with his son in the upstairs playroom.

At times, he feels that despite everything he has, he's missing out on the most important thing. Travelling around the world is great, but if you don't see your child growing up, walking his first steps, speaking his first words, what's the point? Especially since he isn't fundamentally materialistic.

His job gives him an adrenaline rush comparable to a free fall. The excitement that runs through his veins after winning a big client is intoxicating. The same thing happens when he has the foresight to let go of a stock before it collapses. He can ride the adrenaline from those hits for weeks on end.

They hired a nanny for help. They've gambled that he and

Heather can have a successful family life and top-notch careers at the same time. Thankfully, Heather's job requires very little travel since William is constantly in and out of hotels and airports.

He's familiar with several flight attendants. They talk about their families. William's interest for these acquaintances of the sky is inconsequential, he's no philanderer. He strongly believes in fidelity, and he couldn't ask for more than the woman who shares his life. Would he destroy all that he has built for a romp? He's not that stupid. Being a true Cartesian, he takes thoughtful decisions. He never acts on a whim, even if some blame him for his impetuosity. Heather says he should indulge more often, he can afford it. But impulsivity doesn't work for him. He has work with his strengths and weaknesses. Improvisation is not his forte.

He's a proud man. Some would say snobbish and arrogant. He often hears that about him, but when people get to know him better, they realize it's mostly his shyness that gives such a haughty air. He's an unapologetic epicurean. He enjoys evenings with friends over good meals. He's a wine lover and knows a lot about it. He could drop everything and become a sommelier tomorrow if he wanted. He's his family and friends' go-to guy when they have questions about grape varieties. He trains one hour a day, alternating weight training, stabilization exercises, yoga and cardio. His athletic body helps not only to look good on vacation pictures and assuages his narcissism. It's also what enables him to keep up such a sustained pace of work for so long.

A healthy mind in a healthy body. It takes extraordinary energy to accomplish what he does day after day.

People often believe that gym rats do it just for vanity, to build a beautiful, lean, muscular body. Even if it's somewhat true, it affects every facet of life. And it helps to age healthily, to prevent obesity-related illnesses. He harshly condemns those who indulge in their own mediocrity and blame their excess weight on their genetics, or their "glands". Although it's true that genetic baggage has a say in this, it's wrong to believe that people are powerless. Everyone can lose weight, but it takes willpower, consistency, and a good game plan.

Edward is absorbed by a puzzle. William marvels at him as he struggles to match up the pieces. He's nostalgic for the evenings he spent playing with his father between missions for the Canadian Army. Like William, Raymond Primeau wasn't often home. But when he was, he made sure to spend quality time with his children and wife. Things were so much simpler back then. Their conflict didn't diminish his father qualities or his happy childhood memories.

He can see the distinction.

His father was his idol when he was younger. He and his uncle Maurice were his rocks, his role models. When William looked at friends' dads, he knew he was lucky. Raymond commanded respect. He had an aura about him. When he walked into a room, you couldn't ignore him.

It captivated William.

He would never have thought that he would hate him so much one day. That Raymond would turn into the wimp he had become. The Raymond he knew had died at some point to be replaced by a loser who could barely tie his own shoes. He spends his time in his garden, as if his flowers would restore some of his lost virility, his former self. If that's the goal, then the petunias have failed miserably. William has reached a point where he can't stand him anymore. So he has cut all ties with him. It's been going on for years.

Raymond left Nathalie down, and William will never forgive him. He knows what he must do for them to reconnect, but he won't. He would rather waste his time watering flowers and painting tiny cars like a ten-year-old child.

"J'ai fini papa."

I'm done, daddy.

William insists Edward addresses him in French. His agreement with Heather is that he will speak to him in French unless they have to talk to him together. This is the only time William agrees to address him in English. William is proud to hear his son speak the language of Molière with a slight Quebec accent.

This is the greatest gift a parent can offer his child: benefiting from the fact that he is a sponge, hungry for knowledge to teach him languages. The nanny speaks to him in Spanish, so his son will be trilingual before long.

He doesn't comprehend these children from Quebec ice hockey players who don't speak French. This is inconceivable for William. Speaking several languages is an invaluable asset. He himself has learned German over the years, and he babbles some Italian. Heather makes a great effort to speak French because her mother-in-law doesn't speak English. William is tired to be the translator. Heather wants to speak French so badly that she is putting in a lot of effort. She's making significant progress.

"Bon travail, Eddie. T'as bien fait ça. Va te laver les mains, le repas est servi."

Good job Eddie, go wash your hands, dinner's served.

Edward gets up and runs to the dining room. Like his father, he enjoys a hearty meal. William smiles as he sees his child's little legs quickly moving in rapid footsteps. His son doesn't know it, but he experiences the only moments of total innocence in his life. Life will soon enough immerse him in all the horrors this world offers. He misses the day when all he had to do was play, eat and sleep.

In the dining room, under the gigantic chandelier above the table, he hugs Heather as she sits Edward in his high chair. He kisses her on the neck and thanks her for being there for him.

He loves her more than anything in the world.

34

The headline on the news resonates in the apartment where Raymond Primeau had been hiding for days.

"The police have just announced that another person was killed, shot by a sniper. This is the third victim in two weeks of what appears to be a serial killer. "

Raymond Primeau walks near the TV and sees Annie St. Onge's picture on the evening news.

Serial killer.

These words hit him hard. He almost gave in. He sighs and sits on the couch behind him. Suddenly everything seems to slip. He still hasn't decided what to do next. He hasn't been sleeping very well since he fled from his house. Although he loathes the indifferent comfort in which he and his wife have been living for too long, he feels he misses the equilibrium. It's not so bad after all.

He knows very well that going home is tantamount to suicide. The police will soon make the connection with him and track him down. He wouldn't survive in prison. As an outdoor enthusiast, he couldn't bear to be trapped in a cage twenty-three hours a day.

All he has done for his country to end up locked up like a rat? Out of the question.

Better to die.

Monique must be worried sick, especially since he still hasn't called her. He almost did a few times, but he's worried that they monitor his phone line at home.

He uses a police scanner to hear what the police say. Right now, there are only routine arrests or attention-seeking morons who call the police as soon as they hear someone talking a little too loud in an alley.

TV news, newspapers, the Internet and the scanner. Raymond Primeau covers the entire spectrum of possibilities. Information is power, as he likes to remind people. This was true in Vietnam, more so now that he shield his freedom.

His life.

He often thinks about Nathalie lately. All these events have brought him back to his nightmare. He says to himself what he has been saying since he left several days ago. Nathalie is dead. You weren't able to protect her. Watch closely of those still here. Take care of Monique. And even of your ungrateful son.

He turns on his computer, but is disappointed that he didn't get the email he's been waiting for. He closes the lid to his laptop and sighs deeply.

Enough is enough. To know Monique is by herself is too much for him. He can't leave her in the dark any longer.

He puts on his leather coat, zippers up to his chin and leaves to use one of the few public phones still in existence. Nothing under two kilometers from his apartment.

35

The evening was off to a good start and Nathalie Primeau was happy she trusted her instinct and went with the three guys to the party. The music was splendid, and she was having a great time. She had already befriended Geneviève, an eye-catching, tall blonde.

She stayed close to Eric because François Lavoie was a little too clingy for her taste. She had gently made it clear she wasn't interested in him. She had a boyfriend, after all.

Nathalie was dancing like she hadn't in a long time. She drank too much, but since she wasn't driving, it was all good. She would call a cab home later in the evening.

She was fidgeting with Geneviève and they were having a good time, although they spent most of their time chasing away guys circling around them like annoying flies.

At one point, there had been an argument between Eric Gagné, and a man that had escalated.

From that moment on, guys were no longer pushy towards them. Nathalie wasn't fond of Eric's animosity, and she was now keeping her distance.

She loathed violence.

Friendly from the start, Gagné became increasingly demanding as time went on.

The more he drank, the more aggressive he became with those too close to her. Nathalie had to remind him several times that she had a boyfriend.

From the moment she had accepted to go with them, Gagné was sure he would end up in bed with the beautiful brunette. Why was she suddenly so distant? That she had a boyfriend didn't bother him the least. He, too, was seeing someone, but he didn't believe in faithfulness. He didn't mind wrecking other couples when he fancied a girl. Nathalie was more stubborn than he had expected.

He realized that his behavior had frightened her. He knew that his argument with guys had something to do with it. He couldn't help it. Alcohol drove him nuts.

He had several problems in the past with this poison, and each time he swore it was the last time. That he wouldn't drink to the point of losing his shit anymore.

Well, he failed again today, and everything was about to get out of whack. He felt he was losing control and his craving for violence and sex was growing dangerously strong.

An explosive cocktail.

Later, he was alone with Nathalie in the background, and he gave it a go. He wrapped his arms around her waist and tried to kiss her, but she kept pushing him away.

It upset him she wasn't speaking to him, that she was distant and constantly talking about his damn boyfriend.

Nathalie had enough and told Geneviève that she was leaving. Gagné violently grabbed her by the arm to get her closer. His cool, kind face from the early evening had turned into a devilish gaze.

She was petrified.

"Let go of me," she screamed as she tried to free herself from his grip.

"Shut up and stop yelling," Gagné said in a tone that left no room for negotiation.

The music was so strong that she could hardly hear her own voice. She screamed as loud as she could to get attention. Gagné was even more angry. He lifted her up in the air with disconcerting ease and, pivoting on himself, used his body to open the door of an empty room next to them.

He walked forward in the darkness, still holding Nathalie at arm's length, and closed the door with his right foot. He turned to his left and leaned the young woman against the wall with such force that she lost her breath.

Nathalie was freaking out.

"You've been teasing me all night, you slut," Gagné said as he dropped her on the floor while keeping her against the wall. He reeked of alcohol.

"Please, let go of me. There's people around. You're scaring me."

"I don't give a fuck about people."

He had forcefully kissed her as she tried to get loose by hitting him on the chest, but since Gagné was holding her arms, she had no leverage to do any damage.

Trapped, she had bitten his lip. It drove him completely crazy. He screamed in pain, tossing her across the room.

Nathalie's head had struck the corner of a desk, and it knocked out her. She was lying on the floor while she tried to come to her senses. She was at Gagné's mercy. No one would hear the commotion because of the music.

François Lavoie, who saw them enter the room a few minutes earlier, was curious to know what was going on. He came in.

"She bit my lip, that filthy bitch."

"Why would she do that?"

"I was kissing her and she bit me."

Lavoie closed the door behind him.

"What's her fucking problem?"

"I don't know, but now she's about to get one."

The door had opened again. This time it was Stephane Ranger checking out what was going on. Even though he was high to the point he could barely stand up, he followed Lavoie.

Gagné ordered him to block the door with a wooden chair that was near a computer desk.

"She was teasing me all night long, let's show what we do with little whores like her. We will fucking treat ourselves."

Fear crippled Nathalie came back to her senses. How could she fight three men much stronger than her? She was looking for an escape around; she saw no way out, only a closed window. A powerful hand grabbed her by the hair.

She noticed Gagné's fetid breath. He forced her to face him while his lift his skirt with his other hand and quickly tore her g-string off effortlessly. Nathalie cried for help, but the music still covered her voice.

"Shut the fuck up," Gagné shouted, dragging her hair even harder from behind.

Nathalie screamed louder and louder until Gagné's fist broke her nose. The pain was so severe that she lost consciousness for a few seconds.

"I told you to shut the fuck up, you whore!"

He had turned her over on her stomach and sat on top of her, crushing her with all his weight. Nathalie thought she would choke to death. She realized he was taking off his belt and lowering his jeans.

She had felt his erection on her thigh earlier in the evening as he rubbed himself on her while dancing. Gagné instructed Lavoie to help him restrain her by holding her head and shoulders against the floor.

He did so. Lavoie had never seen such a beautiful naked girl for real in his life. He was fired up, aroused as never before. He overheard Nathalie Primeau say something to him while Gagné was reaching out to force himself in her.

"What?" Lavoie said, getting closer to better understand.

"You're a fat piece of shit," she said.

Furious, he lifted her head a few centimeters and crushed it brutally against the ground. The shock was so violent that everything had become silent, except for a lengthy hissing noise. She was totally confused. It took several seconds for her to feel the sharp burn of Gagné's penis piercing through her.

His distant, muffled grunts became louder as she came back to her senses. She had a tremendous headache, but it was nothing compared to what Gagné was putting her through. Lavoie still braced her to the ground while Gagné raped her, yelling every misogynistic insult imaginable.

After five minutes on the merry-go-round, she sensed him coming inside her with a long animal grunt.

"Your turn," Gagné said to Lavoie.

"Fuck she's gorgeous," Lavoie said.

Nathalie felt her aggressor's enormous belly crushing her back. He was struggling to achieve what he had set out to do. He was so excited that he was drooling over her. The obese sweaty smell disgusted her so much that she thought she would vomit. She swallowed big gulps of her own blood instead. Lavoie lifted her up to position her on all four. Gagné momentarily let go of her shoulders. Nathalie tried to punch him in the genitals, but she missed and struck him on the thigh. Gagné choked her by wrapping his right arm around her neck. He then crushed one of her hands with his knee to prevent another blow.

Every part of her body made her suffer terribly.

She had lost consciousness again, just before Lavoie finally achieved what he was trying to do for several minutes.

When she came to her senses, she was lying on her back. Gagné was still holding her down by the shoulders. She had excruciating pain in her genitals. Her breasts were burning as if they had been bitten. She could hear Gagné urging Ranger to hurry. He couldn't get it up.

After two tries, he resigned.

Nathalie assumed the gang rape was over at that point. The three perpetrators were arguing, but she could not hear what they were saying to each other. They scared her to death.

She prayed to God that they would leave her behind and flee. They could run away. She knew who they were; she had their sperm in her, and friends had taken their pictures. She was pretending to be unconscious. She would wait for them to leave and she would call an ambulance.

Oh, there will be an ambulance. Doctors will use a rape kit to collect semen. All this will happen, but only after she suffered more than she could have imagined.

This was far from over.

36

Abygaelle smashes her glass against the wall. She knows she shouldn't get angry like that, but she can't help herself. Some social media posts are abjectly stupid. She can't take it anymore.

People are so ignorant, she thinks. All these armchair quarterbacks with their far-fetched theories about the murderer. Their sketchy strategy on how to catch him. Of course, they'd know what to do, they'd do better than the detective. Reading dumb stuff, like, how many dead teenage girls will it take for law enforcement to do something? As if Davison and St. Onge's lives were less noteworthy because they were adults. As if they weren't doing everything they could to stop the killer.

She quickly dismissed misogynistic comments, claiming that should a man be in charge, it would be over by now. And they say that she's only there because she looks nice on TV. Like smoke and mirrors to cover the police gross incompetence up.

No really, people are stupid.

These freaks don't know what they're talking about. They know nothing about investigative work. They're not the ones having trouble sleeping at night because their brains are constantly looking for solutions, for a lead to pinpoint the killer. Figuring out what they do wrong, what they miss.

Easy from their living room lazy-boy to state that one should violate the rights and liberties of rifle owners to grill them one by one, without a warrant, wasting a tremendous amount of time on totally useless clues.

It's also easy to claim they would drag anyone to justice, ignoring that you can't just do that without protocol or solid evidence. You don't arrest someone just for the fun of it, without probable cause.

Murielle told her several times not to pay attention to this rubbish. She shouldn't read the newspapers, ignore the radio or television. Don't dignify fame-hungry ex-police officers acting as experts on the evening news. They only have vague comments, as they don't know what's really going on any more than the public does. They don't have access to the information.

They should stick to what they know, which is educating the population on standard procedures. They, too, are looking for the spotlight on the victims' expense.

Yes, sometimes law enforcement officials use the media to get their messages across. Aby would have liked their support instead of baseless criticism. Most people are cautious. They say that being a detective isn't easy, that they do their best, but Abygaelle is considerable more hurt by comments from a handful of idiots than from those from the more measured and logical majority.

If only they knew how much she's sick that she can't find a solid lead. How dare they pretend that the Provincial Police don't care about the case? It upset everybody here. All of them are eager to catch this maniac. They are working around the clock on this case. But these pathetic second-guessers vilify all their efforts with a twelve-seconds tweet.

Opportunists who use Ariane's death and that of others to sell their macabre and disgusting rhetoric sicken her. Racist comments about Arabs or migrants whenever something bad happens, while lone wolves Caucasians carry most shootings and mass murders out. Some even claim that secret government organizations are carrying out these horrors to exert control over the population, or the CIA is helping the United States seize the province's water supplies. It takes all kinds to make a world.

Fine.

But can there be less of that kind?

She so badly would like to reply to them, to tell them how ridiculous they are with their silly assumptions which only exist in their sick brains, in their deranged minds, but it wouldn't do any good.

"Don't feed the trolls," they say.

These folks lack attention in their lives. They make up for it by spewing their bullshit on the Internet. The worst thing is that they aren't alone. All these freaks hide behind pseudonyms and fake photos. That's what happens when you don't assume your opinions; you keep out of sight like a coward.

Abygaelle understands this perfectly.

Once settled down, she picks up the pieces of glass from the floor. She hates to lose control like that. She is both Cartesian and logical. How is it she can have such a big outburst of rage to the point of losing her mind for a few seconds? She can't prevent this surge of violence in her, even though she senses it coming.

Like a blackout.

It left her hands before she realized it, as if an evil force had taken hold of her body. She saw herself in slow motion, throwing the glass against the wall with all her strength. One of her former lovers told her she had an alter ego whom he had named Bonnie, like in Bonnie & Clyde.

When she lost control of herself like that, he said her eyes would change color, they would darken, and that's when Bonnie would appear and take over for a few hellish seconds.

Bonnie, Aby's self-destructive doppelganger.

She shakes her head and laughs. She despise dwelling on the past. Mario had a knack for making her feel like shit. Abygaelle doesn't have multiple personality disorder, but, yeah, on the very rare occasions, very brief moments, it's as if someone is taking command of her being.

As if a latent volcano sits inside her, just waiting for a spark to explode. Once it comes blazing, there's no stopping it.

And anything can happen.

As long as it's innocent, like a glass against a wall, there is no harm. But what if Bonnie surfaces for a few seconds as she has a gun in her hands?

Who knows?

She's not sure if she could handle herself. Luckily, she hasn't had to test the concept until now. Her outbursts are extremely rare, but this is the first time they've appeared for something as trivial as some dumb comments about her work written by strangers she couldn't care less about.

Probably because of the anxiety in her new job, and the pressure from the case.

This is no excuse.

This destructive impulse wasn't different. She has lived with it all her life. She felt a similar compulsion as a child when she saw her father standing in front of her on the stairs leading up to their apartment.

But what scares her most about this sudden, vivid fury, are the seconds of total terror she feels immediately after.

37

Montreal, May 17, 2005

THE SIGHT of these beautiful naked girls stunned Stephane Ranger. They dance in front of sweaty men, watching their divine bodies as if they were pieces of meat.

For a few dollars, they waddle in front of them, suggesting they might have a chance to sleep with them. So they lay out their money to get one of her to love them, even if it's a fallacy. They dream that they're theirs, and the girls play along. This exchange of good deeds benefits both unhealthily.

Stephane consumed heroin. He's therefore impotent, unable to have a decent erection. Instead, he pays for lap dances in VIP lounges, with money he doesn't have, buried deep in the vicious circle in which he has been languishing for too long. He borrowed money from his relatives, and worse, from shark lenders.

The trifecta of all his miseries: drugs, alcohol, and hookers.

He works part-time in a pork transformation factory. He's

disgusted by the smell. He can no longer eat bacon, but he needs to earn a living.

His situation has been worse lately. Shylocks have sent out their goons to summon him he better pay up quickly. His mother wondered when she would recover the money she lent him, if ever. At that point, she should have known she won't ever see the color of her money. She's too kind, and he's too manipulative. She lost a fortune funding her son's debauchery, and he will milk this cash cow to the last drop.

His sister figured it out. She cut off ties with him after a dispute over money. She couldn't stand how badly he exploited their mother. She tried her best to reason with her, but she was incapable of bail on her elder son.

He tried to break away from this. Detox clinic managers know him very well. He goes to Narcotics Anonymous meetings and other gatherings, but he keeps slipping back into it. His demons entrench their sharp claws in his throat to bring him down.

Death his only way out.

He thought about taking own life several times, but couldn't muster up enough courage to act.

Maybe one day.

When he'll be sober after a monumental drinking spree. When he'll feel guilty enough of taking advantage of his mother's good heart. When he'll hate himself so much that he would prefer to vanish. When his demons will finally get the best of him and plunge him into an infinite abyss. That gangrene eating away every cell in his body, that filth destroying his brain.

But tonight is party night.

He'd die another day.

Sitting at a table with two of his friends as sick as he is, they comment about the exotic dancers' breasts, asses and legs. Rating their pelvic movements, how beautiful they look when they arch their backs. God, what they'd do to them if they could. Stephane goes along with it even though he knows he couldn't do shit in his condition.

A few meters back, a gentleman is sipping a beer, alone. He hadn't looked at the stage since he came in. He was watching all three men, especially Stephane Ranger, who had his back to him. As time went by, rage grew inside him. All the laughter, the high-fives. Seeing this bastard pay for girls to go with him in the VIP lounge for a few songs, and then come back with a blissful grin on his face.

"Perfect," the assassin thought. "Enjoy your last moments of happiness, you piece of shit."

He had ordered another beer. It would be his last before switching to diet soda. A beer per hour would not impair his reflexes and his intellectual capacities. Since it was half-past one in the morning, and Ranger would leave soon, he prayed he would be by himself, as his friends would impede what he meant to accomplish. He didn't want to follow this jerk to his home. He wanted to act quickly and precisely. Two bullets in the back of the head, then vanish into the night.

Ranger took more money from the ATM, then waved a girl to follow him. The assassin clenched his teeth. How could he live with such impunity after what he had done? He couldn't conceive that some people have so little shame, so little remorse.

Forty-five minutes later, Ranger walked up to someone at the bar and they left together. The assassin kept staring at Ranger's two friends, weighing his options. Then the man from the bar came back by himself.

Where was this moron?

The assassin sipped the rest of his diet coke and walked out through the main door. Ranger was nowhere to be seen. Shit, he was gone. He cursed, furious that he didn't follow his lead. He went around the place. He couldn't be very far.

He turned left to a less busy street, but he wasn't there. He walked quietly, searching every parking space. He was listening for any sound that might point him in the right direction.

When he reached a small, poorly lit alley, he went straight into it with little hope. But it turned out to be an excellent decision, as he heard a conversation between a woman and a guy who sounded like Ranger.

He approached slowly, hiding behind a wooden utility pole. Bingo. There he was, chatting with one of the strippers.

"Pay me first, pal. You've got a reputation. Everybody knows your trick, getting a head job and never actually pay. I ain't doing nothing until you pay me in full."

"Come on. I'll pay you later. I don't have it tonight, but you know me, I come to the club often. I swear I'm going to pay you. Come on."

He pulled down his pants, exposing a tiny, flaccid cock. The girl laughed.

"What the fuck am I supposed to do with this?"

"It'll be hard, trust me. This happens all the time. Come on, get on your knees, I don't have all day."

The woman looked up and down at him, puzzled. Then she walked away and left him high and dry.

"I'm not dumb. You pay first. Jack off if you're broke, that's all. I'm not the UNICEF."

The assassin stepped back into the shade so that the girl leaving two meters away from him wouldn't spot him.

"Come back, you fucking whore. Come back Natasha, I'll pay you, I swear."

Realizing she was gone, he pulled up his pants, still insulting her.

He sat down on the ground and opened a small leather pouch. The assassin crept towards him, screwing a silencer onto the end of his revolver. He monitored Ranger closely, standing by a wooden fence lining the triplex parking lot.

He had an excellent view of the junkie wrapping a rubber band around his arm. He was boiling a substance on a piece of aluminum foil under which he was holding a lighter. Then he sucked the hot liquid into a syringe and injected it into his vein.

He grumbled for a few seconds and collapsed against the wall behind him. His head fell forward, as if he was falling asleep. The assassin thought the sight of him was absurd. He was lying there, unconscious, the syringe still stuck in his arm, his pants undone.

Humanity's underbelly.

He stood there, watching him in all his degradation. He would die sooner rather than later at that pace. Maybe even in the next seconds, right in front of his eyes. How could anyone get to that? He didn't get it. He never felt the need to numb himself to bear his existence, to deal with the burden of life.

Instead, he would rather have full control of his mind, be in command of his abilities. When one feels the need to anesthetize oneself, then one has given up.

He slid closer to Ranger, holding his weapon in his right hand close to his body. Ranger was in terrible shape. The assassin kicked him sharply on the shins to elicit a reaction. Ranger opened his eyes and moaned. Then, when he noticed an individual standing next to him, he opened his eyes wider.

Then closed them again.

More kicks.

"Wake up. I want you to see this," the assassin said.

Ranger opened his eyes halfway once more. Noticing the gun pointed at his face, he stiffened. His stare met the assassin's, his face was displayed. He hadn't deemed it necessary to cover it.

What was the point? He was about to die.

Ranger smiled as he unbuttoned the first three buttons of his shirt. Then he spread his arms out in a cross, as if he was embracing what was coming. It disconcerted the assassin. Ranger wanted him to shoot him.

He pondered what he should do while holding Stephane at gunpoint. Still crushed on the ground, Ranger mumbled something.

"What did you say?"

The assassin came closer so he could hear better.

"Please!"

"Please what?"

Stephane smiled.

"Kill me."

The assassin lowered his weapon. He knew what he should do, seeing him like this, sitting in dry urine, unable to speak coherently.

He thought that the decay in which this human wreck would wallow was a worse punishment than death. That he would do him a favor by killing him like a stray dog in that filthy alleyway.

Ranger rolled his eyes and fainted again.

The assassin kicked him again on the shins, but this time he didn't react.

He knelt down in front of him.

"I know you can hear me, you fucking asshole, so listen to me. You are nothing. You're just a piece of shit I could crush with my foot. But the problem with shit is that it sticks and stinks for days. Hey, look at me," he snaps his fingers. "Do you understand what I'm saying? I wanted to kill you, but your life is so pathetic that I'll just get a kick out of watching you sink into your own shit hole and die like a jackass, alone, with a needle in your arm. Your mother should be so proud to see you like that, eh, Stephane? Hello, can you hear me? So die, you monster."

He took a picture from his pocket

"You see her, right? Do you recognize her? You weren't even worthy of her."

Stephane Ranger's eyes filled with tears. He could understand what the man was saying.

"Kill me," he said once again, begging.

The assassin stood up and looked down at him condescendingly.

"No, I won't kill you. I want you to suffer as she suffered. Like I suffered."

He kicked him hard in the stomach, causing him to scream from pain and fall on his side.

After spitting on him, the assassin gone back the same way he came. He could hear Ranger crying loudly in the background, and it made him smile. But once in his car, he couldn't figure out why, deep down in his soul, he felt so guilty.

Normally, he would have reached out to him and offered his help. It would have been the right thing to do, but he couldn't. His disgust was too strong.

He was glad he hadn't killed him. It would probably have been a solace for this asshole.

There had already been enough victims.

38

Nathalie lost all hopes once Eric Gagné lifted her off the floor. He and François Lavoie dragged her to God knows where. They dressed her with Lavoie's hoodie to hide her face.

The smell coming from the material sickened her.

The smell that would tarnish her forever.

The intense music ringing around them suggested they were back in the main party room. The two men carried her. She wanted to scream and fight, but she couldn't.

She didn't have an ounce of energy left in her.

From the only eye she could see with, she noticed people looking distractedly in her direction, but kept on dancing as if nothing happened. They must have thought she had too much to drink, and both guys were helping her out, taking her home like good samaritans.

Outside, she at least got some fresh air. She still swallowed some blood, but not as heavily as before.

"Where is your car?" Gagné asked.

"Further away," Lavoie said.

Nathalie was horrified. She fought to break loose, but Gagné squeezed her throat so tightly that she froze.

"Stop moving, bitch."

Gagné relaxed his grip as she was about to faint. She heard the typical ringing sound of an open car door and felt being thrown onto a seat.

"Fuck, she will bleed all over the place," François Lavoie said with a grumble.

"No, she won't. We'll hold her head high," Gagné said.

"I don't like it, man. I really don't like it."

"I don't care whether you like it or not. We're getting the fuck out. Start the car and do as I say. There won't be any problem."

Nathalie thought all this was ludicrous. She was violently beaten, and she didn't know what these savages had in store for her, and this idiot was more fearful than she was.

After a twenty minutes' ride, she was abruptly pulled out of the vehicle. Instead of driving her to a hospital as she expected, she was somewhere with no apparent civilization around. Only a huge and endless field. That could only mean one thing. Her aggressors had no intention of taking her home or cavalierly dropping her off in front of a hospital.

For the first time, she didn't like her chances of making it out alive.

She was gradually resigned to her fate despite the urge to fight from her inner voice, to battle for her life. Shouts of discord brought her to reality.

"If you're too spineless to finish the job, wait in the car. I'll take care of her."

"We could leave her here and leave," Stephane Ranger said.

"No, she'll go straight to the police. Trust me, I won't go back to jail."

Lavoie walked away.

"So fix it yourself. I won't have her blood on my hands. Fuck that. Besides, I'll need to wash the car from top to bottom to get all this shit off."

"Fucking cowards," Eric Gagné said.

He grabbed Nathalie by the hair and dragged her to a ravine.

She had the strength to scream.

"Stupid cunt, there is nobody here, can't you see? You can scream as much as you want."

She shouted even louder until Gagné's fist struck her in the jaw.

"Shut your fucking mouth, you crazy bitch."

He threw her into the ravine, then stared at her for a long time, wondering what to do with her. She looked at him with disdain. Gagné lit her face with a flashlight.

"Don't you dare look at me."

She didn't budge. Looking delighted, Gagné jumped into the ditch.

"Well, you had it coming, bitch."

He bashed her three times on the head with his flashlight, but she couldn't feel anything anymore. The light went out on the third blow. The flashlight had broken from the impact.

"Jesus, you've got a tough head," Gagné said with a chuckle.

He walked away from Nathalie, scanning the ravine for something. She got up, stumbling. Then, she sought to escape, but her legs wouldn't comply. She lost all sense of balance.

Gagné came back to her quickly with a heavy tree branch in his hand.

"Enough games, say your prayers."

She saw Gagné swinging the tree branch with both hands to her head before sinking into darkness.

Nathalie was playing ball in the house's backyard. She was happy. The entire family was there. It was the Primeau's annual barbecue. They invited family and friends for a pool-side feast.

The mood was cheerful. Nathalie was having fun with her cousins and the guests' children. William looked at her tenderly. Monique crumpled her hair vigorously with affection as she passed by, like she always did.

Nathalie knew how lucky she was to have such a happy childhood. She and her brother had everything one can wish for. Caring parents who would have sacrificed themselves to give them everything they wanted.

She was swimming with the other kids when an esoteric force pulled her to the bottom of the pool.

Panicked, she swam with all her strength to get to the surface, but she was stagnant. She screamed in the water with no one reacting. She swallowed a lot of water.

Then a hand went into the pool.

Time had stopped. Nathalie wasn't swallowing water anymore. She watched her father's face, deformed by the reflection of the water. He was talking, but she couldn't hear what he was saying. She saw him dipping his arm in the water towards her.

"Fight, sweetheart."

She heard him this time. She stretched out her arm and her father's powerful grip snatched her up by the wrist.

"Fight."

Nathalie woke up startled and having trouble understanding what was going on, where she was. She had a colossal headache. She had difficulty perceiving her surroundings because her puffy eyes hardly opened, and the sunlight was burning her pupils.

A huge dark bird stared at her from the top of a tree with a troubling look, motionless. She wondered if it was a crow or a vulture. The majestic animal flew away with a loud screech, and Nathalie noticed the splendid blue sky for the first time, contrasting with the opaque blackness of the dramatic events she had just experienced.

She slowly remembered what had happened to her. She could feel her heart wringing as she relive the terrible stuff these jerks did to her. Every inch of her body was hurting terribly. Her genitals were on fire and her belly was aching as if someone had ripped her open from her belly button to her throat.

Then she had a thought for her mother.

She must be worried sick. Nathalie didn't have a way to contact her. She did not know what to do. She had to call for help. Telling her mom that she was still alive.

Using whatever limited energy she had, she set her sights on crawling to the top of the ravine. She grabbed the grass on the mound to her right and climbed up slowly. The rise was so strenuous that she doubted she would make it to the top. The ravine seemed higher than the Himalayas.

After about an hour of struggling, fighting to hold on to the grass that gave way under her bruised hands, she could finally see the road above. She rolled over to get out of there and knelt on the roadside. It was cold for a June day. There were no cars on the horizon.

She didn't know what time it was, but based on the sun's location, it was early in the morning. Maybe six or seven o'clock. Her body was full of insect bites and stings. She was dirty and bruised. Even nature had no respect for her. It abused her too. She had never felt so useless.

She felt like garbage, like an object you throw away after use. Her heart pounded when she spotted a car in the distance. She tried to raise her hand, but couldn't do so. She wanted to scream, but no sound came out of her throat. She wept in desperation as the car drove on.

"No one will notice me. No one will help me. I'll die here."

She looked back as she heard a shrill sound further to her right. The car had stopped and backed off the road. A lady in her sixties stepped out on the passenger side.

"Hello?" she shouted.

Nathalie didn't have the energy to answer. She just watched

impassively as the woman approached her cautiously. A few meters away from Nathalie, she had stopped abruptly and covered her mouth with her hand. Her eyes filled with fear. She couldn't believe what she was seeing.

"Oh my God."

Nathalie felt the ground slipping beneath her. Everything had turned black, and she fell back into darkness.

39

In the woods, hidden in an abandoned hunting hideout, the assassin waits patiently for the party's return. The scent of pines reminds him of walks in the forest with his father as a child. These moments of happiness are still well engraved in his memories.

He enjoyed these trips, which invariably ended with a visit to his favorite dairy bar.

Nostalgia emanates from a powerful emotion he hates giving in to. It's so pointless to live in the past. But when he looks back on those days, he can't hold back from the melancholy that fills his mind. Those moments when he was just a young, innocent child.

Those moments when he was still human.

He rests his head against the wooden wall behind him and takes a deep breath. He had tracked Jacques Légaré down and sat down at a table next to his at the restaurant he just entered.

The assassin couldn't believe it when he spotted Madeleine Légaré sitting next to her husband. He could have shot both of them on the spot quickly and crossed two names off his list.

But that would have been stupid.

He would have exposed himself. There were plenty of witnesses. That's the bullshit brainless criminals do, and that's how they get caught. Take the easy way out, instead of sticking to their plan. It won't happen to him.

Madeleine Légaré had her back to him, and Légaré was facing her. The beauty of being a faceless assassin is that you can sit next to your target with no one acknowledging you. All the more reason not to stir up a ruckus.

Patience and orderliness.

Everything comes to those who wait.

Then the conversation got lively. Légaré was gesturing a lot, arguing with his weeping wife. He deciphered only a few bits of the argument. Légaré alleged not to be afraid, that it was an annual thing, and that he didn't care about what could happen to him.

The assassin listened more carefully to figure out what was going on. He got excited when he realized Legaré was planning to go on a hunting trip with friends. He offered him his head on a silver platter. Nothing could be simpler than hiding in the woods and shoot out of sight. Even if Légaré is with people, it's very difficult to locate someone in a forest, even more so if he doesn't want to be seen. There are countless ways to blend in.

Jacques Légaré is on the list, and even if he's the last name at the very bottom, he's still on it. No one said he must tackle the list in order. Madeleine eventually agreed to his retreat, realizing that he wasn't flinching. What an unbelievable mistake!

Sheer suicide.

He thinks he's safe, but God knows he isn't. He became the assassin's priority.

All he needed to do was follow him, and hunt him down like an animal and blow his brains out. His fellow hunters will testify that they didn't see who did it. War is war.

So there he is, several days later, waiting for Légaré and his friends to come back to camp. They left before the assassin had time to strike.

Amidst this sidereal silence, he can only hear his panting breath, filled with excitement. His hands are steady. He takes pride in his ability to handle his emotions. As long as he does, nothing bad can happen.

He will never get caught.

To think that when he was younger, he was a sickly and fearful child. He's now here with a rifle in his hands, ready to carry out once again the worst of barbarisms. His greatest strength lies in his surgical strategic sense.

He thinks about all the fine details that usually slip through a neophyte's fingers. What makes him so commanding is the power of life and death over others.

"Après moi, le déluge."

Few people possess his intellectual skills. People are often stupid, happy-go-lucky. He likes to mention to anyone who would listen, and sometimes even to those who won't. Crackles behind him bring him back to reality. Distant voices and laughter. His heart races, but his hands remain steady. He knows the incoming voices. They come back to the camp.

He smiles softly and licks his chops.

The rising darkness makes his task a little more difficult, but it's still workable. A few more minutes and he wouldn't have had the same easiness to shoot. There still is enough light to make an excellent shot. He's about a hundred yards from his target. An easy shot for someone of his value.

The four hunters sit in a circle on a makeshift seat. Jacques Légaré has his back to the assassin. The discussion that begun before they got here carries on, or rather Jacques Légaré's monologue, as he shares his thoughts with his trusted friends.

Long-time buddies who knew him as a disobedient teenager, always in conflict with authority. They have watched him grow into a relatively successful entrepreneur. He's no pushover.

"I don't care, Pierre. Since the death of my daughter, I don't give a shit about dying anymore."

Out of hiding to get a better shot, the assassin lies down on the soggy grass, the barrel of the rifle resting on a tripod set on an embankment of dead leaves. His prey is in sight, the marker on his rifle scope pointing directly at the center of his neck.

"I will grant your requests," he whispered, gently resting his index finger on the trigger.

"—but it would piss me off if I pass before my idiot brother-in-law. There is no way I can leave Madeleine on her own with that asshole."

The assassin drops his rifle a bit to turn his head so he can better hear what he's saying. Fortunately, Légaré's voice travels well.

It surprises his fellow hunters.

"We knew you didn't like him very much, Jacques. But isn't it a little excessive to wish him dead?"

"No, all he can do is sow sorrow wherever he goes. He made my mother-in-law and my wife go through hell, and now he's crying over Ariane's fate as if she were his own daughter. He was never there for her, and suddenly he got closer to his sister and he's the uncle of the year? I hate him, he hates me, it's been like that since my mother-in-law died. I swear to you, she was a holy woman. Man, did he mistreated her. May God rest her soul."

The guys were listening to every word he says. After a few minutes of frustration, Légaré shakes his head.

"Anyway, fuck him. I gave him too much attention. For everyone's sake, I wish he'd die. It'd be better that way."

Confronted with his friends' stunned expression, Jacques Légaré laughs loudly.

"Jeez, boys, relax. It's just a figure of speech."

They smile shyly as they take another sip of beer.

"Still," said one of them to change the subject, "the young waitress at the bar was something else, wasn't she?"

A hundred meters away, a pile of compacted leaves had kept the silhouette of the assassin who had sneaked out as furtively as he had arrived.

40

Seated at Jacques-Cartier's pizzeria on the street of the same name, Stephane Ranger is nervously expecting a relic of his past. It probably has been three years since he last saw Nicolas Landry, his former drinking partner. He has cut all ties with him when he cleaned up his act. When he stopped drinking alcohol for good. It worked. At least, until everything got out of hand these last few days. He doesn't get Annie's silence; he left her several unanswered messages. He doesn't have the guts to go to her place, because she obviously has something against him. But at the moment he doesn't have time to think about it, he has a new mission: to solve the mystery surrounding his niece and brother's deaths. They are related; he has no doubt about it. He needs to know for sure.

Marc-André had enemies. He was not a choirboy. But Ariane? Killed similarly? It makes no sense. He will figure out this enigma and then leave this world that has nothing more to offer to him. To contribute as little as he can.

Landry is late. He hasn't changed.

Stephane sipped his Coke Zero as slowly as he could and

feels the waitress getting impatient. It's time for Landry to arrive.

He hears a loud and familiar voice outside the restaurant. He recognizes Landry's playful tone. He's eager to see his reaction. Is he still upset that he cut him out of his life, or will it will thrill him to see him again?

"Fucking Stephane Ranger, Holy shit!"

Landry has a big smile across his face and rushes at him. He has put on weight again. He's at least four hundred and fifteen pounds now. He shaves his head and wears grey jogging pants and dirty running shoes.

Ranger was the intellectual of the bunch. A good student, he had a low opinion of himself. He blames his drinking problems on self-loathing. He's always been like that from as far as he can remember. He's fairly reserved and polite.

Landry is a handyman who speaks rudimentary English, even though it's his mother tongue. He's very self-assured and takes up much space. He fully embraces it. This allowed him to quickly join a biker gang and to climb the ladder. Landry's cell phone rings a few seconds after he sits down with Stephane.

"Hold on," he says as he answers.

He's talking way too loud, like those who think that cell phone mikes are cheap. Stephane blushes as he notices how irritated other patrons are.

After a few minutes that felt like an eternity, Landry hangs up.

They exchange the usual greetings, assess their respective lives over the last three years, and then Stephane gets to the core of the matter. Landry's purple face is tinged with surprise.

"The girl was your niece?"

Stephane nods and looks down.

"It has nothing to do with us. We don't mess with children."

Ranger tells him what he knows. He talks about his brother,

shot in the head with a single bullet fired from far away. Just like Ariane. He wants to find out who's behind it.

Landry's looses his smile.

"Now I see why I suddenly heard from you."

Subtlety has never been Stephane's forte.

"I'm desperate, Nick. I want to find the scum who murdered my niece and my brother."

Landry looks at him for long seconds, then sighs deeply.

"I'll never stand for the killing of a child. Especially not someone close to a friend. But we will not discuss such things here. Call me later tonight to tell me what you know, and I'll see what I can dig up. Sorry, but I have to go."

The imposing man struggled to get up from the wooden chair he was sitting on. He has lost his cheerfulness, but it doesn't matter, Stephane needs his help to find whatever lead he can. Landry shakes his hand unconvincingly and leaves the scene, answering another call.

The evening discussion was more enjoyable. The biker regained some of his enthusiasm and, even though the tone of the conversation was more business than social, it was still cordial.

Stephane elaborated on his theory extensively, explaining the connection between both deaths; the anonymous letters with serial killer quotes; etc.

Landry promised to get back to him in the next few days. Stephane fell asleep on his bed, wondering whether he should tell the police about this. Sure, it will delight them to see that a biker is interfering with their investigation, he thinks, rolling his eyes. He decides not to.

He smiles and closes his eyes. There was nothing left to do but hope that Landry would find something useful.

41

The public inquiry was successful. They targeted a young man matching the car dealership's camera picture. Obviously, his name is not Leo Dion. His real name is Kevin Dupont. He has a criminal record for possession of stolen goods and theft. He's a small-time criminal. Dupont wasn't hard to convince to show up at the police station and answer some questions. Jack is looking forward to understanding what happened. He barely can hide his trepidation.

Finally, something tangible.

The young man sounded very nervous on the phone. Far from the image one would have of a cold and calculating serial killer. He tempered Abygaelle's expectations. He's definitely not the murderer.

"I know," she said. "But he holds at least one key to the mystery. It's the best we've had so far. Who knows if it's not what we needed to finally crack the case open and stop the carnage?"

Kevin Dupont came with his mother. Jack grins at the woman's stern look. It's apparent the young man had an earful on the way to the police station. Dupont has his head down and speaks in a low voice. His mother requests to come into the interview room with his son, but since he's over eighteen, Jack declines. He fears that she'll scare him so much that he won't openly speak.

Even the worst criminals don't want to disappoint their mothers.

After the usual introductions, Jack gets to the key aspect.

"Kevin, you have to be honest with me. I'm a kind and gentle man, but I don't have a lot of patience for bullshit. Do we understand each other? So when I ask you a question, you must answer truthfully. I insist that what comes out of your mouth is the truth. If you lie to me, I won't be on your side, and I swear you don't want that."

Dupont collapses in his chair, scared as hell. Jack is convinced Dupont is too scared to lie and act tough.

"Let's start from the beginning. How did you come to buy the Altima?"

Kevin twists and turns in his chair, trying to figure out where to start.

"One of my friends told me—"

"Who's that?"

"What?"

Jack sigh, annoyed.

"Your friend, who is he?"

Kevin lowers his head but doesn't answer.

"Kevin, what did I just tell you?"

"His name is not important, Mr. Morris. He got the request from someone in the Mafia, and he won't tell you who gave him the job. The guy's a pusher. I'd rather not get into trouble."

"Believe me, you'd rather deal with him than us."

Listening from the other room, Abygaelle would like for Jack to drop it, it's not important right now. Let him tell his story. That's what matters.

Since Kevin refuses to go there, Jack instructs him to go on with his story.

"He told me that if I wanted easy money, he had a job for me. I needed money, so I thought he would ask me to rob a house or something, but no, he just required me to get a car. I said OK. He took a picture of my face and said he would call me later."

"Why did he take your picture?"

Kevin shrugs.

"Keep going."

"Honestly, I thought he was making fun of me. Why would someone give me this amount of money just to buy a car? I thought they wanted me as a figurehead. I've done it before, so I didn't have a problem doing it again. A week later, my buddy asked me to come over. He gave me an envelope and told me that everything I needed was in it. He warned me not to fuck up with the money because it came from powerful people, the kind I wouldn't want to mess with. I don't know who those people are in case you ask me. I just know they are related to some mafia."

"What was in the envelope?"

"Five thousand dollars in hundred-dollar bills, the address of the dealership, a fake driver's license with a fake name, but with my face on it, and instructions. I realized they didn't want a puppet, just someone to buy the car. It was even weirder than I thought, but I did it. I wasn't taking any chances. At least that's what I thought."

"Well, now you know why he took your picture."

Kevin doesn't get it. Jack rolls his eyes.

"The driver's license, Kevin. The picture on the driver's license."

"Oh."

Kevin eventually caught the drift of it. Jack realizes that the young man is not the sharpest tool in the shed.

"What did the instructions say?"

"That I had to go to the dealership in a cab. They had already flagged the vehicle they wanted on a website, so I knew what I was going to get. I went to the desk and pulled out the paper. I insisted they show me the black Altima. The guy asked me if I wanted to take it for a test drive and I said no. I wanted to pay for it and take off. The dude couldn't believe his luck, probably the quickest sale of his life. He filed the paperwork, took my driver's license. I paid cash, but at first I signed the contract with my real name. Can you believe it?"

"Yes, I can."

"You can?"

"Yes, I can believe you did that."

Kevin doesn't understand the underlying insult from Jack's response and goes on with his story.

"Finally, I crossed out my name and signed Leo Dion, as specified in the instructions. I then had to park the Altima in an underground parking lot and leave the key on the left wheel ahead. Then I left."

"What happened next?"

"Nothing special. A few days later, I received the rest of the money as agreed. And I never heard about it again until you showed my face all over the news."

"You didn't connect the dots when you heard the killer was driving a black Altima?"

"No. There's a lot of that type of car around."

Later, Jack and Aby showed up at the underground parking lot described by Dupont to look at that day security footage, to see if they could identify who got the car. The parking lot owner swears he didn't have them. They only keep twenty-four hours of footage.

"We can't afford a major camera system here."

Indeed, Aby thought. It's a shabby place. It's not owned by a renowned company. It's the kind of family business that's been passed down from generation to generation.

"The murderer can't do it all by himself," Jack says back at the station. "He needs help. Or maybe he's a member of an organized crime organization, but it doesn't fit the pattern."

"It wouldn't be the first time the mob hired a sniper to kill someone," Murielle says.

"To take out other criminals, sure. But simple citizens? Since when has the mafia been in the business of killing uneventful people? Or teenage girls, for that matter?"

"The only ones who ruthlessly kill children are the Mexican drug cartels."

Jack nods, but there are no Mexican cartels in Canada. At least, if there are, he's never heard of them.

Aby thinks that if the assassin can forge a fake driver's license of this quality, then he has the means to do a lot of things. But he needs support. And somehow he's got it, that's for sure. But from whom? And why?

"Nevertheless," Jack says. "The Mafia is too smart to murder children."

"Unless they didn't know beforehand," Abygaelle says.

42

Stephane Ranger would like to be elsewhere.

He has not yet fully recovered from the drug overdose that got him into a coma for several days. Even though life no longer appeals to him, there are less painful ways to kill oneself.

He holds his head in his hands, leaning against the table in the interrogation room of the Provincial Police. He wonders what the hell he's doing there. He just wants to be by himself. He wants his life back to the way it was before. How could everything get so messed up?

He brought the suspicious emails he received shortly after Ariane and Marc-Andre's death. Maybe it could help. Although he swore to do all he could to help them catch the killer, his time in hospital shed the last bit of energy he had. He ignores how he could be of any use in his current condition.

What could Abygaelle Jensen possibly want from him? She didn't want to explain it on the phone, just reiterating she had questions to ask him. Maybe he could shed some light on some grey areas she couldn't mend, and that it was preferable to discuss it in person.

He wonders how to get out of this nightmare. If drug and alcohol don't ease his pain, what else can he do? Sure, drugs numb him for a short while, from which he hopes never to escape, but his pain is tenfold once the effect wears off.

It's getting worse every time he goes so far over the edge that he ends up in intensive care. Not only does it hit him like a ten-wheel truck afterwards, but his health has deteriorated to the point it's getting harder and harder to recover.

It's more difficult to get the motivation to carry on.

Jensen is very stylish with her tight tailored suit and long, meticulously styled brown hair. She is gorgeous, so much so that Stephane feels intimidated by her. He can't look her straight in the eye for over two seconds at a time before it's too much for him.

She smiles as she sits down across the table. He turns down the coffee she offers him.

"Mr. Ranger, I will be very direct. Do you know who Marc-André Davison is?"

Abygaelle already knows the answer, but she wants to assess his reaction.

"He was my brother."

"How do you explain that your niece and now your brother were killed in the same manner?"

The question puzzles Ranger.

"How should I know?"

"Do you think it's a coincidence?"

He shrugs.

"It's not," Abygaelle says.

Ranger looks at her, intrigued.

"How can you be so sure?"

Abygaelle bends over and picks something out of a bag.

"Because of this."

She puts a piece of a chess set in front of her. An ebony wooden queen.

"I don't understand."

"We found this lying on the ground where the shooter stood to kill your brother."

"And?"

"We found the same thing on the roof where the killer would have been standing to shoot Ariane."

Stephane's head is spinning. He breathes deeply as he clings to the table. He doesn't know if it's his brain that is slow, but he doesn't understand. What does it mean?

"We believe the killer is using it to sign his murders. For some sinister reason, he wants us to link these crimes together. That they are connected. No one knows about the wooden queen except for us, and now you. Please don't tell anyone about it."

"But why would he sign these terrible crimes? What is he trying to prove?"

"We don't have the answer to this question. But we suspect that it's a way to taunt us."

"But why this exact chess piece? Why not a king, or a tower?"

Abygaelle nibbles her lower lip.

"We don't know that either. We thought maybe it would ring a bell?"

"It doesn't."

The detective wiggles her hands as she goes through her notes, as if she were trying to find the right way to set up the next topic.

"Mr. Ranger—"

"Stephane."

"Stephane, I have something to tell you that might shock you."

Stephane straightens up, intrigued and worried at the same time. What now?

Aby glances at the glass window behind him, as if she were

seeking her colleague's absolution from the other side of the reflective mirror.

"There's no good way to tell you this, so I'm going to go straight to it. Sorry if it comes as a shock. Have you spoken to Annie St. Onge lately?"

Stephane closes his eyes. She doesn't need to say more. It can only be one thing. Now he understands why his faithful sister in arms in their war against their demons wasn't at his bedside when he woke up, and why she didn't call him back. It must have happened while he was in a coma.

He sobs silently.

Seeing Ranger's shoulders startled, Abygaelle realizes he understands.

"I'm sorry," she says.

"Why is someone going after everyone in my life?" Ranger asks, yelling.

A policeman opens the door, but Aby signals him to stay outside. She moves her chair closer to his.

"I don't know, Stephane. Can you tell us anything that might lead us to something?"

"I understand nothing anymore. I don't see who could resent me that much."

Through his outburst, he mumbles sentences that Abygaelle can't grasp. Realizing that she will get nothing more out of him in his current state, she apologizes and leaves the room. She asks an officer to get a bottle of water for Stephane, and she joins Murielle and Jack in an adjacent room.

"If we had any doubts it may be him, they're gone now," Murielle says.

Abygaelle knows about the speculation Murielle has been entertaining for the past few days. She never believed it.

"Annie St. Onge's death proves he's central to this case. Before that, it could have been a coincidence. It could just as well have been connected to his sister Madeleine, or to her husband. But Stephane is the only one of the three who knew Annie. They were very close."

Murielle agrees. There is someone out there who has a grudge against this poor guy.

"It remains to be determined who and, above all, why," Aby says.

"It's someone close to him, that's for sure," Murielle replies.

"Why do you say that?"

"How would he know who to target to destroy him? A stranger wouldn't know. It must be someone who knows him well."

"But who?" Abygaelle asks. "His mother is dead, his sister and her husband still wouldn't have murdered their own daughter?"

Murielle has no answer. She can't figure it out either.

Abygaelle watches Stephane through the window. His head is on the table, leaning on his arms. He's still crying.

She started with the softest news, thinking it would set the tone for the next one, which she thinks will be much harder to swallow.

She flirts with the idea of not disturbed him even more, but it has to be done. Ranger must take them to the killer. If Murielle is right, he knows who he is. He just has to realize it.

To do that, he needs to know that his mother may have died at the hands of that same killer two years ago.

Fifteen minutes later, Murielle can sense the vibrations from Ranger's scream of pain running through her heart even though they are separated by a thick brick wall.

Abygaelle has used all the tact she could muster to brief him of the real circumstances of his mother's passing, and he's howling like a wounded animal. Knowing that the same killer shot his mother is the last straw for him and his sanity. It's more than he can endure. He no longer responds to Abygaelle's interactions.

No more contact.

It took five police officers to subdue Ranger and prevent him from hitting his head on an adjacent concrete wall. There is a lot of blood on his forehead.

Paramedics arrived a few minutes later and knocked him out with a strong sedative. Abygaelle's eyes are reddened with grief, while Murielle tries to comfort her as best she can by gently patting her back. It's a lot of emotion for the young rookie.

She's also shaken by Stephane Ranger's pain, despite all her experience.

Standing at a distance, Jack spotted something on the table where Ranger was sitting. He grabbed the printed sheets that were turned over to conceal their contents. What he reads gives him the creeps. These are short quotes from famous criminals. So that means that besides the wooden queens, this sick man is also torturing Ranger with this bullshit? Since he got an email of the same type shortly after his mother's death, it confirms the same creep killed her.

In the adjacent room, Abygaelle whispers something that Murielle doesn't grasp at first glance.

"Excuse me, sweetheart?"

Abygaelle takes a deep breath.

"We've got to find that monster."

Abygaelle's voice, trembling with rage, makes no doubt.

It's now personal.

43

The assassin drives with his side window down. He's in his usual vehicle, a red SUV that he paid in cash using his fake ID. He isn't stupid enough to drive around in his black BMW, probably already targeted by law enforcement. He hides it underground in a parking lot under a large canvas tarp specifically designed for luxury cars.

He relishes the warm wind blowing across his face. Lost in his thoughts, he rethinks his mission, his clumsiness at the hospital. But at the same time, he feels invincible. Who doesn't make mistakes? He simply has to limit them.

Arriving at the exit on highway 132, he allows motorcyclist to pass him before exiting the highway. He saw the biker woman in his rear-view mirror. She was at least a hundred meters behind.

Unexpectedly, the motorcyclist slows down and collides with the SUV, forcing the assassin to swerve to the right. The motorcyclist screams and gesticulates, but the assassin can't understand what he says.

"What?"

"Never cut off a convoy."

The assassin bursts out laughing.

"A convoy? What are you talking about, asshole, you're a pair."

"Shut up, the biker says. I will beat you up. Never cut up a convoy again, get it?"

The biker leaves without awaiting an answer, along with his wife, who had joined him in the meantime.

Still in total disbelief, the assassin quietly presses the gas pedal to go on his way. When he reaches the intersection, he activates his blinker to turn right, but he sees the couple in the parking lot of a gas station. They are drinking water and laughing.

The assassin senses rage rising in him. He disengages his blinker and goes straight ahead. He angles one hundred and eighty degrees out of the gas station building to avoid the cameras under the dome above the gas pumps.

He places himself close to the couple and puts a cap on.

He shouldn't be doing this, it's obvious, but he can't help it. The biker had the nerve to threaten him. Doesn't he know who he is? Isn't he aware that a killer is on the loose? How can he know if it's not him? How can he feel so invulnerable?

The killer admits he should simply drive away and forget about this meaningless event altogether, but it's unavoidable.

Killing gives him a powerful drug-like boost. He plays God, determining who dies and who survives. It exhilarates him. It fucking turns him on. He never thought it was possible. It's dangerous.

Very dangerous.

The public is concerned, though. They are all afraid that he might strike again. If they knew there is no one who is more scared of what he can do than himself. He no longer recognizes himself. From where does this murderous instinct come? He's a good guy, after all.

Simultaneously, he fears he might run out of time to finish

his journey. It can't go on for another two years. Friends and family will wonder what he's up to. His departures will be difficult to explain.

He must finish his mission. Sooner rather than later.

Then a flash. A genius idea. Should the police think he was only after Ranger's relatives, an unrelated murder would put doubt in their minds and distract them enough to allow him time to complete. Then, he will move on.

He feels this is a brilliant idea. And if there is someone to kill out of the list, it might as well be that asshole. Never, in the beginning, would he have dared to kill people not on the list. But Annie St. Onge's nonsense had screwed everything up. This jerk didn't deserve his clemency.

The biker gets on his bike, which makes a hell of a noise. The assassin gets his SUV close to the couple.

"Hey," he shouts at them.

The biker recognizes him.

"The fuck you want?"

In response, the assassin points a long-range rifle he has just assembled on him. The woman moves towards her husband. She hasn't realized how livid he is.

The assassin stares at the biker, holding him at gunpoint, as he silently looks around. The assassin sees the slender look on his face, even though he isn't looking through the scope because he is too close. The woman has just realized what happens when a bullet hits her husband in the forehead. He collapses on his side like a rag doll. The motorcycle slid under him, then jumped forward and fell back to the side.

The assassin moves the barrel of his weapon towards her. Fear cripples her. She begs him to spare her; she has a child. Her whole body is trembling. The assassin holds her at gunpoint for a few seconds. Seeing the biker die filled him with great joy. The look on his stupid face seconds before he shot him.

Dumbass.

The woman didn't deserve to die. She didn't see him close enough for identification. He smiles and puts the gun down. He throws a black wooden queen through the passenger window and flees at high speed down a path to his left.

In his rear-view mirror, he sees her throwing herself at the biker's dead body.

The assassin focuses on what he feels. A fullness comparable to that which one has after an orgasm. He relives the scene in his head a few times before realizing he has a gigantic smile across his face.

An hour later, it strikes him; he has to get rid of his vehicle.

He first parks behind his BMW in the underground garage, and puts the suitcase with the Dragunov in the trunk. He was reckless. Driving around for so long in a truck being hunted by every police force is a foolishness that could cost him dearly. He would never forgive himself if they caught him at a simple traffic stop.

It's too late for that, anyway. He reaches to a gas station and buys a gasoline canister, and fills it up completely. He finds a country road hidden from prying eyes and sets the van on fire. Luckily, he did all this without being caught. He drove through a field and walked for about five kilometers before getting into a cab.

When the biker's wife will recount what happened to the police, they'll even be more confused. The bullet will be identical to that of the other murders. They will discover a wooden queen on the ground.

By setting the vehicle on fire like biker gangs usually do after killing an enemy, the police won't know what to think.

All in all, it's been a damn fine day.

44

Abygaelle brought a coffee to Jocelyne Lamoureux. Her husband's murder still distraught the poor woman. Aby tingles with excitement. The woman may be the first to have seen the gunman they've been looking for. They found a bullet identical to the one that killed Ariane, Marc-Andre, and Annie. And a wooden queen on the ground to boot.

It's him.

Jocelyne details the events as she remembers them, even if it's obscure in her mind. She has trouble separating the true from the false. What she imagined and what really happened. She suffered from a nervous shock, which doesn't help her put the pieces together.

Pete had an argument with the driver of a red SUV a few minutes before he was killed. She doesn't know much except that Pete blamed the guy because he drove between them. Jocelyne thought he was overreacting, since she was quite far behind the SUV. Pete laughed about the confrontation as they were cooling off in a gas station's parking lot. A few seconds later, the SUV came up and pulled out a bit.

She couldn't clearly see who was behind the wheel because

of the distance and the shadows. However, he was alone inside the vehicle; she is adamant. He had a slender figure, not overweight, and had a black cap pushed deep down on his head.

"Pete slowly came towards him on his bike and asked what he wanted. I told him to let go. I hated when he got pissed off. Pete got a kick out of challenging people. Then I noticed the driver leaned over to grab something in the back seat, and then I heard a loud boom. I saw a bright flash of light from the passenger side, and Pete staggered, and—"

Jocelyne is filled by the emotion. Her blue eyes darkened and flooded with tears.

"Take your time, Mrs. Lamoureux. I know it's difficult."

Abygaelle hands her a box of tissues. She tells her she doesn't need to apologize, it's perfectly normal to feel this way. She is very strong.

After a pause, Jocelyne recovered enough of her senses to continue.

"You know, Pete was no choirboy. I know what he did for a living. He had enemies and was impulsive. I often begged him to chill. That you can't nag strangers like that, you never know what kind of lunatic you're dealing with. There are sick people out there, they may be loaded. He said that I worried too much. And now he's dead. Dead from what I warned him about."

"You knew, however, life expectancy is limited in this line of business, weren't you? Unless being on the top of the food chain, your chances of making it past fifty are very slim."

Abygaelle didn't disclose that they were investigating Pete Morin as a suspect in a mega-trial. There's no point putting her through more hoops. After a sip of coffee, Jocelyne returns to her story.

"When I heard the loud noise, I didn't immediately grasp what was going on, but I soon saw Pete fall to his side as his bike fell under him and landed a few meters further down the road once he let go of the clutch. And then everything became blurry. I couldn't hear anything, I couldn't see anything. I realized where the deafening noise that I had heard came from. He had shot Pete. I wanted to rescue him, but I thought I was next. I saw the rifle barrel sticking out of the interior and pointed at me. I froze. I was expecting him to shoot, but he just stood there, pointing his gun at me, doing nothing. I cried repeatedly, pleading that I had a kid, and I didn't want her to be an orphan."

Abygaelle can't wait for her to get to the point.

"Then, he lowered his gun, looked at me for a few seconds and—"

Her throat tightens again, but this time instead of tears of sorrow, Abygaelle sees tears of rage in her eyes.

"And he smiled. That son of a bitch laughed at me, fucking asshole."

"Could you describe him?"

Jocelyne wiggles in her chair.

"I didn't get a good look at him. All I could see were his evil eyes illuminated in the darkness, like fluorescent sapphires. That look will haunt me for the rest of my life. If I saw a picture, maybe I could recognize him, I don't know."

Abygaelle is overjoyed. A sketch would be a major asset to the investigation.

"Jocelyne, do you or Pete know Stephane Ranger?"

From the surprise on her face, she certainly doesn't.

"I don't know anyone by that name, and there was none in Pete's family either

She'll ask Stephane about Pete Morin, but if Jocelyne is right, the biker would be the first unrelated victim.

Aby has shivers down her spine. That would be terrible news. As long as there was a tie between the victims, they could forecast the next potential targets. But if he goes after random people, it will be even harder to stop him.

Abygaelle calls a portrait artist to see what he can do with Jocelyne's description of the killer.

"All we need is to find someone with blue eyes," Jack says with a disconcerting pout. Murielle provides no answer. Although blue is not the most common color in the world, there are about eight to ten percent of the world's population with that eye color.

The sketch resulting from Jocelyne's description is vivid. Abygaelle dissects it. She can't tell the age of the suspect. He may be as old as thirty or sixty based on the sketch. Jocelyne says she couldn't figure out his age from the little she could see, with the damn cap hinder his face.

The man was bulky; she doubted he was older than fifty, but Abygaelle knows very well how difficult it is to tell someone's age without seeing their face.

"We'll broadcast the sketch, and see what happens," Abygaelle says. "We'll see what we get out of it."

"More bogus anonymous calls in the offing," Jack says.

This investigation aggravates him more and more.

45

Magog, Québec. Winter 2007.

JEAN BLACKBURN WAS COMFORTABLY SITTING in his favourite armchair. Large snowflakes flew around outdoors, like huge cotton bales at nightfall. You could rant and rave all you wanted about the Quebec winter, but rarely could you witness such a sumptuous spectacle of nature.

His residence in Magog, built twenty years ago by a renowned Norwegian architect, was set on stilts on a vast lot overlooking magnificent Lake Memphremagog.

It was the house of his dreams, and he worked extremely hard to get it. He had a successful career as a lawyer, during which he pleaded high-profile cases that made him famous. Newly retired, he sometimes was invited as a guest expert on streaming news channels. His straight talk appealed to the viewers.

Of course, he got his share of hate messages, which came with success, but he had tough skin. He wasn't easily intimidated. He had everything he needed to stand up for himself should some lunatic have the bad idea to take it out on him. He learned to fire a gun at a very young age, and he was a skilled hunter. He took long walks every day on his vast estate with his trusty Smith & Wesson thirty-eight caliber pistol, slipped into a holster under his arm.

Like cops in movies.

His weapon lessens the latent paranoia that inhabited him throughout his career. You don't get criminals out of trouble without alienating enemies. Nor were his clients choirboys. Some of them openly voiced their anger at the sentence he negotiated on their behalf.

One can never be too careful.

The kettle was whistling loudly on the stove. He was brewing peppermint tea. A blessing for his stomach. A scholar of classical music, he tuned in to the Twilight of the Gods in three acts by Wagner and read Milan Kundera's Ignorance. To him, that was the definition of happiness.

Music and reading.

His wife Juliette had gone on a cruise with a group of friends. They bought pink "Girls on cruise" t-shirts that they planned to wear all week.

Blackburn enjoyed being alone with his favourite composers, whose melodies resonated in the large living room of the house. He was an audiophile and invested a lot of money in his Bowers & Wilkins speakers to benefit from his home's acoustics. He needed to hear all the nuances of orchestral harmony, to feel the fingers massaging the cello strings.

The fragrance of peppermint filled his nostrils. There was no more soothing smell in his mind. He sat back in his brown leather armchair and resumed listening to Wagner's opera while his tea cooled down a bit. He closed his eyes for a moment to soak up the soprano's voice.

He reached the end of the first act when Brünnhilde heard

Siegfried's horn sounding. She will abandon herself to her man, but Siegfried will deceive her by pretending to be Gunther. Brünnhilde understands she will be handed over as a sex toy to all the gentlemen that show up. This excerpt moved Jean Blackburn every time. It was unequivocal.

He savored the rising crescendo. He had shivers of anticipation as he reveling in the next notes beforehand. The sound was very loud, a luxury he could afford with the nearest neighbor two kilometers away.

He could appreciate the incredible arrangement of the first and second violins, as he loved stringed instruments.

He grabbed his neck to mitigate the mild burn he felt, but instead sensed a warm, viscous liquid slipping through his fingers. He choked within seconds, unable to swallow or breathe. His pale blue pajamas turned a different color as his heartbeat sprayed blood onto his chest at an alarming rate.

He felt the huge horizontal opening across his throat from side to side as if he was looking for a way to shut it. He was drowning in his own blood. Panicking, he tried to get up, but an unidentified force pushed him back into his chair. That's when he spotted a tall man dressed in black standing in front of him. He was wearing a ski hood and silently stared at him. All he could see was his hateful and threatening stare as he bled to death. The man was holding a long bloody knife in his gloved right hand.

The assassin was standing still. He tilted his head sideways, like an artist assessing the quality of his work.

He was waiting for the lawyer to lose consciousness.

When the police showed up on the scene several days later, alarmed by Juliette who had just returned from her trip, they discovered Blackburn's decomposing body. Fortunately, he was still recognizable.

The lawyer was hanging from a banister. His guts had

spilled out from under him. Someone had carved the word RAT on his forehead with a blade.

Probably the same one used to slit his throat, the same one used to open his torso from his lower abdomen to his neck.

46

William Primeau is amused that his day of philanthropy is more strenuous than his typical workout. He carries gigantic boxes of food for fellow volunteers as they hand out baskets of non-perishable food to those in need.

"Thanks again, Will, you're a machine."

Executive Director Ruth Garrison is a friend he knows since forever. William has always made a point of helping people in need, even as a young man in Quebec. His foundation is the proof of that, but he also loves being in the field.

Every year, he sets aside one day in his hectic schedule to support the most important organization in London and to give as many food baskets as possible to those in need. Over time, he managed the work of all the volunteers. Each year, he gives a generous cheque to Ruth on behalf of his foundation.

Heather is here as well, as vibrant as ever. She's focused on the task at hand, with poignant dedication.

He takes a break and watches people in need pick up their food baskets. The sadness in their eyes and their grateful smiles strike him every time. Misery crushes the soul. It shatters the hope one had since they were born. But they go on, bravely heading straight for it. No one deliberately stays poor, people are quick to judge.

There are so many reasons justifying poverty that the common people couldn't possibly understand. It's easy to blame these people from our comfortable lives, but it's beyond logic. It's in the heart, in the head, and in the soul. It swept some into a vicious circle of misery, because it's all they know.

William moves outside to get some fresh air. It's chilly lately. He is scheduled to leave for another country tomorrow. He watches The Gherkin, the bomb-shaped building he enjoys the most. He has a special affection for this building, as it was under construction when he first came to the UK metropolis. They practically grew up together. It went without saying that he set up his capital management firm in this building.

Fighting noises got his attention. At first, he paid no attention to them. William keeps from his Judeo-Christian upbringing to mind his own business. But he can't help but act upon the screams of a woman in distress.

He moves quietly towards the voices. It sounds like a couple fight; the man bawls in a threatening tone. He sees them fighting between two buildings; the man is tall and imposing and the young woman is small and fragile. William comes closer, hesitant to intervene.

He finally shows his presence.

"Is everything all right?" he asks the girl.

"Mind your own business," the man says in a belligerent tone.

"I'm not talking to you. Ma'am, is everything all right?"

She doesn't reply, but her eyes display fear. Tears soaked her cheeks and William walks towards the couple.

"I told you to go fuck yourself, you stupid bastard."

"Shut the fuck up," William answers, raising his voice. "Ma'am? Do you want me to call the police?"

The guy throws her to the ground and rushes towards William, red-faced with anger.

"I told you to—"

The man collapses, stiff as an iron bar after being punched in the face by William. He is unconscious. William learned early on from his dad to always strike first. He reaches to the young woman still lying on the ground.

"Are you okay? Is he your boyfriend?"

The woman responds that he's not. She's shaking like a leaf.

"Come with me."

William helps her to the foundation's office. He gives her a seat and coffee. Heather takes over after he briefs her on what happened a few minutes earlier. He steps out again to check on the guy to see if he has come to his senses. He does, even though he's still buzzed.

"Have you calmed down?"

The man looks at William as if he doesn't realize what this is all about. He's rubbing the back of his head and already has swelling on the edge of his left eye.

William crouched beside him, his face stern.

"Next time a woman says no, it means no, you moron. Do you copy?"

Little by little, the man recalls the events.

"She's my wife."

"She says the opposite. And even if she is, that's no way to behave."

"Okay, Mother Teresa."

William grabs her firmly by the collar.

"Not Mother Teresa. Just a man, a real one. A man would never stoop to hitting a woman, a real man knows how to behave. When you hurt a woman, when you terrorize her. You're not a man, you're nothing but a pathetic worm that deserves to be crushed. I could have killed you, you know that?

You were under my thumb. I could have done whatever I wanted with you."

For the first time, William sees fear in his eyes.

"I will remember your face, and I have an excellent memory. If I ever see you raise your voice to another woman again, I swear I'll kill you. Do you understand me?"

The man signals that yes, petrified.

"Get the fuck out of here!"

William watches him stagger away. Everyone is courageous until they get punched in the face, he thought, smiling. He stayed for several minutes watching The Gherkin, proud of his action.

But most of all, to stop shivering with excitement.

47

Abygaelle tries to see through the thick fog of the case.

What Stephane Ranger just told her was astounding. Initially reluctant to talk, being so close to death seems to give him a new perspective on life. He suddenly is more talkative.

He said he was very close to Annie Saint. Onge. She became the third victim related to him.

Aby asked if he knew who would do this. He knows he has enemies, like everyone else, but no one insane enough to hold a grudge so severe that they would kill him or other people for that matter.

Impossible to be involved in crimes and petty theft for so long without rattling a few. Abygaelle knows that the three victims are not coincidental. Four, including his mother, but why? What is the connection with him?

The only way to find out is to search into his past. What is he hiding that would put her on the right path? He didn't want to venture out, rightly or wrongly, so she has to see if there are skeletons in his closet, and point out what could be responsible for this carnage. She combs through his criminal record, which is less extensive than she would have thought. A lot of juvenile crime, but he settled out as an adult. He was co-defendant in a home invasion trial with one Johnny Marcotte when he was sixteen years old. And they sentenced him to three years in prison for dealing drugs.

Abygaelle discerns the Archambault Detention Center from a distance, emerging from the ground beneath a dark cloud. Prison still gives her the creeps with its fences and barbed wire as far as the eye can see. There's a white control tower soaring above the gray buildings.

It looks like a fortress rising out of the darkness housing bloodthirsty creatures. She abhors to visit convicts in prison, but it's sometimes necessary. Today, she needs to know more about Ranger. Find out what he keeps from her, figure out what is wrong with him, and narrow down the field of investigation.

Johnny Marcotte steps in front of her as if he hasn't had a visitor in a long time and can't believe how lucky he is to see someone from the outside world.

He's a bit of a weirdo, he's got a weird face. With his brush friar tuck hair cut, he looks at her strangely.

"My God, if I'd known you were such a treat, I would have made an effort to look my best," he says from the get go as he mulls over Abygaelle from top to bottom.

"Sit down, Mr. Marcotte."

"You'll be in my thoughts tonight," he says with a mischievous smile. Abygaelle does not flinch. She's used to such salacious comments.

Marcotte is nervous. He swings slightly from left to right, watching her like a piece of meat. Looks like he suffers drug abuse heavy after-effects.

His gaze is intense and empty at the same time. A look that petrifies the hell out of her. Even if he's not a big guy, you wouldn't want to face him in an alley alone at night.

A seasoned criminal, an incurable addict. There's something wrong with him, Abygaelle thinks. But he's one of the few people who knows about Ranger's past.

"Do you know him well?"

"Steph? You bet. How is he?"

"Fine," she says, lying. "Tell me how you met him."

Marcotte wiggles on his chair, brushing his hand over his thin layer of hair.

"My God, we were living on the edge. We did some pretty messed up shit."

"Like what?"

He loses some of his exuberance.

"I plead the Fifth," he says, a hand on his heart.

"There is no such thing as the Fifth Amendment in Canada, Mr. Marcotte. But I certainly wouldn't want you to incriminate yourself. I've noticed that you were both convicted of breaking into homes."

He nods energetically, as if it entertained him to remember this.

"Oh boy, you're bringing back some memories. It's been a long time. Those were the good old days. We had the world right at our feet."

"Would you say Stephane was the leader in whatever crimes you were doing, or was he more of a follower type?"

Marcotte puffs his chest.

"I was the brains of the two. He was there because he was very good with doors, if you know what I mean," he says, winking.

Abygaelle scoffs at the criminal's ill-conceived pride. What's next? He'll pretend he was the mastermind for Jacques Mesrine's jailbreaks?

"I see. After this conviction, I see nothing else in his record, except trivial stuff like public disturbances, drunk driving, drug possession, and so on. How long did you two hang out together?"

"Until he turned into a priest," he says, disgusted.

"I don't understand."

He rolls his eyes.

"He turned his life around," he says, mimicking quotation marks with his fingers. "Shit, he's become boring. A real bore."

"So as far as you know, he's cooled down."

Marcotte screams with laughter. Abygaelle stiffens.

"I thought you said 'so fooled down'. Sorry, I heard wrong."

He's laughing way too loud than he should, Abygaelle thought. He's high as a kite.

"Yes, he has calmed down. He did detox and then got a job. I think his last stint in jail really scarred the shit out of him."

"What do you mean?"

"Well, he got pretty shaken up in there. He's a quiet guy, a bit of a pussy. The sharks in here smell that, and you become an easy prey."

"Did they sexually abuse him?" Aby hasn't lost her vice squad instincts.

"Could be, I don't know. All I know is that they beat the crap out of him. Then the prison isolated him until his release for exemplary behavior. So after that, he did everything he could to clean his act. Pretty sad if you ask me. I mean, who would like to work nine to five? What's the thrill?"

Aby almost said: "Do you know where you are? Everything is better than this place. How can you judge those on the outside?"

"Anything else?" she asks.

"Not really," he says, pondering.

"Thank you, Mr. Marcotte. How much time do you have left?"

"Six years. Hey, don't you want to go in a trailer?"

Abygaelle looks at him in amazement. How can he expect for a moment that he has a chance to sleep with her? These guys are definitely disconnected from reality.

"I'll pass, thanks."

"Your lost," he says with a straight face.

Aby puts her notebook back in her bag and she hears a voice in the distance. It's Marcotte's who was about to walk through the heavy metal door to the hallway.

"Oh, I forgot. He was charged with gang rape, too, but he was cleared. Him and two other guys."

Marcotte blows her a kiss from afar, smiles and disappears for good.

On her way back, Abygaelle wonders how it could have slipped through the cracks. How can Ranger mean nothing to her since she was in Vice Squad? She would remember something like a gang rape. And above all, why didn't Ranger mention it?

While waiting for the green light, she dials Roland Michaud's phone number.

"Roland, I'm going to need to pick your brain."

48

Abygaelle tries to collect herself, but thanks to her discussion with Roland Michaud, she has new hope. Her mentor vaguely recalled the case. Since there aren't that many gang-rape cases, he didn't have to look long. He quickly pointed her in Nathalie Primeau's direction after double-checking that Stephane Ranger was one of the co-accused.

Reading the trial transcript, Aby realizes that justice has failed again. She has seen this type of verdict all too often, with no reasonable doubt.

Most of the time, it is because of a lawyer successfully raising doubts in the jury's mind, taking advantage of the victim's helplessness to expose her and make her bear the brunt of her own misfortune.

No wonder women are reluctant to press charges against their abusers. When you're treated like a whore, it's natural not to put yourself through the wringer.

In rape cases, prosecution is not only about the accused but also about the victims. Someone saw you flirting with the man you denounce. How do you explain that? Didn't you have it coming a little bit? People say you enjoy one-night stands, is that true? An ex-lover testified you like animal sex, almost to the point of violence. Isn't it rather a game that slipped out of control? And what about your sweater showing off your abdomen, don't you feel you've been responsible of your own demise? Wasn't this skirt too short?

It's hard enough to go through a trial when the aggressor is found guilty. It must be hell when he's not.

Nathalie saw not only one, but three of her aggressors exiting the courthouse as free men. Some of them smiling and taunting her relatives on top of it. Enough to wreck any human being, no matter how tough he may be at first.

Abygaelle calls Murielle and Jack into a conference room. She wants to revisit the entire case.

She presents three co-accused profiles: Eric Gagné, François Lavoie and Stephane Ranger. She reads the gruesome details of the case: the trial; the jury failing to agree on a verdict; the defendants pestering the family; the guards intervening to restrain Nathalie's father.

"It's horrible," Murielle whispers.

Aby carries on.

"François Lavoie was murdered by several bullets in a wood clearing, his genitals in his mouth."

The smile on Jack's face doesn't go unnoticed. But Aby let it go.

"Eric Gagné was repeatedly stabbed, practically beheaded, also had his reproductive organs in his mouth. These two crimes were perpetrated a few years apart. We didn't catch the culprit."

"All were violent murders. It comes from profound rage," Jack says. "It's personal. Not at all the same as the homicides we're dealing with."

"You're right," Abygaelle admits. "On the other hand, the latest hits have targeted people who had nothing to do with the rape. Perhaps that's the reason for the depersonalization.

Assuming that Nathalie's rape was the spark that ignited this slaughter years later."

"It makes sense," Murielle says. "So how do you explain Ranger is still alive? Why kill everyone but him? Why go after his loved ones."

"Not to mention his mother. They killed her in the same fashion. A round of the same caliber went through her chest. They shot her on her way to the prison to visit her son."

Murielle and Jack are focusing.

"The strange thing is the trajectory of the bullet. According to the medical examiner, the shot came from the front, not from the side, but directly in front of her. As if the shooter was in a vehicle ahead. The bullet went through the windshield, through the woman's body, through her seat, through the back seat, and ended up in the trunk's metal."

The three discussed potential suspects and virtually identified everyone near Nathalie. Anyone with an emotional connection to her. Her family, her lover, her friends.

"We've got work to do. We need to interview all these people and see where you go from there," Murielle says. "Since it takes someone proficient with a sniper rifle, it will narrow the potential suspects."

"And above all, we need to understand why things have changed," Jack adds. "And why Ranger is still alive."

Aby puts the file aside with a satisfied smile. She finally has a lead and her instinct tells her she should bet all her chips on it.

49

Abygaelle worries about what is in store for them at the Primeau's residence. Jack warns her that anything can happen: a hostage situation, belligerents barricaded, or, on the other side of the spectrum, a completely normal encounter.

It depends on whether they have something to hide. And if so, it will mean that they have finally found the right lead, or at the very least, that they are getting closer.

Aby sees it as a beacon in the dark. What if this is the culmination of this nonsense and she could finally take her bearings in her new role? She will settle with Picard not to get another case for a while. She would like to support Murielle and Jack, enough time so that she can relax.

It's been way too intense since her arrival.

She relaxes as she looks at the cozy Primeau neighborhood unfolding in front of her eyes. Suburban houses, nothing special at all. Huge mature trees overlooking the street showing a poignant reverence. Aby suspects they bought their house before their children were born and have been living there ever since.

"Here we are," Jack says in a deep voice.

Abygaelle feels as nervous as she did coming near a residence where there were reports about child abuse.

Different reality, same dread.

A car is parked on the side of the brown brick house. A white shelter covers most of the parking spot and give path to a metal door on the side. There is another door in the front, but Abygaelle assumes it's only for special occasions.

They'll knock on that door, anyway. It looks more official. People usually restrict access from the side to family and friends. A petite woman answers after a few seconds. She becomes anxious when she sees they are cops.

"Mrs. Primeau, I'm Abygaelle Jensen, Detective Sergeant at the Provincial Police. This is my colleague, Jacques Morris. May we come in for a few minutes?"

The lady collapses in tears.

"My God, what is going on? Something has happened to Raymond, hasn't it? Oh my God."

"No ma'am, we're not bearing bad news," Abygaelle assures her with the softest voice possible. "We just have a few questions."

Monique beckons them in and keeps whining. Jack assumes she's on edge.

What immediately strikes them is the extreme cleanliness of the house. Plastic wrapped furniture, latent scent of cleaning detergent. The silence in the house emphasizes the clatter of the old grandfather clock sitting in the passageway to the dining room.

It feels like a museum.

Abygaelle notices the large number of pictures on the walls as they follow in the woman's footsteps. A beautiful girl whom she presumes to be Nathalie, and a handsome young man smiling. Probably their son William.

After serving them coffee, Monique sits and watches them

silently, apprehensive of what they have to tell her. Jack breaks the silence.

"Is your husband at work?"

She lowers her head.

"No, he has been away for several weeks."

"Where is he?"

She plunges her sad eyes into the detective's, then shrugs.

"He left me this note before he vanished," she says, pointing at a piece of paper on the kitchen counter.

Jack picks it up and reads aloud: "I'm gone, don't look for me. I have my reasons. I'll be back soon. Wait for my call. I love you. Raymond xxx." He glances incredulously at Abygaelle.

"That's strange, Aby says. Has he contacted you since then?"

"No," Monique says, "I don't understand what's going on. I was hoping you'd have some answers."

"Was he with you on June 3rd, around 4:30 p.m.?" Abygaelle asks.

"It's been a while, I don't remember," Monique Primeau says. "You know, Raymond didn't leave the house much, but sometimes he could escape for hours. He loved walking in the wild, getting some fresh air. He needs his space from time to time."

Abygaelle moves her chair closer to hers.

"Has he seemed more distant than normal lately? Concerned about something in particular?"

Monique smiles for the first time.

"Like all men of our generation, Raymond shows very little emotion. He's not the type to open up. If something is bothering him, you know about it several months later, when he finally talks about it, but even then, he only gives you snippets. I did everything I could to help him open up more, but eventually I let it go. That's the way he is, and I eventually came to terms with it. I enjoyed being the chief of the family. I wield the authority in the house when the kids were here. Raymond was away a lot because of his missions abroad."

"He was in the military, wasn't he?" Jack asks.

Monique Primeau raises her head and looks at him blankly.

"Yes, he first started in the sixties. He went up the ladder afterwards. He was in charge of troops for most of his career."

"Does he still have weapons around?" he says.

"Yes, well, I think so. I don't like these things, so he hides them. I couldn't tell where they were. Why all these questions?"

Jack was about to answer, but Abygaelle stopped him with a wave of her hand.

"We're talking to people in the neighborhood about events we can't disclose at the moment. Would you allow us to search around for any weapons?"

The lady wiggles in her chair.

"No, I'd rather not. Raymond doesn't like people snooping around in his things, and neither do I. What exactly are you looking for?"

Jack sighs in exasperation. Abygaelle puts her hand on his colleague's forearm and continues.

"Clues, simple clues. We have no reason to suspect anyone at this point. But we must investigate the surroundings. Has William come to see you recently?"

"No, Will is very busy. He's been living in London for years. He married a girl from there, but I didn't go to the ceremony."

Aby feels in her tone that something troubles her. She asks for an explanation.

"Because of his wife, she's keeping him back. He can't see straight since he's been with her. I would have been more comfortable with the situation if he had married here. But he preferred to pay for the flight so that I could be there."

"And why didn't you go?" Jack asks.

"Because, for one thing, I'm afraid of flying. And two, he wanted me to go by myself. It was too much for me."

Abygaelle has an interrogative pout.

"What do you mean?"

Monique Primeau frowns.

"Him and his father don't talk anymore."

"Since when?"

"Several years. A little after his exile. I don't know why, they both refuse to tell me any more, simply stating that something has happened, but that they don't want to drag me into it. If you only knew how much their clash impacts me. My worst nightmare would be that they don't reconcile before my husband dies. Oh, my God, I—"

She covers her face with her hands, sobbing, as if she had just realized the magnitude of the situation. Abygaelle pats her shoulder with empathy.

After giving her time to calm down, Abygaelle asks for William's phone number. Monique doesn't get the connection between her son who lives in London and their investigation in the neighborhood, but Aby says they want to know more about the strained relationship between him and his father, to find out more about it.

She also informs her they may come back with a warrant to search the house if they find out that Raymond's departure is related to their investigation. Finally, she asks Monique to advise them as soon as Raymond shows up. And also, instruct him to call them. They absolutely must talk to him.

"Well," Aby says as she stands up, "we've taken up enough of your time. We must go on with our investigation. Thank you for your collaboration."

Monique vows she will do everything in her power to help them, but they are wrong if they presume Raymond had anything to do with something fishy.

"He wouldn't hurt a fly."

"Before he disappeared like he did, would you have imagined that he could just vanish like that?" Abygaelle asks.

Surprised by the question, Monique says no, looking down.

"Sometimes people have secrets, Mrs. Primeau, even when you think you know them inside and out, they still have their own secret garden."

On their way back, Abygaelle tells Jack she didn't want to push Monique too much for a first visit, not knowing whether her husband is involved or not. Of course, his disappearance is suspicious, but that proves nothing.

They have to tackle this situation strategically, compel Primeau to come out of his lair, even if it means coming back and pushing his wife harder and searching the house from top to bottom, forcing her to recall if he was with her when Ariane was killed. But for now, let's wait and see what happens.

"He may have killed himself too," Jack says. "You know, realizing what he'd just done?"

Abygaelle shrugs.

"Maybe, but assuming our theory is right, what does that have to do with Ariane, Marc-André Davison, Pete Morin, and Annie?"

Jack finds no explanation.

Abygaelle regrets she was a bit cavalier with Monique, about not really knowing people. She feels like she left her in worse shape than before the visit. She decided they would stick superficially, that they wouldn't talk about their suspicions about her husband. But the answer came out of her mouth like that, and that's unfortunate.

But if there is one thing she is sure of, it's that Raymond Primeau didn't kill himself. She doesn't know why, but she has a hunch that he's hiding somewhere and that he follows them in the shadows.

50

At the morning meeting, Murielle cheerfully reports that she has new information about Raymond Primeau.

"Quite an impressive track record," she says, almost admiringly. "He enlisted in the U.S. Army for the Vietnam War and then worked on peace missions with the UN peacekeepers. He was leading several operations near the end of his career, which was over when his daughter died."

Jack and Aby listen carefully. Murielle is relishing the attention.

"A very respected man, it seems. A true leader."

"Nothing else?" Abygaelle asks.

Murielle scans the file she holds, as if she's trying to find something more juicy to relate.

"Yeah, well, he was an idealist and could be a little awkward," she adds.

"What do you mean?" Jack says.

"Mood swings, a lot of intensity. Sometimes overreactions, a crazy outlook on life, stuff like that. Still, you could count on him."

Murielle keeps silent for a few seconds so that her colleagues can digest everything before moving on.

"After his daughter's death, he suffered from post-traumatic syndrome, which he feels results from his missions in Kosovo, but many believe it's related to Nathalie's suicide."

"Is that all?" Aby asks.

Murielle smiles.

"Not quite. Ask me what he was doing in the army, especially in Vietnam."

"What was he doing in the army, especially in Vietnam?"

"He was a sniper."

51

Sitting in her living room, Abygaelle savors a chamomile tea. After her shower, she tackles the case file of Nathalie Primeau's rape trial. She reads from top-to-bottom everything related to this event. She hopes that the key to finding the killer is in there.

Johnny Marcotte was telling the truth, after all.

If there's one valid explanation why someone would torture Stephane Ranger, it's definitely the one. She has to grasp everything about this, master the smallest details. Read everything that has been said and written about it. Who were the key players, the important witnesses. Who were Eric Gagné and François Lavoie, what role did they play?

Perhaps she will uncover extra details about Ranger? She can quickly absorb information and connect the dots. Just a few more readings, and she will know everything there is to know about this, as if she attended the trial.

This is especially important since this is her first homicide case. She will do everything in her power to keep it off the cold case files. All three men had a different recollection of the evening than Nathalie. Gagné and Lavoie swore she consented to a foursome with three guys, an unlikely narrative given Lavoie's shoddy look. Whether a pretty young woman like Nathalie fell for Gagné, Aby could believe it. Ranger? Perhaps if she were really drunk.

But Lavoie? No chance in hell.

He never had a regular girlfriend, and he often hooked up with prostitutes. Ranger said he only remembers parts of that evening, but that he's commonly incapable of getting an erection when he does drugs.

Unlike Gagné and Lavoie, Stephane was polite and remorseful. He hadn't taunted Nathalie's family after their acquittal.

Several people testified Nathalie was all over Gagné that night. Some thought they were a couple. Other witnesses remembered them leaving the party together arm in arm, even though Nathalie had a hard time walking was covered by an oversized anorak.

They thought she was drunk.

Some reported she was barely standing up while dancing. And that she relished other guys' attention. One of Nathalie's friends mentioned she urged her not to leave with these guys. She had a bad feeling about them. She knew her friend and didn't buy the defendants' story one bit.

But Nathalie was over eighteen and vaccinated. She couldn't coerce her not to go. Her only regret was that she didn't call her father to tell him about all this.

The defendant's defense lawyer did an excellent job at discrediting Nathalie's deposition. He portrayed her as a scatterbrained party girl who would do anything to have fun and who had suddenly felt guilty about her boyfriend. She regretted her wrongdoing, so she lied about the three poor guys to save face.

The co-accused Eric Gagné, François Lavoie and Stephane

Ranger were suspected to have cruelly ganged-raped, beaten and left the young girl for dead.

Gagné, a careered delinquent who had perpetrated several offenses as a minor, had not calmed down as he got older. On the contrary, his crimes became increasingly violent.

Abygaelle got chills at the sight of his photograph. She saw that look so many times working on sexual abuse cases in her former life.

Those predatory eyes.

The frightening detachment of a rattlesnake's gaze. How did a smart girl like Nathalie failed to see this right from the start? She didn't have good instincts. Psychopaths are certainly the greatest manipulators and charmer on earth. They also dismiss any authority; they become excessively angry when someone turns them down, which Nathalie claims to have done on multiple occasions, putting Gagné more and more in a rage. They also feel no guilt. Again, a behavior fully displayed by Gagné, both during the aggression and at the trial.

They entice gullible young girls with fancy words. Gagné was physically attractive, with his square jaw and athletic shoulders.

Nathalie was doomed from the start. It was only a matter of time before the snake devoured her.

François Lavoie had a few minor crimes under his belt, but nothing comparable to Gagné. He was rather a cowardly follower hanging around in his friend's shadow. He was overweight, suffering from severe baldness, hollow, dark circles around his eyes, crooked teeth, and a flagrant personal hygiene issue highlighted by yellowed teeth and a dull complexion. Like a parasite, he would come behind Gagné to pick up his crumbs.

Stephane Ranger, the trio sole survivor, was thinner and looked sicker in those photos. The scrawny face of a Crystal

Meth addict. Ashen skin, emaciated eyes. He swore he was in no condition to molest Nathalie, but she said he was.

Nathalie had memory lapses that negatively impacted her testimony. There were some inconsistencies that the defendant's prosecutor jumped on like a piranha over a drop of blood.

Even though doctors confirmed the many blows to her head may well have caused her amnesia, Nathalie was helpless against the defense attorney's surgical destruction of her deposition.

Things got worse after the acquittal. Raymond Primeau had stepped over the railing separating him from the defendants and rushed at them, but three guards had subdued him somehow just before he reached Eric Gagné. They required reinforcements to restrain him while they extracted the suspects.

Maxime Fauvette had also threatened the defendants, to the point of almost getting convicted of death threats, but the judge gave him a serious warning.

The doctor's statement detailed a long list of chilling injuries: bruised genitals, torn anus, severe bites to the breasts, extensive bruising to the head, three broken teeth, severe concussion, fractured jaw, two cracked ribs, collapsed lung, multiple insect bites and stings, major dehydration.

The woman who found her lying on the side of the road reported that she and her husband were driving quietly on a sunny Sunday morning when they saw what they initially thought was an injured animal on the roadside. As she drove past Nathalie, she realized it was a human being and told her husband to stop the car. She went up to Nathalie to see if she needed help, but she immediately grasped the seriousness of the situation. Nathalie was badly injured, with her face heavily swollen, and she had difficulty standing up straight. The woman kept in touch with her and became deeply fond of her.

Nathalie then had a severe depression and had several stays at the hospital. Some time after her convalescence, she expressed her gratitude to the woman for stopping by that day. She also apologized for dragging her into her misery, as she said.

The woman told her that not only didn't need to thank her or ask her forgiveness, but that she was thrilled to have rescued her, because she saw what a beautiful young woman Nathalie was, full of potential. Nathalie told her a little about her recovery and then hung up, promising to call her again the following week.

A few hours later, she hung herself in the family residence's garage.

As she closed the file, Abygaelle notices the photocopy of a handwritten letter. A nice fine artist's calligraphy.

Nathalie's handwriting.

"Hello my parents, who I adore. First, forgive me for putting you through this. I can barely imagine the horror it must be to find my lifeless body in the house, but it's the only place where I felt safe. So, to the person who found me like this, I'm sorry.

There is no justice in this world. I always have been honest, as you taught me. I applied those values of respect and self-sacrifice every day. I believed in karma. That if you do good deeds, life will reward you! But that's bullshit. Karma doesn't exist. Good people go through evil and bad people get away with crime. So what's the point? Assholes can harm a helpless girl like me and get away with it with no consequences. Those scumbags who have poured out their stinking seed in me and used me like an insignificant object, just good to quench their worst instincts. Just useful to be thrown away after use, like a tissue. I'm damaged. I don't have the strength to reconstruct myself.

They killed me that night. I just didn't die right away. My soul is still in that cold, muddy ditch. I never came out of it.

I love you. I hope you'll understand my choice and not judge me. I can't live like this. I ask you to accept my decision and above all to go on with your life as if I were still here because, in a way, I will. I don't want you to be miserable or waste your energy loathing my aggressors; they don't deserve your attention. Understood Daddy? I loved your protective instincts at the trial, but if you live in resentment and bitterness, you will be the one unhappy. Not them. You're the one who will ruin your life, not them.

I will wait for you on the other side, where I hope the world is better and brighter. Where the good and the gentle are rewarded, where the wicked go to hell for eternity.

Sorry again for doing this to you. I know it will come as a shock, but I will be happier over there. I won't suffer anymore. I no longer hope for anything out of this life. It has let me down.

I'll see you on the other side. Tell William and Max that I love them and I apologize big time.

Nath xxx"

With foggy eyes, Abygaelle folds down the folder and breath profoundly. Nathalie's lucidity and courage a few hours before she killed herself moves her. How sad, but how strong at the same time!

Aby is ambivalent about suicide. Whether it is an act of bravery or cowardice. It's hard to understand what goes on in someone's mind when they reach this irredeemable conclusion.

How do you explain people kill themselves even when they have everything in life? Why do others carry on despite all the terrible hurdles that fate puts in their path? Maybe sometimes despair is so deep that death seems soft.

Abygaelle went to the homicide squad because she could no longer stand the sexual abuse she witnessed day after day. It's ironic that her first investigation had the same effect on her.

That it highlights the depth of her own scars.

52

Abygaelle paces around waiting for Stephane Ranger to arrive.

She has questions for him, lots of questions. She is curious about everything related to Nathalie Primeau's gang rape.

Murielle Bouchard is with her in the interrogation room. She didn't want Jack to be there. They need Stephane to be calm, to realize that they see him as a witness able to help move the investigation forward and not as a potential suspect.

Jack's crude methods could put him off.

Murielle will stay on the sidelines, leaving Abygaelle to lead the interview.

About ten minutes later, Ranger sits down in front of her, looking annoyed.

"Stephane, tell me about Nathalie Primeau's rape."

He straightens up on his chair, surprised by the harshness of the opening. He takes a few seconds to put his ideas back in place.

"I have already disclosed what I knew at the trial. Read the verbatim transcript."

"I've read it," Aby says. "But I want to hear it from you since you felt the need to keep it from us."

"I hid nothing from you. Why would I talk about this since the court cleared me?"

Abygaelle and Murielle look at him sternly.

He sighs, annoyed.

"I don't remember much. I took enough heroin to kill a horse. I only remember bits and pieces of which I—"

He stops, as if already said too much. Aby orders him to carry on. She assures him that the aim is not to reopen the investigation. She only wants to understand.

"You won't find anything about this rape," he says. "The other guys are dead, so is the girl."

"We know about Eric Gagné and François Lavoie."

"And Jean Blackburn," Ranger adds.

Murielle and Abygaelle are confused. Jean Blackburn? What does he have to do with it?

"He was our prosecutor. He, too, was murdered," Stephane says as the sight of their puzzled faces.

Listening on a closed-circuit monitor, Jack vaguely remembers the famous lawyer's death.

"Tell us what you remember," Aby says.

"Only that we were at a party at a house up north. At one point, Gagné and Lavoie were fucking a girl. The only image that comes to mind is that she was face down on the ground, her lower body naked, and Lavoie just came in her."

He notes the discomfort on both women's faces.

"Sorry for the sordid details."

"Go on," Abygaelle says, undaunted.

"They made me fuck her too, but I couldn't. When I've done heroin, I can't get a hard-on."

"Did you try anyway?"

"I don't know, maybe. It's a blur. Then we all left together with the girl. Then I just remember waking up at home with a hell of a headache."

Ranger's account matches what Abygaelle read. His version has not changed.

"How did you find out about Gagné, Lavoie, and Blackburn's murders?"

"For François, it was on the news for a while. They found him shot in front of his truck in Saint-Hélène-de-Bagot. His girlfriend, Annie, told me about Gagné. Blackburn's disappearance had been all over the news as well."

"Wait," Abygaelle says while grabbing a pen, "Annie who?"

"St. Onge," he says, lowering his head.

Aby stares at him, motionless, stunned.

"Are you saying that Annie St. Onge was Eric Gagné's girlfriend?"

"Until his death, yes. She was there when they killed him."

"She was there during the murder?"

"Yes, the murderer ambushed her in their living room. According to what she told me, she fell asleep on the sofa waiting for Eric to come back from a night out with friends. The killer held her hostage with a knife at her throat. He asked her when Gagné would be back. She did not know. The killer had turned off all lights and ordered Annie to shut up. She attempted to talk to him, try to figure out what he wanted. She begged him to let her go, but he told her to keep her mouth shut."

Abygaelle takes notes.

"When Eric came home, he froze when he saw the man sitting next to Annie. It was the first time she ever saw him so powerless. The first time she sensed terror in his eyes. Gagné was the ultimate alpha male, always looking for trouble. He would often get into fights. He wasn't afraid of anyone, but Annie told me that this time he was petrified. She said that at one point, the killer told her to run away. Then everything happened quickly. She recalled she could not make it to the door. She was paralyzed watching the killer dominate Eric. He had stuck his knife in his throat. Afterwards, the man came back towards her and forced her into a wardrobe. He tied her wrists and ankles with duct tape and put some over her mouth. He closed the door. Then she heard him talking to Gagné, but Eric didn't answer. She didn't quite understand what the killer was saying, but there was noise for approximately ten minutes. Then the front door opened and closed gently. After about half an hour, she untied herself and escape from the closet. She exited the apartment, not looking at Gagné, but she noticed that there was blood everywhere. Then, she called the police. Oh, poor Annie, she didn't have any chance in life. And now she's dead."

For a moment, Aby thought Ranger was going to cry. She waited for a few minutes until he came to his senses.

"Stephane, Annie left us a voice message saying that she absolutely needed to talk to us. But she passed away before we could reach her. We found her dead in her apartment."

"Do you know what she wanted?"

"Unfortunately not."

Ranger looks forward, pondering.

"How did you find out about Nathalie?" Abygaelle says.

"About Nathalie?"

"Nathalie Primeau's suicide."

"In the news, too. She took her own life in the family home's garage. That's awful. We really destroyed this girl."

Abygaelle feels Stephane has genuine remorse. She looks at him and is reluctant to share her idea with him. She thought long and hard about their failure to catch the killer.

It's intolerable.

They need a different strategy to tackle this psychopath who seems to make no mistakes. They have two choices: wait for him to have a misstep—at the risk of increasing the death count in the process—or go all in, put all their chips in the center of the table and hope for a miraculous flop. It was all or nothing.

Once Stephane Ranger calmed down, she put her hands on his.

"What I'm about to tell you may sound incredibly weird, but please listen to me until the end."

53

Jack Morris moves towards Abygaelle Jensen, looking gloomy.

"Listen Aby, if you don't mind, I'll have to cancel our plans for tonight at my place."

He invited Abygaelle and Murielle for dinner earlier in the week, as suggested by his wife, Francine. Aby, who is not fond of these social gatherings, agreed anyway for the sake of team spirit and to get to know his colleagues better.

You can see the true nature of homo erectus by analyzing where it lives, she thinks. But now that Jack has cancelled, she is disappointed.

"Everything's fine, Jack?" she asks.

"Yes, don't worry."

The detective's one-stringed tone sounds wrong. Something has been wrong with him for the past few days. Proof of that is the rescheduling of the evening. She seeks answers from Murielle, but she sees nothing but weariness.

By late afternoon, Murielle seizes a moment of lull to ask her to take a stroll outside.

"You know, Jack often plays tough, but deep down, he's a big teddy bear. At home, he doesn't run the show at all, if you get my meaning. It's Francine. She's hard on our pal. He's at her feet like an obedient little puppy. Sometimes it's not fun to see, I assure you. It makes no difference whether or not there are people around. I have never understood why he condones such conduct."

Several minutes after she's back at her desk, Aby watches Jack. He reads a file, but the sadness on her face strikes her.

She feels sorry for the man. How can people cope with such a toxic relationship? She would never accept such a thing. If a guy made her feel like dirt, she would dump him right away.

She's done it before without ever looking back. She would rather be alone than with a man who treats her like shit. It's all about self-esteem. One must cherish oneself to let others love them, as Roland Michaud often told her.

He was right.

"He can't be that miserable if he stays," Murielle says.

"But look at him, have you ever seen anyone more miserable reading a file?"

Murielle doesn't answer. She looks at Jack too.

A few hours later, a man in his forties follows Abygaelle to an interview room. She beckons Murielle to go with her.

Maxime Fauvette doesn't look nervous in any shape or form. He has the typical accountant look with his round glasses on the tip of his nose, his black curly mop with some grey streaks, his flowery shirt too large for him, and his beige corduroy pants.

Aby reassures him, they do not charge him with anything. They speak with everyone who was close to Nathalie Primeau. Simply trying to glue together a gigantic puzzle bits and pieces.

"You've heard about the murders in recent weeks, about the sniper?"

"Who didn't?"

"We believe it's connected in some way to Nathalie's rape."

Maxime looks at the two investigators, skeptical.

"I don't understand," he says. "Nathalie? Who is dead since over fifteen years? How can it about her?"

Abygaelle notices that man's hand shaking.

"This is one of our assumptions," Murielle calmly says. "We don't want to leave anything to chance, so if it's not related, fine, we'll rule it out. However, there are some interesting coincidences."

"Like what?"

Abygaelle outlines her theory about the murderer going after Stephane Ranger acquaintances, the last surviving defendant in Nathalie's case. Three of Ranger's relatives were killed one after the other.

The explanation didn't provide the desired effect. Fauvette is incredulous.

"After all these years, a man would suddenly decide to attack not the rapist himself, but his loved ones? I'm not a cop, but it seems far-fetched to me."

Murielle shrugs.

"I've seen crazier shit than this," she says.

"Do you think it's the same guy who killed Gagné?" Fauvette asks.

Abygaelle and Murielle look at each other in surprise.

"What do you mean?"

"You don't know who Eric Gagné is?" he says, perplexed.

"We do," Aby replies.

"Then you know what I mean."

"My question more about what you know of Gagné's murder?"

"Just what I heard on the news back then, someone killed him. They found his genitals in his mouth."

The image makes him smile.

"You think it's funny?" Murielle asks.

"Yes," Maxime says with poise. "Actually, I don't think it's funny that a rotten bastard like him died with his own balls in his mouth, Mrs. Bouchard, I think it's hilarious."

"You profoundly hated the three accused, didn't you?" Abygaelle says.

"You bet I did, but Gagné in particular."

"Why him more than the others?"

"Because, according to Nathalie, he did most of the damage. And because he shamelessly mocked us in the courtroom. As if this monster hadn't already done enough."

"You would have wanted to kill him, wouldn't you?"

Maxime leaned down on the table and approached Abygaelle, gazing longingly into her eyes.

"Yes, I would have liked to at the time. But I didn't. He had many enemies. He was a career criminal. Someone finally took action, and I'm delighted about that. When I heard the news, I uncorked a bottle of champagne. I won't lie to you."

"And François Lavoie?" Murielle asks.

"The fat pig? No idea what happened to him."

"He's dead."

Fauvette shrugs.

"Okay, Then I guess I'll get another Dom Perignon."

"He was murdered."

"Even better!"

"He too had his testicles in his mouth."

Fauvette freezes. After some thought, he concedes it's a strange coincidence.

"I don't believe in coincidences," Abygaelle says, crossing her arms.

"I do," Maxime answers curtly. "I've had several examples of that. Coincidences happen all the time."

He didn't flinch; she thinks.

"I must ask you the question, Mr. Fauvette," Abygaelle says.

"Did you have anything to do with the deaths of Ariane Légaré, Marc-André Davison and Annie St. Onge?"

Maxime answers no, in a very assured tone, swearing that he does not know these people.

"What about those of Eric Gagné and François Lavoie?" Murielle adds.

Maxime smiles wickedly.

"Unfortunately not."

There is no reason not to believe him. He has no criminal record; he lives a quiet and orderly life in the suburbs with his three children and his wife. He has been working at the same accounting firm for thirteen years. No wonder he doesn't care about three thugs who robbed him of the girl he loved.

"You named your daughter after Nathalie?"

The question took Maxime by surprise, and for the first time since his arrival, he shows emotion.

"I had to," he answered softly, lowering his eyes.

"Why is that?"

"I don't know. I thought it was inconceivable that a person as extraordinary as Nath, with such great potential, would be so cruelly cut down when she had so much to offer, to life, to all of us. In doing so, I hoped that somehow she would never die. That a piece of her would still be alive. It's ridiculous, I know."

"Did it work?"

He looks up and looks into the Abygaelle's eyes.

"Yes, in a sense. In her own way, my daughter looks like her. Or I assume she looks like her. I don't know."

Even though Maxime Fauvette left the police station more than an hour ago, the two detectives are still in the same room, lost in their thoughts. It was as if the last part of the interview had drained them emotionally.

"My God, what's with you?"

Jack Morris startled his colleagues with his loud, deep voice.

"Look who's in a good mood now!" Murielle says in a mocking tone.

"Pff, what are you talking about?" he says as he moves back to his desk.

Abygaelle and Murielle look at each other and smile.

54

As soon as Jocelyne Lamoureux opened the door, she got an awkward apprehension. That kind that makes your blood curl, but you wish you had it before it was too late.

It's too late.

She's crippled by fear as she peeks at the legs of a man in the dark, calmly cuddled up in the living room couch.

She contemplated leaving, but there is one problem: she doesn't know where Myriam is, but more importantly, where Maripier is?

Myriam is her young neighbor babysitting her eight-year-old daughter, Maripier. Did she run away with her? Or did something bad happen to them? My God, please make it that Myriam ran away with her.

The man doesn't move. He doesn't speak either. She slowly puts her bag on the ground, weighing each of her movements. She evaluates her options. She moves one step towards him. Fortunately, the darkness hides the trembling of her legs. They could give way at any moment.

"Good evening Jocelyne."

The man's voice startled her. How does he know her name?

Surely it's not the voice of someone she knows, perhaps one biker from Pete's chapter?

She knows how to deal with them. She takes another step in his direction. Thanks to the moonlight, she can see her daughter's tiny feet lying on the couch out of the corner of her eye.

Her heart stops beating for a second. It's Maripier. Dear God.

She feels a parental fury rising in her, interspersed with deep fear. She doesn't know how to react. Her thoughts jostle in her head.

"What did you do to my baby?" she says authoritatively, taking another step forward.

The reflection of a gun coming out of the shadows stops her dead in her tracks. She needs to be cautious, at least until she knows her daughter's condition.

But if he hurt her, she would have nothing to lose and would jump on him like a rabid hyena. Who cares if he kills her? Pete and Maripier's death a few weeks apart would be too much for her.

"Sit down, Jocelyne."

The man's voice is measured, but authoritative. It leaves no room for negotiation. Even more so because even if the silvery reflection of the barrel of the gun vanishes in the half-light, she can tell it's still pointed directly at her chest.

She obediently sits down and keeps staring at his shadow.

"That's better."

The deafening silence filling the room puts an enormous pressure on her. But she can fee it. She can't deny it. What is the point of all this? He's certainly not here to chat, so what does he want?

"What did you do to my daughter?"

"Everybody's okay."

"Who the fuck are you? What do you want from me!"

The man bends his torso quietly toward the light to expose his face to the light.

Jocelyne stiffens and feels her blood drain from her body.

She would recognize that crazy look in a million. These demented blue eyes which have haunted her for days. They are there, in front of her, piercing her like a long, sharp sword. This time, she fully looks at his face and registers it in her memory. If she makes it out alive, she will go back to Detective Sergeant Jensen.

What does he want from her? Hasn't he done enough? His tight grin just as he pulled the trigger. His draw, as if he had just done something trivial.

There he is, illuminated by the night light. The same mad smirk that had paralyzed her. He's Pete's killer.

"I can see by the look on your face that you recognized me, Jocelyne" the assassin says. "Good, you know what I can do."

She feels filthy every time he says his name. Like a rape. As if he's stripping her from her soul. She notices his hand rubbing Maripier's hair. She is motionless, her eyes are closed, her head resting on a pillow near the man's thigh.

How dare he? She couldn't tolerate the hands of her husband's murderer patting her head. The heavy and calm voice of the killer echoes throughout the room. How is it that Maripier doesn't wake up? She's breathing normally, that's all that matters right now. Now it's up to her to get them out of this mess.

"And Myriam?"

"The babysitter? In the bedroom. Also sleeping."

"What do you want?" she asks unemotional.

"That you wipe me from your memory."

"I don't understand."

"I want you to forget about me, to go on with your life, to act as if nothing had happened."

Jocelyne has a sneer of contempt. As if nothing

happened? You're right, nothing serious. You only shot the love of my life in the head. But other than that? Nothing extravagant.

"Is it a bad joke?" she asks seriously.

What he's asking from her is unthinkable. The nerve he has to ask for this? As if she could forget the sight of her boyfriend being shot, for no logical reason. Even if she wanted to, it was impossible.

"I'm afraid not, dear Jocelyne." he sits comfortably in the armchair and continues to stroke the girl's hair. "What would you do if you were me?"

She doesn't react.

"It's a heartbreaking choice for me, Jocelyne. What would you do if you were standing next to someone who could ruin your life, and you could stop her? I know you talked to the police."

"I'm standing next to someone who has already ruined my life," she says tacitly. "And if you do what I think you're about to do, you could wreck it forever. But unlike you, I don't have the luxury of stopping anything."

"I mean, I made a mistake. I got caught in the moment. I shouldn't have killed your boyfriend—"

"My husband," she says, correcting him.

Even though she knows he doesn't give a rat's ass about it, it's important for her that he knows.

"Your husband, whatever, I shouldn't have done that. I let my feelings get the better of me. But, Pete wasn't a choirboy, was he?"

She clenches her teeth. How dare he speak his name so casually after what he did?

"I mean, drugs, money laundering, and what else? Normally, I kill people who deserve it, but this was a fluke, but let's face it, I was lucky."

"You asshole."

She whispered these words so hatefully that she's afraid he will react violently. But he doesn't.

"I accept your contempt. I probably had it coming. You have every right to be angry at me. But it won't bring your husband back. I thought it would nip it in the bud, and we could move on, but imagine my surprise to see a sketch of my face on television. Fortunately, it looks nothing like me. I thought it was proof that you were on a mission to destroy me, that you wanted to hunt me down. So you can't blame me for taking the lead and meeting you beforehand. Here I am today sitting in front of you, with young, uh, Maripier? Yes, that's right, Maripier lying next to me. So, Jocelyne, I know you don't want to, but you'll have to make up your mind. I'll ask you a favor and I strongly advise you agree to it. I implore you not to work with the police again."

"Why would I do that," she says, even though she knows the answer.

"Come on, Jocelyne. You're smart. Your baby girl is sleeping peacefully right now. We wouldn't want that to be permanent, would we? Such a beautiful little girl with her whole life ahead of her. Look, I'm willing to pay for my other crimes, but in Pete's case, it was a mistake. Ironically, you'll agree, that's why I'm against these overly liberal gun laws. If I hadn't had my rifle, I would have just beaten him up like in the old days. He would have gotten away with what, a broken jaw? A broken nose? Nothing comparable to what he got. You should never carry a gun around when you're pissed off, Jocelyne, never. Don't you agree?"

She's not answering. She refuses to play his sick game.

"Let's be honest, how many innocent victims have the bikers killed compared to what I've done so far. A lot more, right? Honest mistake. Let's leave it at that. Okay, Jocelyne?"

Total silence.

"Hello? Okay, listen, I need you to play along. I enjoy chatting as much as the next guy, but at some point you'll have to tell me if we have a deal or not."

After a few seconds of silence, he raises his voice:

"Do we have a deal, Jocelyne, yes or no?"

She sighs at length. Does she really have a choice?

"We have a deal."

"Perfect," the assassins says, excited, as if he has closed a major deal. "I knew you were a savvy businesswoman, Jocelyne. Can you imagine? I was coming here to get rid of you and the rest of your family, but I thought, "Buddy, why don't you try to come to an agreement? Do we really need more casualties? Am I right?"

Jocelyne nods.

"Of course, you can imagine that I won't leave walking to the sunset whistling like the end of a movie. I'll have to take precautions."

She hears him rummaging through a bag at his feet, then the deafening sound of a rubber band being stretched makes her startle. He instructs her to put her wrists together, and he ties them. Then he sticks another piece over her mouth. He secures her ankles against her chair's rails.

"Jocelyne, I would piss me off to come back here. You'll agree that it's better if it's the last time we see each other. We'll both be better off. But if I find out that you've gone to the police again, I swear I won't for one second think twice before putting two bullets in the back of your daughter's skull. Are we clear?"

The tone leaves no doubt. For the first time, the man's voice was alarming. The intention is obvious. She's knows he'll carry out his threats. Tears flows softly down her cheeks, reluctantly nodding in agreement. She feels like she's giving up on her husband.

"In about thirty minutes, the drug I gave your daughter will fade out, and she'll have no after-effects. It may be another story for the babysitter. Let's say she went hard with the creme de menthe. I didn't have to do anything. You should really lock up your bar downstairs, Jocelyne, kids these days, right?"

He walks out the door and quietly closes it without saying another word.

Jocelyne couldn't swear, but she thinks she heard him giggling as he left.

55

Abygaelle is completely overwhelmed. Every time she thinks she holds all the pieces of the puzzle, they found a new one. This time it's as the high-profile murder of lawyer Jean Blackburn.

She recalls the case very well; it was a big deal at the time. Although not the first famous defense attorney to be killed in Quebec, it's rather unusual. His constant media exposure after his retirement earned him a great deal of public notoriety.

His death had ignited strong interest.

His murderers were never identified, nor were those of Frank Shoofey, another prominent Montreal defence attorney who was gunned down on his way out of his office.

Except that the assassin's fury over Blackburn's body was baffling. Officials said that the killer must have been furious at him for killing him in such a way, carving "rat" on his forehead with a knife. It wasn't your run-of-the-mill break-in going wrong.

It was a deep, visceral rage.

Initially, Aby didn't make the connection between this murder and her investigation, even though she knew Blackburn was the prosecutor for all three defendants in Nathalie Primeau's rape. But now, knowing Eric Gagné and François Lavoie's demise, that Stephane feels that the same killer is responsible for Blackburn's death, it makes sense.

Jack wonders how three seemingly insignificant young men could afford such a prominent lawyer. An excellent question indeed. The case was not particularly high profile, so Blackburn didn't take on the case for the fame, as he usually only took on popular cases.

Murielle learned that Eric Gagné's parents are very rich. His father, Marcel, was a senior executive at Gaz Corp, a Canada-wide oil company. He has since retired, and lives with his wife in a vast estate on the Montreal North Shore.

Abygaelle contacted them to confirm they hired Blackburn, which they confirmed right off the bat. They wanted the best defence for their son once he swore he was innocent of the crime, stating that the young woman was consenting.

Although he was not proud of his son's way of life, Marcel Gagné wanted to protect him from very serious allegations of rape, aggravated assault, and attempted murder. He couldn't leave him like that.

Jean Blackburn was an acquaintance. They went to the same university. The litigant agreed to take on the case wholeheartedly. When he found out that they assigned the other two defendants incompetent lawyers, he elected to represent them as well at no extra cost since they were all in the same trial. Blackburn was adamant that the two inadequate prosecutors would be detrimental to his client.

Gagné still believes that his son was innocent. Although he had great sympathy for the young woman, he didn't think his son was capable of such atrocities. He believed Nathalie was telling the truth, that she had been assaulted and left for dead that night, but he refused to consider that his son was to blame.

Eric didn't want to be a snitch, but he revealed to his father shortly before his death that it was François Lavoie who beat Nathalie and left her lifeless in the ravine because she turned him down.

He drove Gagné and Ranger back to their apartment, and was about to do the same with her, but everything had gone off the rails.

Abygaelle listened to him, raging. She knows the truth. Both Nathalie's testimony and Stephane Ranger's show that it was indeed Eric who did all the damage. But it would be useless to burden Marcel Gagné and his wife with such details. They are not responsible for their son's wrongdoings. They, too, are collateral victims of this monstrosity.

They too have lost a child.

Although Blackburn probably helped the three defendants get off the hook, they did what any parent would have done to save their offspring. Their son lied to them too. Aby doesn't have children, but she knows that if she did, she would do anything to protect them.

Eric was murdered, so there's no point in reopening that wound.

Stephane Ranger told Abygaelle that he got back in the car when he realized he wouldn't convince Gagné to leave Nathalie alone. He stated he had to turn up the radio volume in the car so that he could no longer hear the screams of distress.

To this day, he still feels guilty that he didn't call the police as it was happening, and that he didn't reveal the horrors perpetrated by Eric Gagné, but he terrorized him. Gagné was much stronger than he was, and he was insane. Stephane was weak and will have to live with his cowardice for the rest of his life. Even though Gagné didn't kill the girl that night, he made her endure an inhuman fate.

Abygaelle asked Marcel Gagné if he knew who killed both their son and Blackburn. He pondered for several seconds but admitted he didn't, because Eric had multiple enemies. But he had a hunch that it was the same assassin for the three of them. The crimes were quite similar, a knife attack, a vicious assault, a hate-filled murder.

He has no proof of that, and he has since moved on. He knew his son might end up that way someday. He doesn't comprehend why he turned down that road instead of doing something meaningful with his life, why he became a bum. He had everything one could wish for. He was handsome, tall, strong and had everything he needed with the family fortune.

But he craved adrenaline, addicted to narcotics and alcohol, which were destroying his life. Even at a younger age, he had burst of rage. Marcel Gagné was very tough himself, so he easily overpowered his son, but it was as if an evil spirit consumed him.

"Life is weird," he said. "Kids with very little in life sometimes do better than rich ones. It's like life hasn't allotted them to the right families."

Luckily, the Gagné have two other children who are doing very well, but for the eldest, Eric, that hasn't been the case. However, all three have had a similar education, the same environment, the same opportunities. There was something wrong with Eric's brain. It was like he was never satisfied. Never comfortable anywhere unless he was doing drugs.

Despite his resigned tone, Aby suspected that deep down inside, Marcel Gagné felt guilty. It's as if, by confessing all this to her, he tried to convince himself more than anything.

She felt that even tragic, Eric's death was salutary. He brought his share of problems and worries to the family. They were ashamed of what he became. Having a hard-core criminal and substance abusing son was a stain on their reputation. They hid him as best they could, but it wasn't always possible to pretend he didn't exist.

Despite all this, when Eric needed him, he didn't hesitate to use all his contacts to get his son the best lawyer he could. He didn't know that by involving his old-time friend; he was sending him to the slaughterhouse.

That Eric would drag him into the abyss of his wasted life.

This is something he'll have to live with for the rest of his life. Blackburn's wife feels the same way, and she still holds a grudge against him.

Abygaelle is surprised that neither the Gagné's nor Blackburn's widow have expressed their suspicions about the murders to the police. She had found no record of it anywhere. Marcel Gagné confirmed to her they never talked about it because they wanted to move on. They had suffered enough because of all this.

Eric's death marked the end of a dark chapter.

When she hung up, Abygaelle was glad she hadn't revealed Eric's role in this barbarism. The more the discussion developed, the more his voice softened. She felt as though he were reliving these painful events again and again.

Indeed, they had suffered enough. Why bring more pain?

Jack disagrees.

"They should have realized they've created a monster."

"They know that, Jack. Believe me, they know."

Murielle is more sensitive. She grasps Abygaelle's logic; she agrees with her, even if it's not as clear-cut.

Aby is at peace with her decision. At least now they know why Jean Blackburn ended up at the center of the quagmire that ultimately cost him his life.

56

On the way back under a torrential rain, Abygaelle is lost in her thoughts. For ten minutes she has been watching the wet pavement slip under the car driving by Jack. They are silent.

It didn't go as well as she would have liked.

They came back to Monique Primeau's house with a search warrant. They searched everywhere. The woman was sobbing. Abygaelle attempted to comfort her, but conceded that there was nothing she could do but let her live out her emotions.

Then, Jack showed a blatant lack of tact in coming after her. He said he didn't believe her, that he was sure she knew where her husband was hiding. How could she not recall if he was with her when Ariane was killed? She swore he was home when the evening news mentioned the murder, but was he home when the murder occurred, she didn't know. She was out in the backyard.

Jack's reaction upset Abygaelle. That was not the agreement they originally had. Jack was there to ensure things would go easy during the search. Abygaelle would stand by Monique Primeau, deal with her the best she could.

Then Monique said something about her rights, or complained that she was being harassed. Aby can't remember what made Jack go off the rails, but he burst towards them to pick on the poor woman. Aby had to step in, but it was too late. Monique was no longer responding, no longer interacting. There was nothing more to be done. She took refuge in a profound silence.

Technicians compared the soles of Raymond Primeau's shoes with the mould taken from the Marc-André Davison murder, but found no correlation.

"The size of his shoes is similar, however. He may have disposed of the boots he wore that night."

That's one possibility. And that his foot matches the mold doesn't eliminate him as a suspect, on the contrary. Except that he's part of a large stratum of men who wear that shoe size.

"How many people could blame Stephane Ranger for their daughter's death," Jack asks.

That's the crux of the matter. Although this is the current hypothesis that everything is connected to Nathalie Primeau, they have no proof. Before Monique shut down, Aby asked her if Raymond played chess. She said no. They found nothing in the house either, no board, no chess pieces anywhere.

"Was there any relationship between Nathalie and chess pieces? You know, like a queen?"

Monique Primeau shook her head with a perplex look. Obviously, she did not know what Abygaelle was referring to. Aby bite her lower lip, reflecting on what these wooden queens meant to the assassin.

The silence in the car was heavy. Jack glances furtively at her, unwilling to speak first. He knows he screwed up.

He would have a hard time explaining why he snapped like that. It was pure instinct. He, too, is on edge. He realizes these events shook and completely overwhelmed Monique Primeau.

If she knows where her husband was, then give her an Oscar, she's a goddamn talented actress.

Meanwhile, he's worried about Abygaelle. He senses she's fragile, on the verge of breaking down. He sees through the phony confidence she uses as a shield. He shared these concerns with Murielle the other day.

"We're about to lose her," he said to her.

Murielle nodded. He wasn't crazy. His intuition was good.

"Every time we hit a bump," Jack said, "I have the feeling she's more confused. We must do all in our power to help her."

"That's what we're doing, aren't we?" Murielle said.

"Yes, but we need to find a way to help her, bring her hope that we're on the right track. To be honest, I sometimes share her sense of inadequacy."

"I know," she said with a timid smile.

Jack glanced at her interrogatively. Murielle kept on speaking:

"When you can't make sense of things, you become impatient and angry, you jump to conclusions. Don't act insulted, it's not a secret. We have discussed it many times. You've been on a plane before, haven't you?"

"Of course," Jack said, not seeing the connection.

"When there's turbulence, what's the first thing you do? You look at the flight attendants to gauge their level of concern. Their deadpan allure comforts you. You assume that they've been through worse and that this brief moment is perfectly normal. You realize everything is going to be okay, that it's just something we need to work through."

Jack smiled.

"True."

"So imagine if there was turbulence and the flight attendants freaked out, you wouldn't be as confident, would you? You wouldn't be optimistic about your chances of making it alive. We're Aby's flight attendants, and when the going gets rough, we're the first people she turns to. She seeks solace in our eyes, in our physiognomy. So we have no right to panic."

Jack looks down.

"You're right."

"I'm always right, Jack. Stick to that principle," she said with a giggle.

Murielle is the voice of wisdom in their duo. He wonders what place Abygaelle will take in their dynamic. Youth and energy perhaps. Of course, it's more than that. What Abygaelle brings to the table is intuition and courage. He doesn't know her very well yet, but her tenacity strikes him. When you strip away the layer of self-doubt and fake confidence she displays, you see the determination of those who would rather die than give up.

If she gets through this, she'll be an incredible asset to the department. He's confident about this. He has a shiver down his spine thinking that she might fail. It would be disastrous. This is her ultimate test.

It's make or break.

But it's not by acting the way he did with Monique Primeau that he'll help her. By bursting out in anger, he hurt her. She was in control, squeezing snippets of information out of the woman until she shut up for good.

She's right to scowl at him right now. Her contained rage is palpable in every cubic centimeter of air in the car.

They drive in complete silence. No radio, no talk, no music. Only the sound of the tires tearing through the water on the pavement.

When they reach the office, Jack takes the key out of the ignition and stays seated next to her. They stare straight ahead, mute. The rain keeps on tinkling, pounding the sheet metal of the car.

"You know, Aby, I—"

She looks at him with no animosity.

"I know, Jack."

She gets out of the car, but he can't do the same. She knows he's sorry, that he repents what he did. But the tremendous disappointment in his young colleague's eyes tears him apart.

57

William Primeau chuckles at Murielle Bouchard's inadequacy with technology.

"No, click further down where you see a speaker icon, on the right, no no, at the bottom right," he says, pointing frantically with his finger at the bottom of the screen. "I can't hear you. Can you hear me? No, I can't hear you, don't you have an IT department?"

Murielle signals him to wait for a minute and gets up furiously.

"Get me a fucking IT tech support, it's urgent," she says, screaming across the hall.

Everyone freezes and look at her. She fumes at the damn technology that's supposed to make everyone's lives easier. She can't figure it out for the life of her.

She misses the days when a notebook, pen and phone were all you needed to do your job. And you can't have a conversation nowadays with someone under thirty without their face glued to their smartphone.

After a technician got the thing working in about three seconds, the interview finally can start.

William Primeau has a sympathetic, cheerful face. He makes a good impression on Murielle. She notices his undeniable charisma.

"Nice view," Murielle says, admiringly pointing behind William.

"Yes, Big Ben is mythical. But believe me, London is not only made up of royal carriages and the Beatles. There are also bad parts, like in Quebec."

"How long have you lived in England?"

"Fifteen years."

Murielle is surprised. Fifteen years for someone that young is a big chunk of life. She thanks him for his the time and to respond to her questions. They chat about his life in London, his parents in the Montreal area. He doesn't sugarcoat his relationship with his father.

A man who achieved great things, but turned out to be a pain in the ass to everyone after Nathalie died. He mutated into a hermit, and is now only happy with his miniature cars and his gardening.

"It's a kind of normal, isn't it?" Murielle asks.

"Maybe the first year. But at some point, you need to go on with your life," William says, speaking really fast. "That's what Nathalie would have wanted, anyway. She would have been the first to ruffle him and tell him to live his life. I tried, but after a while I gave up."

"What about your mother?"

William's face softened.

"Poor thing. She's so sweet. She has no malice. Nathalie's death destroyed her, but she went on with her life as best she could. Unfortunately, she has to drag this gigantic ball and chain around with her."

"You mean your father."

"Correct."

Abygaelle Jensen watches the scene from a nearby room.

He impresses her with his demeanour. Smart, talkative, good-looking despite his nascent baldness. He's dashing and successful.

She read an article in The Economist about successful expatriates, and it mentioned him. He has a wife.

"We have a young boy and my wife is pregnant with our second child. I'm trying to work less. My wife keeps criticizing me for it," he adds with a laugh. "But she's also busy with our foundation."

They don't challenge him the way he thought they would. The silver-haired policewoman only asks him about his life.

"How often do you visit your parents?"

"Not as often as I would like. I mean my mother. I regularly invite her to London, all expenses paid, but she declines because I don't want her to bring Raymond along."

Murielle notes that he referred to his father by his first name several times since the start of the interview. This is a good illustration of the gap between them.

"When was the last time you came to Canada?"

"A little over two years ago."

"To see your family?"

"No, for business. An European client wanted to invest in artificial intelligence, and there are emerging companies in Montreal. It's always a pleasure to come back to home. I'm still attached to my country despite my exile. Of course, I seized the opportunity to visit my mother and friends."

"Maxime Fauvette among others?", Murielle asks.

Her question puzzles William. He explains he hasn't talked to him for several years.

"Do you see other family members?"

"No."

"Not even your uncle? Maurice?"

William frowns.

"Maurice died a few years ago, Mrs. Bouchard."

She didn't know.

They talk about Nathalie's death, how it affected him. His entire family was affected, but differently. William threw himself headlong into his education like a bulimic, cutting off all other activities in his life. He stopped playing ice hockey, ceased going out with his friends. His father shut himself up, and Maurice spent his time writing letters to the Attorney General to overturn the three defendants' acquittals.

It made him so sick that he died of colon cancer. William thinks it's because of the grudge he bore for all those years. Maurice was probably the most angry of them all about the situation. He didn't have any children, so Nathalie and William were very dear to him.

"And Maxime, how did he cope?"

"It devastated him, that's for sure. Nathalie was the love of his life. He worshipped my sister. He's rebuilt his life since then. Married and father of three, one of whom named Nathalie, as a tribute to my sister. A great guy. I sometimes think about him even though we don't speak to each other anymore."

Murielle says she would like to meet him in person next time he's in Canada. William tells her he doesn't intend to come anytime soon, but intends to visit his mother with his wife after she gives birth, as she hasn't seen his hometown yet.

"When was the last time you spoke to your father?"

"Have a casual discussion with him? I mean, besides saying hello? Not since my exile."

Murielle can't believe it. That boy's a real grudge-holder. She told him about it.

"Not holding a grudge," he says, correcting her. "We rather have nothing in common. As much as he was my idol when I was young, I have no respect for him now."

"Harsh words for a son towards his father, wouldn't you say?"

"Maybe, but that's the way it is."

"Do you think you'll eventually reconnect with him?"

"Doubtful, but I guess we never know."

William doesn't fully understand why the interview suddenly turned into a psychoanalysis. Since he doesn't want to sound rude, he answers questions about his relationship with Raymond vaguely.

Murielle finally gets to the point.

"William, we have a favour to ask of you. We can't locate your dad right now. He seems to have vanished."

William rolls his eyes. Of course he did.

"I need you to let him know we're looking for him," Murielle says. "We want to talk to him."

"Talk to him? About what?"

"We have some questions about certain events that took place over the last few days."

"Like what?"

Given the woman's reluctance, he persists.

"If you want me to help you, I need to know what it's all about."

Murielle looks through the window where Abygaelle is. She nods approvingly.

"William, we are concerned to find out why your father went missing immediately after Ariane Légaré's murder."

William still doesn't understand.

"Who's Ariane Légaré and what does she have to do with Raymond?"

"Ariane Légaré is Stephane Ranger's niece, do you know who Stephane Ranger is?"

William's gaze stiffens.

"If it's the Stephane Ranger I'm thinking about, yes, I know who this scumbag is. But, once again, what does this have to do with Raymond?"

"We want to talk to him about Ariane's murder."

"You don't think he has something to do with that, do you?"

"That's what we're trying to figure out."

William chuckles loudly.

"I assure you that Raymond is absolutely incapable of shooting someone. He's not a murderer. He doesn't have the balls."

"Yet, in Vietnam—"

"Not sure if the legend is true," William interrupts her. "I can't imagine Raymond killing anyone."

"If he had nothing to do with Ariane Légaré's death, then he has nothing to worry about."

William nods.

"What exactly do you expect me to do?" He asks.

"Surely you have a way to reach him, phone, e-mail, whatever. Tell him we want to talk to him."

"I can do that."

"That's all I'm asking for, William, and I look forward to seeing you the next time you're in Canada. You know how to reach me."

"I will definitely let you know when I've delivered the message, then it's up to him."

The detective's face disappears from the screen, but William stares ahead, lost in thought.

The interview went well. He was self-assured. You never know what to expect. Police sometimes jump to conclusions. Often, in order to botch an investigation, they look around and accuse the first suspect who stutters too much.

He can't understand how they can even think that his idiot father could kill a teenage girl.

He turns a hundred and eighty degrees on his chair axis and faces the panorama of London.

He crosses his arms and smiles.

58

Abygaelle wipes the foggy mirror in her bathroom with the back of her hand. She took a shower, and starts her night ritual, like the perfect metronome she is. Routine makes her feel secure. She doesn't relate to change or improvisation. Although at work she has no trouble getting out of her comfort zone, it's quite the opposite in her personal life.

She needs anchors.

She sighs as she pores over the slight wrinkles at the corner of her eyes. She is not happy about aging. It's paradoxical, since she wanted so badly to be older when she was young. But since she has grown up, time has been slipping away from her. She feels like life creeps by.

She waddles to Lady Gaga's music, while her half-empty glass of wine decants on the bathroom counter. She applies night cream to her face.

Previously, she went through Ariane Légaré and Marc-André Davison's murder files for the umpteenth time. As if this new pass would hand her the key to the case on a silver platter while the previous ones did not.

She also reflects on her last encounter with Monique

Primeau. She feels totally helpless by her husband's disappearance. Aby knows that she does not know where her husband is. Aby visualises her alone, wondering why her world suddenly collapses. She imagines her crying with sorrow, all by herself without her husband, her only remaining child a thousand miles away. How cruel, Aby thinks.

She feels immeasurable pity for the woman.

She must resolve the case. It doesn't matter if she offends people in the process. She devotes all her energy to stop this lunatic firing at people whilst hiding like a coward.

Then she questions herself again. She doubts her own means. It keeps coming back like a train right on time. This damn impostor syndrome, this damn uncertainty. Will it ever vanish? It was the same in Vice Squad.

She sometimes wonders what she could have achieved with more self-confidence. She shakes her head to take her mind off it. She grabs the glass of wine and sniffs at the pungent smell of the Chardonnay she loves so much.

She jumps at the sight of a shadow slipping behind her through the mirror. She regrets living alone at such times. She's so vulnerable. She hates feeling like this; her stomach in knots, her head spinning, the tingling in her legs.

She's not naturally anxious, although the thought of an unknown presence near her, not knowing if she's hallucinating or if it's real, makes her uncomfortable.

She should get a dog.

She calms down. There's no way someone could have come in. She has locked the doors. The windows are tightly closed. She sneers for courage and drinks the rest of the wine. She inspects her reflection one last time and turns off the lights.

Back in her bedroom, she has no time to react to the crackling sound behind her before being thrown flat on her bed by a powerful force crushing her. A powerful hand covers her mouth as she feels the warm breath of a man on her face.

The feeling of cold metal on her throat paralyzes her. She could twist to tip her attacker, but he would slice her neck.

She stops moving.

Her 9 mm gun is close by, in the drawer of the bedside table. She's familiar with this sense of despair, this feeling of helplessness. She has experienced it on more than one occasion.

Suddenly, she's eight years old.

Suddenly, she's trapped.

Suddenly, that fear overcoming her every time her father entered her room and stole her innocence.

She is plunged back into the nightmare she thought she had escaped from.

"Listen to me very carefully, I'm only going to tell you this once."

Abygaelle stops breathing. The individual's voice quivers with anger.

"Don't ever, ever bother Monique Primeau again. If you or one of your dumbass colleagues even comes near her again, even driving in front of the house, I swear I will kill you. Is that clear?"

Abygaelle is out of her mind, angry.

"Is that clear?" the man shouts.

Abygaelle nods. It could only be Raymond Primeau. Who else would be in such terrible mood because a simple visit to Monique Primeau?

"You want to talk to me? Fine, we'll talk. I'll reach out to you. But don't ever contact my—"

He stops.

"Never contact Monique Primeau again. I mean it. I could have killed you ten times today. I see you at your work, I see you in your car, I even see you in your shower. Don't underestimate me, don't make that mistake. I will kill you before you can see me. I will kill you in the dark. You won't know what hit you."

The voice of his assailant had suddenly softened, as if there was some kindness in his terrible threats. Once again, Abygaelle is powerless and physically owned by a man. She had sworn it would never happen to her again.

Fear gives way to rage.

If he doesn't kill her, she will. She will make him pay.

The attacker tied her hands behind her back with a rope. He stands up quickly. She was looking for clues. She noticed a tattoo on his right forearm right after he leaned over to get up. She doesn't remember if Raymond Primeau has one. She will look for a picture where his arms are displayed. The man quickly leaves the scene without saying a word.

The door closes quietly.

Abygaelle screams furiously in her pillow. All she can hear now is the sound of her rage echoing through the room.

All she can feel now is an immense wrath overtaking her.

59

Sitting in a secluded corner of one of the four Internet cafés he hangs out at, Raymond Primeau hasn't touched his espresso yet. He reviews for the sixth time the e-mail his son sent him.

"Raymond,

The police are looking for you and until they speak to you, they will harass mom and me. Make a man out of you for once and contact them. Ask to speak to Abygaelle Jensen.

Can you imagine they think you have something to do with the girl's murder from the other day? I couldn't help but laugh, because you and I both know you're incapable of doing anything like that.

I told them you don't have the balls to kill someone, but they didn't believe me. They want to meet you anyway.

Go ahead, they will know by your dull look that you couldn't murder a teenage girl and you could quit hiding and go back home.

Why are you hiding anyway? Do you really think you're in trouble? Honestly, as always, you're giving yourself far too much credit.

Go see them and then you can go back to your lousy miniature model cars and your fucking petunia.

Hopefully, I won't have to deal with you again.

William"

His son's belligerent tone is no surprise to Raymond, even if his hypocrisy annoys him. By his tone. By the unspoken words.

Yet he's glad to hear from him. He believes William will eventually get over his hostility and reconnect with him. They were so close to each other before all this. People can't hold grudges their whole lives. That's what Monique always says.

"You'll see Raymond. One day, he'll come to his senses and speak to you. Of course, you haven't lost your son. Come on, stop talking nonsense."

She mentions William confesses that he sometimes misses his father, that he would like to move on, but that it's impossible for now.

Raymond wonders if William is really saying this or if Monique is embellishing the truth so that he doesn't lose hope. Still, Raymond feels like he lost both of his children when Nathalie died. His son criticizes him for a lot of things. Raymond tried to explain the situation to him, but he keeps saying that he didn't condone his betrayal of Nathalie.

The sound of a horn startles him. He must decide what to do next. The police want to talk to him, that's what he was afraid of. He won't jump into the lion's den by himself. The detectives have made the connection between Ariane, Stephane Ranger and the rape of Nathalie.

Do they know about Eric Gagné and François Lavoie? And about the lawyer?

They don't have a suspect; they are certainly desperate to find one. The media puts a lot of pressure on them and they seem unable to deal with it.

People are more and more afraid and frantic. The trash talk radio shows and vox pop clearly show this. The first person with even the slightest conceivable motive will have a hard time out of this mess. People's court doesn't bother about evidences. It doesn't care about presumption of innocence. If you are arrested, you are guilty. To the bonfire at once. Until the next thing that will feed the mob's inexhaustible appetite for tragedy.

"Raymond? Where are you for the love of God?"

He called Jean Mantha, his most faithful friend, his lifelong ally. He needs his insights. The roles are inverted. Normally, Raymond is the mentor. He's the brain of the duo. But today, Jean is his only hope. Monique is smart, but far too emotionally involved to provide counselling. It would take forever just to explain why he fled without warning. He doesn't have so much time to make up his mind about his next move.

~

THERE'S JEAN.

After telling him about his situation, William's email, the police wanting to talk to him, there is a long moment of silence.

"I don't know what to tell you, Raymond. It sure looks suspicious that you ran away. I respect you too much to ask you if you killed the girl, you're my buddy. I know you'd never do that."

"Can you talk to Monique? Tell her I'm fine. I will contact her soon, but I don't have the strength to cope with her tears and worries right now. I need to put my efforts in the right place."

"Of course, I won't tell her that speaking to her means you're not putting your energy in the right place."

"You know what I mean, Jean. You know Monique, you know that when she gets emotional, things get tough."

"OK. I'll tell her you're fine and you'll call her soon, and that I don't know more. But Raymond?"

"Yeah?"

"Why the fuck are you hiding for?"

"It's hard to explain."

Silence on the phone.

"I don't trust the police, Jean. The victims were relatives of one of the accused in Nathalie's rape."

"Fuck."

"You understand now?"

"Yes, but you can't run away for the rest of your life. You'll have to face them someday. Why don't you call them?"

Primeau bites his nail while he thinks.

"I guess I could."

Mantha asks Raymond to meet him somewhere to talk, but he flatly refuses. There's no way in hell he wishes to be seen in public or implicate more people than he needs to.

Thank you, but I'll pass.

Lying on his bed, Raymond stared silently at the ceiling. The sound of cars outside is the only soundtrack, but Raymond has grown accustomed to it.

All he hears is the noise of his ideas colliding.

The next day, he goes back to another Internet café and reads William's e-mail again. After several minutes, he addresses his reply.

"I'm sorry, kid, but I'm afraid I have to turn it down for now. Give me a few more days to assess the situation and I'll let you know. If they get back to you, you'll tell them exactly that.

I love you, Daddy xxx"

60

Abygaelle nibbles her lower lip, thinking about what Stephane Ranger just told her. He doesn't want to go along with Abygaelle's plan. He doesn't wish to stay on the sidelines. He promised his niece he would find his assassin, and that's what he's going to do.

She tried everything to make him change his mind, but he won't budge. Aby hung up before saying things she might regret. Fortunately, they got a promising first lead, since the warrant on Raymond Primeau was issued. The challenge in these matters is to separate the truth from the fake. There's a lot of misinformation, a lot of misidentification.

It's not the time to look anything like Raymond Primeau right now, Abygaelle thinks. But this time it's serious. A man called, mentioning that he was an old Raymond Primeau's military mate.

Jean Mantha enters the interview room following Abygaelle, who signals him to sit down. The man looks ten years older than his age. He talks in a hushed voice and pauses for long before answering questions, as if he's reluctant to share his feelings. He says he spoke with Raymond a few days ago, and the discussion they've had has been haunting him ever since. He has weighed the pros and cons of contacting them behind friend's back.

He cannot conceive that anyone could kill a child. He agrees to meet Abygaelle. He's nervous, but open and collaborative.

Aby discloses from the start that Primeau is not only suspected of the murder of Ariane Légaré, but also of three others. Mantha can't believe what he hears. Raymond, a serial killer? If it's true, it has nothing to do with the man he knew. Even in the army, he was reluctant to shoot at enemy combatants, although they wouldn't hesitate to shoot him at sight. He's highly sensitive, just the opposite of the image one would have of a bloodthirsty predator.

Of a child killer.

"Are you saying that Raymond killed people during his time in the army?"

"Yes," Jean Mantha says, surprised by the question. "In Vietnam, it's not like we had a choice. It was them or us."

"Strange. His relatives certified that he killed no one, not even in the army."

Mantha smiles.

"Raymond wouldn't brag about it. He probably said that to spare them. He was a sniper, he was on missions. He took care of them. He was very gifted."

"Did he pass on this passion to his son?" Abygaelle asks.

"William? Not to my knowledge. But his father was his idol back then, so who knows?"

"Do you know about their conflict? Do you know what caused it?"

"No idea, but I can tell you that William is the one having a beef with Raymond, not the other way around. Raymond would very much like to reconnect with him. It goes back to after Nathalie's death."

"Let's go back to your call with him, if you don't mind."

Jean Mantha summarizes the nature of the conversation. He elaborates on their bond since Vietnam, that their wives were initially getting along well, but Monique's somewhat peculiar personality had turned his wife off. They have since distanced themselves, but he and Raymond have remained close.

In fact, until Nathalie's death.

From then on, their friendship shifted. Raymond has drifted. He was never the same, at least not completely.

Mantha states he doesn't believe Raymond is responsible for the murders in question. He has no reason to go after these people.

"Even if, let's say, it would mean avenging Nathalie?" Abygaelle says.

He frowns.

"Over twenty years later? Hard to believe."

"Don't you think it's suspicious of him to flee from his home? That he wouldn't give you a straight answer? I mean, if he had nothing to do with it, why would he behave like that?"

"That's the thing," Jean Mantha admits. "It makes no sense."

Abygaelle tells him he probably used a Dragunov to shoot his victims. Jean Mantha rolls his eyes.

"What is it?" Murielle asks.

"There's no way Raymond would shoot anyone with a goddamn Dragunov."

"I don't understand," Aby says. "Wasn't he a sniper in the army?"

"Yes, and in Vietnam."

"So why does that make no sense to you?"

Mantha leans over to the table closer to her.

"Raymond would never shoot a Dragunov," he says condescendingly.

"Yes, but maybe the reason is that it's the easiest weapon to find on the black market?" Murielle says.

"Maybe, but I would be shocked."

"According to your recollection of him, would he be capable of a shot of this difficulty? At that distance on a moving target through a crowd?"

Jean Mantha wedged himself in his chair, looking for the right words.

"If you had given me this mission and told me to dispatch the best man to make this shot, I would have recommended Raymond Primeau."

"Assuming he was the murderer. Why do you think he did it?"

Mantha thinks for seconds. He admits that if he is guilty; they are right, it must have something to do with his daughter's death.

"Sometimes, there are tragedies that drive people crazy. There are tragedies that turn a man into a monster."

61

Abygaelle can't sleep. She sits in her living room in the condo she bought two years ago. She put a lot of effort to arrange everything so the apartment would suit her taste after her difficult break-up. It's her haven.

At least, it was until Raymond Primeau tainted it. She thinks back of Primeau pictures on his house wall, the tattoo on his forearm identical to that of his attacker. She spent the last few days figuring out how he found out where she lives and how he got in stealthily.

He crossed an indefensible line that day.

Instead of frightening her, he infused a rage and determination in her she was missing since her debut at the homicide unit. Roland Michaud is right, she's a good detective sergeant. She has no reason to doubt herself.

She'll put in the effort and do her best, that's all she can control, anyway. Trying to be someone she's not won't help her.

She puts her 9 mm back in her bedside table drawer. It's not the aggression that bothers her the most. She'll get over it, and it will soon be a distant memory.

What upsets her the most is the reopening of wounds she

thought were healed. This frightens her the most. The rage she felt when she was trapped. If she had her gun on her, she would have killed him. She would have lost control and shot him like an animal.

Bonnie would have killed him.

The images that took her years to repeal were playing in her head repeatedly since the assault. She had forgotten the vile smell of his cologne, his face, his aroused gaze. Wipe away that look she had spared her younger sister.

She used to lure her father into her room when he drank too much so that he wouldn't hurt her younger sister. She knew when he was in that state, knew the signals.

Feeling him inside her made her want to kill him. The taste of his foul, acidic phallus made her sick to her stomach. On over one occasion, she threw up after he came in her mouth. Each time, he hit her.

"I repulse you, is that it?"

Aby didn't answer, defying him in silence.

She killed him every time with her eyes.

But he would never die.

She was angry at her mother for abandoning them. For leaving them with that monster.

Today, she tries as hard as she can to reconnect with her daughter, but Aby can't get past what she did. One day, she told her about the atrocities her ex-husband, a pedophile, was inflicting on her. She declined to get them out of that mess, claiming she couldn't take care of them.

She told her to call the child protection agency and put them in a foster family. Like a complete stranger, deprived of any emotional bond, would advise.

Sophie, Aby's sister, has long since forgiven her mother, but she hasn't lived through the effects of her neglect, the horrors Abygaelle has endured all these years.

Surprisingly, these abuses didn't repel Abygaelle from men.

She has normal sexual relations. No barriers, at least on the surface. She always has excellent comments about her sexual prowess. But what her lovers don't know, partly because she doesn't want to hurt them, is that she completely disengages herself from her body while they have sex.

She's never made love once in her life, she fucks. Like a pornstar, Aby acts out. But in reality, she's in the background waiting for it to end, after which she reclaims her body to benefit from the after sex tenderness, her favorite moment.

Even when men fall asleep, satisfied, she stays nested in their arms, listening to their breathing and the beating of their hearts. She tries to ideate what it's like to make love for real. Maybe one day she'll experience it.

She'll understand why people make such a big deal out of it.

As she got older and entered puberty, it was harder to take her father's thoughts away from Sophie. Teenage girls were not his forte. He preferred them younger.

Aby was six years older than her sister and time was running out. Sophie didn't have her strength. She was fragile. She couldn't detach herself from her body and let him do what he had to do. She, too, would no longer endure a man's pungent sweat without flashbacks of her father on top of her, the oozing hairy chest crushing her face to the rhythm of the sickening back-and-forth motion from the one who should have protected her.

When police arrived on a chilly January evening, their father was lying in a pool of blood on the sidewalk in front of their triplex. Aby watched the corpse, impassive. For the first time, she was breathing freely. As if someone had pulled out a sheath that had been strangling her forever. She was taking deep breaths.

And smiled.

The downstairs neighbor went out to see what was going

on. She must have heard her father's scream, then the heavy sound of his fall. She shouted to her husband to call 911 and held Aby in her arms, thinking she was in shock. Aby followed her to her apartment.

"Poor child, this is awful. Where's your sister?"

Aby pointed to the ceiling, and the lady ordered one of her sons to stay with the little girl upstairs. Sparing her this terrible sight.

Abygaelle thought it was indecent for the woman to take pity on her since she was living the happiest moments of her life. She wondered if she heard her father urging her to hurry with the grocery bags. She couldn't have known that Aby had pushed her father down the third floor spiral stairs and that, by some divine and unexpected force, he had toppled over the railing. His excess weight sped up his fall, and he crashed like a pancake, face down on the ground.

Abygaelle laughed at the sound of the enormous mass smashing against the pavement. Like a balloon filled with water. He hadn't moved; he hadn't grumbled. The night was icy and silent. As if they were meant to live this between the two of them.

The victim became the executioner.

To this day, Abygaelle can't point out what force drove her to do what she did that night. Perhaps it was Bonnie's first apparition? Or maybe it was herself.

Aby bumped him with her shoulder while he was off balance on one foot, but either way, she feels it's a shame that the happiest day of her life is when her father died. Normally, someone happiest day is the birth of a child, or remission of cancer.

Aby hopes that her father understood she killed him as he fell. That he knew she killed him because he was a monster.

To protect Sophie!

He perished as foolishly as he lived. She hoped he suffered.

The police asked Aby a lot of questions about what happened that night, but she swore she saw nothing wrong.

Sophie couldn't understand why Aby was so stoic. She never mourned his death, expressed no grief. She wouldn't talk about what happened, would change the subject when someone brought it up.

Sophie couldn't get it, and it was for the best. Aby swore to bring the secret to her grave. She kept that promise since then.

They placed them in a foster home for a few years, and when Abygaelle left for college in another region, she took an apartment. She asked Sophie to live with her, but she had many friends and was at the age where hanging out with her older sister wasn't very cool.

Their foster parents, the Métivier, were decent people, so Aby wasn't reluctant to leave her sister behind. Their relationship suffered as a result. They don't see each other very often. As if instead of strengthening their relationship, tragedy created a gap between them.

Something was broken that night.

Aby doesn't care. Roland Michaud is the only person who knows about her past, and she has full confidence in him. He doesn't know about her responsibility in her father's demise. She told him he fell because he was drunk.

They never talked about it again. She appreciates his secrecy.

Roland knows she entered the vice squad because of this. To protect little Sophies from this world. To support the courageous and fighting young Abygaelles.

To lock up the scums who put them through hell.

The attack in her apartment would have devastated any woman. But not her. She had seen worse. So Raymond Primeau is trivial.

But he lit a flame in her. And that was the worst thing he could've done.

62

Abygaelle can't wait any longer. She has finally received the message she was waiting for so long. An email from a Hotmail address to join a private chat site. She requests that the police technical team be on hand to trace the connection location.

Abygaelle asks his counterpart to prove he's indeed Raymond Primeau. He replies that his wife's name is Monique and had a career in the army. He mentions the names of his children. That's all he agrees to disclose. If this isn't enough, the discussion will end as quickly as it began. He doesn't have to prove anything to them; they want to talk to him, not the other way around.

"Did you kill Ariane Légaré?"

"I will not answer that kind of question. You want to talk to me? Then talk. I have very little time."

"Why did you come to my house?"

"I don't know what you're referring to."

"I know it was you, you told me to leave your wife alone."

"Again, I don't know what you're talking about."

Primeau doesn't want to incriminate himself, she thinks. Leave no trace.

"Did you kill Marc-André Davison?"

"If that's the discussion you want to have with me, I'll cut it short. Am I clear?"

"Okay, Mr. Primeau."

"What do you want from me?"

"To meet you to rule you out for the murders of Ariane Légaré, Marc-André Davison and Annie St. Onge."

"I don't care if you rule me out or not."

"We'll meet at some point, Mr. Primeau. Whether willingly or unwillingly."

"Good luck with that, Mrs. Jensen. I'm way too intelligent and cunning for you. But I commend your determination. We have that in common. Our will to get the job done."

"What about the chess pieces?"

"Sorry?"

"You heard me. What is the meaning of the wooden queens?"

"No idea what you're referring to."

"Your ego will be your undoing."

"Has your technical team tracked me down? They should have by now if they were proficient."

"No one is trying to track you down."

"Ms. Jensen, let's not play each other for fools. I'm asking you to extend me this courtesy."

"Alright, I will. They haven't tracked you down yet."

Meanwhile, the IT team tells Murielle that the contact's IP address changes regularly from a server in Bulgaria to servers in China, Ivory Coast and Russia. Impossible to track him.

He's no amateur. He knows what he's doing.

"Mr. Primeau," Abygaelle says, "you asked me not to take ourselves for fools? That's fine. Quit pretending you don't know what I'm talking about."

"I'm giving you an honest answer."

"Why are you doing this? Why are you targeting innocent victims?"

"Innocent people die every day. Nathalie, for instance."

"Your daughter committed suicide."

"No, she didn't, they killed her."

"That's not what I heard."

"I don't care what you were told—it was the first time since the beginning of the interview that Primeau was belligerent—the day those animals raped and beat her, leaving her to die, they killed her."

"Why not just kill Ranger himself? I'm trying to understand. You killed Lavoie and Gagné. Why did you spare Ranger?"

"I don't believe in the death penalty."

"Why would you go after Stephane Ranger's relatives?"

"Draw your own conclusions. You are an intelligent woman."

"You would have wanted them sentenced to death, I presume."

"I told you I don't believe in the death penalty."

"What do you mean you don't believe in the death penalty?"

"I don't believe in it anymore."

"You no longer believe in the death penalty?"

Aby looks at Murielle to see if they are making progress. She signals they are not.

They won't succeed.

"You catch on quickly."

"Why not?"

"Before, I thought it would discourage anyone who thinking about killing someone, but that's not the case. You won't frighten a murderer from killing. He's either too sick to worry about it, or too arrogant to believe he'll get caught. I thought it made economic sense not to shelter them expensively for twenty-five or thirty years, but with all the recourse, postponements and appeals, it ends up costing as much as life imprisonment. So it left me with death as a punishment, but what if it wasn't a punishment? No one knows what goes on beyond death. What if it was salvation? So, if we are not saving money, and death penalty isn't a deterrent, what's the point?"

Abygaelle notes that Primeau makes very few spelling mistakes.

"This is a valid opinion."

"Based on this, the only motive for the death penalty is to quench the people's thirst for vengeance. Let them fulfill their primary desire for punishment by executing those who have committed revolting crimes. This is the equivalent of reducing ourselves to their level."

"On your level."

The response rattles the assassin. She's right. He has killed. He is a murderer. He feels a certain weariness.

"I can't blame you for feeling that way."

"How can I convince you to stop?"

"Stop what?"

"Do you intend to kill more innocent people?"

No answer.

"Mr. Primeau?"

"Enough talk. You've wasted enough of my time."

"No, I have more questions. Wait—"

A notification on the screen shows he has left the conversation.

While chatting with Murielle, Aby thinks back to what Jean Mantha had mentioned. That Primeau didn't confirm nor deny the murders.

Why being ambiguous?

What's the point?

63

The assassin stares at the sunset through his living room window. He woke up with a pit in his stomach, and it's still lingering. It happens to him sometimes. Jolts of humanity and remorse resurfacing from time to time.

He has become a monster. Killing both the biker and Annie St. Onge weren't the plan. Yet he cold-bloodedly shot them. Like business as usual. It's what troubles him the most; his lack of emotion in the action.

His absence of doubt turns him into an onlooker of the events. He sees himself perpetrating the unthinkable, as if he were watching a movie, as if everything were happening in slow motion. What distinguishes him from the evil monsters against whom he takes revenge? The more he kills, the more insensitive he becomes.

And the more he turns into one of them.

The last glimpse of conscience he may have knows he transgressed the last vestiges of human morality by shooting the teenage girl. Once he witnessed the little blond girl's head explode through his rifle scope, he felt nothing. No guilt, no remorse. It was natural. He aimed at her and pulled the trigger. Period.

He's a skilled marksman. What did they expect?

That it was a bad dream. That's what he was wishing for. That this evil impulse that crept insidiously into him never existed.

He would be relieved to wake up one morning and find that it was all a figment of his imagination. His mission has brought him nothing but disenchantment and a rupture, both with those he loves and with himself. A cleavage between what he was before and what he has become.

Once caught up in the spiral, there is no turning back. To stop now? That would be insane. He never does things half-heartedly. But God, would he rather put the gun away and forget about it.

To move on.

He's not immune to mistakes. He's too arrogant. Why did he go to the biker's wife and show his face? For what purpose? To prove how powerful he is? For his bravery? To see her shiver with terror? As if killing wasn't exhilarating enough anymore. He needs more, like a drug addict constantly increasing his dosage to recover the initial thrill.

He is addicted to dominance. To overpower those stupid cops wading in the fog, totally scorned. They have no clue, nothing to hold on to.

To dominate his victims, those who had the misfortune to cross his path. To dominate the mafia, his relatives, his colleagues. Beat the odds. The perfect crime doesn't exist?

Just watch me.

However, he can't deny the emptiness of his soul, the pit in his guts. He is no longer the man he once was. He is no longer human. No normal person would do that.

Everyone used to be proud of him. What a force of nature,

what a scholar, what an individual. Using his superior intelligence to get to this point?

To end up like this?

To be a simple serial killer like any other imbecile? Nobody relishes his achievement. No one admires his work.

He's his only audience, his harshest critic.

Drop everything and go back home? It sounds so good to him. He shakes his head to quit daydreaming. He gets soft and weak.

Focus on the mission. Get your shit together, cry-baby.

He takes a deep breath.

I'm not who I used to be anymore. What I'm doing is magnificent. I have to remind myself that all the time.

He watches the sunset one last time, colouring the sky with a touching red splendour. He tightens his lips, disillusioned. He no longer knows how to enjoy even that. The beauty of the world, a world he no longer recognizes.

How can he get rid of the deep melancholy that tears his soul apart?

64

Sitting around a table in a meeting room over coffee, Abygaelle, Murielle and Jack go through the record of potential suspects. If the Primeau family's lead is right, they must go through the clan members one by one.

They quickly eliminated Monique from the list.

A fragile woman by nature, she had trouble managing her emotions when they saw her. Raymond Primeau felt the need to threaten Aby in her apartment so that she would be left alone. This proves she's not the mastermind behind the murders, and especially not the perpetrator.

William Primeau's passports prove he wasn't in the country when the murders took place. He cooperates, and the video conference showed a magnificent panorama of London. Even the technical team confirmed the IP address William used to connect to was from the UK.

That leaves Maxime Fauvette, Nathalie's ex-lover. But he, too, has a solid alibi, eliminating him as a suspect. On the other hand, he has no alibi for the Annie St. Onge murder. It's obvious to them that only one person handled those crimes. The signature and caliber of ammunition are the same.

Nothing in Maxime's past exhibits skills with high-range firearms, unlike Raymond Primeau, the number one suspect.

Raymond has motive, skill, and ran away shortly after Ariane's murder without disclosing it to his wife.

His unwillingness to cooperate is suspicious. It all fits. It has to be him. They have issued an arrest warrant in Canada and Interpol, but he's elusive at the moment.

"Should we put more pressure on Monique to bring him out of his lair?" Murielle asks.

Jack agrees, but not Aby.

"I don't think it's a good idea. She's upset enough as it is. It could backfire."

"I don't give a shit what the killer wants or doesn't want," Jack says.

Aby raises her hand.

"It's not so much about what he wants, but that I feel like it won't work out. Do you really think he will simply give himself up if we keep harassing his wife? He would have done it the first time, wouldn't he?"

"The kid has a point," Murielle concedes.

Abygaelle smiles every time Murielle calls her "the kid" even though she's in her mid-thirties.

"I believe that if we do that," Aby adds, "he will target us, camouflaged as he does well. And Jack, he might shoot you while you're quietly sitting in your living room listening to your beloved Montreal Canadiens this winter."

"Being shot as I watch a lousy team getting stomped would be a deliverance," he says.

Murielle chuckles.

"He has nothing to lose, he's already killed three people. Nothing will worsen his case. You know better than I do sentences aren't adding up here in Canada."

Jack looks down. It makes sense.

"But why kill Ariane, Marc-André and Annie this way, but kill Lavoie, Blackburn and Gagné differently?" he asks.

"That's what we need to find out," Abygaelle says.

"Maybe he's tired," Murielle says.

Seeing her colleagues' puzzling look, she elaborates:

"The first three murders were highly physical. He was close to his victims and exposed himself. But it's been over ten years now. He may have had the strength and ability to do it then, but it may be easier and safer now to kill from a distance, to avoid the risk of being disarmed or physically dominated."

"By Ariane Légaré?" Jack says, ironically.

"Come on dummy," Murielle says. "From witnesses or people playing heroes. If he had been subdued after firing at the girl, he wouldn't have been able to carry on with his rampage."

Jack and Abygaelle nod. It makes sense.

Aby says it may have been difficult to lure the victims to recluse places. It was much simpler to shoot from a distance.

Like a ghost.

"Like a coward, you mean," Jack says.

"Killing a fifteen-year-old girl is despicable, no matter how you do it, Jack." Murielle replies.

"You know what I mean."

A clamor draws the three investigators out. There's a commotion near the front desk. Abygaelle precedes her two colleagues, making her way through the commotion. She reaches behind a couple of cops, some of whom have drawn their weapons.

Then, behind the silhouettes, she sees Raymond Primeau with his hands in the air.

After a few seconds of scrutinizing the mass of officers, he meets Abygaelle's gaze, and fixes her with a defiant grin on his face. He looks older than the photos she flipped through, but it's definitely him.

"We won't need to drag him out of his lair. The fox came to us," Jack says, whispering behind her.

"At least, we'll get answers to our questions," Murielle adds.

Although Aby hopes they're right, something tells her it won't be that easy.

65

Charles Picard doubted that this moment would ever come, but they finally have their killer. The press conference is about to begin. Hidden behind a curtain, he looks at reporters and cameramen setting up their equipment.

The media clustered several of their microphones on the stand. Public pressure was becoming intolerable. They have constantly talked about this affaire in the evening news in the country and around the world for months. He denied several interview requests from major U.S. media outlets.

The Provincial Police's head of communications starts the press conference, asking everyone on the podium to introduce themselves one by one. They show a picture of Raymond Primeau on a giant screen behind them. It reveals the man up to the waist, looking pale and with his arms crossed. They took the photo shortly after his arrival.

Watching from the back of the room, Abygaelle can't take her eyes off the picture. Primeau looks tired, as if he hadn't slept for several weeks. She stares at the tattoo on his forearm, the same tattoo she saw far too close the other day.

A huge phoenix.

She wonders from which ashes Primeau emerged stronger.

Seeing him pondering on the image shows he may have a conscience after all. Yet he confessed to the murders with such detachment that she believes he's a psychopath. At the podium, the Police Chief is supported by Picard and Martin Fignola, the director of communications. They offered Abygaelle to join them on the stage, but she declined. The last thing she wants is attention. Anyway, she's not pleased with how much time it took to catch the killer.

Moreover, since he turned himself in. She couldn't stand there with her chest puffed up when she wasn't even close to arresting the murderer before he surrendered.

"Police Chief Richard Sirois, will make a statement. Then we will take questions from the floor."

Sirois clears his throat and grabs the page in front of him, and he puts on his glasses.

"At 7:30 p.m. last night, we arrested the prime suspect in the homicides of Ariane Légaré, Marc-André Davison and Annie St. Onge."

He pauses to create a dramatic impact.

"We also suspect that he committed murders in the 2000s. Raymond Primeau, an army veteran, has confessed to being the perpetrator of all these crimes. He therefore is one of the most prolific serial killers in the province's history, if not the country."

Murmurs in the room. The media are eager to get more details.

"These murders have never been solved until now. They are the homicides of Eric Gagné, François Lavoie, Louise Laflèche and lawyer Jean Blackburn."

The room turns cacophonic. The famous prosecutor's assassination captivated the population for several months and fueled the craziest conspiracy theories.

Sirois asks the journalists to calm down so that he can

finish. He can't imagine their reaction when he'll drop his next bomb. He clears his throat again and proceeds:

"Mrs. Laflèche was Ariane Légaré's grandmother."

That's it. Some reporters grab their cell phones, others leave the room in a hurry. The director of communications unsuccessfully seeks to bring all these people to order.

This is unexpected news for the media. A gift from heaven that will boost sales in a struggling industry. Advertisements will definitely increase, and so will the audience for the 24-hour news channels.

A story like this is a dream.

Those who stayed have many questions for the PP officials. Did Primeau explained why he did it? What is the motive? Was Primeau a sniper in the army? What about his record as a veteran? Officials kept their answers brief, simply repeating that the investigation is ongoing and they will disclose more information as things evolve. Even if Primeau confessed to the murders, he's innocent until proven guilty. The usual stuff. Some journalists spotted Abygaelle and demanded an interview, but she quickly slipped away, simply saying she agrees with everything her bosses said.

A few minutes later, Chief Sirois walked up to her to congratulate her. Picard, smiling from afar, winked at her with a complicit eye. Once the clamor had dissipated, Abygaelle stood aside, thoughtful. She thinks of Jack's demeanor, who is just as ambivalent as she is about all this circus.

Murielle told them they worry too much, that the important thing is to have the killer out of the picture. But Abygaelle trusts her instincts. Seeing Jack sharing her uneasiness reinforced her belief that she has reason to be careful.

It was all too much.

A gloomy spectacle to amuse the mobs.

The next morning, Abygaelle listens to a message on her office voicemail. An individual wants to talk to her about

François Lavoie's murder. He mentions that even though it has been over fifteen years ago, he still remembers when Lavoie left with a man dressed in black.

"I don't know what your guy did or didn't do in his life, Mrs. Jensen, but if the man who left with François that night killed him, he's not your guy."

Abygaelle is puzzled.

"How can you be so sure?"

"For one thing, he didn't have a tattoo on his forearm. He was at least in his late fifties. That would make him almost seventy-five years old today."

Almost ten years older than Raymond Primeau, she thinks.

Primeau had his tattoo done before the Vietnam War. It's visible in one photo she saw from that time.

"How tall is your guy?"

Abygaelle doesn't understand how this is relevant, but upon insistence, she says that he's five feet eleven inches tall.

"François Lavoie was at least six feet two. He was quite a big guy at 375 lbs."

"What does it have to do with Primeau?"

"The man that left with François that night, his alleged murderer—"

"Yes?"

"He was taller than him."

66

Jack Morris holds his head in his hands. He's gone through all the investigation details for the thousandth time and still nothing conclusive. No leads. Of course, he could speculate and find a motive for anyone, but speculation won't convince DPCP to file charges.

It wouldn't even clear Picard's desk, anyway. There's got to be a loophole somewhere. He doesn't believe the perfect crime exists, there's always a mistake in the end. Sometimes it's not enough to press charges, but you know deep down that you got the murderer. You just don't have enough evidence to convict him.

Watching Raymond Primeau, Jack has his doubts. Really? This seemingly harmless man is the bloodthirsty killer we've been seeking for weeks? The same one who shot Eric Gagné and François Lavoie?

Murielle rolled her eyes at his skepticism.

"When no one believes something, you do, and when the evidence is undeniable, and there are confessions, you're overly careful."

She's right, but he can't risk another mistake, another false accusation. He can't stand the reproving looks of his colleagues. He's sick of them rolling their eyes and saying Morris at it again with his fantasies.

Even if he's rarely mistaken, his reputation is no longer what it used to be. He can see in Abygaelle's scowl that she's not fond of his impulsivity. At times, he judged suspects by their appearance. Other times by their extensive criminal record.

Either way, he can't shake his doubts about Primeau's guilt. And since his work partners seem confident that he's the murderer, and he has confessed to them, he must ignore his nagging doubts.

Sitting ahead of him, Raymond Primeau feels bored.

"What now? Do you need me to repeat the same things over and over again?"

"I restate my advice, Mr. Primeau. You should talk to your lawyer. We can use anything you say against you in a court of law. You are about to make an official confession."

"I don't need a goddamn lawyer. I know what I have done. It has to stop, and as long as I'm free, it won't. I already confessed to my crimes. What more do you want? I would have picked Jean Blackburn, but I'm told he's not available," Primeau says with a chilling smirk.

Jack looks at Abygaelle to see how she feels about it. She shrugs.

"Let's get on with it then," she says.

"Mr. Primeau, I'd hate to put words in your mouth," Jack says. "Can you specify what murders you intend to confess about?"

"I have told you a thousand times."

Primeau's angry tone doesn't faze Jack. He clenches his jaw.

"Say it again," he asks.

"Eric Gagné, François Lavoie, Ariane Légaré, Marc-André Davison, Jean Blackburn and an elderly lady I can' t remember her name."

"Louise Laflèche."

"I guess so."

"And Annie St. Onge?"

Primeau pauses for a moment.

"Yes, Annie St. Onge too. And the biker."

Jack stays silent for a moment. He reads over his notes about the killings Primeau has just confessed to. Gagne and Blackburn were killed by a knife, Lavoie by a bullet. Both weren't choirboys. They found both with their genitals in their mouths. A couple of years went by between each murder. Then Primeau switched to sniper rifle mode.

"You said you killed them at random, right?"

Primeau simply smiles.

"You refused to tell us why you picked these people. Did you change your mind?"

"No, I haven't."

"You said: I'll bring this to my grave."

Primeau grins despite his grim look.

"Why not give the families a rationale? So they can grieve?"

"They can do it knowing it was a coincidence. They picked the wrong number. There is no logical reason."

"Are you trying to tell me you killed Gagné, Lavoie, and Blackburn by accident?"

"No, I targeted them."

"Because of Nathalie."

Raymond Primeau doesn't answer.

"And Ariane was just unlucky that you shot her outside of her school?"

"That's right."

"Don't play us for fools, Primeau."

Jack's voice thundered through the room. Raymond Primeau smiled again. Of course, it wasn't a coincidence.

"You didn't know that Davison was Ariane's uncle."

"No, I didn't."

Jack feels rage building inside him even more. He controls himself the best he can.

"And you didn't know they were related to Stephane Ranger. Oddly enough, the third person charged with your daughter's rape. Oh, and you also killed his mother by mistake, I presume."

Primeau smiled at him, looking defiant.

"You're scum," Jack says.

Abygaelle interjects.

"Jack, I think Murielle wants to talk to you. I will take it up with Mr. Primeau if you don't mind."

Jack looks insulted, but he stands up and leaves.

Abygaelle opens her file, then looks at Primeau's forearm. She would recognize that tattoo out of a million.

"Close the mics," she yells for someone outside.

She waits a few seconds, glaring at Primeau.

"Why did you attack me in my house?"

Primeau is taken by surprise, but doesn't show it.

"I told you. I wanted you to leave my wife alone."

"Yes, but you have to be out of your mind to take such a risk. I could have shot you with the gun I keep on my bedside table. You must have expected us to question her. I can't understand your anger."

Raymond Primeau looks down.

"Afterwards, I understood I was mostly angry at myself. You were only a scapegoat. I was mad that she had to go through this. I know Monique. She is very sensitive. She's been through a lot of stuff in the past. I'm sorry about this."

Abygaelle didn't think she would get an apology. But it appeased her immediately. She swore revenge, but now that she faces him, with a defeated look on his face, jail time might be enough."

After asking to turn the audio back on, Abygaelle continues:

"Can I explain my theory?" she asks.

"Your theory?"

"Yes, my theory about why you choose your victims. Because in all transparency, I do not buy your coincidence story one bit. I don't believe in coincidences."

Primeau looks at her without flinching. His silence is an invitation to proceed.

"I assume you killed Davison and Légaré because they were Stephane Ranger's relatives."

Raymond snickers nastily.

"You're talking nonsense. Why would I kill them, but not him?"

"I have my own hypothesis, but I would like to hear it from you."

"I won't explain anything to you. It makes no sense. You can fabricate any conspiracy to make it more palatable to you, but the fact remains that it is a coincidence. It's very easy to understand, even for cops."

Jack Morris, who had been back for a few minutes, stands up and laughs.

"You don't like us much, do you, Raymond?"

Primeau shrugs and pauses for several seconds, as if he wanted to assess his words.

"Let's just say you didn't impress me with my daughter's case," he says. "The lack of evidence and mismanagement of the crime scene have ruined everything. Nathalie killed herself because she couldn't cope with the verdict. You have blood on your hands. So no, I don't like you. For me, you are only fit to give parking tickets, and even for that, it's a bit too much. You don't believe me? I had to turn myself in because things were getting out of hand. I could have gone on for a long time like this."

Jack impulsively tries a distraction

"If you really are the killer."

"I'm sorry?"

Abygaelle wonders what he's getting at. Jack signals her to let him go on. He slides a chair near the suspect's.

"You see, Raymond," Jack speaks softly for the first time, "I don't believe for one second you are the killer. Even your friends who know you well don't buy it."

Primeau laughs loudly.

"You're even dumber than I thought."

Jack carries on, pretending he didn't hear. He wants him to realize that this is a lecture, not a discussion. When finished, Jack will get up and walk out of the room.

Primeau will go back to his cell with this in mind.

"I don't think you can murder a young girl. Davison? Yeah, okay, why not? But your daughter is dead, killed according to you because unscrupulous men targeted her, and you would do the same to Ariane? Non sense."

Primeau crosses his arms, amused. Jack Morris continues:

"Your wife told us about you. It doesn't add up. You are very diffuse in your confessions. You don't comment too much, as if you didn't want us to know that you are wrongly incriminating yourself. You don't give us anything. You hide behind your stupid theory about taking stuff with you in your grave. But what are you doing here? What are you trying to prove? Who are you trying to convince? And why? That's what I don't know yet, but I intend to find out."

Raymond looks at him silently, as if waiting for the monologue to end.

"My colleagues think you did it. But you don't fool me. So you can stick to your silly story as much as you like, but I will prove that you are lying and expose your morbid little game in front of everyone. I'm just waiting for the right opportunity to come along. And Raymond? I will seize it."

He's playing his last card:

"When the killer strikes again, you'll have some explaining

to do, pal. And when that day comes, you'll find me on your way."

"There will be no more victims."

Jack smiles.

"We'll see about that."

He picks up his file and stares at Primeau for several seconds. He then storms out of the room, instructing the constable at the door to take this lousy comedian back to his cell loud enough for Primeau to hear him.

Abygaelle doesn't interfere. She won't get anything out of Primeau, anyway. He will shut himself up.

Back at his desk, Jack is a little doubtful about his hunch. Primeau has shown no signs of weakness. He doesn't know if he's right or if he's going crazy. One way or another, he will do everything he can to prove whether Primeau is indeed the killer or not.

After all, many thrill-seeking lunatics have previously incriminated themselves for crimes they didn't commit.

The case is so widely covered by the media that the killer will instantly become famous around the world. His name will be all over the news. They will want to know his story, what could have driven him to do it.

Netflix will produce a documentary about him, which will increase his fame.

And all the while, no one will care about Ariane and other victims of this madman. This makes Jack sick every time there is a killer on a rampage. They talk about him at length, ignoring the victims in the process.

There are still colossal morons praising Columbine High School shooters. Humans can sometimes be awful. Mental illness is more common than ever.

Jack has nothing to lose. If Raymond Primeau is really the killer, then people will say he tried something and life will go on.

Abygaelle goes through the whereabouts of Nathalie's ex-lover and his brother William. Both have strong alibis.

William has not set foot in the country for over two years, as he mentioned in his conversation with Murielle. Maxime Fauvette was taking university classes when Marc-André Davison was killed and he was at work during Ariane's murder.

Raymond Primeau is the only one who doesn't have an alibi.

67

Raymond Primeau is in the middle of a book about Italian car history, sitting snugly on his bunk behind his tiny cell bars. Since he confessed to the murders, including that of the young girl, they isolated him from the other inmates who openly threaten to make him pay with his life.

Even worse, since the media widely broadcasted the case. What better redemption for a prisoner than to inflict the death penalty on the killer of a beautiful, innocent teenage girl? No one is against virtue, anyway.

Primeau scoffs at these hypocrites who suddenly find themselves with a conscience and a bogus code of honor, despite having committed similar atrocities.

He's in a wing for defendants awaiting their trial. It will be short since he recognized the crimes.

He occasionally wonders if he made the right choice. His mind wavers from one extreme to the other. Sometimes he thinks it's the right thing to do, only to consider a few seconds later that he should have let the cops work out their mess and have fun watching them struggle to put the pieces of the puzzle together.

After all, many homicides are never solved.

He honestly believed the cops were much closer to solving the case than they actually were. The look on their faces as he told them the chronology of events was astonishing, and they didn't know what was going on.

But since they made the connection between the murders and Stephane Ranger, they were on the right track. They would have eventually figured out the common denominator underlying all this and things would be the same today, or maybe worse. It was better for everyone if he turned himself in.

Since the big, gruff detective looks as if he wanted to jump at his throat, which shows that they were leading his way.

And this Abygaelle Jensen is dazzling, very brilliant.

Some people have an unmistakable lucidity showing through in the way they express themselves, in the way they look at you. As if they could read your soul, pull you back into a corner, push you back into your final recesses with a snap of their fingers.

Then there's that stupid attack at her apartment. Beyond the foolishness of the gesture, it's the inner turmoil he felt that disturbs him the most. How much she reminds him of Nathalie, what she would look like if she were still alive.

Even though Abygaelle was slightly younger, he felt her daughter's presence as he tackled her on her bed.

Of course, he regrets it. It was stupid. His emotions went out of control, as did his rage at the police officers when they were only doing their job. Nothing more natural than interrogating a fugitive's wife. He ran away after Ariane's murder. What did he expect? By running away, he painted a huge target on his back.

He panicked. A rookie mistake. It wasn't the first time he lost control. His impulsiveness has always been his worst enemy.

Justice is not very lenient for police officer assailants, but that's the least of his worries. The sentence for his breaking and entering Jensen's home will be concurrent with the punishment he faces for the murders. He has already apologized for his actions, but didn't get a warm response from the detective.

He gets it.

So far, everything is going as he expected before turning himself in. He believes Nathalie would be proud of him, no matter where she was right now. He hopes that Monique, and especially William, will understand.

Raymond had a hard time answering Abygaelle's questions since he was so obsessed with her resemblance to his daughter. Nathalie, too, was tall, slender, with long brown hair. The only difference was that she had blue eyes, contrasting with the detective's emerald pupils.

Nathalie had the same confidence in her voice, the same assertive tone, fast and fluid delivery. He feels affection for Detective Sergeant Jensen.

They have had several encounters over the past few days that turned out to be quite friendly. Abygaelle relaxing a little more each time and lowering her guard. It's easier than with her colleague, who thinks he's intimidating him with his loud voice.

Raymond wonders if this method works with anyone. One thing's for sure, it has no effect on him except to entertain him. He's seen too many horrors and evil beings in his life to fear a belligerent policeman. He smiles every time he raises his voice, and it seems to make him even angrier.

Let's just say that no one would invite Jack Morris and him to the same party.

Abygaelle tried to corner him on a couple of occasions by asking him very specific questions about the crimes, forcing him to shut down. She won't get anything out of him by playing this game. But since it's quite rare, he doesn't hold it against her. Again, she has a job to do; he respects that. But he quickly showed his hand, and set the rules of the game: he won't talk about the scabrous details of each of the murders.

For several good reasons. And no, he doesn't mind the victims' families not knowing what happened to their loved one. It's actually better that way.

This nature enthusiast can't imagine how he will survive in prison. He needs the outdoors to recharge his batteries. How will he survive with only one hour of sunlight a day? Humans have unsuspected resources, he thinks, to reassure himself.

We shall see.

There's nothing that a noose made from a sheet won't be able to fix in time and place if it's too difficult.

He lived a noble life, experienced more than most of his fellow men. His dysfunctional family, his abusive father, who beat him, and who did the same with his mother, his hasty departure from his parents' home, his joining the army, his voluntary enlistment in the Vietnam War.

He still has nightmares about it today. The heads of his victims exploding through the lens of his rifle are still imprinted in his memory.

Then there is Nathalie.

He did everything he could to wipe the image of her bluish skin and her tongue hanging out of her mouth from his brain. But above all, the serenity on her face, as if liberated. As if it were the only solution to break free from her misery. He may have made it all up, but that's what he saw on his daughter's face: an absolute abandonment to the great reaper.

When he laid her down on the ground, his tears ran down her face. Her eyes were half open, as if she was staring at him, but there was no light in them. Her body was there, chilled, her soul was gone.

Even today, he wakes up abruptly, his arms in the air, as if he wanted to unhook her from the ceiling. He doubts that many humans on this planet have gone through as many atrocities forever stamped in their minds.

How do you go on with your life after experiencing all these things, seeing all these corpses? After you have killed those people, and after you have lifted your daughter's body so that her neck is no longer crushed by a rope, praying that it isn't too late, that there is still hope to save her.

He should have known that he was doomed to a terrible life the day when, at six, he first took his father's fist in the face. He should have understood that his life story would eventually end in a cage for mad soul.

If he had grasped it earlier, he would have made different choices.

He wouldn't have lost his family.

And all those people would still be alive.

68

What a lovely August evening. The assassin is overwhelmed by the number of stars in the sky. Since childhood, he believes each star represents the spirit of every dead person. Each individual becomes one when they die, and they watch over the living for eternity.

That's why he's not afraid of dying, even though he doesn't believe in reincarnation. He doesn't know what comes after life on earth. He's convinced that our time on this planet is only a mandatory transition to something else. Existence is so tightly structured, everything is interconnected. It wouldn't make sense for things to be over after that, that it's the end. That would imply that life is pure luck, like some kind of lottery. Why does one person live for almost a hundred years and another die from birth? Non sense.

Once he reached his destination, he quit thinking philosophical thoughts useful only to entertain pseudo-intellectuals at social events. He must concentrate on his mission. Over the last few days, the assassin has focused on the next name on the list: Maryse Letarte.

She's Stephane Ranger's ex-lover, according to his data.

They split three years ago. This has created a huge dilemma. Would eliminating Maryse, under these circumstances, help him reach his goal? Although he initially thought it wouldn't, admittedly, Ranger would feel guilty about her loss. Maryse apparently moved on with someone else, but he saw Stephen talking to her a few days ago, and they seemed to get along just fine.

The assassin concluded that they still have an affection for each other.

He regrets he spared Jacques Légaré's life the other day. The original aim was never to validate the list before taking action. The intent was to go through the list, regardless of their current relationship with Ranger.

That's what he'll do.

He parks his gray Hyundai Elantra in the same spot he spotted the day before. He already has the gear to burn the car next. He has targeted an embankment between two residences for positioning. From this location, he has a perfect view of the inside of the house.

A large window overlooks the living room where she is sitting right now, next to her boyfriend. They are watching television. After assembling his weapon while keeping his eyes on Maryse, he points it at her. From his scope, he frames the young woman's laid-back face. Her kind features touches him. This woman has probably wronged no one in her life.

Stick to the list.

Don't validate the list.

Ariane Légaré didn't have a mean bone in her body either, and you shot her without a second thought. Why would Maryse get a pass? You're getting soft, man.

Come on, focus.

He rests the butt of his weapon on his shoulder, then notices a shadow-like figure near his target. He shifts his scope and tightens his lips. A little girl of about five years old has emerged in her pajamas. The boyfriend gets up to walk her away. He will tuck her back in, the killer thinks, based on his experience as a father.

Stick to the list.

He refocuses on Maryse Letarte. The intersecting lines cross exactly in the middle of her forehead. He puts his finger on the trigger, then realizes that his plan has flaws. He didn't expect that the target wouldn't be alone. How is he going to get away unnoticed? He can't predict how the man will react. Maybe he will freeze or hide behind a piece of furniture. Or yell, or worse, run out of the house to confront him. Maybe he will scream at the neighbors to call the police.

The assassin lowers his gun and curses. How could he be so stupid? Chances were she wouldn't be on her own. And now he figures it out? He berates himself for not being thorough. That's how criminals get caught, by being stupid, by acting like idiots. He's very smart, he can't afford to be intellectually lazy.

Once it's all over, once the list is finished, he'll vanish in nature and never show up again. This will be his greatest achievement. But for that, he has to plan everything right. He has to have a plan A, B, C and D.

He can feel it. The further he progresses in his quest, the more untouchable he thinks he is. And the more he drapes himself in an aura of invincibility, the more risks he takes, and the less prepared he is. This has to change. He needs to revert to the metronome he was in the beginning. A well-oiled killing machine. He considers his options, and one becomes obvious: kill the boyfriend too. The question is who to shoot first. Who might fail to react quickly enough to allow him to kill?

He must take advantage of the element of surprise, hoping that the other person will not lie down on the floor or hide behind the couch. He didn't intend to kill the man at first. He's not on the list, and there are a few too many collateral victims for his taste.

Even if the biker deserved it, he wasn't on the list, nor was Annie St. Onge. He could think of a valid reason for each of these murders. Nevertheless, they weren't on Ranger's list.

He was pondering his options when the man got up and walked out of the house. He got in his car and drove away quietly. He probably went to get cigarettes or something. Who knew smoking could save your life? He's relieved that he doesn't have to kill him. That's one less thing on his mind. Once the man's car turns the corner, the assassin moves back into position. He holds his aim, no sign of the child. He attached a suppressor to the end of his rifle, just like with Davison and St. Onge.

With his finger on the trigger, the assassin takes a deep breath and holds it to stabilize his weapon. Maryse changes position slightly and the assassin also moves to target the head again.

He pulls the trigger.

Blood spurts onto the wall behind Maryse Letarte as if a balloon full of red paint had blown up, shattering the upper half of her skull. The bay-window didn't explode. The assassin can see the small hole left by the bullet in one pane through his rifle scope. The woman's body remain seated, as if what was left of her head didn't want to miss what was playing on the television. A zany and grotesque image at the same time. As enjoyable as he imagined it to be.

He drops a wooden queen in the grass and puts his gun back in its suitcase. He is about to leave when he hears a car approaching. He kneels down to wait until it passes, but as he sees the car slow down, he realizes it's the victim's partner returning.

Bad timing.

The killer waits as the man enters the house before hopping on the sidewalk and moving away as quickly as possible. He does everything in his power to stay in the shadows.

Finally, next to his car, he puts his suitcase in the back trunk and shuts it gently. He took off his ski mask on the way, so as not to attract attention if he should run into someone.

A death scream echoes in the night as he gets into his car. He saw several exterior lights turn on and people running up to the porch of their house. Maryse Letarte's boyfriend gets out, yelling, "Call the police, call the police," and then rushes across the street to where the assassin was standing a few minutes earlier. He bravely searches for the killer.

The assassin turns back and drives away, wondering how long it will take for the provincial police detectives to learn of this new murder. Or he can force fate. He has an idea.

Murielle Bouchard walks into her office to find Abygaelle Jensen thinking.

"Are you okay?"

Abygaelle looks at her colleague, her eyes reddened with tiredness.

"Do you remember messages Stephane Ranger used to receive? The serial killer quotes?"

"Yes."

"Take a look."

Abygaelle rotates her computer screen towards Murielle. The message is from a few hours ago.

"I just wanted to see what it was like to shoot Grandma.

- Ed Kemper."

After a few moments of reflection, she asks Abygaelle what it means. No one has a clue. Is it from the killer or a prankster? Is it related to the murder that just happened?

"Is the victim related to Ranger or Légaré?" Murielle asks.

"Not from what I can tell," Abygaelle says.

"Then it's probably a hoax."

Abygaelle bites her lower lip and nods.

"It's still strange that someone would pull a hoax like this. Nobody knows that the killer sends out such quotes."

Murielle concedes she is right and looks worried. Maybe he has struck again.

"Stephane Ranger may have talked about these messages, and some joker thought it was funny to send this to us."

An hour later, a rumor spread through social media that the murder was in every way similar to the others.

Soon, the confirmation came. A hole in the window, a woman's head blown off, found by her boyfriend as he went back. The police are filing this as a suspicious death for the moment.

But the e-mail Abygaelle received puzzles her. It can't be a coincidence. Why target a woman in a quiet suburb? There are no photos of Jacques, Madeleine, or Stephane in the house. The boyfriend claims he doesn't know who they are.

"There must be a connection," Aby says.

"Don't forget that he kills strangers, too. We assumed the sniper was targeting Stephane Ranger's relatives, but what if we were wrong?"

Abygaelle nods. Even though she believes there is a connection to Ranger, she can't rule out any scenario.

~

RAYMOND PRIMEAU LISTENS to television in his cell distractedly as he reads a book. The John McCain's biography that he reads fascinates him. Heavy footsteps draw his attention coming towards his cell.

"Primeau."

The loud voice of a man approaching. The man's face emerges from the bars of his cell.

Jack Morris.

"I knew it. I saw through you and I exposed you. I swore I would uncover your little game. And now, buddy, you've got blood on your hands."

Raymond Primeau sits down on the end of his bed to look at him.

"What the hell are you talking about?"

"There's another victim, Primeau. You told me there wouldn't be any other, right? Well, you were wrong."

"Are you going to blame me for all the murders in the area?" Primeau asks with a defiant smile.

Jack nods, still smiling angrily.

"I won't. Not all murders. Just those of a woman shot through a window while she was quietly listening to the television. Like Annie St. Onge."

Primeau feels blood rush down his legs.

"A copycat," he says unconvincingly.

"I thought of that," Jack says. "But there's only one detail that makes it unlikely."

"What's that?"

"The victim is Maryse Letarte, Stephane Ranger's ex-girlfriend."

Raymond Primeau buries his face in his hands.

"It looks like your silly scheme failed, and now you owe us some serious explanations."

69

Maxime Fauvette is yelling all by himself in the interrogation room. He requests to know what they charged him with. He was rudely dragged to the Provincial Police precinct after declining several times to come by himself.

Abygaelle and Murielle watched him on closed circuit after cutting the sound. Jack was so irritated by the screaming that Aby worried he might lash out at the man at any moment. Instead, he got himself a cup of coffee, just to clear his head.

After about fifteen minutes, Fauvette finally gave up bitching. Abygaelle entered the room with Murielle. She told Jack to stay on the sidelines for this one; she wants to keep everything under control. After several minutes of talking, Murielle steps in as she notices Fauvette is constantly interrupting Abygaelle.

"Listen to me carefully, young man. The sooner you answer our questions, the sooner you can go home. But if you keep acting like a smart ass, we will call your wife and tell her you will spend the night in a cell because you are too stupid to comply. Kind of like when your elementary school principal called your mom to tell her you weren't being nice to your classmates. Do we understand each other?"

"No need to be condescending," he says in an angry tone. "You can't keep me against my will. I'm not charged with anything."

"You gave up that right when you pushed us to get a warrant to bring your ass here," Murielle says. "So no, you can't simply walk out as if you were here willingly."

"What am I doing here, then? You told me you had questions about a murder. Are you completely insane?"

"No, but if you answer our questions calmly and we see that you have nothing to do with it, we'll let you go," Abygaelle says. Maxime sinks into his chair and crosses his arms. Aby opens her file and grabs her pen.

"Where were you Tuesday night?"

He frowns.

"Why?"

"Answer the question!"

"I was at home."

"Who can confirm this?"

"My wife."

"We'll check it out," Abygaelle says. "Where were you on July 2?"

"I don't know, I was probably also at home."

Jack has dialed Fauvette's home phone number. Murielle takes notes.

"Why? What happened on July 2?"

"What do you think?" Murielle says.

Maxime has a smug laugh.

"Are we playing guessing games, Ms. Bouchard?"

"Don't mess with us, Maxime. I advise you not to. You're already in trouble."

There's a knock at the door. Abygaelle joins Jack outside.

"His girlfriend claims he spent the evening with her watching movies on Netflix. He left for about ten minutes for a convenient store and came back. He stayed home afterwards until they went to bed."

"Around what time?"

"She said around 8:30 pm."

Maryse's murder took place at 8:45 pm. Except it happened on the North Shore, forty-five minutes from where Maxime lives. If this is true, then it can't be him.

"Physically, no," Jack says, "but he may have called the killer to give him the go."

"Let's get his phone call log from that day and also ask for a triangular analysis to find out where he was, if he was with his wife, as she claimed."

"I will check for a video footage from the convenience store."

Abygaelle sits back down in front of Maxime, who has settled down.

"Your spouse says that you went out on Tuesday night."

Maxime swallows with difficulty.

"What? No, I... oh yes, I went to buy bread and cigarettes."

"When did you go out?"

"I don't know, around 8:00 pm? 8:30 pm?"

He grabs his cell phone. After a few seconds of typing, he hands her his phone.

"Even better, check this out."

Abygaelle sees the transactions from Maxim's bank account on the screen. There is a purchase of $14.78 at a convenience store at 8:27 pm.

"May I have a look at your call log? We're going to get them anyway, but if you don't mind—".

After contemplating the situation, Maxime nods.

She writes the three outgoing phone numbers as of Tuesday. She will compare them with the cell phone provider's report. If there is a number missing from Mike's log, it means he's hiding something. She slides the phone over to him.

"Would you like to test my hands for gun residue?"

Murielle smiles.

"You know a lot, don't you? You seem much too prepared for a guy who doesn't know what we want from him."

Maxime smiles back at her.

"Maybe I'm watching too much CSI."

"So I will disappoint you. We no longer use this kind of stuff. Now we use atomic absorption spectrometry. I'm sorry."

Maxime has an admiring pout.

"Maybe you didn't pull the trigger," Aby says, "but that doesn't rule you out as a suspect. You may well have hired the killer."

"That's the only way I could be involved," Maxime agrees. "Because I wouldn't even know how to handle a gun. I've never used one in my life, except for a BB gun when I was a teenager. I'm more of the intellectual type, Mrs. Jensen. You can tell by my bookkeeper's appearance. I'm not getting off on tanks, guns, or whatever douchebags normally enjoy. I'm more of a reading and movie kind of guy."

"Which makes you even more dangerous," Murielle says. "The smarter people are, the more they cover their tracks."

"You greatly overestimate my intelligence, Detective Bouchard," he says, laughing.

Murielle glances at her colleague.

"It's a surprisingly self-critical statement from a guy who's been cocky from the start, isn't it?"

Abygaelle nods.

"Yes, it's weird indeed."

Maxime settles back into his chair.

"You're trying too hard, ladies. I have nothing to hide. I have only one level. What you see is what you get, as Churchill said."

"I'm pretty sure Churchill never said that," Abygaelle says.

"He certainly used this expression at least once in his life. Come on," Maxime says with a smile.

Murielle exhibits a devastating pout.

"I don't get any amusement out of the idea that lots of people are being brutally shot dead, Maxime. I really don't."

He frowns.

"Don't put words in my mouth. I'm answering your questions openly, and here you are trying to get at me, trying to make me say things I didn't say, searching for another meaning to my words. Go to the convenience store and ask them for the video, check where I was with my cell phone data, analyze my calls. I have nothing to be concerned about.

After a few minutes of silence, Abygaelle gets up and takes a few steps in his direction.

"You're really into CSI, aren't you?"

"I never miss an episode. Do you?"

"Nah, I don't like crime fiction, it's often over the top, and since I'm in it every day, I'm not particularly interested. Would you watch a series about an accounting firm?"

"It depends if one dies in the process," Maxime says, thinking he's funny.

"Not the kind of jokes I would make if I were you," Murielle says.

Fauvette shrugs.

"I told you, I'm not very bright."

Abygaelle leans back, putting her hands flat on the table.

"You're smart enough to know what a burner phone is, especially if you watch CSI."

"Of course."

"So, everything you've taught us so far, your sudden openness to let us look in your phone, is worthless if you used a burner phone to communicate with Maryse Letarte's killer, Pete Morin's killer, Ariane Légaré's killer—".

Fauvette leaps to his feet.

"You won't do to me what you did to Raymond Primeau. I

won't be the scapegoat for something I didn't do. I was at work when the girl was killed."

Jack storms into the room.

"Sit down," he yells as he rushes over to Maxim.

"I know my rights."

"Sit the fuck down!"

Maxime stares at Jack, then complies.

"I'm willing to let this piece of shit rot in a cell for the night, aren't you?" Jack asks his fellow officers, keeping his eyes on Maxim.

Abygaelle watches Maxim, biting her lower lip.

"No. He can leave. But Maxime, don't stay too far away. If you intend to leave the country, let us know."

"Why would I do that?" he says, defiantly.

Abygaelle sighs with impatience.

"You know what? Maybe a night in a cell isn't such a bad idea after all," she says.

"OK, OK. I will stay around. I don't have a trip planned, anyway."

"That's what I thought," Abygaelle says with a devious smile.

Later in his car, Maxime notices his hands still haven't stopped shaking. That's why he declined every drink they offered him and hid them under the table. He didn't want his nerves to show so clearly. Except that he goes home empty-handed. He doesn't know what they have on him.

He wonders if they know.

70

Abygaelle Jensen daydreams in her car as she watches passers-by rush across the street. Many of them cover their heads the best they can, caught short by a rainstorm. Granted, the forecast was for a thirty percent chance of rain, nevertheless, many were betting on seventy percent good weather.

A monumental mistake.

The sound of the raindrops on the car's frame calms her down. She loves the rain. It's like therapy for her, a form of meditation. A pause, a moment of recollection. Even though she tries to think about other things as best she can, her investigation is the only thing on her mind.

Twenty-four hours a day.

She thinks about Raymond Primeau, who they released on parole. They will probably prosecute him for hindering a police investigation. She and Jack interrogated him for hours, hoping to get him to spill his guts, to explain why he made the false confession. But he cowered in a stubborn silence.

No way to make him flinch.

Then his lawyer got involved and forced them to let him go,

because even though he had confessed to the murders, he was obviously not the serial killer that had been on the loose for the past few weeks. He also admitted that he lied about the early 2000s murders. The whole thing is back to zero. The chances of him still being prosecuted for the murders are great given his confession, but a judge deemed him an insufficient risk to keep him locked up.

It devastated Jack.

She is eager to see the sixty-year-old man she has been waiting for almost an hour. She rehearsed the scenario in her head so many times that she could deliver it all by heart. She just has to be careful with her reactions, keep her composure, avoid getting upset.

It's not an official interview.

Then she sees him. She second-guesses her decision. Maybe it's not such a great idea after all. What the hell. She gets out of her car, covers her head with the top of her long beige raincoat, and rushes to the other side of the street.

"Mr. Primeau."

He looks back, dumbfounded to see her standing next to him. Totally normal, since she probably is the last person he thought he would face today.

"Detective Jensen, we had an appointment?"

"No, but I would like to talk to you."

Primeau looks at his watch, exposing part of his forearm tattoo.

"I don't think that's a good idea."

"I'll only be a few minutes, let's go in," she says, leading him to a small, near-empty café.

Primeau sighs. He grants her ten minutes, no more. He has an appointment with his lawyer.

Abygaelle smiles and follows him. Once inside, they each order a cappuccino.

"Do you have your cell phone with you?"

Primeau frowns.

"My question is simple," Abygaelle says. "Do you have your phone with you?"

"Of course I do."

"Take it out, turn it off, and put it on the table."

"I beg your pardon?"

Abygaelle sighs. She grabs her own mobile device, demonstrates that she is turning it off with the condescension of an adult patronizing a child, and sets it down beside her. After a few seconds of figuring out the point of this, Primeau shrugs and does the same.

"Great, our discussion is off the record. So I want to keep it that way. Let's talk human to human."

"Listen, I have nothing more to tell you than what I've already said."

Abygaelle looks at him, smiling.

"I know, that's not why I'm here. I know why you confessed to the murders. I understand what you were trying to achieve."

"You do? I didn't know I had a plan."

The detective's face hardens.

"Don't play dumb with me, Mr. Primeau. I want to talk about us."

"About us?"

"Precisely. You must wonder why no one has charged you with assaulting a law enforcement officer, trespassing, death threats—"

The man loses color as Abygaelle lists potential charges.

"What are you getting at, Detective Jensen?"

She takes a long sip of her coffee and keeps her eyes on him.

"That you have nothing to worry about. No one knows about your childish act, your cowardice. No one will charge you for this."

"Well, if you want to insult me—" Primeau says, standing up abruptly.

"Sit down, Abygaelle says in a tone of voice that leaves no room for negotiation."

He tries to look cool, never will he show all the fear that ran through his spine. The detective's eyes darkened so much that it seemed like an evil spirit had taken over her body. He obeyed after several seconds of silence that served mainly to show she didn't intimidate him.

It was, of course, a facade.

Abygaelle gulps another sip. Her face softens.

"This is a public place, Mr. Primeau. You have nothing to worry about. But you will do me the favor of listening to me until the end. Are we clear?"

"What do you want?"

"That's better. When I said you had nothing to worry about, I may have been hyperbolic. You don't have to worry about the tribunals interfering with our, shall we say, little impromptu meeting at my apartment."

Primeau watches her with restraint.

"Justice would be too gentle."

This time, besides her darkened and stormy gaze, Primeau notes the aggressive features of her face and her clenched jaw. If a look could kill, he would be dead in a heartbeat. He knows he must maintain a casual look. She's about to jump at his throat. Her hand shakes as she takes another swig of her cappuccino. Primeau has seen this many times with soldiers coming back from battle. Adrenaline flooding your veins to the point where you are no longer in control of your heart rate and nerves.

Abygaelle pauses for a few minutes, just looking at the man who shows no sign of animosity. That changes nothing for her. She feels astonishes by the fury she experiences. She gets closer and shifts her elbows forward on the table.

"Maybe one day I'll resolve to get even and slit your throat in your sleep, or shoot you down like a stray dog in an alley. Or maybe I'll move on. Life is full of surprises, doesn't it make it exciting?"

Raymond Primeau is dazed, but he holds his ground. This girl can sink deep into the abyss of her soul, he thinks. He has seen this look more often than not. But it was among hardened criminals, bloodthirsty dictators, cruel and shameless murderers. He is shocked to see it again in a seemingly gentle young woman.

"My God, what happened to you, detective Jensen, to bring you to this point?"

She doesn't react, only clenching her teeth.

"Normal people don't go so deep into the darkness. You must have seen something horrible up close to get there. What exactly did you see, Abygaelle?"

She screams and smashes her cup on the floor.

"ENOUGH!"

Raymond Primeau is petrified. For a guy who has lived through the worst of humanity, this is no small feat. For the first time in a while, fear grabs him in the gut. The vein in the policewoman's forehead is so prominent that it's ready to burst at any moment. There is only one thing to do:

Keep quiet. Avoid to worsen the situation.

Abygaelle shivers. What just happened? Asking is the answer.

Bonnie.

She signals the waiter to stand back. The cup was empty, it's best for him to stay away. Patrons seated further away watched her for a long time before swinging back to their discussion, glancing at her with concern here and there.

She's taken aback by what Raymond Primeau said, as if he read her mind. All her life, she did everything to mask her dark side. And he spotted it in a matter of minutes. She understands the army teaches you how to untangle people's souls, to decipher what they tell you, but above all, what they don't. She suddenly feels exposed.

She showed up with a plan, intending to scare him, to give him nightmares, and now she's the one shaking. She's unsettled. She doesn't have the strength to go on, but she does.

"Did you understand me clearly, Mr. Primeau?" she says with no conviction. She doesn't look at him.

Primeau smiles. But not in a condescending way.

A kind, gentle smile.

"Please look at me, Abygaelle."

She looks up at him.

"You have every reason in the world to be mad at me and to seek retribution. And I know you can do me harm. Your wounds are deep enough to cast a violent and dangerous torrent towards me. We are more akin than you think. We have similar traumas, we've experienced things no human should. We're cut from the same cloth, Abygaelle. I'm not the monster you think I am. I know I shouldn't have done what I did, but I wanted to protect my wife from a world she knows nothing about. You understand that, right? Haven't you ever sacrificed yourself to protect a loved one?"

Abygaelle looks down. Sophie comes to mind.

"I knew it. You're a fighter. I felt it the other night in your apartment. You can kill me if it will set you free. If you think it will make your life easier. But I implore you. Risking your life and your job in the belief that killing me will satiate your rage, that it will provide you with the salvation you've been looking for, is heresy. You have a brilliant career, you are gifted and have a lot to bring to society, don't make this mistake. I'm a bitter old man, don't follow me down this road.

He observes Abygaelle, fragile, biting her lower lip.

"How can't believe how you remind me of Nathalie. It struck me when we were struggling on your bed, like a revelation. Like she was sending me a message. Since then, I have grown very fond of you. You are what she would have become, I'm certain. A beautiful, confident and intelligent woman. I look at you and it comforts me. It gives me hope. What she went through was terrible, but I wish she had the strength to go on, like you. I'm convinced that she would have achieved great things, like you. Of course, she would have struggled with her own demons, as you and I have. But, who doesn't?"

Abygaelle hasn't looked at him for several minutes. She listens quietly. She has nothing to contribute. She won't tell him it moves her, that being compared to Nathalie is a compliment. She has become close to her through her readings of the drama, through what she went through, through her assertiveness during the trial, through the strength of her suicide note.

Raymond Primeau tells her they would have been great friends, and she agrees.

He left the café and laid his hand on hers. Contrary to what she would have expected, she wasn't disgusted.

He was gone for several minutes when she came out of her torpor. She wipes a tear, then gets up. She apologized to the waiter for the broken cup, left a generous tip, and walked back to her car.

The rain has given way to bright sunshine breaking through the clouds.

Beyond Raymond Primeau's unexpected speech, Abygaelle took his advice on revenge and deception. She knows for a fact that he didn't say that casually, that he was referring to something deeper.

This speech was not random, it wasn't meaningless. He was referring to something real, something cruel. Something that haunts him and that he must live with day after day.

All that remains is to figure out what it is.

71

When Nicolas Landry called him back, Stephane Ranger realized that his old friend was deliberately withholding information. He had to remind him a few times that an innocent teenage girl was killed before he would be more forthcoming.

Landry reached out to his contacts and learned that the mafia was somehow involved. Stephane didn't understand why they would target his niece and brother, since he had no business with them. Why would the Italians do something like this, it's not their style?

"Not the Italians," Landry said.

"Then who? The Chinese? Nick, I need your help here. I'm sure you can't stand that. Why are you covering for them? I'm just trying to understand what's going on."

Stephan's voice was agitated. Nicolas Landry stayed silent for a short while and finally said:

"Fuck it, I'll tell you. But you must swear never to disclose where you got it from. I've already asked too many questions, I've exposed myself."

"I promise."

"Look at the Russian mafia."

"The Russians? What do they want?"

"I don't know. But I heard that one of their top men is working with your guy."

It makes no sense, Stephane thinks.

"I've never been in trouble with the Russians. I don't get it."

Landry sighs.

"I'd like to help you more, but I don't know much more."

"How do I get in touch with these people?"

"You don't. Don't talk to them, Steph. They are very dangerous."

Ranger thanked Landry for his help, but he wouldn't settle for so little. It was too sketchy to implicate the cops. He recalls that one of his buddies worked with the Russians for a previous job. Stephane called him to find out more. He had made up a story to smooth things over, and his friend referred to a very popular café linked to the organization.

The Michkhin café.

The next day, Stephane went to the restaurant to get a cappuccino and see if he could find any clues that might shed light on the case, or meet with someone who could help him. He knew Marko Gusarov because he met him a few times over the years. He didn't know if he was a member of the mafia, but that's what he was told through various sources. He obviously worked at the café, or owned it. There was a computer and filing cabinets in an office at the back of the place.

Ranger then went to the bathroom and looked around. An alarm panel draws his attention. There was nothing on the digital display, as if someone shut it off. Normally, a light shows that the alarm is disarmed, but not this time. Stephane saw these in some of the wealthy homes he had broken into, alarm systems that were inactive. He figured he'd come back after hours to check if he couldn't pick up something in the files or on the computer. Apart from the organization's headquarters, which he didn't know about, this was the most likely place to look.

This is it. The café has been closed for an hour. Since he didn't want to attract attention, Stephane took a cab to a few blocks from the bistro. His plan is all set. He will begin with the filing cabinets in the office. He dresses in dark clothes and puts a dark blue wool ski mask on his head.

This will allow him to go incognito past the surveillance cameras that are potentially surrounding the building. Earlier in the day, he typed the address into Google Maps to scan the surroundings through photos. He saw the front of the establishment. Using the navigation feature, he looked for the best places to sneak in undetected. He looked for discreet doors or accesses. He spotted a frame on the wall to the left of the building and a service entrance.

Stephane dashes to the side of the building where he locates a window in poor condition that would be impossible to tamper with quietly. The metal back door is locked. There is no point in wasting energy on forcing it open. He heads to a wooden door in the back of the café that is easy to break into. His petty theft past still comes in handy sometimes.

He looks through the area to make sure he's out of sight. He carefully slides the tip of his flat, hardened steel screwdriver between the frame and the latch. There's no extra reinforcement, so if he succeeds, he'll have a clear path. His biggest fear is that the alarm will be functional, unlike what he witnessed earlier, and that it will go off as soon as the door opens. He has an escape plan, just in case. He handles his tool delicately and creating no noise, except for the almost inaudible cracking of the wood frame as it crumbles under the pressure.

Still a little more, and he will be in the clear. He smiles as he hears the satisfying click of the door opening. He hasn't lost his touch. He takes a deep breath and quietly enters, gritting his teeth.

No alarm.

Not very secure for a mafia hideout, he thinks. He glances inside, lingering on the corners of the walls near the ceiling, looking for active sensors. There are some, but they don't have a halo showing any kind of functioning. He quietly infiltrates the café's kitchen, closing the door behind him. The brightness outside lights up the rooms through the side window, but he has enough shade to move discreetly to where he wants. That the alarm is inactive is a sign of fate.

Ariane is watching over him.

He crouches down, measuring each of his steps. He must be careful not to trigger a secondary surveillance system, or run into someone still on the premises. He has no way of knowing if there are any employees left, but the silence reassures him. He's most likely alone. He walks quietly along, turning left at the end of the hallway. He goes past the wall, and on his right is an entrance to another room of the café. Reached at this level, he recognizes the place. The dining room isn't far away, and there's the table where he was sitting at earlier in the day. Directly on his left, Gusarov's office.

From his vantage point, he sees a filing cabinet and a desk in front of which there are two chairs on wheels. He squats down to the room and notices a computer screen on the desk. An old white cathode-ray screen faded with age. There are two other metal filing cabinets to the left, standing side by side, about six feet tall. Most of them are unlocked; really for a secret organization, security leaves a lot to be desired.

After going through all the drawers finding nothing relevant, Stephane feels frustrated. It was silly to think there would be any clues about Ariane. He sits down at the computer and moves the mouse to get off the screen saver.

A password, obviously.

He tries a few things with no luck. He hangs his head as if a flash of genius would strike him. He's in a dead end. There is nothing here. He tried and failed. Nothing more to do but to get out, neither seen nor known. He squats quickly under the desk. Someone has just turned on the lighting in the dining room. Maybe they are smart lights activated at regular intervals to pretend that someone is present? He puts his hood back on and slides further under the desk. He brings the chair closer to him. Fortunately, there is a partition shielding him from the outside. Voices in the distance suggest that there are at least two people on the spot. They are speaking in a language he doesn't recognize.

Probably Russian.

He doesn't recall closing the door on his way in. If he didn't, they will search the place from top to bottom. He's done. The voices approach. He recognizes Marko Gusarov's husky tone from earlier in the day when he heard him talking. He's chatting with another man. Stephane prays they don't walk on to the office.

Tough luck.

The lights come on, and from where he is, he can make out the shadows of the two guys walking to his left. He doesn't need to hold his breath, as their conversation and the flickering neon lights cover the sound of his breath. He doesn't speak Russian, but he senses from Gusarov's tone that he has noted something fishy. He hears the cabinets' drawers opening and closing, then the characteristic sound of a gun being cocked.

He's as good as dead if they catch him underneath the desk. They will shoot him like a stray dog in the back alley. If Gusarov sits at the computer, his feet will hit him. Space is limited under the desk. Luckily, he had the foresight to turn off the computer screen before he hid. After what seemed like endless minutes, they left the office and turned off the lights. Ranger waits several more minutes, enough time to make sure that Gusarov and the other man have left in order to leave as quickly as possible. No more noise, and the main door is locked.

He nuzzles the chair and comes out of his hiding. His limbs are numb from the peculiar position he was in. He remains seated on the floor, rubbing his legs to get the blood flowing. Near the wall, there is a paper basket made of metal mesh from which he can see the contents inside. He sees though it is half full. A crumpled document catches his eye. The header reminds him of something. He grabs the sheet and unfolds it.

Then everything becomes clear. As if the pieces of the puzzle were falling into place all at once. His heart races as he reads the printed names. He steps out of the office. As he turns the corner, he just has time to react as he hears heavy footsteps stamping towards him. He bends down as a big silhouette rushes to attack him. He stumbles against Stephane, and crashes on the door by which he entered a little earlier.

It's not Gusarov, but it doesn't matter. He won't chat with him. He doesn't have time to ask him questions either. He gets up and looks at him, although he's still wearing his hood. The man yells something in a foreign language and rushes towards him. Stephane takes a step to the side and runs towards the bistro's dining room. He has always been a very fast and agile runner. This is perhaps what will save his life tonight. He turns sharply to his right toward the front door, but it's locked. He sees the glint of a rifle in the glass's reflection and bends down just in time to avoid the shot. The shooter is about thirty meters behind.

Under the impact, the main door's window shatters and Stephane slips in quickly. Seeing his pursuer running towards him, gun in hand, Stephane sits down on the ground and smashes the lower part of the second glass door with his two feet. It's a risky bet, because he could tear his calves and cut himself deeply. Fortunately, he broke the window unharmed.

The opening in the door is large enough for him to squeeze through, but not enough for his towering pursuant.

He gets on all fours and goes through the hole. He feels a burn on his belly, but keeps going. Once outside, he runs away, zigzagging to make it harder for the gangster to shoot him. The shooter fires two bullets at him from inside the café, smashing the window of a car parked nearby. Stephane runs at full speed and crosses a large cedar hedge on the corner of the street, out of sight of his assailant. He jumps over a smaller hedge, and over a metal fence. He pulls into an apartment block parking lot and crosses a nearby park, glancing behind him.

No one is chasing him.

Given his size, there is no chance in hell that the man will catch up to him running. His only chance is to get to him by car. Stephane stays off the lit-up streets and goes through the nearby house's backyards, and across grassy fields. About twenty minutes later, he finally reaches his place. He looks at the fir tree as if waiting for its approval, a confirmation that he did the right thing, a confirmation that it will lead them closer to catching this monster. The tree dances in the wind, Stephane sees it as the sign he was waiting for. He smiles at the conifer. Thank you for being there despite everything. It's the only one that hasn't given up on him, that never will, that will love him unconditionally no matter what.

He heads to the bathroom and locks the door. He crashes to the floor against the wall, catching his breath and coming to his senses. He removed his hood as he approached near his home and tossed it into a recycling bin near a residence. He has a long gash on his stomach, but his shirt has absorbed most of the blood. He doesn't think he'll need stitches, but he's concerned that he left blood at the scene. A simple DNA test will disclose his identity. As an ex-convict, he's on file and the mob probably has the means to get their hands on DNA analysis. He gazes through the paper he took from Gusarov's office one more time to make sure he's not delusional. Focus Marketing, McGill Street, Montreal. He recognizes the name of this company because it was the firm that interviewed him and his fellow inmates a few years ago.

He has since forgotten that day, but now that he has the document in hand, he remembers it as if it were yesterday. If this is the survey the killer used to target his victims, it sickens him. How can someone be so Machiavellian? He turns on the taps to take a shower and, after stripping completely, he disinfects his wound. He observes the reflection of his face in the mirror.

He has never looked so old.

72

Marko Gusarov smokes a cigarette while watching two of his men pick up broken glass from the ground. He's livid. Who had the nerve to break into his café? Don't they know who he is? He rants against his carelessness with his alarm system. He thought no one would dare to break into his business. Everyone knows it's a Russian mafia hideout.

He'll have to report this to his bosses. Tell them what happened, and why his security was so deficient. It will stain his record, that's for sure. Fortunately, nothing was stolen. All the money is there; the equipment, too. He doesn't understand what the intruder wanted. Why would he risk his life breaking into his business if it wasn't for the money?

The worst part is that he was there at the same time. He went back to the shop to get his laptop, and he saw that things had been shifted. Something was wrong, but he couldn't put his finger on it. He asked Sergei to wait inside once the door was closed to ensure that no one was there.

Then a skinny guy in a cagoule came out of the office, but escaped Sergei. He lost sight of him. Apparently, he was running extremely fast. Marko assumes they scare the guy shitless. He absolutely must know who it was. And especially what he was doing there, what he was looking for. He violently closes the shutter of the panel of his security system. He instructs his manager to arrange for everything to work on this very day. The manager lowers his head and walks with a quick stride to the nearest phone.

Marko paces back and forth. If word got out, the organization's top brass'd label him a sloppy soldier. He has worked too hard to get there. He signals Sergei to follow him outside.

"Find that bastard, you hear me? How could you miss him?"

Sergei stays mute. This is a rhetorical question. He looks down. Marko breathes like a caged animal. His brain is boiling. He should have taken care of this himself. The contractor responsible for repairing the main door glass should be here any minute.

Marko is working his cell phone, making multiple calls to subtly check if anything has been leaked within the organization.

Apparently not.

He relaxes a bit. It's not too late to do damage control.

He looks at the crushed glass at his feet, and crushes a few pieces with his heel, sweeping the crumbled glass with a brisk motion. He thinks back to what Sergei told him, that when he realized he wouldn't catch the intruder in a foot race, he got in his car, but lost sight of him. He believes he swooped through the park.

The workers were getting the work started when Marko spotted something on the ground.

"Stop!"

He motions for the two men to step aside and he crouches down, lingering at a sharp piece of tile in the lower part of the metal door.

"What's that piece of a different shade? It looks like blood."

Sergei confirms that this is where the guy came out. So if it's blood, it's the fucker's. Marko smiles. He signals the workers to wait in their truck for a few moments and calls Chris Myles, a doctor he knows, who advises him to use a cotton swab and take a sample.

Marko doesn't take any chances. As the stain is dry, he breaks the piece of glass, making sure not to touch the bloody part, and puts it in a handkerchief and places it in a desk drawer. Let's hope this idiot has a criminal record or is on file somewhere. He knows where to get a DNA test done, and he's connected to someone with access to the RCMP's National DNA Data Bank.

He suddenly breathes a little easier.

Sergei will take care of getting the test results as soon as possible. Marko doesn't need to mention that it's urgent. Sergei already feels guilty enough as it is. He understands that this is his only task for the next few days. The square park antique clock in front of the café marks eight o'clock in the morning. He scans around him and when he looks up; he sees Darya in a short robe looking down at him from her balcony. She smiles and instructs him to join her upstairs.

Marko looks at the men working to replace the glass, then figures there's no harm in spending a few minutes warming up between the pretty blonde's moist thighs. With a nod, he instructs her to go back to her apartment; he goes up the stairs to the second floor, rubbing his hands.

This day won't be completely shitty after all.

73

Laurie Métivier stares at the ceiling for several minutes. As has happened all too often in the last few years, Maxime Fauvette has taken her from behind with such violence that it has upset her. He has been snoring next to her for the past half hour, satiated from having fucked her.

Because that's what it was: fucking.

It wasn't making love.

They don't really make love anymore. Maxime finds his pleasure in fucking her with intensity, as if he didn't care for her. Laurie still feels him inside her so much that it makes her uncomfortable. Even though they have started a family, a safe and cozy home, she feels Maxime has become like a stranger.

As if she had met a man she didn't know on a dating site, and fucked him with an unsettling detachment.

Not so long ago, everything was fine. They made love slowly, without rushing things. Maxime pampered her like a princess, a term he loved to use when talking about her.

All that changed.

As if something had broken between them. They make love less and less, and he fucks her more and more, as if she were his object. Every time he rolls over on his side after using her as his sex toy, she feels like a fool. Contrary to what she thinks, Maxim has not fallen asleep. As always after sex, he's in an unbearable lethargy. He never admitted it, but he always felt guilty about what had happened to his teenage love. He will never tell Laurie that Nathalie is still the love of his life. Laurie is something like a consolation prize. He's happy with her, but not as happy as he would have been with Nathalie. The one brutally stolen from him so long ago.

He never understood how she could have gone off alone, without her friends, with strangers she met in a bar. It was so not like her. It's no use anyway, he'll never get a satisfactory answer. He asked her several times what had crossed her mind, but Nathalie shut down. She took her secret to the grave. The trial baffled him. To hear witnesses claiming she spent the night glued to that scumbag, Eric Gagne. How she was flirting with him. Gagné, who had confirmed all this with his fucking triumphant look that made him so angry.

Yet, they were living something wonderful together. She so often reassured him he was the love of her life that he couldn't conceive that she would fall for someone else. She told him it was only girls' night out, which is why he couldn't join them. He agreed right away, because he trusted her completely. He knew her, or so he thought. She wasn't a giddy little girl who would fall for a bad boy. She wasn't an idiot who, under the influence of alcohol, would blow a stranger into a downtown bar's gruesome bathroom.

He's certain that someone slipped something into her drink for her to act that way. Like someone she wasn't. At the end of the day, he concluded it was his fault. Because he was too sweet. Because women secretly want a romantic and respectful man in life, but a domineering chauvinist in bed.

Over time, he came to only take his wife brutally, pulling her hair to make her arch her back. The whole thing will end in mutual discomfort once the bestial sex is over. He understands Laurie's concerns, but he can no longer make love to her. What if he loses her, too? What if she went out to a party and fell in love with another Eric Gagne? He couldn't survive this again. Never again will a woman have to look elsewhere for dominant sex. He can deliver it until he's blue in the face.

He can play that role. Even if it's not him, he can become one. The survival of his wife depends on it. The problem is that Laurie is no longer enough to satisfy him. He has to prove himself all the time. To whom? He doesn't know. But it's an impulse. He fucks with prostitutes just as savagely as Laurie, because they, at least, seem to enjoy it. He admits that it's wrong to ask for girls who look like Nathalie, but he can't help it. It's as if for an hour he gets back what they took away from him. He pictures himself with Nathalie. And he fucks her with authority so that she stays. He fucks her with vigor to protect her, so that she gets back with her friends instead of with those three scumbags.

He visualizes them in their apartment. The one where Nathalie lived with him almost all the time, towards the end. She was supposed to move in with him after college. He doesn't make love with Laurie anymore; he fucks her like crazy. It's violent, it's energetic. He orgasms like a wild beast before falling back on the bed, panting loudly, his body beaded with sweat. It's the only way he's found for Laurie to never experience what Nathalie has gone through. It's his unhealthy way of protecting her from herself.

Even if it means ignoring the silence of her tears.

74

Stephane Ranger strolls into a park next to his place that he goes to when he needs to recharge his batteries. Some people travel, others go to the country. He sits on the same bench and watches children playing. It relaxes him. Sometimes parents look at him suspiciously. They think it strange that a man his age is watching their offspring from afar. They're right, he thinks. But I don't have any malicious intent. I just want to sort out my thoughts.

A blond girl around five years old who plays with a boy of about the same age draws his attention. It's amazing how much she looks like Ariane when she was a kid. His eyes track the young girl and he's smiling as he feels a nostalgic tingling in his nose. He has long since realized he is not the kind of man to start a family. He cannot take care of himself. How could he take care of a toddler and give it everything it needs? It's best for everyone to channel that love back to Ariane and Marco.

Well, that was the plan until life decided otherwise.

He snaps out of his ramblings by shaking his head. He looks out into the clearing to his right. The wind dances with the foliage in a soft and soothing choreography. He closes his eyes and goes over the scene in his head one more time. He went to the provincial police station to meet Abygaelle Jensen, but was told that she was out for lunch. Since he didn't have time to wait for her, he sought to find her by going around the surrounding restaurants.

After a few minutes of seeking, he finally spotted her through the window of a well-known stuffy bistro. She was with an older, well-groomed man. Unexpectedly, Jensen was far from thrilled to see him. He was disturbing her during her meal. Despite the importance of what he had to share with her, she was distant, almost to the point of being mean. She instructed him to schedule an appointment for later in the day. She seemed troubled.

He would have liked to tell her about the list, but she wasn't listening, just interrupting him and telling him to make the damn appointment.

He was doing everything he could to support this bunch of incompetents and they were picky? She reassured him that his help was welcome, and now that he finally has something concrete in hand to give them, she was not receptive?

This list is important. What were they waiting for? For this sicko to kill again?

The man eating with her stared at him for several minutes as if he was attempting to read his mind. Was he afraid that he would lash out at her? He conceded he was intense and agitated, but he wasn't threatening. He just hoped she would listen to him for a few seconds, and grasp the importance of the list. After all, he risked his life to get a hold of it. There was no time to wait quietly for her to finish her tuna salad. We're past that stage, right? Are they a team or what?

How many victims will it take before someone does something? The cops have other matters to deal with, he knows, but this one has to be at the top of the pile. Everyone should work on it. It's all over the 24-hour news channels. Every other front page is about the murders and their failure to make progress. They must feel the pressure.

He realizes he's been clenching his teeth for several minutes now, and he loosens his jaw. He shouldn't get carried away. He needs to keep hunting for the killer. He made a promise. He's broken his word many times in his life, but this time, there's no way he's going to betray his oath to his niece. Even if it means alienating the cops. He doesn't give a damn if it's helping solve the case and stop this son of a bitch. He keeps thinking he has nothing to lose. Not to convince himself, but because it's true. He literally has nothing left in his life. It's not like he had much to his credit before, anyway.

When you have nothing to lose, you are free.

There's nothing more scary than a fearful animal, backed into a corner, fighting for its life. A dark force hunts him down, he's under attack. He's in constant danger of death or of losing another person dear to him. Pushed to the limit, he's now on a mission. Nothing and no one will stop him.

Fortunately, the individual eating with her stepped in and invited him to join them. There was a soothing kindness about him. A man of great stature, he exuded a genuine authority. There was a disconcerting warmth in his figure. Stephane could finally articulate his story, what he had done at the café, what he found in the wastepaper basket, about the man who shot at him.

As soon as he mentioned the names on the list, Abygaelle Jensen's attention shifted completely, and she was now listening to him as if he were giving the gospel word. Stephane slid the document next to the woman's glass of wine. He told her about that day when a research firm did a focus group in the clink, though his memory was hazy about why they were there. He recalls that all the prisoners attended voluntarily.

The list resulted from one of the many questions they asked him and the other inmates. If his memory serves him right, it revolved around ranking the ten most important people in your life in order.

He had played along.

But what he failed to grasp is why the mafia would use such a list, and if the killer really uses it to identify his victims? All he knows is what Nicolas Landry told him: that the Russian mob was providing confidential details about the victims to the alleged killer. Stephane knows the list by heart. First, he wrote the name of his beloved mother. Then that of Ariane; of his nephew Marco; of Marc-André; of Madeleine; of Maryse, his girlfriend at the time. The last name on the list was Jacques Légaré, his brother-in-law. He included him because no one else came to mind. The others were comrades of the time that he no longer sees. He does not wish them dead, though. They, too, need protection.

Annie St. Onge was not among them, even though he knew her a bit for having met her a few times. That was before they became good friends. Before their respective demons brought them together. If the list feeds the murderer, then why murder Annie? And why not kill him, directly?

He doesn't see why anyone would want to hurt the people he loves. After all, he's just an insignificant ex-convict who has lived a boring life for the last years.

Who could hate him that much? Is it really related to that fateful night?

75

From where he is standing, the assassin has a perfect view of Madeleine Légaré's apartment. For lack of a better hideout, he climbed a thick tree behind the triplex parking lot. He blends in beautifully with the leaves, but anyone paying the slightest attention to the ash tree would easily spot him. He already screwed a silencer to the end of his weapon.

Everything is set. Just wait for the right moment.

He parked his car behind, on the other side of the street. Once he's done with Madeleine Légaré, he'll climb the fence along the cedar hedges and slowly make his way to his car.He's been watching her for several minutes now, looking as she goes about her business in the kitchen. She makes slow and delicate gestures, with minimal effort. Like a death row prisoner. The assassin doesn't know if it's a coincidence or if she has a sixth sense to foresee her future, but he feels like she gets what is about to happen, and gives in to her fate.

He wonders how people can live with three other relatives in such cramped apartments. I guess one gets used to anything; he thinks.He zooms in on the woman's face through his rifle scope, then flicks the trigger with his index finger. A shot of disconcerting ease, even for a poor shooter. Madeleine's glowering face mystifies him. Is it tears sliding down her cheekbones? It's awfully hot. Maybe she's sweating? But her reddened eyes don't lie.

She is crying.

The assassin sighs with relief as he realizes he will put an end to her misery. Not that he needs a motive to rationalize his action, the purpose of his gesture is clear and amply justifiable. But to know that he will end the suffering of a brave woman to whom life has not been kind fills him with an inexorable serenity. She has suffered like few people in their lives. You don't know what genuine distress is until you lose someone you love more than yourself. It can't be explained. You must experience it to understand. Those who have lost a dear one acknowledge each other, almost nod at each other like bikers passing by on the road.

You know when you know. And the assassin knows.

He feels compelled by his mission. He realized that Madeleine's husband and her son had gone away from the house through his previous days' watch. He waited for them to come back to kill three birds with one stone, but they have definitely vanished. Maybe they are traveling, maybe they are hiding.Could that be the reason for her tears? Never mind. It will all be over in a few minutes and she will rest in peace next to her daughter.

At last.

He focuses on his target again, steadying his rifle by pressing the stock firmly against his shoulder. He takes a deep breath and... what the hell is she doing? Madeleine's right hand clenched and her face twisted in pain.

An intense pain.

The assassin tries to grasp what is going on. Her hand darkened.

Then he understands.

He realizes she doesn't need him; he read the situation perfectly. Seeing the blood flowing from Madeleine's wrists, a thick dark red blood, typical of a deep cut, he clenches his lips. Suddenly empathetic, the urge to rescue her, to call the paramedics, surprise him. Madeleine sits and stares ahead, crying silent tears. A sly smile appears on the assassin's face as he lowers his weapon. No need to do the dirty work, after all. His plan works, except that instead of Stephane Ranger suffering to the point of slitting his wrists to the bone, it's his sister.

This disappoints him deeply. If she suffers so much that she sees no other way out than death, how come her useless brother doesn't feel the same? The death of his sister may be the last straw he needed. The satisfaction the assassin gets from this thought is beyond anything he has experienced by killing his previous victims.

A life full of torment is the worst punishment one can experience. Worse than death. The grief he sees in Madeleine's eyes is like the one he watches every day in the mirror. Even if it has nothing to do with his own pain, he understands what she feels and is in complete symbiosis with her.

Madeleine stares ahead, as if she were looking into his eyes. As if she was talking to him telepathically. He puts his rifle under his left armpit so it doesn't slip out. He pulls on his Bushnell to watch her more closely, to scrutinize her face, digged with deep wrinkles.

He notes the total abandonment in her look. An abandonment peculiar to those who have surrendered. Those who have suffered too much. She heads for death like an incurable automaton resigned to her fate. How beautiful. How poetic. He has seen nothing like it and immediately embraces the powerful emotion it inspires in him.

He feels like he's at her side. He thinks she's beautiful, pushed to her limits. He would like to take her in his arms, to listen for her heart to stop beating gently and to kiss her tenderly on the forehead. Swear that everything will be okay. That it is for the best.

He thought he'd never experience a moment like this. But there it is. Like a gift. As if she had been waiting for him. As if she said that she understands and gives him what he has hoped for all these years. A deathly pain. He knows exactly the path she took to get there; he has walked the same route so many times. Like an elegiac labyrinth denying happiness. Forbidding inner peace.

He reacted by seeking redress. Madeleine felt that nothing in the world was worth sticking around for. Not her son. Nor her husband. He wondered if she knows. If she understood what happened. If she perceived that all this was because of her loser brother. And if she approves of his mission. After all, wouldn't she have done the same to him if she knew who he was? If she had the means and the guts? He liked to think so.

She would agree with him, for sure.

She embraces her fate with a moving dignity. He grants her what is rightfully hers: she is greater than him, stronger than him. She has the courage he doesn't have. He dismantled his rifle and put it back in his backpack. Madeleine is pale. She has stopped crying. Her eyes are half closed. The assassin offers her the courtesy of guiding her to her last breath. Even if he is not with her physically, he is metaphysically. Never has he felt so close to one of his victims. He takes the moment with humility and respect.

"Yes, that's right. Close your eyes, love. Go to your daughter. You will sympathize with my action, I'm sure. You would have done the same thing. You're a fighter, like me. I don't know where you're going, but I hope you'll find the answers and comfort you're looking for. That you understand I had no choice, nothing against you. Nothing personal. But know that I must finish what I started. Sorry you had to cross my path. Sorry you drew the wrong number."

Madeleine collapses on her side, out of the assassin's sight. A powerful melancholy lashes him. Again, these damn feelings. At least it proves he's not dead on the inside. He didn't know Madeleine, but he respects her. She was damaged, like him. He doesn't think she's weak. Suicide is not always a sign of cowardice. He experienced that. Sometimes he wondered if life was worth living.

He gets it.

He had just climbed down from the tree when three police cars came barreling into the parking lot, all sirens blaring. The cops raced up the stairs two at a time toward Madeleine Légaré's apartment.

The killer disappears behind the cedar hedges, drifting from rage to relief.

76

Abygaelle went out to get some fresh air. The image of Madeleine Légaré lying in her blood made her sick to her stomach. Each new ordeal increases her perceived incompetence and makes her feel more guilty. The media, hungry for everything about this case, will pounce on the investigators like wild animals.

But she doesn't care.

Nobody is more severe than she is about her work. Not the media, not Picard.

No one.

She didn't expect when she took this job that every new body would be like a punch in her stomach. Even if it was the same with each new sex crime victim in her other role. At least the victims could reconstruct themselves, even if the road was long, winding and full of hurdles. A possibility that murder and suicide victims will never have. The power of this fatality gets to her.

Madeleine left two notes on the kitchen counter. One addressed to her husband, another to the killer. She wrote that although he took away her daughter, the apple of her eye, she wouldn't allow him to kill her, from afar, like a gutless wimp. She took matters into her own hands.

So she was serious. Fortunately, they came on time. It was close. A witness notified them that there were lamenting noises in the apartment. The neighbors know what happened to Ariane, and they were worried. They monitored their good friend whom they have known for long. The children have played together since elementary school. Every breath of fresh air helps Aby to gradually calm down.

They interviewed the neighbors, including the one who called 911. A woman said she saw someone climbing the tree behind the parking lot, but she doesn't have good eyesight. She couldn't give any more details. It could have been a teenage boy. They looked around, but found nothing conclusive.

No clues.

Madeleine slashed her wrists so deeply that the bones were visible to the naked eye. She didn't want to miss. Nothing to do with a half-hearted suicide attempt disguised as a cry for help. Madeleine's letter also specifies that her husband and son went to a secret location, and that they will not return until they catch the killer. She wrote a phone number at the bottom. Jack called and reached Jacques Légaré, whose was sobbing, relieved that his wife was alive. He knows about her plan. When he heard the phone ring, he thought it was it.

"We tried to talk her out of it, but she wouldn't listen," he says. "We wanted her to come with us, but when Ariane died and she found out that her stupid brother was on drugs again, she just snapped. I thought it would fade away after a while, but she never came back as herself. Gone was the sparkle in her eyes. She was on autopilot the whole time. She told me that if I really loved her, I would go with Marco to protect him and allow her out of this messed up world. That all she wanted was to go back to Ariane. She made me swear not to contact you, not to put her in an asylum. I did everything I could to persuade her. I had a long internal struggle about whether or not I should give in to her request. But finally, I left, hoping that she would change her mind. That she would come and join us here. I was naïve.

The man takes a pause.

"For Madeleine, her children were the most important thing," he says. "She put her career on hold to raise them. She was totally committed to provide them with the best life possible, and she was doing great. But she blamed herself for Ariane's death. I kept telling her there was nothing she could have done to change the outcome, that she had nothing to feel guilty about, but she wouldn't listen."

"How is your son doing right now?" Jack asked.

"He doesn't know yet. When I heard the phone ring, I asked him to leave me alone for a moment. I don't know if I'll tell him. When we'll get back, the three of us will have a big talk. Decide what we are going to do. I'll call her when I can. Try to convince her again to come with us. But I know Madeleine. When she sets her mind on something, no one can convince her not to do it. Even if she had been forcibly institutionalized, she would have tried to commit suicide upon her release, or a few months later, when the thought of Ariane would have been too painful. There was no room for negotiation. She thanked me for understanding. I said nothing, but I didn't understand. In fact, yes, I did, but I didn't see how she couldn't foresee a way out."

Jack gets the impression that Légaré tries to find a meaning for all this. A justification that would make sense to him, that would justify his choice. Jack can't help him. He knows that he would have dragged his wife to a psychiatric hospital hoping that adequate medication and treatment would make her realize that suicide wasn't the answer. At the same time, who is he to judge his actions?

He looks at Abygaelle outside; she's daydreaming. He feels sorry for her. She had the misfortune to have the worst case the province has seen as a christening in her new role. He wouldn't wish that on his worst enemy. Knowing that the killer was free and could strike at any time was unbearable for an experienced investigator like him. He can't imagine what it's like for a rookie. They do their best to support her, to reassure her, saying they've seen nothing like this before. That they wouldn't do any better in her place. That they are as helpless as she is.

She says they are sweet to try to make her feel better, but she can't shake the feeling that she's incompetent. If she only knew how inept everyone feels about this. No one related to this matter is sleeping well right now. It's not the first time this has happened to him and it certainly won't be the last. But with age, Jack has found a mechanism to get over it. To desensitize himself.

It's a matter of survival.

He joins Abygaelle in the parking lot and puts his hand on her shoulder. He guesses words are useless. She stares at the tree in front of her, as she awaits the answers she seeks from it. She smiles wistfully, not taking her eyes off the huge ash tree. It reminds her of the tree next to her uncle's cottage where they used to go when she was just a young girl. The leaves dancing in the wind make her feel nostalgic.

Jack knows she needs consolation, but sometimes a simple presence is enough. Being there for each other. She hasn't brought it up with him, but she's confident that Jack will never give up on her. He will be there for her, no matter what. They will succeed or fail together.

They are a team.

Through her desperation, Aby feels for the first time that she is officially part of the group. It fills her with a fullness that churns deeply in her soul.

77

The image quality is mediocre.

It stuns Jack that with all the technology available, commercial security cameras are so terrible.

"It's obviously him," Abygaelle says.

There is no denying it. Indeed, they see Maxime Fauvette at the convenience store checkout where he claims he went, picking up bread and cigarettes. He is even smiling at the cashier when leaving. The outside cameras capture him acting casually. He doesn't linger in his car; he doesn't use a cell phone.

"If he spoke with the killer," Aby says, "it wasn't then."

"He doesn't look like someone setting up the murder of a woman," Murielle says, sitting in the back.

"How does someone planning a woman's murder look like?" Jack asks with a bit of sarcasm he doesn't shield.

"Stop it, buddy. You can see he's laid back. He buys what he needs, gets back to his car and quietly vanishes out of the camera's reach."

Jack shrugs.

"He's a smart guy. He knows about the cameras. He played

his part perfectly. There's no evidence that he didn't stop and call the killer off camera. Nothing proves he didn't call the murderer from home and that his wife isn't an accomplice."

"Indeed," Abygaelle says, "but nothing shows the contrary either. And as we are in a lawful society in which people are innocent until proven guilty—"

Jack brushes the argument aside.

"Yes, and that's often a load of crap. How many times have we seen someone we knew committed a crime go free?"

"No system is perfect," Murielle says. "But it's the best we've got, and that's what we've got to work with. You know that more than anyone."

Jack takes offense.

"What's that supposed to mean?"

"You know what I'm talking about, Jack," Murielle says, unfazed.

Abygaelle looks at them, not grasping what they are referring to. There is an underlying account that she ignores. Murielle waves her off, but Aby thinks she understands. She noticed Jack is quick to jump to conclusions. Perhaps it has hurt him in the past. Who knows? But since both are on edge, Abygaelle deems it inappropriate to dig any deeper.

"So what do we do?" She says.

"I'm sure he's not as innocent as he claims," Jack says after thinking of a logical answer. "But then again, we have nothing on him. We need to keep looking. We will find something."

Abygaelle smiles. It's her way of hiding her despair.

"You see, I don't think he's involved in any way," Murielle says.

"Of course you don't," Jack says, hissing.

"Listen, you saw how he was the other day." Murielle says. "Out of control, vindictive. It took several minutes to calm him down. You even had to play tough to get him to sit down and answer our questions. He was panicking"

"The more you talk, the more you increase my suspicions."

"Murielle is right," Abygaelle says.

Jack sighs with irritation.

"What are you, a tag team?"

"I'm persuaded that the killer is cool and methodical," Aby says. "I'm sure he controls his emotions. He has made no mistakes yet. At least none that have cost him enough to get caught."

Murielle nods approvingly at every word Abygaelle says, much to her veteran colleague's chagrin.

"The image I have of him, is someone who would speak in a low tone. He would be affable and collaborative. He wouldn't put a target on his back like Fauvette did."

It hurts Jack to admit it, but she has a point.

"When I saw Maxim lose control the other day, he struck me as far more frightened than anything else," Abygaelle says. "Afraid of being blamed for something he didn't do. What I saw in his eyes was not arrogance, but confusion and fear. His account of the evening when Maryse Letarte died is consistent with what we saw on the video. His wife says he was with her, so impossible for him to have pulled the trigger himself, because he was about fifty kilometers away from the crime scene, a few minutes before it happened. Instead of agreeing to that, we're coming up with far-fetched theories to pin the crime on him."

She pauses, weighing her every word.

"Like him or not, we still have to prove he had something to do with the murders. It's simply not feasible right now. And he'd be the first serial killer to get someone else to do his dirty work."

Jack falls back in his seat. Nothing makes sense anymore. The killer is like a slippery eel. Every time you think you've got him, he slips through your fingers.

78

Abygaelle struggles more and more with obstacles getting in her way. Every time she thinks she's finally on a strong lead, hope slips away like sand in an hourglass. The lack of mention about the list firm Focus Marketing on Internet search engines is a sign that it no longer exists.

"Indeed, it has been closed for two years," Murielle Bouchard confirms.

"Of course," Abygaelle says, irritated.

An overwhelming discomfort weighs heavily on her heart as she reflects on what Stephane Ranger said at the restaurant. She's sorry she acted so cavalierly with him, but she needed to be alone with Roland. She wanted to get it off her chest, disclose her wish to come back, to quit homicide, that it wasn't for her. Many scenarios were running through her head regarding his impending response. Roland would understand, Roland would object, Roland would be bitterly disappointed.

Of the three, the last would be insufferable. It would break her heart to disappoint him. The thought of it brings tears to her eyes. She had to cough it all up, because Ranger popped up like a rock in a shoe. Aby only wished he would wait for her after lunch. She couldn't have known he had something important to drop off. Out of the blue, was this list for real? Or was it the product of a young man's troubled mind? There was only one way to be sure: to corroborate the information he provided. Find this so-called marketing agency and see what comes of it.

And even if it exists and that all this is real, it is still circumstantial. Yes, it looks suspicious that the victims' names are all on the list, but Annie St. Onge's is not, nor is Pete Morin's. In any case, she doesn't have the option of ruling out any leads. Even if they can get a hold of legal documents from Focus Marketing, it won't be easy to track down those who worked in this focus group. Two years is a long time. Chances are slim that anyone will remember anything. Who would recall a pointless research project in a prison?

No one.

She uses her connections in various organizations to find one of the company's former executives, Raymond Garrison. She learns he now lives in San Francisco. Semi-retired, he made his fortune in marketing and communications. He was vice-president at Bell Canada and worked as a minister for a few years in the government of Daniel Johnson junior.

A man who has had a brilliant career and has surely earned the right to enjoy his life in California. If he was honest, of course. Life has made Abygaelle cynical. Successful business people have too often succeeded by exploiting others through shady shenanigans. But she was careful not to jump to conclusions. Especially since he was rather jovial on the phone. He fully enjoys retirement by playing golf twelve months a year. He takes some contracts here and there to distract himself, but mostly to share his experience with Silicon Valley startups.

Young people inspire and excite him. He's seventy-one, but judging by his voice, she'd have bet he was in his fifties. Focus Marketing was his baby. He started the firm with his wife. They grew to become one of the three largest marketing firms in

Montreal. His voice gives away his pride. His wife is working in the garden right now. It's her new passion. She has the most beautiful garden south of the bay, according to him. No grocery store can compete with her zucchini.

They're big and luscious.

Aby gets to the key aspect, emailing him a scanned copy of Stephane Ranger's list. Garrison smiles as he recognizes the Focus Marketing logo on the document header. He's sorry that he doesn't remember this particular piece. It's unfortunate, because he had hoped to help the friendly policewoman. Quite normal, Abygaelle reassures him. With the size of the company, he couldn't have been aware of all the ongoing campaigns. It wasn't exactly a high-paying contract anyway, stuff you delegate to interns. Garrison gave her the names of three former directors from the firm, just in case. Perhaps they will know. He suggests she begin with Mathieu Boulerice; he handled focus groups. If he doesn't remember, chances are no one will. He doesn't know how to reach him, though.

"But I'm sure you'll find a way to reach him," he says, a hint of mischief in the voice.

As she hangs up the phone, Aby is still thinking about the word Garrison used to describe his wife's zucchini.

Big and luscious.

She's not sure if that term really applies in that context, but she understood what he meant. That's what words are for anyway, so in that sense, he nailed it. If the zucchini were as lovely as she pictured them, his wife is excellent at it. Her hope quickly dissipates when Mathieu Boulerice claims he doesn't remember the Archambault prison case. Let alone who had sponsored it. He apologizes and mentions the same thing as his former boss. If he doesn't remember, no one will.

Abygaelle hangs up and curses. Will they ever have luck on their side in this damn case? For her first investigation, she could have stumbled upon a passionate crime in which the husband is undoubtedly the murderer. But no, it had to be a million piece puzzle you must crack without looking at the original picture. "Deal with it, girl," she shouts. She feels weary and discouraged. She has to face the facts, she's only good at busting sexual deviants. It's not too bad after all. She doesn't know what she was trying to prove by chasing killers. And more importantly, to whom?

She doesn't have what it takes to play in the big leagues. She'll tell Picard to hand over the investigation to someone else, stop wasting everyone's time, and get back to Vice. She misses Roland anyway. She should never have left. She slept on it, hoping it was some kind of twist of fate that Ranger showed up just as she was about to tell her mentor she wanted his old job back.

It was all smoke and mirrors. Her first instinct was right.

She had no business in homicide.

79

Stephane takes his morning stroll. He forced himself to get out of his apartment at least once a day. He usually takes the same path. It takes forty minutes to complete the circuit, and he gets home feeling much better. Fresh air is pleasant for him and helps him sort out his thoughts.

He reported to his boss earlier in the day that he was taking a leave of absence. He doesn't have the strength to work with all that's going on in his life. One hundred percent of his energy needs to be focused on tracking down the killer, backing up the cops and ending this carnage. Even though his manager gave him a thinly veiled threat that his job might not be there for him when he comes back, he knows he'll return to it. He's always helped him so far, and he appreciates him. Stephane never skipped a day of work, or almost. He's performing very well. There is no argument not to hire him back.

In fact, when he told him the reason behind his request, his boss mellowed and understood. A shrill noise startles him. Two large men emerge from a car blocking his way.

"Hello, Stephane," a deep voice says from inside the car.

It's Marko Gusarov.

He feels his legs go limp like rags. Shit, they know. Gusarov pats the back seat next to him.

"Let's go for a ride."

Stephane has seen enough gangster movies to know that people rarely come back from these rides in one piece. He quickly weighs his options, but the most logical thing to do is to comply. The two big guys will easily stop any escape attempt. Stephane notices their guns inside their coats. He gets that his quest ends here. That he won't be able to fulfill his promise to Ariane. He grasps all the irony to perish at the hands of organized crime just as he quit dabbling in this filthy world. He who had no trouble with them when he was a full-blown criminal.

Gusarov's face hardened.

"Get in, I won't tell you again."

The two bodyguards approach him. He has no choice.

A deathly silence submerges the cabin of the vehicle, heading for an undisclosed location. He must not, under any circumstances, confess that he broke into the café and gave the list to the police. Deny until his last breath, even under torture.

If he confesses, he's done.

"Can you tell me what I'm doing here?" he asks without expecting an answer.

Gusarov gives him a look that makes him shiver. He doesn't insist.

He sees his survival odds diminish as the car turns off onto a dirt road, far from any civilization. It's obvious they'll kill him and dissolve his body in a bin full of acid or something like that. He bows his head and sobs silently. Not because he will die. He doesn't really care about that. But because of Ariane, because of his broken oath.

He puts it all on the table.

"I don't care if I die. I don't know what you want from me, but I have done nothing wrong. All I wanted was to find my niece's killer. I understand you won't let me. But that's what I would have liked to do. And then I was leaving this rotten world, anyway."

"Excellent," Gusarov whispers.

Unknowingly, Stephane is relieved he confessed about that. It was the plain truth. They must have sensed it. Find the killer, then disappear. That's how he planned his next move. They slow down as they approach an empty barn. A huge, old-fashioned structure with no door in the front. Stephane probably wasn't even born the last time it was being cared for. The two in front get out of the car, and one of them opens Stephane's door. He gets up despite the fragility of his legs. He wants to go out with dignity. He won't beg them for mercy or cry like a coward. He will stand up straight like an oak tree and face his fate like a man.

The two behemoths lift him from the ground and drag him into the dark barn. Gusarov follows. They throw Stephane hard on a chair in the middle of the barn, illuminated only by the sun's rays seeping through the many roof cracks. On the ground, there is old hay and dry mud. Stephane looks around, but there is no way out. His only option would be to flee from where they entered, but he won't take three strides before they shoot him in the back.

"Stephane, I think you know why we're here," Gusarov says in his thick Russian accent.

Stephane pretends he thinks about it, then shakes his head.

"Don't play dumb with me. I'm not in the mood."

"I don't know what the hell—"

Gusarov's fist crashes into Stephane's jaw and he falls backwards. He is dazed. One goon picks him up and sits him back down on the chair. Gusarov says something in Russian, and the man goes into the car and comes back with a long rope. Stephane tries to recover his senses while the man binds him with the rope and sticks him against the backrest.

"So, I ask you again. Do you know why we are here?"

Stephane opens his mouth very wide. His jaw isn't broken. He looks at Gusarov.

"Apart from my complaint that your coffee tastes like piss, I don't see. Is that why I'm here? Look, don't take it personally. I have a particular taste. You shouldn't make a big deal of it."

Gusarov smiles, but his eyes have a demonic look. Another right jab, this time on Stephen's nose, makes him lose consciousness for a few seconds, until he receives a strong and icy water jet on his face. He opens his eyes and sees one man holding a large hose aimed at him. This isn't the first time they've done this, he thinks.

The pain is unbearable, but since he's been in many fights before and wasn't what you'd call a defense whiz, it's not a pain he ignores. He can take it. A bullet in the head, on the other hand, is a different story.

"Get to the point," he says after coughing up some blood. "Tell me what you want from me so we can have an intelligible discussion."

Gusarov looks at his companions, laughing. He says something in Russian, and they all laugh. Stephen smiles.

"What did you say? It sounds funny. I'd like to laugh too."

Gusarov comes closer.

"Of course, here is the translation."

He hits him with a powerful punch on the skull, making him fall on his side. Once again, the three of them laugh. Gusarov overhangs him.

"Do you get it? You think it's funny?"

Stephane hears what he says, but as if he is far off, and speaks in a muffled voice. A long crackling sound fills his ears. Someone lifts him up to straighten him out. His head falls forward, dragged by gravity. Blood flows from his mouth. His head hurts and he feels nauseous. He spits out blood.

"What did you do with the list?"

Stephane has a long shiver that runs down his spine. He doesn't answer. Gusarov put a finger under his chin to lift his face so he can look at him.

"What did you do with the list?"

"What list? What are you talking about?"

Another punch, but Stephane feels nothing anymore. He is semi-conscious. As if his face were anesthetized.

"The list," Gusarov shouts.

"Buddy," Stephane replies with difficulty, "I'm telling you, I have no idea what you're talking about."

Gusarov sighs angrily.

"If you don't tell me what you did with it, I'll kill you."

Stephane spits out a good deal of blood.

"You'll kill me, anyway."

Stephane ears the cracking sound of a gun being cocked. The barrel is pressing against the top of his head. He closes his eyes, ready to accept his fate. But it doesn't come. Instead, he takes another round of punches to the face. But he sticks to his plan. Since he has no strength left, dying will be most welcome.

After about an hour of this travesty, in which Stephane almost confesses a few times, he seems to be completely elsewhere. He inhabits his body, but feels nothing anymore. He only wants to die. To be put out of his misery like a sick dog. He begged Gusarov for it several times.

Finally, the beating stops.

"Well, we won't get anything from this bastard," the mobster says. He points his gun at Stephane.

"Last chance."

Stephen shrugs it off.

A gunshot, then everything goes black.

80

The next morning, Abygaelle daydreams for several minutes at her desk. She isn't in the mood to work. She still plans to quit homicide. She is used to running away from difficulties; she has done it since she was a child; she bails out when there is a hitch in her love life, but it's the first time this poison grabs her by the throat in her professional life.

She can't help it. She would like more than anything to disappear, to be forgotten. But she can't bring herself to drop everything amid the investigation. Although every fiber of her body urges her to take off, to say "Fuck that, they'll work something out, I don't give a rat's ass", she can't do it.

She owes it to Ariane and the other victims; she owes it to Jack and Murielle, but above all, she owes it to herself. She wants to look the killer straight in the eye when she catches him, defeats him, and knows he can't hurt anyone anymore. Her departure will have to wait. In fact, she dodged the subject during her lunch with Roland. Then came Stephane and the list.

She goes over the names and cusses at her bad luck. She is

more and more convinced that this is the key. It is not just a coincidence! Call it women's intuition. There are too many pieces that don't fit in this scenario. Why would a marketing firm ask a question like "Who would you save from a shipwreck?" How does it help? Who benefits from knowing that? What company would use these answers to draft a marketing plan? If only she could talk to someone to confirm her suspicions.

Aby contacted Sami Nazri, who worked in business development for Focus Marketing, but he wasn't part of focus groups at the time. She left a half-hearted message on Martine Choquette's voice mail, the last name on her list.

This will go nowhere.

Ranger knows no more about the list than they do, other than its origin. Although she is grateful for his contribution, it bothers her to think he could have been killed in the Russian mafia hideout. If they had killed him, their chances of cracking the case would have suffered. Especially since he seems central to the whole affair.

Ranger mentioned he recalls the focus group moderator was beautiful, which caused quite a stir among the inmate population. They hadn't seen such a stunning woman in the flesh in a long time. She was with an older man who didn't faze anybody. There had been a lot of questions on many more or less relevant topics, including this question about the ten people to save in a shipwreck.

An hour later on the phone, a soft, shy female voice confirmed she worked at Focus Marketing. Abygaelle gets excited when Martine Choquette mentions that she vaguely remembers this marketing campaign, because it was her first experience in a clink. It had impressed and terrified her at the same time; it was, in her own opinion, an uncanny experience. Of course, she was aware of the salacious comments about her from the convicts, the perverted looks from wild animals looking at her like a piece of meat.

She thought it was fascinating to survey over fifty inmates for half a day. They were genuinely happy to be sought for their opinions on a variety of topics. After a few minutes of saucy remarks, they were fully cooperative. They lost interest in her and were completely committed to the process. Focus Marketing was not very enthusiastic about this study, which they considered banal and insignificant, but Martine wanted to get something concrete out of it. That's why they asked her to do it, as she was just starting out in the business. It showed how little regard the agency had for this assignment.

However, she was delighted by one sponsor's interest in a series of tests that she had designed especially for him. Especially the topic of the ten people to be saved from a shipwreck, as this was one of the client's requests. It was quite peculiar. You don't probe these kinds of individual questions. It's worthless from a marketing angle, and it's not statistically useful. But if someone is willing to pay a lot of money, why not?

When it was time to submit the findings, Martine produced a report with standard deviations and a compilation of the results, but the client only wanted specific inmate responses. Reluctantly, she had given him the files at the behest of her boss, as the man was providing to pay a generous premium for them. She felt that this was unethical and violated the respondents' privacy. She never saw him in person, phone or email did everything. She recalls that he spoke in a confident tone, seemed extremely intelligent and had authoritative words. The type you can't refuse anything.

The three investigators go over the latest information, trying to make connections with what they already have, but other than the strangely high number of dead people on the list. There were none. Annie St. Onge wasn't on it. Marco

Légaré, who is on the list, is still alive, so are Madeleine Légaré and Jacques Légaré. Jack is skeptical about this. There are too many gaps. Too many blurs. But Murielle and Abygaelle can't help but think that there is a connection to all these crimes.

They still have to find out what it is.

81

Abygaelle got another coffee, sitting by herself in the audiovisual room. This is her fourth coffee in the last two hours. She re-reads all the documents, re-listens to all the audio and video tapes. There's a flaw somewhere. Why can't she figure it out?

She flips through her chat with the murderer again. His lecture on death penalty puzzles her even though she understands the logic. Jocelyne Lamoureux's testimony, the only one to have physically seen the killer, can't really help. Aby is frustrated, but she understands; she was in shock; the shooter was relatively far removed and wore a baseball cap. Nothing in what Jocelyne mentioned gives her anything substantial to fall back on other than that he had blue eyes. But since then, Aby has had a doubt. How can Jocelyne possibly know for sure the shade of the killer's iris if he was at a distance and in the shadows? Perhaps her imagination plays tricks on her.

And with colored contact lenses now, it's easy to fool the naked eye. Maybe that's why they glowed in the distance? A reflection on the lenses? Anything is possible. That's why

Maxime Fauvette can't be ruled out right away, contrary to what they thought.

"Think, Aby. Think. What's wrong with this picture? It's right there in front of you. Focus."

She watches William Primeau's video conversation again. She listens to his words peppered with tiny British intonations in his voice, wonders if she too would develop an accent living so long abroad. It's very subtle, but it's there. In the pronunciation, in the transitions.

The young man is striking, and not just physically. True, he is handsome. His fine features highlight the softness of his face, of his beautiful azure eyes, like those of his father. A hypnotizing blue. He gave himself up without hesitation. His answers were direct and straightforward. No hesitation, he looked at the camera with force. The way he laughed at his father's name as a potential suspect showed how little respect he has for him.

How can he claim his father is weak? And how can he be so sure he didn't kill anyone in Vietnam as a sniper? Is that what Raymond told him and he believed it?

Abygaelle examines her own reactions, what she feels when she sees young Primeau. After a few minutes, she has to face the facts; he tells it like it is. This boy has an undeniable natural charisma.

So captivating.

She opens her internet browser to uncover everything about him, even if she has already done it several times. She scans the pictures of his wife Heather again; the couple is worthy of Hollywood red carpets. They have style. She is beautiful. She could be a model or an actress. Aby has done some research on her as well, but everything she uncovers is related to her Foundation. Nothing about a previous career as a model. Nothing really before the creation of the foundation. As if her public life began at the same time as her relationship with

William. She wonders how they met, what their deal is? Does Heather know about Nathalie? Or has he kept it from her?

William is a model citizen. No criminal record, dual British and Canadian citizenship. Neither of his passports show any recent travel to Canada. Obviously, he uses his European passport when he travels outside North America. Aby assumes there is a reason for this that she doesn't know about, especially with his European travel. It's easier to get through customs in the European Union.

She is less fond of Maxime Fauvette. This man with a peculiar look didn't leave a good impression when they met. Something fishy about the look in his eyes, but he has a rock-solid alibi for all the murders except Annie St. Onge's.

Then she thinks maybe it was staged? William is extremely intelligent. What if his alleged hatred for his Raymond, his bias to portray him as weak, is just a cover-up? To take the pressure off him? She plays the interview again, focusing on the part where he talks about how certain he is of his father's innocence.

She plays the interview repeatedly. She focuses on his eyes, the muscles of his face. She knows some of the liars' pantomimes: overuse of sarcasm or humor, discomforted by moments of silence, small rigid movements, gestures that don't match the speech, parasitic moves like scratching his face, arms and neck.

She doesn't notice any of this.

Either he's telling the truth, or he's a great actor, or he's a psychopath. Granted, psychopaths are charming, she thinks. She should not look for things that don't exist. There are many lovely people in life who aren't psychopaths either.

Let's not jump to conclusions.

Abygaelle sighs. She hears William snicker again as Murielle mentions the possible liability of his father. Nothing pops up. He really hates him, has no respect for him, pays him no credit. But why? Why so much hatred? What happened between these two? Perhaps the key resides there. Then, like an epiphany, Abygaelle stares at the screen and her heart races. She gets up from her seat, keeping her eyes on the image.

It is impossible.

She reviews the scene, and yes, there it is. She tries to find a logical reason for what she sees, but there is none. She plays the sequence over and over, and William's eyes darken more and more. Abygaelle's imagination plays tricks on her. William's face remains unchanged. His eyes are joyful and frank. But she feels deceived. Perhaps that's why her mind senses a shift in William's physiognomy, so that it matches up with what she senses. She watches the sequence several more times, but needs to face the facts.

William Primeau has deceived them.

She storms out of the room. Murielle and Jack have to see this.

82

Jack is staring at the Focus Marketing list. His discomfort is palpable. He can't get past the disgust in the action of the man responsible for these horrors. To plan in such fashion, years in advance in a Machiavellian way, is beyond his comprehension.

There are so many sick minds in today's society. He can't decide whether it is worse or better than before. After all, they publicly executed people in the Middle Ages. Nevertheless, he feels that collectively we aren't going in the right direction.

Jack has often been angry to the point of extreme aggression, but never enough to seriously consider killing someone. Let alone once he calmed down. So how can someone carry that level of hatred and rage around for all these years without fading? Never moving on. It takes a deep despair to wallow in this state of mind day after day, month after month.

Year after year.

He still feels a twinge of sadness upon seeing Ariane Légaré's name at the top of the list. He knows one should not rank victims or tragedies, but humans being what they are, it automatically occurs to us. Whether or not we like it, we are more upset when a hunter poses next to a deer or a lion than next to a pig. We are more infuriated by the murder of a child or an elderly couple than by a white, middle-aged man. By definition, people feel more sorry for Ariane's death, an attractive young teenager, than for François Lavoie, even if he wasn't the criminal he was. Nature is like that, and it would be extremely hypocritical to pretend otherwise.

"Jack, follow me."

Abygaelle whizzed past him, putting on her Provincial Police coat. She is pale as a ghost.

On the way out, she talks about Stephane Ranger, who was found lying face down in an old barn. Someone shot him in the head. He is on life support in intensive care.

"Did our killer finally elect it was his turn?" Jack asks.

Abygaelle shrugs. She knows no more than he does.

"But there are still names on the list," Jack says.

At the hospital, things aren't looking good for Ranger. Abygaelle doesn't believe that their killer is the culprit. First, his skull did not explode like Ariane and Marc-André's. Second, they found no wooden queen at the crime scene.

"Is it only me or we spend too much time at the hospital?" Abygaelle asks. "Madeleine Légaré, and now him."

"That's pretty much our reality," Jack says. "Several suspects or witnesses have the annoying habit of ending up here."

Then, Abygaelle has a revelation. She leads her colleague out of the patient's room.

"The mob."

"Huh?"

"I'm sure the Russian mafia is behind this. Ranger broke into one of their facilities to steal the list. Sounds like the M.O. of organized crime, right? A remote location, a bullet in the back of the head?"

Jack ponders for a moment and agrees that it's entirely plausible. Abygaelle is tormented. Jack massages her shoulders.

"I'm going to stir some shit up, Jack says. I know a high-ranking member of the Russian mafia. I know where he hangs out."

"Maybe it's not them either," Aby says.

"Maybe not, but they had the list."

"You can ask them about Marko Gusarov. According to Ranger, he is in the middle of it all."

A clamor emerges from Stephane's room. Nurses run in and out.

Abygaelle and Jack rush in immediately.

83

Jack and Murielle follow Abygaelle in an audiovisual room. They wonder what their junior colleague has discovered to be so excited about.

"Watch closely."

The video shows William Primeau talking with Murielle. He replies to her questions with aplomb and energy. Aby fast-forwards for a few seconds.

"Right there, see?"

Jack and Murielle approach the screen.

"Do you see anything," Jack asks his old friend.

"No," she answers. "What are we supposed to be looking at, Aby?"

Abygaelle sighs. In her excitement, she rushed things a bit. She rewinds the recording to the beginning, where Murielle appears trying to activate the video conference sound.

Jack chuckles.

"Quit it, big boy," she says, irritated.

Abygaelle pauses the video.

"Look at the time on Big Ben."

"Quarter past four," Murielle says.

"When did you have the videoconference?"

"It was ten o'clock and change, our time."

"Ten o'clock in Montreal means it was three PM in London."

Murielle thinks. Is it possible that there was a problem with Big Ben that day?

"That's what I thought, so I kept watching the interview, but this time focusing on the image behind."

She fast-forwards the footage again, then pauses it.

"What time is it now?"

"Almost half past four."

"Perfect," says Abygaelle. "Keep your eyes on Big Ben now."

She restarts the video. After a few seconds, Murielle and Jack finally see what Abygaelle wanted to show them.

"Son of a bitch," Jack rages while standing up abruptly.

The clock displays again 4:15 pm.

"That's not all," Aby says by rolling back the image to the moment just before the time switches. "Look at this red car."

In the lower left corner, a car is about to make a left turn. Abygaelle starts the video.

"Abracadabra," she says after it magically disappears from the screen.

"A looping image," Jack says through clenched teeth.

Abygaelle smiles.

The two sergeants-detectives try to understand. So he wasn't in London that day, but wanted to make it appear that he was. But why? His passport doesn't show any travel to Canada. If he wasn't in Canada, why pretend to be in London?

"That's what we have to find out. Where was William Primeau, and why this staging?"

"We aren't done talking to him," Jack says.

"Let's look at his holdings. Does he have a private plane, could he have used it to leave and come to Canada without going through customs? I don't know, through a clandestine airport?"

"It's still slim evidence," Murielle says. "A video on a loop, big deal. It doesn't give us much to go on."

"Agreed," Abygaelle says. "But he's moving rapidly up on my suspect list. Because as the saying goes: if it sounds like a duck and it walks like a duck—"

"It's a duck," Murielle says.

"I want to talk to his business partners, his wife, his nanny, his dog, everyone," Abygaelle says. "I want to know his schedule for the last few months. And most importantly, I want us to set up a call with this comedian."

84

Vadim Gregorov is sitting on his favorite bench at Skara, along with his two bodyguards. He is seated at the far end of the restaurant, with his back to the wall so he can see customers' comings and goings. His henchmen are sitting on either side of him, also scanning the place, ready for anything. Gregorov is glad that he recruited these two former KGB agents for his close protection. They are well trained and have a lot of experience protecting politicians and oligarchs.

He is discussing one project from one of his legal businesses on his cell phone. For mob-related talks, he speaks in Russian and in a coded language. As much as possible in person or from a secure line. He would never discuss this kind of business on a mobile device. The number two guy in the Montreal Russian mafia didn't get this far in his late sixties by acting like a clown or a hothead. He's serious and extremely strict. He doesn't allow any misbehavior from the most influential group members. The rest are replaceable. They can eliminate them with little consequences.

The organisation favors keeping a low profile. They maintain cordial relations with law enforcement, and avoid drawing the public's attention. Spotlight is bad for business. The mafia has traditionally championed the shadows. Gregorov notices a tall individual entering the restaurant. A man he knows well and would rather not hang out with. He watches him, hoping he's only here by chance, to get a meal, preferably to take out. He is quickly disappointed watching him walk towards them.

"I'll call you back," he says to the man he's talking to before hanging up.

He takes another bite of his luscious lamb chops, pretending he didn't see Morris approaching.

"Vadim, my friend," Jack says, standing at his table.

The bodyguards get up to block his path and slip one hand into their jackets. Gregorov signals them to sit down.

"Exactly, stay put, little doggies," Jack says in a dry tone while sitting down in front of the mobster.

"Mr. Morris," Gregorov says in a strong Eastern European accent, "to what do I owe the displeasure of your presence?"

Jack Morris unbuttoned his coat and looked him straight in the eye. He always liked the russian's passive aggressive character.

"I think we have a problem, buddy."

"I don't have a problem with anyone."

"If you don't know already, I suggest you talk to your people."

Gregorov looks at Jack sternly.

"Why don't you get to the point, Detective Morris. My lamb chops are getting cold, and I hate to eat them cold."

Jack dips his hand into his inner coat pocket, alarming the bodyguards in the process, and pulls out a photo.

"Do you know her?"

"Of course," he says. "How can anyone ignore her? Ariane Légaré is on the news every day."

"She's your problem."

"I don't think so."

"You don't, eh? Tell me, Vadim, since when has the Russian mafia been in the business of murdering children?"

Vadim Gregorov gritted his teeth. The question had its effect.

"What are you talking about, Mr. Morris? We don't kill children. Is this a sinister joke?"

"I hope it were," Jack says, "but unfortunately it's quite true. Does the name Marko Gusarov mean anything to you?"

"Let's stop playing games, Mr. Morris. I know that you know Mr. Gusarov very well. If you wanted to question me, I would have preferred you to invite me to your splendid police station, renovated at great expense by the taxpayers, instead of insulting me by interrupting my meal."

"This is not an interview. If I had ordered you to do it, there would be a record of us together in an official context. And the public would wonder why the police are meeting with a high ranking Russian mafia official, while someone randomly shot people in the past weeks. But in this case, we're just two old friends chatting."

Gregorov's sharp gaze is locked on Jack's. He really doesn't appreciate the tone of the conversation, but Jack doesn't care.

"As far as we know, Marko Gusarov not only provides ammunition to the person responsible for this massacre, but also information that allows him to locate the victims. He provides the address of their residence, where they go, where they work, that kind of thing. Vadim, you have blood on your hands. I need to single out who the killer is, and fast."

"We have nothing to do with this, detective."

Jack snickers evilly.

"You probably don't know this Vadim, but I am a project guy. I hate routine, that's why I enjoy working on projects so much. And you see, I'm lacking some right now because apart from these gruesome murders you're somehow involved in, I have nothing to keep me busy. And when I find a project that interests me, I go at it like a pit bull over a bone."

Gregorov looks at him quizzically.

"Why are you telling me all this?"

"Because you don't want to be my next project, Vadim. You don't want me to mess with the Bolshevik mob."

Gregorov smiles.

"Bolshevik? Mr. Morris, haven't you heard of perestroika?"

Jack stands up.

"You have forty-eight hours," he says. "After that, you become my new project. I'll come to your house with warrants and we'll snoop around. In the current climate, with corpses piling up, including that of the girl, I'll have no problem getting a judge to sign an order for me, even if it's for looking through your mother's underwear."

"I wouldn't recommend it, she's long dead. I'm not sure you'll like what you find," Gregorov says with a sneer.

Jack stays put.

"Forty-eight hours."

"I'm telling you we have nothing to do with this, but you'll hear from my lawyers. I will not let you bully us like this."

"Talk to Gusarov. If you don't know what I'm talking about, he does."

Jack walks over to leave, but stops.

"By the way. Stephan Ranger is dead and a little bird tells me you have something to do with it too. You guys look bad in this, Vadim. Very bad."

Gregorov waves him off. Jack complies by greeting him. The Russian stuffs another lamb chop, then stops.

"Call Marko and tell him I want to see him," he orders one of his bodyguards in a voice trembling with rage.

Marko is known as a loose cannon who doesn't always do things the right way. Gregorov warned his organization against him when they promoted him. His love for drinking, money and women makes him vulnerable, but still he got his promotion. If he had anything to do with it, if he really did what Morris claims he did, he's no better than dead.

"Mudak," Gregorov says, taking another bite.

85

Abygaelle watches the news reports about Stephane Ranger's death. They broadcast the clip several times in all the media outlets. Ariane's uncle also gets killed. Is this the act of the serial killer? And above all, when will he stop?

This family really suffered.

The media show Stephane Ranger's footage from an interview a few weeks earlier discussing the death of his niece. Madeleine's husband blamed him for wanting the spotlight, which he categorically denied. Commentators are coming up with various theories. The shooter did it; the mafia did it; he owed money to pawnbrokers; he killed himself, etc. Police refuse to disclose too much at this time. The press is pushing for details and more transparency, claiming that the public deserves to know.

The hospital where he was treated before his death will not discuss confidential patient records. The communications department is redirecting journalists to the police pending the autopsy report.

The press will have to wait.

"We don't want to impede the investigation. The less information we disclose, the better for the investigation," Abygaelle said laconically when chased by a horde of reporters camped outside the precinct.

Deep down, the media gets it. Police have already mistakenly picked the wrong suspect once. Social networkers are not bothered to make fun of their huge press conference with Raymond Primeau as a punch line. Stephane Ranger's murder is another bizarre chapter in this bizarre tale.

Aby is disgusted with the way the media is working up the case. They seem to forget that people died in all this, including a young girl. These vultures are hungry for more, too happy to sell newspapers and airtime. It's the nature of the beast, she knows it, but she has a hard time coping with it. She also didn't like how they raided neighbors and friends of Annie St. Onge after her death. Or how they practically set up camp in front of the Primeau house, forcing Monique to go into exile in England with her son, and her husband to hide out God knows where.

What will they do with Ranger's death? Dig up his mother from her grave to check if she'd have a comment on the matter?

"I understand," Murielle says, "but they have a job to do. I know several journalists, and most of them are okay. Sure, there are some rotten eggs in the bunch, but I can say the same of all trades, including ours."

She's right, Aby thinks, but she still thinks it's a shame. Although she worked with the media when she was in vice, she never had to deal with this kind of pressure before, and she never had to deal with this kind of thing. As they wheeled Ranger out of the hospital on a gurney, his body fully covered with a burgundy sheet, she heard the whispers of the crowd. Several onlookers witnessed the scene. They sold video images captured by cell phones to the news organizations. In one image, she is standing next to Jack Morris in dismay. She wonders what the killer will do now that the tables have turned. She hopes that this will persuade him to stop, and they can finally track him down and bring him to justice, without fearing more deaths to come.

But nothing is for sure.

Why kill Lavoie and Gagné in the mid-2000s, take a long break, and then do it again?

Questions that remain unanswered.

86

Murielle and Jack spoke to some of William Primeau's colleagues. They all corroborated that he is regularly on business trips. Especially in the last few months. They also confirmed he wasn't at the office on the dates given by the cops.

But as one of his associates said, chances are you'll find him on a plane rather than at home in London. It's a long shot, Abygaelle thought. If people had seen him at work the same day one murder took place, they could have eliminated him as a suspect, but he was away. The firm declined to release the names of the clients William saw unless they had an international warrant. They jealously protect their confidentiality. That would be very difficult to get, according to Murielle, on circumstantial evidence, let alone on mere supposition.

Even though he has agreed to talk to them again, this time on the phone, William Primeau is much less cordial than during the first meeting.

"I don't appreciate all the questions you're asking about me to my family and friends. I don't understand your fascination with me. The success of my business is based on my credibility.

With your inquiries, you are propagating suspicion about me among those around me and I can't accept that."

"Indeed, we got the warning from your lawyer not to bother people about you anymore."

"Exactly."

"You still claim that you haven't come to Canada in the last few weeks?"

"I told you the first time. That hasn't changed."

"It's been over two years, right?" Abygaelle says.

"Right. So what do you want from me now?"

"Mr. Primeau, were you in London when we first interview you?" Murielle asks.

William thinks for a few seconds before answering. He feels the question is peculiar.

"Of course, why are you asking me that?"

According to his passport, he was in England at the time, just back from Thailand a week earlier.

"Because your London background was a fake."

They perceive the discomfort in William's giggle,

"That's right. I apologize. I'd rather show you this than the ugly wall behind me. The view from my office is nice, but I was at home. You would have seen a disappointing plaster wall. Is that what tipped you off?"

"Yes," Abygaelle says. "Let's just say that if you have nothing to be concerned about, we think that this staging is odd."

"I admit I have a particular sense of humor," he says laconically.

"If it was a joke," Murielle says, "it was a bad one."

"It's a matter of taste, Ms. Bouchard."

The police goes through his whereabouts over the past few days. He answered with annoyance. Yes, he spends a lot of time in Brazil, India and Thailand, three emerging markets he's explores. He spent time in some friends' apartments. He refuses to give out their names.

"Didn't you hear me when I told you about not involving my friends and family anymore?"

Abygaelle gets it.

It sure raises doubts when the police ask about you. People jump quickly to conclusions. However, she has homicides to investigate, and she doesn't care about people's sensitivities, whom she may offend in the process. But when you deal with someone who can afford the best lawyers in the world, you ought to be careful. She also feels that the DCPC's legal department is very nervous about this matter. They'll need sound evidence. Eyewitnesses or confirmation that he was in Canada at the time of the murders.

Something specifics.

Before hanging up, Primeau told them he would no longer answer their questions unless forced to do so by a warrant.

The next morning, Charles Picard called Abygaelle to his office to tell her what she already knew. To leave William Primeau alone if she didn't have solid evidence against him. The order comes from higher up. Aby passed the message to Murielle and Jack. The latter burst out in anger.

"How many people have to die before we can work freely? Can they stop obstructing us?"

Abygaelle tries to reason with him, but he won't listen. He's going to give Charles Picard a piece of his mind.

"Not a good idea, big guy," Murielle says.

He grabs his coat and leaves abruptly. Murielle looks at Abygaelle and rolls her eyes.

"He always had a flair for the dramatic, that one. His theatrical nature."

Abygaelle smiles, but deep inside, she challenges William Primeau's story. His explanation about the looping background didn't convince her. There's something fishy.

"You see, it's Maxime Fauvette I can't stand," says Murielle. "His arrogant attitude, his shit-eating grin. He stares at you as if you weren't worthy of talking to him. There's something in his eyes that gives me the creeps."

"You're right, he seems dishonest," Abygaelle says, "but not so long ago, we all thought Raymond Primeau was the killer. We need to stop guessing around and trust our senses, and find reliable evidence, either for them or for the actual killer, if it's someone else."

Abygaelle is right, Murielle thinks. Because we have nothing tangible to hold on to, we settle for twisted narratives. But in the end, it doesn't add up to anything concrete. Jack can get furious all he wants, but it helps nothing. There is a loophole somewhere.

They just need to find it.

87

Abygaelle has been hiding in her office since the beginning of the day. She watches the flock of journalists waiting for her outside, at the bottom of the police station's stairs. She has peaked through the dusty white Venetian curtains several times, as if it would make them go away suddenly. Besides Stephane Ranger's death, reporters learned his sister tried to kill herself.

Charles Picard strongly advised her to speak to them. The communications department no longer knows what to do to keep them at bay. A simple scrum, and everything will be back to normal in no time. She wonders what they want from her. You're in charge of the investigation, remember? That heresy that got you on an endless roller coaster in your first few minutes at homicide? Aby says to herself as she sighs in discouragement.

"Talk to them already," Murielle says in a reassuring tone. "The longer you wait, the more anxious you get. You remember your class presentations at school?"

Abygaelle looks at her suspiciously.

"Yes?"

"Remember how stressed you were as your classmates took turns and yours was coming up? And how liberated you felt once it was over?"

"Yes," she giggles, "but that's a long time ago, you know."

"Tell me about it," Murielle says, mischievously.

They both laugh. Abygaelle relaxes a bit. She's right. Might as well strike while the iron is hot. She grabs her jacket and heads outside. The deafening rush of journalists and freezes aggravates her.

"Everyone calm down," she says in a firm voice. "If we are to have an intelligible conversation, we must go one question at a time. Yes, you," she says, pointing to a lady with a stern look.

"What can you tell us about Madeleine Légaré's suicide attempt and her brother's murder a few days apart?"

"It shows how distressing it is for people to lose a child or a parent tragically. For Mr. Ranger, we are still working to understand what happened."

"Do you think the same killer got to him?"

"I doubt it. If it is, he switched his modus operandi. Not the same caliber of bullet, fired at close range."

"So who killed him?"

"That is what we are trying to determine. The investigation is ongoing."

Abygaelle knows she'll use that all-purpose phrase often in her new role.

"Do you have any new clues about the killer?"

"The investigation is still ongoing. We have some interesting leads."

"How does Ranger's death impinge on your investigation?"

"Of course, we are very sad about the whole proceeding. We wish things had turned out differently."

"What about the rumor that it was all related to a rape back in the nineties?"

Abygaelle is caught off guard by the question, how do they know about this?

"As I said, we're looking at several scenarios."

"Why does the killer drops wooden queens at the crime scenes?"

"You'll have to ask him."

"Are you still confident that you can catch him?"

"More than ever."

"Why did Raymond Primeau confess to the murders if it wasn't him?"

"We are still trying to figure that out."

"Will you charge him with obstructing a police investigation? After all, his false confession wasted valuable time."

"Indeed, it is not ideal, but at that time, we had reason to believe that what Primeau was saying was genuine. Now, whether charges will be pressed or not, I refer you to the DCPC."

"Are you really sure he didn't play a role in this?"

Abygaelle stares at the reporter as if he were stupid.

"Raymond Primeau was in prison when Maryse Letarte was shot."

"Yes, but maybe he killed others first and his actions inspired some attention-starved copycat?"

Abygaelle has a condescending smile.

"You watch too much late night movies, sir. Thank you for your questions, that will be all."

She goes back inside, ignoring the hubbub coming from the mass of journalists.

When people are coming up with far-fetched theories, it means the subject has been covered.

88

Anxious, Jocelyne Lamoureux bites her nails as she sits in the provincial police precinct's waiting room. She glances furtively at her daughter, who is busy on keeping within the lines of a drawing provided by the front desk agent using orange and black wax crayons.

Jocelyne almost changed her mind three times since she arrived, and dragged Maripier outside to her car parked in front of the building. She packed the minimum of her and Maripier's belongings to hide somewhere in Lac-Saint-Jean as soon as she is done with Abygaelle Jensen.

She hasn't slept in the last several days, using her nights to weigh her options. On one hand, the assassin's recent visit tormented her, petrified by his threats. But on the other hand, she can't stand for this monster to go about his everyday life with impunity, without consequences for his wicked action. It doesn't sink in.

She couldn't live with herself, couldn't justify her cowardice to her daughter. She would not be capable of looking at herself in the mirror. She can't tolerate staining the memory of the man of her life like that. She can't condone the retention of information that would help catch this sicko.

But most of all, she's pissed out of her mind.

Furious that he drugged Maripier, that he broke into her home, that he threatened her, that he threatened her child, the apple of her eye. She can't forget what he did to Pete, his terrifying grin after he savagely murdered him. He should have killed her, too. He had plenty of chances. Now it's her turn. He had the nerve to show her his face, so sure of himself, convinced that she would never dare turn him in.

He's in for a goddamn surprise.

She's here to tell all, and then disappear until they get a grip on this creep. Even if it means escaping for years. Even if it means they have to change their identity. Abygaelle Jensen greeted her with a warm smile. It helped her decompress. Someone took care of Maripier and moved her to another room. Jocelyne wanted to speak freely and spare her daughter horrible details. Words that a child her age should never hear. It took her several minutes to put her thoughts in order. Where to start? How not to look like a total fool and look solid? Not assume she had come up with all this, even if she has doubts since the situation was so surreal.

Abygaelle talks about casual stuff right off the bat so Jocelyne would relax. She offered her a cup of coffee, which she refused. After a few minutes, the detective renews her offer, and this time, Jocelyne accepts. Abygaelle feels overly excited since she has learned that Jocelyne Lamoureux wanted to meet her again. She has a good feeling that her doubts will be proven. She gets an idea as she watches the coffee slowly brew in the percolator and asks an assistant to do her a favor.

Who knows?

She goes back into the interview room and slides the cup of coffee towards the woman. Jocelyne relaxes after a few minutes of talking about the weather. She rubs her hands together and starts her testimony. She describes in great detail what she saw upon entering her house; the assassin sitting next to her sleeping child with her head on his thigh, the threats to her life and that of her daughter, the insult he made by showing his face to her for a few seconds in a trickle of outside light, his steel-blue horrifying gaze. But this time, she snapped a mental picture of his face. It was quick, but she had time to imprint every feature of his features in her mind.

Every wrinkle, every skin pore.

Her photographic memory that helped her get out of trouble so many times in college may save her life. Because Jocelyne doesn't believe that Pete's killer will leave her alone at all. He could come back anytime and say, "You know what? I changed my mind" and kill her and Maripier. There's no way she will spend the rest of her life with that Damocles sword hanging over their heads, constantly looking over her shoulder. They say the best defense is offense.

So she strikes bravely with all her might.

She flinches when someone knocks on the interview room door. She's on the edge.

Abygaelle gets up and talks with a woman in the doorway for a few seconds. She comes back with a file, which she puts down beside her. Jocelyne carries on with the details of what they talked about that evening.

Abygaelle takes notes.

"Give me as much detail as you can about his face. What does he look like?"

Jocelyne smiles.

"Of course. He's a guy in his thirties or forties, piercing blue eyes, neatly combed brown hair, straight, perfect teeth. A handsome man, but totally terrifying. No empathy in his eyes."

Abygaelle's heart is beating quick. She does everything in her power not to get carried away, but she is now convinced that it's him. His description is similar. She notices her own hands shaking.

Calm down, for God's sake.

She excuses herself and leaves the room to drink a large glass of cold water, but mostly to collect herself. She looks for Jack and Murielle, but they aren't around. After a brief moment, she returns to the interview room.

"Aren't you afraid he might go after you?" she asks at once.

"Yes, but I've planned to sneak away for a while."

"Can you tell me where you are going?"

"I'd rather not. The fewer people know, the better my chances are to succeed."

"I understand. May we reach you on your cell phone?"

"I won't have a phone either. I know how cell towers work and how you can pinpoint someone in a fairly specific area. I'll leave you my email address."

"I'll have our technician show you how to use a VPN. Someone could track you down using the IP in your email header."

Jocelyne smiles shyly, though Abygaelle detects in her grim gaze that she is resolved to hide out, even though she has done nothing to deserve it.

To flee from a monster.

They discuss more about Pete's murder, to see if she has any extra elements that she would have missed the first time. Aby discloses that they found a burned van a few hours after the crime that the killer could have used. Jocelyne is still angry at herself that she didn't memorize the license plate number of the SUV. She instantly ran to her dead husband, lying in a pool of blood.

"Perfectly normal. You were in shock. Anyone would have reacted the same way."

The words didn't have the desired effect. Jocelyne

Lamoureux was still devastated. Abygaelle takes a sheet of paper from her file, showing only the back of it.

"Mrs. Lamoureux, let me try my luck. I want to see if you can identify the killer in the set of pictures I'm about to show you. Do you feel up to it?"

Jocelyne is stunned. She didn't expect them to have a lead yet. She nods. Abygaelle slowly flips the page to display six color photographs. They show six white men, about the same age, of similar build. She watches Jocelyne's reaction. She initially scans the photos, but then her eyes freeze. Her face hardens, and she clenches her jaw. Then, her eyes fill with tears and she buries her face in her hands, sobbing. Abygaelle tries to keep calm despite her excitement, like intoxicated. She recognized him from the list, it's undeniable. Abygaelle doesn't need her designation of the murderer's picture. She already knows that it's him.

When Jocelyne comes back to her senses, she points with no hesitation at the one Abygaelle was hoping for. William Primeau. Except that there is a major problem. According to his passport, Primeau hasn't set foot in Canada for two years.

This is the last mystery she needs to solve.

But Jocelyne Lamoureux has just confirmed her doubts. Abygaelle still doesn't know how she'll prove Primeau is the serial killer they've been looking for, but she'll figure it out.

She always does.

89

Marko Gusarov is in trouble. He just got off the phone with a senior member of the organization who told him to report to the headquarter immediately. The tone of voice of his interlocutor wasn't reassuring. Despite his past mistakes and good deeds, Gusarov has always kept his nose clean and made no trouble. Sometimes he works on his own on extensive projects. He isn't doing this to be deceptive, but rather to prove he can take initiative and deserves consideration for an influential position in the organization.

He is highly ambitious, but he also has a rebellious streak; an explosive cocktail that can blow up at any moment. Is that what is happening? He thinks through, but he can't find a serious enough offense that requires a disciplinary meeting at the top. However, as he walks down the stairs to the basement of the Miralov restaurant, Gusarov realizes that there is something rotten in Peteroff's kingdom.

Sitting at the back of the room, Vadim Gregorov stares at him with a disdainful look. Next to him are members of the staff and a few bodyguards. Some people regard Gregorov as the most ruthless Russian mafia boss. He has life and death power over everyone except the boss. Gusarov would have rather met the godfather. There is something creepy about Gregorov's features. He's dressed as if he were going at the Oscars. A dark suit with subtle gray stripes, a neatly fitted tie and gold cufflinks. Coal-black hollow eyes, prominent and pointed cheekbones, thin pursed lips that point downward. As if this man had never smiled once in his entire life. There is a peculiar smell in the Miralov's basement.

Pungent and damp at the same time.

A smell of death.

Gusarov can hardly go down the last steps, his legs are so limp, he has a lump in his stomach. This isn't the time to act defiant. The answer is yes to everything. Whatever it is, you apologize. Your goal is to get out of there alive and as soon as possible. Gregorov doesn't beat about the bush. He is very upset. The discussion is in Russian. In fact, it is more like a lecture.

He is furious. What is this story the police are spinning about him? Is he colluding with the murderer who killed that child? The Russian mob was so happy to have the public's attention focused on something other than their business, only to learn now that they are up to their necks in it? Unbeknownst to him on top of it all?

Gregorov's heavy, powerful voice echoes off the walls of the gloomy basement room. Then he looks at Gusarov in silence, obviously waiting for answers to his questions. Gusarov swallows his saliva, takes a deep breath and starts talking:

"One of my contacts at the port of Montreal called me one day to tell me someone was looking to buy weapons and ammunition," he says in a precarious voice. "We first spoke in a darknet chat room. I didn't ask him why, he offered me a lot of money so I took the business opportunity. Then he told me he had a list with names on it and he needed me to use contacts to give him some intel on them. Follow them, record their habits, their address, their car, where they work, etc. He was paying a lot of money for each person."

"Was Ariane Légaré on this list?"

Gusarov lowers his head. Gregorov slams his fist on the table, startling everyone around him.

"How could you be so stupid? You know we don't mess with civilians, let alone children. When you saw who it was, that it was a teenager, what did you do?"

Gusarov wrings his hands.

"I stopped looking and told him I couldn't keep up with him if he was going to go after that girl."

"And?"

"I slipped, revealing where she was studying, but he would have found her by himself, anyway. He didn't need us for that."

"What do you think, I'm stupid?" Gregorov says, leaning his elbows on the table.

"No, I don't."

"You want to be a smart ass?"

Gusarov says nothing.

"Who is your client?"

"I don't know."

"I beg your pardon?"

Gusarov lowers his eyes.

"I don't know."

Gregorov sits up straight and looks around at the other eminences grises, stunned.

"Are you saying that you cooperate with someone who knows who you are, but you don't know who he is?"

"He doesn't know who I—"

"SHUT THE FUCK UP. He knows you're with us. Even if he doesn't know your name, he knows how to get to you."

Gusarov didn't see it that way at first. Indeed, he was extremely careless. He should have found out who the man was, so that he could have a hold on him, so that he could keep him in check if things went south, so that he could blackmail him if necessary.

He cut corners because of greed.

He should have stopped when he saw the girl on the list. Even if he didn't know what his client wanted to do with the information, an easy rule of thumb would have clarified that he didn't want to buy them flowers. That he would shoot them with the gun and ammunition he had sold to him.

"What else?" Gregorov says stiffly.

"I issued him a false passport and set up some trades for him. With aliases and contacts."

"Is that all?"

"That's it."

"Are you sure?"

"Yes, Mr. Gregorov. I'll fix everything."

The elderly man raises his hand to interrupt.

"You've done enough already. Get lost for a few days. I'll fix it. And Marko? I don't want the police to come to me ever again because of you. Is that clear?"

Gusarov nods yes.

"Is that clear?" Gregorov repeats in a loud voice.

"Yes, Mr. Gregorov. I'm sorry."

The senior member of the organization looks at him for a long time silently and then waves him off.

Two days later, Jack Morris sits down at the very same table in front of Vadim Gregorov as before. The same bodyguards are sitting in the exact same place, and Gregorov is eating lamb chops again.

"I hope you have good news for me, Vadim."

Gregorov looks at him sternly. Obviously, he doesn't like this situation, and he doesn't appreciate the detective's company.

"First, let's get things straight," Gregorov says calmly. "We had nothing to do with it. It was not an order from us. We have a soldier who acted alone, thinking he was doing the right thing."

"Gusarov?"

Gregorov proceeds without answering.

"We will settle this matter internally. As a sign of good faith, what I can tell you is that your individual is using false papers, and a false passport under the name of Richard Béliveau. If you find Béliveau, you find your man."

"There must be several passports in that name, don't you have more details?"

Gregorov nods to one of his bodyguards. The latter slides a paper towards Jack. It contains a series of numbers and letters on it, which the detective assumes to be the passport number.

"Don't you have a picture?"

"You'll find it easily."

"Is that all?"

Gregorov nods.

"Not much."

The mobster looks at him with an amused look.

"I won't do the work for you. Now fuck off."

Jack smiles. He'll immediately go back to the office to tell Abygaelle about his finding. He gets up to leave.

"One more thing, Mr. Morris. Never threaten me again."

Jack observes him blankly, then leaves the restaurant. The look on Gregorov's face chilled him to the bone. He knows what he can do, and even though the Russian mob has never historically targeted Montreal law enforcement, Jack isn't stupid enough to think he's untouchable. There is always an exception that proves the rule.

These are the risks of the job.

Normally, one prefers to keep one's nose clean with the upper echelons of the mafia, but sometimes you have to stir the pot. It's a risky gamble, but in this case, it could be the last piece of the puzzle they're missing. Abygaelle stormed out of the police station. She scribbled down the name and number Jack gave her and was on her way to see what she can find out from Customs.

There is only one person on her list of potential suspects who would need a fake passport.

William Primeau.

If it's him, that was the proof she needed since the beginning.

90

Upon hearing the news about Stephane Ranger's death, William Primeau felt completely fulfilled. He relished the image of Ranger moments before they shot him like a rat. He wished he could have been there. It was finally over. He got away with murder like a boss. No one knows who he is. The killing will stop as drastically as it started. This will join the list of things no one understands, of mysteries that won't be solved.

William will go back to his regular life, his mind at peace for the first time since Nathalie's death. He will carry on in osmosis with his mission, which he has accomplished much better than expected. He has made very few mistakes, and they prove not costly. He turned out to be far too smart for the police in this province of idiots. Like the Zodiac Killer, his legend will stand the test of time and fuel passions. People will spend decades struggling to figure out who he was. What was the significance of those wooden queens?

He feels a twinge of sadness when he thinks about Jocelyne Lamoureux, about what he did to her. But at the same time, her husband was a criminal. It was written in stone that he would end up like that at some point. He called his wife to tell her he needs to extend his travel a little more than he had planned. He will be back in two days. He stops at a St-Hubert restaurant, the one that brings back his childhood the most. That time when he was happy.

Before all this.

He has wiped out everything linking him to the murders. His good old Dragunov in pieces at the bottom of the St. Lawrence River, the remaining bullets thrown in a huge ice hockey bag in a garbage can several kilometers away. He threw his BMW down a ravine and took a cab back to town, dragging a backpack with clean clothes. He felt like Bruce Banner walking solo with his bundle after turning into the Hulk. He closed his post office box and his bitcoin account. He would so much like to hug Nathalie right now, to stroke her hair, to tell her he kept his promise, that he took care of the last scumbag who soiled her. He wished she knew Heather. They would have gotten along so well.

He had not felt such a plenitude since his youth. For the first time, he breathes thoroughly, as if someone had lifted a tremendous weight from his shoulders, as if that sheath of bitterness that was squeezing his chest had vanished. It had been a long time since he had woken up in the morning and not felt enraged. Without this huge fury that poisoned him for what seemed like an eternity. They say that time sorts things out, and in most cases, it's true. But sometimes time fixes nothing and you have to take matters into your own hands.

This would be the last time he would use his fake passport. He doesn't know who Richard Béliveau is, but he's grateful. Unknowingly, he has been a key part of a quest that is bigger than life.

Once in London, he will shred it over a glass of champagne. That will be the end. For real. The last vestige of a mission he handled like a general. He will resume his life with his wife, his son, his partners and his clients. It will all be a regrettable relic.

Of course, it would have been easier to kill Ranger, but it wouldn't have satisfied him. When he killed Eric Gagné, he thought it would free him. But the grudge still clutched him by the throat. The same empty feeling. The day after that piece of shit death, he wasn't any happier. He was still in pain. It hadn't brought him the satisfaction he expected. That Gagné only felt pain for a few seconds before he died was nothing compared to the agony that had been ripping him apart from the inside out since Nathalie's death.

Her absence was unbearable. And to realize that no one would pay for the harm done to her, for crushing her soul so much that she saw no other way out than to hang herself in the family garage. He couldn't live with that. He would want people to see that he tried to move on, that he wanted to prevent it from coming to this. He wasn't a monster once, just a brother shattered by the murder of his own flesh and blood. His heart disintegrated every time he heard a song that brought her to mind, every time he saw a location, smelled a scent, and she emerged before his very eyes, almost materialistic. It was like a stab in his chest. He left Canada because it became untenable. At least in another country, there would be nothing to remind him of her. He could have some semblance of a normal existence.

Then one day, he had an epiphany. It struck him. The only way to get revenge was to take an eye for an eye, a tooth for a tooth. Not to cope with the death of a single loved one, but of many. The ultimate pain. The one you can no longer bear. The one where death is like a deliverance. When it becomes a sweet way out. For William, there was no worse pain than the kind that would drive you to kill yourself. His creativity subjugated him by the precision of his execution.

The death of Ranger freed them both. He would have wished he killed himself, but the result was the same. The original plan was to only target his mother, the first person on the list he had arranged for a few months earlier. He bought a van cash and parked it for a few days near his target's residence. He knew she visited her asshole son at the same time every Tuesday afternoon.

Habit kills.

William followed her a few times to study her habits and patterns. He noticed that the old lady only drove in the right lane, between 90 km/h and 100 km/h, probably worried about missing the exit to the prison. He picked out a hot spot on the service road where cars were slowing down momentarily. By parking at an angle of about twenty degrees, he was in the best position. He drilled a hole in the metal door behind the van, and he made himself a tripod to secure his rifle to the floor of the vehicle. He set up a makeshift bench to steady himself. He mounted a modified scope and welded into another hole higher in the door, giving him an ideal vantage point of oncoming traffic.

In theory, foolproof, the strategy had been more challenging to execute than expected. On his first attempt, a vehicle driving by obstructed his angle close to his target. It wasn't until the fourth attempt that he finally had the perfect opportunity to shoot. At first he thought he missed, as the vehicle kept going, passing him by several meters before veering quietly to the right and falling heavily into a ravine. William got back behind the wheel of his van and slowly approached the car to make sure she was dead. The sight of flames devouring the car's interior quickly soothed him within seconds. He was back on the highway, flabbergasted by his good fortune.

The fire would get rid of evidences.

The media reported the incident in a blurb on their website. The charred body of the victim would complicate the coroner's task. William was proud of himself for his efficiency and went about his daily life as if nothing had happened.

Two years later, he learned Ranger was out of jail, had a job, and had taken charge of his life. William wanted to confirm this information for himself when he visited Quebec a few days later, prior to a business meeting in Toronto. He followed Ranger to a party and was beside himself to see him having fun and laughing with his friends. If his mother's death was torturing him, he was keeping it well hidden.

So if one death wasn't enough to wreck his life, he'd keep going until he couldn't see any hope. So that he would understand the pain of losing a loved one. There was surely someone on that list he loved to the point of devastation.

He had gone back to the drawing board. To become more efficient without exposing himself. The van would slow him down and eventually they would track him down. Everything was thought out, surgically planned and executed with a master's touch. He had to improvise a few times, but even in those moments, he couldn't have done it better.

After looking out the cabin window and seeing the city of Montreal slipping away under the plane's wheels, he chugged a gin and tonic and closed his eyes. The smile of satisfaction on his face said it all.

Mission accomplished.

91

Marko Gusarov is sitting outside the hideout house where he lived for the past week. Even though the place is remote, he can still see cars passing in the distance. He spends his time listening to TV, radio and watching birds. He received a call from someone in the organization earlier today. This is the first time he spoke with one of them since he got here. They asked him to go with two other guys he knows on a "courtesy" visit to a client late on his payments.

Gusarov did this type of mission before. He intimidates people with his massive built, even though he's small in stature. He's known as the tank in the organization. He feels he's too important for the mafia to be disposed. That they already involve him in a new mission this soon is a proof of that. Normally, it takes longer to get back into action in these situations. It can take months. Gregorov surely realized that he didn't intend to embarrass him. Should he had known his contact would kill a child, he would have told him to fuck off.

Gusarov rehearsed his speech several times in front of a mirror before he went to the Miralov. He needed to be concise and look honest while answering Gregorov's questions. This man is a living lie detector. He can spot a drop of sweat in your underwear just by looking at you.

So you might as well be totally forthcoming.

He paces around the house, impatient for something to happen. The mafia has a few houses they use to keep people hidden while they figure out what to do with them, or just so they can get lost. He wonders how the police reacted to the information Gregorov leaked. He listens to the news on television every night, but nothing has emerged yet. The only thing reported is that the killer is still at large, and that there are no new leads. Gusarov believes the police know more than they are telling the media. This is a good thing.

They too have their omerta.

The house is bland. An ordinary one-story bungalow in a remote village. No neighbors around, a large lot serviced by landscapers. He gets some fresh air and groceries, but he must alter his appearance as much as possible. He pulls his cap down to his ears, turns up his jacket collar, wears sunglasses, and a fake mustache. He felt ridiculous, but it is the right thing to do. It's a far cry from his plush, nearly two million dollar home in Montreal's north shore. He was told that someone would take care of it until he gets back. He has no wife or children, so it's less of a hassle for the mafia to deal with than having to take care of a family and explain what's going on.

Gusarov requested hookers from time to time, but he's still waiting. They have forbidden him to call anyone, and although he's eager to get in touch with Daria, he's walking on eggshells. Now is not the time to disobey a directive from the big bosses. He must act perfectly, avoid attention.

Be forgotten.

He hears the characteristic sound of a car driving on gravel. He pulls a curtain and recognizes Pavel Lunchenko at the wheel. He's with another person he had met before, but doesn't remember his name. He puts his jacket on and leaves to join them.

On the way, he's relieved to sit in the backseat. In the front seat, he would be opened to an attack from behind, with no chance to fight back. He's unarmed. He doesn't need one for the job at hand, but he would still prefer to have one on him, just in case.

The two men sitting up front discuss the last time they saw this man. He peed himself; they recall laughing. The mood is casual. The weather is great, this is the last vestiges of summer. Trees already display their colors, the fields are dry.

He savored the warm wind blowing across his face as he walked from the house to the car.

He couldn't wait to put it all behind him. He's been doing a lot of thinking and decided to shift his entire attitude, to work on altering perceptions. He needs to keep to himself for a while, do what he's told, and take no initiatives. Then he can start doing everything in his power to move up in the organization and, above all, in the eyes of his bosses. No more sneaking around to prove himself. He got the message loud and clear. They do not appreciate such actions. So he will concentrate on growing his business and being a good and trustworthy soldier. He presumed that Raymond Primeau was his mystery buyer by looking at his picture in the media. Even though his contact never exposed himself, the swagger in Primeau's face is consistent with the idea he had of him.

He didn't bother to look at his photo before handing it over to the guy in charge of creating his fake IDs. Gusarov doesn't waste his time with such petty stuff. He has full confidence in his suppliers.

They never betrayed him.

He knows how it works. One singles out a homeless man around his client's age, gives him a good sum of money for his ID cards and forged documents by changing only the picture. Then, you have a legitimate passport application. It doesn't get much more secure than that. The homeless are far too busy surviving and doping to care. It works every time. No one's going to complain about it.

Gusarov is resourceful and has multiple connections that his organization has taken advantage of several times. They even praised him for developing a network of such reliable collaborators. His connection at the port of Montreal is one of the union bosses. His contact with counterfeit documents is the best in the country. The hitman he uses is so efficient that he thought for a while he was behind all these murders. But he had no motive to do that. This guy is a ghost. Not the type to taunt the cops. Not the type to intentionally leave stuff at the murder scenes. Only an amateur would do that, it's so "show-off". A professional killer would never waste his time with this kind of nonsense.

Only a raving lunatic looking for attention would.

When the car slows down after venturing onto a country road, Gusarov gets it. No need to paint him a picture. His courtship with Gregorov didn't work out, and we won't have another chance to make up for it. They won't provide him the opportunity to get his act together.

No chance to prove his worth.

He realizes he overestimated his importance in the organization, or underestimated the impact of his actions. As a Russian proverb says: the dead can do no harm. He looks down as the car comes to a complete stop. One man opens his door, silently staring at him. Marko could plead for his life, beg to be spared, but that would be acting like a coward.

That's not how he wants to leave this world.

If he can't do anything to boost his stock while he's alive, he can at least ensure that his legend lives on; be remembered as a man of courage, a man who stood tall in the face of death.

A man of honor.

He struggles to make his way towards the field, stretching as far as the eye can see. His legs are limp, but he keeps his composure. He got tears in his eyes.

Like a courageous man. Like a man of honor.

The two individuals follow him in reverent silence, then one of them orders him to halt. Gusarov looks at the sky and wonders what's in store for him up there. He doesn't fear death; he fears suffering. Make it quick. These guys are pros. If they wanted to torture him before killing him, they wouldn't have taken him out to a country field.

He isn't afraid to die, he just thinks it's a shame he couldn't redeem himself. Not being able to reestablish his image and prove his worth. He killed Stephane Ranger for his impudence, and his arrogance to presume he could deceive him.

Like a rat, Ranger handed the list to the police and told them they were involved. Another blunder on his part. He couldn't figure out who tipped him off, how he ended up in his restaurant. How did he know? Mistakes here and there created a butterfly effect, and that's why he is here today, living out his last moments in bright sunshine.

He gets a tap on the shoulder. He understands what that means. He kneels in the dry grass, clasping his hands behind his back. He's annoyed that his legs are still shaking. He wishes he were more sturdy, but he's terrified. His senses are on high alert to the point that he can hear his tormentor's arm rise to his head.

It's true that everything happens in slow motion and you see your life flash before your eyes. Gusarov thought it was a romantic myth, but it's real. His mother is there, clear as day, even though she died twenty years ago.

Still beautiful and radiant.

He's proud of what he accomplished with the cards life dealt him. Poor family in a miserable country. The former Soviet Union was not kind to those of his kind. But he got out of it. As if in a state of grace, he feels a strong inner wholeness. Suddenly, he's at peace. He leaves for a better world; he hopes.

A flock of small sparrows flies away at the sound of the gunshot resounding through the sky. Two more shots, then silence. Lunchenko looks at Gusarov's body and takes a few seconds to collect his thoughts. How sad it is to lose a soldier, no matter the circumstances. Rest in peace, comrade. You served the cause well. You died with dignity, courage and honor.

After burying the body in a hole previously dug for that purpose, they drove a few kilometers, then stopped on another deserted road.

A car coming from behind parked in front. The driver opened the trunk and took out two cans of gasoline. Lunchenko signals to his colleague to do what he needs to do and sits in the front passenger seat.

Several minutes after leaving the scene, he still sees the thick, opaque smoke rising into the sky through his rearview mirror.

Black as Marko Gusarov's soul.

92

Life is back on track for William Primeau. It's back to normal for him, and for Heather, it's one of those precious moments she cherishes so much, when he's home. He has been away so much in the last few months, working on important matters that he hopes will pay huge dividends.

To celebrate his homecoming, Heather invited some of his closest friends over. Her husband appreciates their company, and it's been ages since they've spent time with them.

Monique has been in London for a few weeks to flee the pressure from the media, literally camping outside her house. William is proud to introduce her to his friends, and they all attempt to speak French and use the translation app on their mobile phones. She's glad she finally came along for the ride. She hasn't spoken to Raymond since his time in prison. She will in due time. She is now the one unwilling to talk to him. She will have plenty of time to figure out what happened. Why was he accused of these monstrous crimes, and why, according to rumors, did he confess to being a serial killer?

But not tonight.

William is right. Away from the house, she can clear her

head and think straight. Put all these things in perspective. Tonight, Monique wants to enjoy the party with Heather, her son, and his friends. She came to know her daughter-in-law and likes her very much. She realized she didn't steal William from her. He moved to London before he ever met her. It's not fair to hold that against the girl. To her astonishment, she enjoys it here, close to her son in this beautiful villa, a short drive from London, the magnificent. Heather is helping her learn Shakespeare's language, and she's making substantial progress, even though she thought she couldn't learn another language.

Heather prepared a succulent turkey with mashed potatoes and brown gravy, which everyone is raving about. It's a family recipe passed down from generation to generation. William is relaxed. He's laughing with Andrew, a friend from Oxford. His wife Elizabeth is equally charming.

Enjoying a respite alone in the kitchen, William relishes the moment. It's been a long time since his mother looked so happy and radiant. He shook his head out of spite, thinking about Raymond's attempted sacrifice. This ridiculous suggestion to blame himself for murders he didn't commit. No one understood what he was getting at with his phony confession. As usual, he didn't think it through.

If this was a way to redeem his cowardliness, it was useless.

As if William would let him take credit for everything he achieved. Succeeding in what he was too weak to do himself, wallowing in pathetic excuses and sanctimonious speeches. Through the kitchen porch, he watches the guests discuss, and he smiles. He's not used to this freedom. His life was on hold for almost two decades, his mind compressed by torment, unable to fully appreciate each cheerful moment.

He lives again for the first time.

The chapter is closed. He carried out his plan to perfection and everything has gone according to plan, or nearly so.

Heather is radiant. She has a special aura since the start of her pregnancy. She's overjoyed with the impending arrival of their second child.

How beautiful she is.

As always, he gives her all he can. Even though he pockets several million pounds a year, she is the workaholic of the two. What she has accomplished in such a short time with the foundation is nothing short of amazing. He sometimes felt guilty about his double life over the years. An alternate reality that would devastate her if she found out about it. To figure out that she was living with some kind of bloodthirsty monster all this time would be enough to kill her. They will never talk about his mission. It's a secret he'll take to the afterlife.

The only way she could find out is if... no, that's impossible. She will never know who he really is. No one will. She'll have to deal with the image he fabricated.

Launching his own business gave him the flexibility to move around as he saw fit. No one dared to question him. Everyone trusted him whenever he pretended to travel for business, to meet clients. That's what his associates told the police and Heather whenever they questioned them, they had no reason not to believe him. Technology allowed him to work from anywhere in the world, so he wasn't deceiving, except for the part where he claimed to be at clients' offices.

Just to have been able to achieve his mission, it was worth it.

He's amused to think of those assholes running through the murders one by one with no clue as to what happened. He didn't leave a single trail, other than the wooden queens. He was methodical and thorough. The perfect crime exists. He proved it time and time again.

Stephane Ranger is dead, and life is now worth living. He's at peace with his actions. He never thinks about his victims. He speaks to Nathalie every day. She can now rest in peace. At her funeral, William vowed to avenge her. He kept his promise. His word is his bond.

He kept a photo of them when they were teenagers in his wallet. They were so close, like the two fingers of a hand.

"Honey, could you bring more wine, please?"

Of course, my love. Not only that, but I'll crack open a bottle of 1959 Chateau Laffite I kept for a special occasion. There is no better time than now, with the most important people in my life around me. Even if only he knows what they are really celebrating. He climbs upstairs where he built a huge, perfectly weathered cellar.

His wife calls out to him again.

"Honey?" says Heather as she walks halfway up the stairs towards him.

"Yes, I'm coming."

"Look out the window, there's something strange."

Something strange? William puts the bottle down on the old secretary near his desk, and heads for the window overlooking the long gravel path leading to his home. The path emerges from the forest about eight hundred meters from his house.

Initially stoic with the spectacle unfolding before his eyes, he suddenly feels his legs give way under him as he grasps the magnitude of what is happening. He maintains just enough of his composure not to break down.

He turns to her, in control.

"Go back downstairs, don't panic. I took care of everything, you'll know what I mean soon. Don't forget how much I love you," William says.

She didn't quite comprehend why he said that, but he once again instructed her to return to the guests downstairs. She complies. There is no point to contradict him when William is speaking in such a tone. He returns to the window, secretly hoping it was just an illusion. But it's real. He counted twice:

there are seven Scotland Yard cars coming in a hurry, leaving a vast cloud of rock dust in their wake.

He smiles.

The smile of the defeated. He was mistaken. For a rare moment in his life, he has misjudged a situation. Abygaelle Jensen is more cunning than he thought. He would like to know how she found out about him. But he'll never know. He must grip to a dresser to keep his balance. He thinks about the unborn baby and Edward. Never in his worst-case scenarios did he think he would make two orphans.

His brain is running at a hundred miles an hour. What did he do wrong? What gave him away? It certainly wasn't Jocelyne Lamoureux, there's no way she would have put her daughter's life in danger. Suddenly, the mistakes he minimized looked precarious now. Revealing his face to Jocelyne, the hospital, the roadblock, the wooden queen he dropped after shooting Pete Morin.

Seven cars.

This is the treatment saved for the heaviest, most twisted, most dangerous criminals. William feels genuine pride. Tomorrow, his name will be all over the world news. People will wonder how a young, powerful fund manager with unlimited potential could have done it.

Fortunately, he has it all figured out. He will control the message. He wouldn't stand for media meddling. He shot a video justifying his behavior, as well as wrote a letter. They will understand. Heather will too, he hopes.

And Edward. And the unborn child.

He has little time to think. He must put the emergency plan into action, as he has rehearsed it in his head hundreds of times. He goes back to the secretary to pick up a steel box. He dials the combination with his adrenaline-shaking fingers, and picks up its contents: a CD labeled "For Heather, my love" on which there is a recording with his instructions and justifications. The kind of ridiculously dramatic video that opens with "If you're listening to this, it means I'm dead..."

Sometimes you have little to no choice.

He says that he has arranged a large sum of money for her in a trust. He gives details of his funeral arrangements, explains why he went after all those people and takes the blame for all the murders listed in the letter he will leave on his desk. Eric Gagné, Louise Laflèche, François Lavoie, Ariane Légaré, Marc-André Davison, Annie St. Onge, Jean Blackburn, Pete Morin and Maryse Letarte.

This list is overwhelming.

Another CD labeled "For the Media" in which he placidly explains the basics of his mission, and at the bottom of the box is his old Ruger with a single bullet inserted in it, ensuring it is in front of the muzzle. He enters the barrel of the gun into his mouth to destroy everything in its path as he has studied. He grimaces at the taste of the cold metal. The gray cars are three hundred meters from his house. He can hear their tires crushing the gravel.

It disturbed him to leave his wife and children so abruptly in such a mess. He hears the guests talking to each other in a disbelieving clamor. He would have liked to say proper goodbye. To kiss Edward one last time on the forehead. Sad, too, for his mother, who probably won't recover from the loss of another of her children, nor from finding out what a monster he was. But he's happy to reunite with his sister he misses so much.

He prays that it's true we reunite with our loved ones when we die. When he embarked on this adventure, he assumed the remote possibility that he might fail. He's at peace with ending it all.

He's not afraid to die. It's better than being locked up like an animal for even an hour. Better than being paraded around for the media like a circus animal. This is not the way he wants to go out.

Settling into his favorite leather chair, he closes his eyes.

"William?"

He smiles, glad that the last thing he heard before he died was his wife's sweet voice.

Sitting in the back seat of the convoy front car, Abygaelle Jensen glances at a shadow that stealthily passes in front of a window on Primeau mansion's second floor. Then, a bright and quick bolt of lightning lit up the room before going pitch-black again. Abygaelle sighs as she closes her eyes. William Primeau will go out of the house on a stretcher, a tarp covering his body. He will bring his secrets into his grave.

With a twinge of sadness, she looks away to her right and gazes at the thick black forest in the distance. She is disenchanted. Why did it have to be like this? Why all these dead bodies, and collateral victims? Why was his revenge more important than his wife and son? Why couldn't he go on with his life like most people would after experiencing a tragedy?

As she arrives near the house, she stares at the beautiful luxury cars parked in an adjacent lot. She hears screams from inside the house as she opens her door. A confirmation of what she suspected. She sits back in the car, resting her head on her seat. She watches the British police officers run towards the residence, guns drawn, as if in slow motion. Straight ahead, an image breaks her heart.

A child bicycle overturned on its side.

No matter what she runs from, no matter what she does.

She can't stop the children from suffering.

93

Jocelyne Lamoureux has just returned from her long daily stroll. Every day, she goes for two kilometers with her daughter to get some fresh air, to clear her head and to reflect on her life. She also doesn't want to work out in a gym or go to public places. She hasn't ridden her motorcycle since Pete's demise. Her life comprises worrying about her child and startling whenever she hears a noise up close.

Since she talked to Abygaelle, she lives with Karine Tremblay, a friend in Saint-Félicien, Lac-Saint-Jean. She looks out the patio door to monitor Maripier. The girl is playing with Léa, one of Karine's children. Jocelyne is in constant eye contact with her daughter. She can't stay over five minutes away from her without checking on her, making sure she's safe and sound.

She lives in constant fear the murderer will track them down and get to them, although she can't see how that would be possible. No one knows about her friendship with Karine. They had not seen each other for over fifteen years, only sending scattered emails from time to time.

Pete and Karine's husband were not crazy about each other,

so that kept them apart for a long time. Fortunately, her childhood friend didn't hold it against her and readily agreed to let them stay. She has been divorced for two years.

It smells good in the house, and Jocelyne is hungry as a wolf. Her stroll has given her an appetite.

"What are you cooking for us?" she asks, taking off her coat.

"A broad bean soup," Karine says with her strong accent characteristic of the people of the region.

Jocelyne never tasted this soup before she came, but since, she has eaten it three times, and loves it. Karine is cautious to show her mother's recipe to her friend, mockingly saying that it should stay in the family. It felt good to reconnect with Karine. Their complicit humor didn't fade with time and they quickly picked up where they left off, as if they had never parted.

They met at the University of Montreal over two decades ago. Karine returned to her hometown, to which she was very devoted. She is now taking care of her aging parents. As is the tradition in the Tremblay household, the television is on all day, like a friendly background noise. Jocelyne listens to the news casually as she stares at Maripier jumping on the trampoline by the cedar hedge. No matter what happens, Jocelyne won't let anyone keep her from hanging out with whomever she wants, from isolating her from her friends. Not to mention that her daughter has just made a new buddy. She gets along wonderfully with Léa.

The temperature is chill for an early September day. Jocelyne's hands are still cold, and she warms them by squeezing them tightly between her thighs. The news casts begins with a breaking story, dramatic music to boot: the police have finally tracked down the raging sniper who was rampaging through the city in the past months. Jocelyne stops breathing. Abygaelle revealed that the serial killer they were after was the same who shot Pete. She feels her legs giving out. Is she hallucinating? She must have misunderstood. She slowly makes her way to the living room to have a closer look at what it's all about. They couldn't have gotten to him already. She thought she would have to hide for months, maybe even years.

Knowing that the murderer had been located in England dampened her optimism. It can't be him. London is far away. The man who threatened her in her own home was French Canadian. She doesn't get it.

Then she saw the picture.

She sits because otherwise she might fall apart. My God, it's him, they got him. Jocelyne's heart is pounding. She would like to jump up and down with joy, but she's shaken up. Hot tears stream down the prominent cheekbones of her smile. Images of William Primeau flash across the screen, shots of him in magazines, others taken at charity events. But the softness in his eyes confuses her; and his plastic beauty. Far fetch from the coldness and the absence of compassion he showed.

Karine looks at her, puzzled. She sits down next to her, trying to understand what is going on.

"My God, Jocelyne, what's wrong?"

"He's dead."

"Who died?"

"The serial killer."

"The one who killed the girl?"

Jocelyne had not yet told her friend that the serial killer was also the killer of her husband. In fact, she didn't want to talk about his death. She didn't have the energy. She nods slowly.

"Yes, he committed suicide in his house."

She sobs loudly and puts her hands on her face.

"For God's sake, Joce. Tell me what is going on? Why are you so upset?"

After a few minutes of sobbing, of feeling the weight of the world lifting off her shoulders, Jocelyne notices Karine is smiling slightly. She puts her hand on hers.

"It's him."

Karine frowns.

"What do you mean, it's him?"

Jocelyne pauses, realizing the enormous secret she is about to disclose.

"Pete's killer."

Karine gasps.

"Oh my God, you poor thing."

Jocelyne gets up and walks to the patio leading to the backyard. Maripier waves at her, not seeing her wet cheeks and reddened eyes. Jocelyne sits on a chair in the kitchen, trying to clear her head. Karine respectfully gives her space. Jocelyne doesn't know how to deal with all this, it's unexpected. And now what? She's just supposed to go home and go on with her life as if nothing happened?

She turns on her laptop to check her e-mails. She hasn't read them in days. She catches an email from Abygaelle Jensen dated from the day before. It is short, just one line.

"We got him. You have nothing more to worry about now."

Searching for her words, Jocelyne can think of nothing better than to simply reply, "Thank you." She closes the lid of her laptop and looks outside again. The sun has come out of the clouds and a ray falls on Maripier, who is sitting in the grass, contemplative. Like a sign that everything will be fine, that the future will be bright for them.

Even if Jocelyne knows she will need years to reconstruct herself. To heal. She spared at least her child. Karine approaches Jocelyne gently, massaging her shoulders.

"How are you doing?"

Jocelyne smiles. It's the first time she's done it sincerely since Pete's death. The grin of a death row convict who has just been absolved.

"I'm okay," she says, her voice still trembling. "But you'll have to give me the damn soup recipe."

94

On her flight back to Montreal, Abygaelle replayed the last events in her head. William Primeau's suicide leaves her with a bitter aftertaste. She would have so much wished that he would explain himself, to understand, that he answered her questions. His justification on the video didn't convince her. She has a hard time conceiving that he could have shot François Lavoie if the witness in the bar was telling the truth. She checked with him several times, and he was adamant that the mysterious man leaving the pub with Lavoie that night was taller than him.

Lavoie was 6'2 and William was barely 6'0.

This is assuming that he was indeed Lavoie's killer. Nobody knows for sure. Nothing more than suspicions that wouldn't stand up to the scrutiny of a court of law. From this point of view, nothing can disprove Primeau's story. They would never have the chance to repel him. But nothing can diminish the doubts she has. Even today, she struggles to regard William Primeau as a cold-blooded killer.

But he was.

Sometimes people aren't exactly who they seem to be.

Some have an unflappable ability to blend in, to live like anyone else, and then strike when you least expect it. Once she figured out his motivation, she found a way to stop him and buy some time to track him down. Although those who died, shot by him or because of him, will never come back, others survived. It all depends on how you look at it.

Abygaelle sees the glass half empty. One death is one death too many. She can't help but feel a distressing melancholy when she thinks about the deaths. She should have realized before what it was about, should have grasped William's motives more quickly. Her inexperience probably cost the life of a few people, and she won't forgive herself for a long time.

Perhaps never.

She recalls when she shared her plan with Ranger a second time, after he refused the first time, which probably cost his former lover Maryse Letarte her life.

Ranger regained consciousness and, by some unimaginable luck, had no severe consequences despite the projectile lodged somewhere in his head. He was very weak and had trouble sustaining a long conversation, so Abygaelle had done most of the talking. Stephane confirmed that Marko Gusarov handled his beating. As for the bullet in his skull, he does not know. He doesn't recall that happening.

Abygaelle seized the opportunity to introduce her plan a second time, and this time she wouldn't take no for an answer. In the condition he was in, he couldn't possibly contribute in any meaningful way to the investigation, anyway. The best thing he could do was to help incapacitate the killer while they were tracking him down. Spare other people's lives on the list. He could still make a difference.

The discussion had been strenuous, with Ranger settling for monosyllabic answers. It was a risky gamble, but they had nothing to lose by trying. In football, it's called a Hail Mary. You toss the football to the end zone in the last seconds of a game and cross your fingers that one of your players will catch the coveted object. Abygaelle determined it would be faster to do that than trying to find the last people on the list, whose location they didn't know, explaining to them what it was all about, persuading them to leave everything behind, and cutting them off. In her opinion, this was the only way to stop an unknown and untraceable assassin at that moment. A ghost. The point was to discard what she believed to be the killer's motivation. Assuming that she fully understood what was driving him.

"Stephane, here is my theory. The killer means for you to suffer. I think it's connected to Nathalie Primeau rape, but all our suspects have solid alibis. I could be wrong and it could be unrelated, but someone is targeting your loved ones and you are the common denominator. I don't think he'll stop until you're dead. Every time you'll fall in love with someone or have a little fun with someone, he'll kill them."

Stephane looked at her blankly.

"Do you understand what I'm saying?"

He nodded.

"Good. Then I'd like you to come with us. We'll use your mishap to achieve this goal. We will get you out on a stretcher, into an ambulance, show the world that you are dead. Hospital staff won't talk to the media beyond referring them to us. The hospital's communications department is already in the loop.

We'll take a picture of your fake corpse, fake an autopsy report, and I'll do the rest. We'll leak the picture around the criminal underworld and see what happens.

"It won't bring Ariane back," he said in a weak voice.

"Maybe not, but there are still people you can save. I'm trying to prevent them from suffering the same fate. I'm sure that if he thinks you're dead, he'll have no reason to keep on killing. And that will give us time to track him down and lock the son of a bitch up."

Stephane wasn't sold on the idea.

"You told me you promised Ariane that you would do everything you could to find her murderer. So that's exactly what you're going to help us do if you agree. You will avenge Ariane, your mother, Annie—"

For the first time, Stephane's face had brightened. She had his attention. She had pounded him like a boxer about to knock out his opponent. She had Stephane on the ropes.

"We'll keep you at a distance in an anonymous location where you won't be seen in public. You will still get the care you need. We will compensate you financially, for your time, take care of your groceries, meals, etc."

He looked away, but Abygaelle approached and put her hand on his forearm.

"Stephane, look at me. I need you. Don't think about lost lives, think about those you can salvage. Think about Marco and Madeleine. The killer murdered people off the list too. Nothing can prevent him from going after people you care about, even if they are not on the damn list. Remember Annie, she wasn't on it. He shot her anyway. I know you feel like crap right now, but I swear you have the power to stop this. Although I could coerce you, I would much rather getting your endorsement."

On the way to the country house they arranged for him, Abygaelle was sitting in the back of the ambulance next to his stretcher. He was lost in thought, looking out the small back windows, the beams of light interspersed with raindrops drawing shadows dancing across his face.

He's completely destroyed, she thought. His swollen face is almost unrecognizable. She wonders how he'll go on with his life once this is over. She doubts she could if she were in his situation. She's glad he agreed this time. It's too bad he dismissed her plan to fake his suicide the first time. But the past is the past. All that matters is the present. Aby instructed the police officers on duty to keep an eye on him. She feared he might try to take his own life. She is committed to save him. She wanted no more victims, be it him or anyone else. Abygaelle promised to come and see him a few times a week to update him on the progress which she did. As time went by, Stephane gradually recovered, despite his perpetual gloomy mood. She suggested he write to the assassin about his feelings, what he would tell him if he had him in front of him. He refused.

He had made significant progress quickly, to the point where he could sit down long enough to eat a meal at the kitchen table or have a discussion. Then one day, she met him in the living room and told him that the killer was William Primeau, Nathalie's brother. She told him about the false passport, the misleading trails, the wooden queens, his fury over the rape, and his confession to the murder of his mother, Lavoie, Gagné and Blackburn a few years earlier. Stephane fell back into a catatonic state. It was as if acknowledging his link to all these barbaric crimes was too much. He secretly hoped that it wasn't related to him, so that he would feel relieved. He kept asking the same question to the point that Aby didn't know what to answer anymore. She realized it was rhetorical, that no one would give a satisfactory explanation.

"Why didn't he kill me?"

Aby looked at him in silence.

"Why didn't he just shoot me like the others? I'm the only one who didn't rape his sister. The only on who did nothing to her."

Abygaelle came close to pointing out, full of rebukes in her voice, that he had let Gagne and Lavoie act with impunity, but she restrained herself.

"Why can't I die? I've done everything possible, whether or not intentionally. I can't die while those around me are being slaughtered one after the other. Not even a damn bullet in the head could get me. It's ridiculous."

A few days before Abygaelle's trip to London, Stephane contacted her to announce he recorded a video on his cell phone for William Primeau. Abygaelle watched it on the plane. It depicted an angry and hurt Stephane, sometimes apologizing for not assisting Nathalie, sometimes insulting him and calling him a coward. Aby also had little sympathy for William and his cause. She would never condone hurting children. She built her career on it. It was no more acceptable with the other victims, but Ariane's case had particularly upset her.

But she couldn't tell him. It was over before she even got out of the police car.

She wished she could have looked him in the eye, told him "I got you," told him everything that was on her mind, that he was less intelligent than he thought. She would have liked to show him Stephane's recording so that he could hear what he had to say, that perhaps a simple, frank discussion between the two would have prevented this savage absurdity. That he would understand she had deceived him, that Ranger was not really dead. But he deprived her of that pleasure. He planned it all. His exit was quick and smooth. Exactly as he planned it.

Exactly like his homicides.

She told Stephane about William's suicide before her flight home. She told him that William had friends for dinner and that his mother was there. That she is in a severe state of shock in a London hospital, and Heather, his wife, is sedated. She lost her unborn baby.

William will have left nothing but chaos and devastation on his trail. This will be the legacy that his family and his son will have to live with for the rest of their lives. They say there is always good to come out of tragedy. But sometimes there is none. William Primeau made sure everyone suffered.

But little did he know that those he would wreck the most were the ones he loved.

95

Abygaelle Jensen is fuming.

Despite her pleas not to do it, her bosses handed Primeau's footage to the media.

"People have a right to know," Charles Picard says. "It would be worse to conceal information."

"I'm not saying we should have hidden some information, but we could have summarized what he said in the video and controlled the message."

"I don't think it will make a difference. People above our heads decided. Both the recording and the letter are already in the possession of the media."

Abygaelle nibbled her lower lip.

"And you agree with that?"

"Absolutely," Picard says before walking away.

Abygaelle abhors the tendency to idolize killers, even more so for serial killers. She worries there might be a ripple effect. Maybe some crazy wannabe will resort to this surefire method of becoming famous and finally be somebody.

A quick way to fame.

It is well documented that there is an increase in suicides

when a famous person takes his or her own life. The same goes for murders or carnage, making headlines and give ideas to the sick minded. She shudders thinking about the coming feature stories about William Primeau. Who was he? Why did he kill those people? They will publish the transcript of the video in all the newspapers and magazines. The video itself will be available on all platforms. His picture will be on the front page of print and electronic media. Everyone will forget about Ariane, Marc-André, Annie and the others. But everyone will know all there is to know about William. This is exactly what he hoped for when he filmed this video. He left nothing to chance. Journalists will regurgitate his message for months to come. After all, aren't people still referring to Marc Lépine's misogynistic letter? Yet, he was renowned in his field. Finance magazines featured him. It's not like he was a complete stranger. But that wasn't enough for him; he wanted to be a legend.

Jack feels the same. He doesn't agree with the release of the recording either. He says that no one should ever name the killer, no one should ever put his picture in the media. There should be a global consensus in the world media. They should refer to him as "the killer". Instead of his picture, they should show the victims' pictures, talk about their lives.

Instead of feeding the legend of a madman.

Abygaelle agrees. How many mentally ill people take a gun and kill a large mass of victims to get out of their anonymity? The cult of celebrity has many more bad sides than good. She no longer cares about the video. She saw it at least a hundred times. She doesn't want to see William Primeau's face anymore, to hear him speak in his assertive tone, as if he wanted to convince someone that his actions were justified. Abygaelle cringes realizing he made this video months in advance. The evil premeditation, the trivialization of human life.

Disgusting Machiavellianism.

She will also stay off social media for several weeks, because she knows that a handful of morons will defend the horrors, that they understand, and that the victims are just collateral damage.

They were in the wrong place at the wrong time.

People are such idiots sometimes, she thought. They all need psychiatric care, because no normal human thinks like that. Those fools are most likely to their guns, thinking that it's a good idea after all to kill those who have made other suffer.

At home, Raymond Primeau watches television. Although he too watched the video several times, he wants to see his son alive again. Even if his words are intolerable, even if he looks like a cold and calculating monster, he is still his boy. Monique can no longer stand these images. She locked herself in her room for days. Raymond brings her food in a wooden tray, the same one that Nathalie and William used when they wished to surprise them by fixing breakfast in bed. It's amazing how the most insignificant objects suddenly take on an inordinate importance once the memories attached to them are all that hold you back to your former reality. A peaceful time where everyone was happy, where everything worked flawlessly. A past when you didn't understand you were living on borrowed time, in an artificial happiness. They never saw the tsunami coming.

They never saw the horror creeping in.

Monique lost a lot of weight. If it's true that the human body is sixty-five percent water, she was evaporating through her tears. Raymond would never have thought one could cry so much. He knows she'll never get over it, just as she never got over their daughter's death. If he's honest with himself, he hasn't overcome it either. For William, it was less of a shock, because he saw it coming, like a train accident in slow motion.

Maxime Fauvette listens to the evening news with Laurie. She didn't know William. Maxime didn't invite his ex-brother-in-law to his wedding. He thought it was too weird to have his former girlfriend's relatives over there.

They didn't get along so much, anyway.

Laurie knows that this is Nathalie's brother. She asked Maxime how he felt about the whole thing. He said he felt sorry for him. That William was a good guy. She was very surprised when Maxime told her he understood why he did it.

"You agree with that? That he killed the young teen and all those people?"

"Of course not," he said. I'm telling you I understand his fury. Where he's coming from. Maxime didn't lie. He doesn't approve of what William did. If he killed Stephane Ranger, he would have concurred. But not to kill innocent people.

William's face emerges on the television, crouched forward, as if he were thinking about how to begin his diatribe. Raymond's heart sinks.

Abygaelle eats by herself at Babylone, a Turkish restaurant that she particularly likes. She waits for her Adana Kebab plate, then she looks at William's face on a screen in the distance out of the corner of her eye. The couple next to her discuss the matter, how awful what he did was. Abygaelle needs privacy. The last thing she wants is to hear about Primeau and his delusion. The waiter moves her to a more secluded table where she won't see the television or hear people's comments. Anyway, she could recite William's speech by heart. It makes her nauseous.

On the video, William raises his head and looked at the camera.

"Ladies and gentlemen, I know you think I'm a monster. As I record this video, I don't know how many victims there have been. So, excuse me for not talking about them. I want to justify my actions without expecting you to agree with them, but to understand my motives. I'm not asking for your forgiveness, but only to understand why I did it.

He takes a pause to collect his thoughts.

"First, the context..."

He explained at length what happened to Nathalie, the defendants' arrogance, and the work of the defense lawyer. William's face twists with rage as he recounts what they did to his sister not only during the rape, but also at the trial.

Without realizing it, Maxime Fauvette clenches his jaw as he listens to the account of Nathalie's aggression, as if he relives it. This kind of wound never completely heals. Laurie realizes the trauma that this speech entails, but says nothing, too horrified to hear what Maxime never dared to tell her, about what happened to his ex-girlfriend, only talking about it on the surface. Maxime hadn't felt such rage rush through his veins for a long time.

Hello darkness, my old friend.

"When those bastards got away with it," William says, "I have lost faith in the justice system. So I took matters into my own hands. If I had to sacrifice myself to avenge my sister, I would. Tonight, I make the ultimate sacrifice. I confessed my murders on a list given to the police, but I can tell you about the first few I did. First, I killed François Lavoie in a vacant lot, shooting him like a mutt. Then I cut off his balls and stuffed them in his mouth. I did the same with Eric Gagné a couple of years later, but this time with a hunting knife. That rotten bastard ate his testicles, too. Finally, I took care of Jean Blackburn, the lawyer, with the same knife I used to kill Gagné, I carved the letters R, A and T on his forehead, and then I cut open his belly so that his guts would drip on the floor.

Abygaelle runs her fork through her orzo rice without eating a bite. Even though she isn't listening to the video, she can hear the clamor of the employees in the kitchen reacting to the killer's every word. She is no longer hungry, aware that the public is listening to this horrific tale. Even though he only confesses to the murders before Ariane's, he takes responsibility for the murders of the people in his letter. Unfortunately, Abygaelle will never know why he shot Annie St. Onge. For Pete Morin, she knows since Jocelyne Lamoureux told her the whole thing. Abygaelle hopes that the poor woman isn't currently watching her husband's killer expose the extent of his insanity.

But she is.

Jocelyne hears William's speech, shaking like a leaf. His bright blue eyes still terrify her, even though he's dead and can't hurt her anymore. She still has nightmares of his violence-filled gaze piercing her like an X-ray. His curt smile is enough to give you goose bumps. She strokes the head of her daughter sleeping with her head on her thigh. She's glad she defied the killer's threats and went back to the police. This time, she had a clear memory of his grotesque face. It was a breeze to spot him in a series of photographs. Detective Jensen told her that without her, their case would have been much weaker and they probably wouldn't have had enough to arrest this sicko.

"Contrary to what I thought," William says, looking straight at the camera, "Lavoie, Gagné and Blackburn's deaths didn't provide me the release and joy I expected. I was as miserable as before. I still missed my sister. Like coitus interrupted, I didn't have the ultimate orgasm. Yes, killing them filled me with an immense satisfaction, sorry for their family, but like mine, they spawned a monster. Except that afterwards, I found myself helpless, with the same resentment, with the same latent sadness plaguing my life. Einstein said that insanity is doing the same thing repeatedly, hoping for a different result. I'm not crazy, so I had to try something else. Then I realized that the best revenge would be for my target to feel the pain that my family and I were experiencing because of his actions. I wanted him to feel the same pain, but a thousand times worse."

Stephane Ranger wasn't listening to the murderer's monologue, either. He couldn't tolerate it. He saw it once and walked out of the police station room to vomit. His guilt slowly eats him alive. He will live a hellish life for the rest of his days. People will know about Nathalie's rape. People may want to make him pay to complete this maniac's mission out of sympathy for him. Again, the cops suggested protecting him by isolating him for an indefinite period, even proposing to get him a new identity. But with his family practically wiped out except for his nephew Marco and his sister, there was no need. He understands he won't see them again. Marco won't forgive him for being related to his grandmother's death, his uncle's death, but above all, Ariane's death.

If Stephane thought he was alone in the world before, it's nothing compared to what awaits. It hurts to admit it, but the assassin achieved his goal. He took away all reason to live; he suffers as never before. He has no anchor.

He is lost.

Since watching the video and confirming that Madeleine no longer wants to see him, he has been dancing with his demons every day. Why stop now? The only way he can survive is by numbing himself. Impossible to go through this sober. Welcome, my dark angels. I have missed you so much. I expect nothing more from life. I might as well live it to the fullest until the end, which I hope will come sooner than later. His gamble that Madeleine would forgive him since he was central to catching Ariane's killer turned out to be a bad one. She didn't even thank him. She won't talk to him, despite all that.

"I commissioned a prison survey that included a questionnaire asking inmates to name the ten people they cared about most. The ones they would save from a shipwreck in order of importance. Obviously, I didn't care what anyone else said. I used this list to identify the targets to kill. First, I killed his mother by shooting her from a truck while she was on her way to visit her son in the slammer. I have no doubt that she was a good, kind lady. But her son caused her death. I was just the messenger.

William Primeau pauses for a few seconds before carrying on.

"My goal was to kill the rest of the people on the list until everyone was dead, or until he killed himself. If, once the list was complete, he was still alive like the coward he was, then I would shoot him myself. In either scenario, this scumbag wouldn't hurt anyone else. As of the release of this video, I don't know if he's dead and if so, if I killed him myself, but I hope with all my soul that he died before I did."

William's face softens.

"People will ask, why a wooden queen? It's to honor my sister, to honor the girls from Polytechnique, and all the women who have fallen into the clutches of a misogynist. I know you'll say I'm no better than them, that I'm like Marc Lépine. But don't make the mistake of putting me in the same category as that creep. I didn't kill the women on the list because they were women. I would have preferred it if they were all men. Not because I hate them more than women, but because it didn't align with what I did. Killing women to avenge other women, I'm sure you'll agree, makes little sense to a logical man like me. But these are the cards that were dealt to me at first. I had to do with it.

Abygaelle walks and inhales fresh air on her way home. She almost didn't touch her dish after all. She paid the bill, apologized to the waiter she knows well, and left. She was suffocating in this bubble where she was imprisoned. She had to get out, and fast. She walked home with her head down, thinking of a thousand things at once. She saw William's face again, oscillating between rage and kindness as he went from one subject to another. Like a bipolar.

"I'm not crazy," William says in a low voice, "but I'm sick. No one could do what I did and be totally sane. I lost my morals the day Natalie died. I committed to avenge her, but I know she would be angry at me right now if she were here. She would never have approved of that. She was good, my sister. Too naïve, of course. That's what got her killed. Those sharks were hungry for sex and blood. I will end by saying that no one in my family knew about the mission. They are surely devastated today to see what their son, who was so successful in life, did as an ignominy. The bodies he left behind. For that, I ask their forgiveness. I know they share my pain and suffering about Nathalie, but they don't share my rage. Don't put them through what you did to the Columbine killers' parents. Let them experience their pain and grief. They had no way of knowing my purpose. The same goes for my wife.

Raymond's eyes are wet. His son protecting him and his wife, even though he hated him. It shows that he had a shred of affection for him that was still there, buried somewhere deep inside. He's already less tense. His son took a weight off his shoulders. He didn't hate him fully. He hinted at an ultimate sacrifice; he did. He took a bullet for everyone. He threw himself in front of the enemy's heavy fire and protected his brothers in arms. Why? Raymond will never know, but courage was one value he instilled in his son. The lesson resonated. Even if he doesn't agree with what he did.

It's not much, but at this point, Raymond will take everything he can for this ordeal.

"That's it," William said in closing. I've taken up too much of your time. I already apologized to my wife in another video, and to my son who is still too young to grasp the abominations his father carried out. I don't expect you to forgive me, but I hope that deep down you'll understand a little better why I did this. And that even though I'm sick and lost, I'm no monster.

The image fades away.

Laurie turns off the television, speechless.

She looks at Maxime, who keeps staring at the black screen.

96

All the family gathered around Maurice Primeau, just out of the palliative care center where he's been for the previous two years. He was nearing death and wanted to die surrounded by his loved ones, in the home he lived in for over thirty years.

He called for a farewell party. He wanted to express how much he cherished each of them.

"He always enjoyed having people over," Johanne Lafontaine told Monique, his sister-in-law. "He enjoys the mood, the music, and hearing people laugh and have a good time."

She could hardly hold back her tears. Monique patted her back affectionately. What that poor woman had to go through since her husband was ill. It's inconceivable. Raymond and his brother joked around as Maurice was laying in his orthopedic bed. William chatted with his mother and aunt, occasionally peeking at the two men. He and his father were estranged, merely extending courtesies for Monique's benefit, so as not to upset her further. He was waiting for his father to leave his uncle's bedside to pay his last respects. He had a flight to London that evening.

"So? How is the huge career?"

In her fake good mood, Johanne gently nudged him with her shoulder like she used to when she would tease him as a child. He had a caring smile on his face. Johanne and Maurice were very important in his life.

"I'm fine, Auntie, thank you."

William was usually an imposing figure. He was always in control of every situation. But with his aunt, he regressed to the shy, docile boy he was as a child.

"And how is your girlfriend? What's her name again?"

"Heather," Monique said from the background, with a pout that irritated William.

"That's right, Heather. She's so pretty."

"She is," William said. "Again, she apologizes for her absence. She has an urgent matter at the office, but she swears that next time—"

Johanne interrupted him with a wave of the hand.

"We understand, William. Your uncle understands."

He smiled. He tried to convince Heather, pointing out how important it was that she was there, but he gave in. It caused a rift between them.

Raymond Primeau passed behind him, putting his hand on his shoulder on his way out. William stiffened and his face turned bitter. He saw the sorrow in his mother's eyes. Their conflict deeply hurt her. He smiled at her.

"That's okay, Mom."

She smiled back at him, and followed her husband into the kitchen, along with Johanne. William looked at his uncle, who was looking at the ceiling, lost in his thoughts. The powerful giant of his childhood had given way to an emaciated and weak man.

A giant of clay.

Heartbroken, he walked towards him. His footsteps brought Maurice out of his daydreaming. He warmly smiled at him.

"Hello, big guy."

"Hello, Uncle."

"How is my superstar?"

Maurice and Johanne had no children. William spent so much time with them they were like his second parents. Nathalie felt the same.

"Stop with the superstar stuff, please."

Maurice chuckled loudly. His characteristic laugh. His eyes were rich of affection.

"You know I'm proud of you."

William laid his hand on Maurice's arm. Even weakened, he was imposing. He was 6'5" tall. An anomaly in a family where men were barely six feet tall.

"You worked hard for everything you have, don't let anyone tell you otherwise."

"I'd like to see them try," William said, looking falsely defiant.

Both chuckled.

"When are you and your beautiful, tall wife going to have babies?"

"Well, you know, I don't think I will. I have little time to raise them, and I don't think I'd be such a good father."

"With the money you make, hire a nanny or something."

"I'd rather have no kids than have someone else raise them."

Maurice understood. There was no obligation for anyone to have children, anyway. It would have delighted him to learn that William since changed his mind.

"You would have made a good father, though."

Maurice looked stern.

"I settled for being the best uncle I could be."

"To me, you're like my father."

William said this out of an emotion as he saw his idol lying there dying. He forgot it was a sensitive subject.

"William, you have such a good father. Don't make me angry."

He didn't argue, because he didn't want to make things worse.

"You can't blame him for the rest of your life. What happened happened."

William snapped.

"Maurice, I adore you; you know that, but let's change the subject. Let's not go there."

Maurice looked at him for a long time before lowering his eyes.

"If I had to do it all over again, I wouldn't."

William felt a powerful wave of anger wash over him.

Maurice noticed.

"William, hear me out. This isn't a knock against you and what we've done."

"Oh really? What is it then?"

His harsh tone took Maurice aback.

"Calm down, let me finish."

William listened, crossing his arms, looking coldly at him.

"When you are about to die, you think about what you have done in life. When you're about to meet your maker, you want your things to be in order."

"Not me, anyway."

"You don't know that, you're perfectly healthy. I used to be like you. I was proud. I felt invincible. I used to find solace and logic in it all. But now when I look back, I'm sad."

"I am not."

"I'm sorry I turned into a demon."

"You are not the demon, for fuck's sake."

"Yes, William, by sinking down to their level, we aren't any better than they are."

"Nonsense."

"You'll figure it out."

"No, I'll regret nothing."

Maurice was disappointed in his nephew's attitude.

"If you say so."

William shook his head and smiled mischievously. Maurice looked at him with sorrow. His soul was adrift, and it was his fault. All this shit was his idea.

"I can't believe you're telling me this," William said in disgust, looking away.

"I know, buddy. But it's the truth."

He felt betrayed. As if his uncle had stabbed him multiple times in the heart.

"All those years I was angry at my father. I thought that at least you got it, that you were with me. That fool Raymond understands nothing with his nickel-and-dime morals. With his conscience right before he was supposed to take action. But hell, you also don't get it."

"No, I do William. I get it perfectly. But I'm sorry—"

"Stop it!"

"I'll clear my conscience before I leave. I'll ask Johanne to call a police investigator tomorrow, and I'll confess my wrongdoing. Don't worry, I won't say anything about you."

William was livid.

"Have you lost your fucking mind?"

"I won't say anything about you, I promise, but the family must know what I did."

"What the hell is wrong with you? They'll make the connection, especially if you elaborate."

"I'll make things up. I've got it all planned out."

"Say nothing, please. You'll ruin my life."

"Of course not, they won't trace it back to you."

"Take your secret with you, Uncle, I beg you."

"I can't," he said, his voice broken with emotion. "I can't have it on my conscience."

William's eyes filled with tears as he realized that his stubborn uncle would not change his mind. He never thought he'd hear those words from his most trusted ally. It totally crushed him.

"Okay, Maurice," he said in a soft voice. "Does Joanne know?"

"Not yet. I'll share it with her just before she calls the cops. She'll be very upset, that's for sure. I hope she'll understand."

"I see."

William bent down to kiss his uncle on the forehead. Discreetly, he grabbed the pillow next to his head and clutched it in his hands.

Maurice looked at him, begging. He knew he would not have the strength to counter the power of his nephew.

"I'm sorry, but I have too much to lose."

"William—"

Bringing the pillow close to his uncle's face, William stared one last time into his steel-blue eyes. Maurice raised a defensive hand with great difficulty, but it was useless.

After several minutes of pressing the pillow against his uncle's face, William was sure he was dead. His face was inert, his eyes half open, his cheeks soggy.

William didn't need to check his pulse. He was dead.

He was crying his eyes out and clinging to his uncle.

"I'm sorry uncle, I'm so sorry."

He was sobbing like a child.

"Are you ready for dinner?"

Johanne's voice startled him. Her smile faded as she saw him weeping.

"What in the world is wrong with you?"

"He's gone, Johanne. Maurice is dead."

Johanne walked towards her husband, screamed, and collapsed beside him.

The others ran over to them upon hearing the screams. They quickly realized the tragedy unfolding.

"He was having such a good day, I don't understand," Johanne said tearfully.

William watched his aunt and uncle, two of the most important people in his life, and couldn't stop crying.

Feeling scrutinized, he turned to his right and met his father's enraged gaze.

William was in too much pain to care. When he tried to go back to Maurice, Raymond stepped in.

"Get the fuck out of here."

Rarely, William saw his father so livid. He was so scared that a shiver of terror ran through his body. Raymond knew about Maurice's plan. He realized he opened up to his son and, like the egomaniac that he was, William wouldn't allow it.

He put his sunglasses on and went out to sit on the top step of the front balcony. He couldn't stop bawling. The pain was too sharp.

He hadn't cried this much since Nathalie's death.

97

The mood in the provincial police interrogation room is intense. Jack watches Raymond Primeau with unequivocal sternness from behind the scenes as Abygaelle struggles to get any information out of him.

He's acting dumb, Jack thinks. There's no way he didn't know.

"You will agree, Mr. Primeau, that we struggle to believe you weren't aware of your son's plan," Abygaelle says.

"He confessed to the murders. I'm as stunned as you are," Raymond answers in a neutral voice.

Jack hisses angrily.

"Yes, but something's not adding up," Aby says. If you didn't know what he was up to, why did you take the blame? To protect him? If you wanted to protect him, you must have thought he was somehow involved."

Raymond Primeau stares at the ground before answering.

"I didn't know it was him. But yes, it was a distinct possibility. Since we were at odds, let's say I wasn't his primary confidant. He admitted nothing to me. But I knew about Stephane Ranger. When I found out that a long-range fire killed his niece, I thought someone would single me out because of my military background, and because I tried to go after the defendants after the trial. So I took off to assess my options. Then there were more murders. Victims I didn't know. I thought it couldn't be him because it would be too complicated for him to be here, still running his business in Europe. Then he sent me an email saying you wanted to talk to me. I looked at the header of the message and saw that he sent it from Europe. That made me feel better. But, it was definitely a possibility.

"But why did you suspect it? Only because of Ariane Légaré?"

He nods.

"After Nathalie's death, he swore to avenge her. But you know how it is. You say things on the spur of the moment, then time passes and you go on with your life. I, too, would have wanted to kill the bastards. When I heard that Gagne and Lavoie were dead, I must admit I was thrilled. The list of potential suspects was quite short in my mind."

"Who were the others?"

"It doesn't matter now," Primeau whispers.

Abygaelle wonders if he's hiding something. She feels like he's not telling them all he knows. But if his crime is keeping his suspicions about William to himself, that won't fly in front of a judge.

"He stopped by you recently, didn't he?" Abygaelle asks.

Primeau's face stiffens.

"Yes, he did"

"And you didn't think it was worth telling us?"

Primeau smiles.

"No, I didn't."

Jack sneers wickedly as he looks away.

"Did he confess to the murders at that point?"

"Not at all."

"What did he want?"

"Well, the same old stuff. Telling me how bad of a father I was, reiterating all the things he blamed me for."

"And your head injury?"

"That's him. We fought, but he's stronger than me."

"Would you have told us if he had confessed to the murders?" Jack asks.

Primeau stretches his neck, then looks intensely at him.

"Do you have children, Detective Morris?"

"Yes, I have a son."

"How far would you go to protect him?"

"Not to the extent of covering up a homicide."

Primeau chuckles.

"We'll see if it ever happens, it's easier said than done. To answer your question: no, I wouldn't have told you. Why would I?"

"We were looking for him.

"Rat on my son? That's not in my values, Mr. Morris. I'm sorry."

"I still don't get why you confessed to the murders," Abygaelle says.

"No matter how many times I flipped this around, I figured that if it was William, then he might stop seeing that I was taking the blame. He would see this as a helping hand and stop his carnage. And if it wasn't him, maybe the perpetrator would stop too. Either way, I was your number one suspect. It was the perfect situation for me to step forward to save my son's life."

"I hope you get busted for obstruction of an investigation," Jack says.

"I understand. I'll do my time if that's the case. But I really hoped the killer would make the most of my sacrifice to stop all this."

Once the interview was over, Abygaelle followed Raymond Primeau outside.

"Mr. Primeau," she said, putting her hand on his arm.

"When we met the other day at the café, you told me about the heresy of believing that revenge is a necessary balm to heal our wounds. I thought about it a lot, because I knew it wasn't some far-fetched theory to calm me down. I wondered what you were referring to. Now I understand you weren't talking about me, but about William, right?"

Raymond Primeau's eyes moisten despite his tense smile.

"Maybe, Detective Jensen. Maybe."

He grabs her shoulder with affection and wishes her good luck for the future.

Abygaelle returns inside, realizing that she won't know all the secrets this man is holding back. He has only told her what he wanted her to know and he will keep the rest of his secrets deep in his mind.

Raymond Primeau is pondering on the way home. The police asked him all the questions they can think of. They attempted to have him confess he knew about William's implication. What did they expect? That he would concede his son was a monster? He juggled the idea of ratting him out a hundred times. Of telling them to look up William, he had something to do with it. He immediately knew it was him when Ariane died. He wasn't shocked to learn that most of the victims were related to Stephane Ranger.

William was a gifted shooter.

As soon as Raymond brought him to a shooting range, it was as if he was born to shoot a gun. Then he asked him to take it to long distance shooting. His father was his idol and at that age, he wanted to do everything Raymond did. It wasn't until he started high school that Raymond finally agreed. It quickly became a passion. William pestered him to go shooting every week. He even joined a shooting club. He entertained the idea of starting in biathlon, but being a poor cross-country skier, the plan didn't stick for long. Raymond learned that William kept shooting even in England. If he had it to do over again, he would never have put a gun in his hands.

That was his biggest regret.

That and that William didn't take the olive branch he offered. Because his heart was too dark, too full of hate. He responded to his action by hurriedly murdering a woman, like a huge middle finger, as if he were telling him to fuck off.

Despite all this, Raymond was incapable of turning on him. He so hoped it wasn't him, even though there was no way it could be someone else. William had an alibi, but that was only because his passport showed no travel to Canada. That's why he wasn't surprised when his son pointed a gun at the back of his head and ordered him to kneel down two weeks before his death. Raymond thought that was the end. All the resentment against him because of what he did, or rather, what he didn't do.

"It was so simple, William told him. We had a deal. Everyone complied except for you. You had to kill Ranger. We all did our damn share, except for you. You screwed up. You forced me to do it instead of you. You have the victims' blood on your hands. Raymond was crying silently. Tears of sorrow, tears of rage, tears of despair. How could his son, so intelligent, so generous, who had everything one could wish for in life, be so ruthless? How could he bring himself to murder innocent people so easily, while he was still having nightmares about the enemy combatants he shot in the Vietnam War?

"You killed those people, William. I didn't. You could have done what I did and moved on. But no, you have so much resentment that it's clouding your mind. I tried to make you understand, but you wouldn't listen."

"You're such a spineless, weak old man," William told him. "I did the work at your place."

Every word tore at his heart.

"No, you didn't do the work in my place. Doing the job

would have meant killing Ranger and packing up your things, then getting on with your life. That was the deal. Not the girl, not the other victims. What was your motive in killing all those people?"

Raymond asked, even though he knew the answer.

William knew Raymond confronted Stephane Ranger in an alley, found him unconscious with a needle stuck in his arm. That he hit him hard, but decided that life was a worse punishment than death. For a while, William agreed with his logic. But as the months went by, he felt the rage welling up inside him, and he blamed his father for his inaction, his flawed and foolish morality.

"At first, even though I was opposed to your cowardice, I let things go, see how I lived with it. See if Ranger would really mope around in his miserable life. Then I learned he turned his life around, that he was getting a second chance, an opportunity that Nathalie didn't have. So I did the dirty work for you. I wanted him to suffer. I wanted him to die, but at the end of horrible emotional suffering. I hoped his pain would kill him. Unfortunately, someone killed him before he did, but I'll settle for that.

"And now you feel better? You don't feel sorry for Nathalie anymore? You live in joy and cheerfulness?"

William didn't answer.

"And Maurice, when you murdered him, did that make you feel better, too? You regarded him as your idol and you killed him with no hesitation, you monster."

There was a long silence, then Raymond got struck in the back of the head with a powerful blow that knocked him to the ground.

William was still standing over him when he lost consciousness. By the time he regained consciousness, he was gone.

Raymond Primeau couldn't believe he was still alive. He truly thought he was dead.

98

Kneeling in front of his petunias for the past half hour, Raymond Primeau wanders in all directions. Gardening is like meditation for him. He feels the need to be anywhere but in the present moment when things are still too painful, too rough. He still regrets breaking into Abygaelle Jensen's apartment, especially since they met at the café. Despite everything, he's worried about her. There is something sinister and dark in her soul. He wouldn't know what exactly, but one day, something terrible will happen, a huge suffering will ensue.

Something like the overwhelming urge that gripped him to the core and drove him to her place. This dark rage that led to his poor decision. He wonders if William inherited this same impulse, if this fury turned him into a savage killer. William's funeral took place five days ago. He was buried in a lot next to his Uncle Maurice and his paternal grandfather, two men he admired. Raymond is sad that they couldn't figure a way to come to peace. All he can hope for is that wherever he is, William understands why he did what he did and forgives him.

His post-mortem video gives him some hope.

Feeling sad, he struggles to stand up. Being on his knees for so long at his age is no picnic. He lifts his face towards the sunlight and closes his eyes. The next few months won't be easy for Monique and him. She is devastated, completely shattered. One would be at less. Not only did her son, whom she cherished the most in the world, die, her second child to take his own life, but he was also the filthy serial killer rampaging through the city. He spread death like an unstoppable tsunami, sweeping away everything in his path. Leaving nothing but mangled corpses and grieving families behind. It wasn't unusual for him to find her sitting in silence, staring straight ahead, tears rolling down her inert cheeks. Her face emaciated with pain.

A presence behind him snapped him out of his torpor. He recognizes a face sprung from his past, a hard and cold one, Maxime Fauvette's figure. The last time he saw him was at a party in Nathalie's memory about five years ago. He would recognize him in a crowd. He was like a son to him.

After observing him for a long time, Raymond shifted away from him and return to his flowers.

"What are you doing here, Maxime?"

Fauvette is standing a few meters behind him, a black cap screwed on his head, sunglasses on and his hands in the pockets of his gray sports jacket.

"I see your petunias are still splendid."

Raymond doesn't react, carrying on, plowing the earth with his little shovel.

"Come on, Raymond," Maxime says in response to his ex-father-in-law's silence. "I won't be long."

Raymond gets up and walks towards him.

"You didn't answer me," he says. "What do you want?"

The reflection in Maxime's sunglasses reflects the severity of his face back to Raymond.

"William is dead. I'm sorry. I know it must be hard for you, and especially for Monique. I just offered her my condolences.

Poor thing, what she's going through right now. She invited me to dinner, and of course I accepted. But first, you and I need to talk. Then we can go on with our lives as if nothing had happened."

Raymond slowly removes his dirt-stained gardening gloves.

"Get to the point, Maxime."

"I will. I've invested a lot in my family, in my career. I have a wife and three children. I'm a senior manager in a financial institution—"

"I already know all that," Raymond says.

"If you know all that, then you'll recognize that I don' t want to lose it all."

Maxime is holding the handle of a knife hidden in the right pocket of his jacket. Raymond has noticed the movement of his hand. He has a belligerent sneer.

"What are you going to do with that?"

Maxime smiles back at him.

"Nothing, I hope. I want your word that I won't have any unpleasant surprises. That the police won't come to my house and ask me about an old topic that we all thought was gone just because someone suddenly had a case of conscience!"

"Are you done?"

"Yeah, I'm done."

"OK. So listen up, fucker. I attempted to take the blame for everything William did, and it almost worked. I gave him a chance, protected him against himself. If he hadn't had such a disproportionate ego, he'd still be alive and kicking today. But no, he needed to prove that he was smarter than everyone else. Unfortunately, in life, there is always someone smarter than you. We are all someone else's fool. I am well aware of his opinion of me, and he surely persuaded you the way he almost convinced my brother."

Maxime listens to him attentively, an insolent smile hanging on his face.

"You can think that I was a coward, that I left Nathalie down, but you're just pretentious young guys who think they know everything. You don't know shit, and William paid with his life for his arrogance. That's what I wanted to avoid. That's why I intended to protect him from himself. The question you must ask yourself now, Maxime. Is whether you'll be smarter than him, or whether you'll be just as dumb? Because I swear, if you follow the same path, you'll end up in the same place. You say you worked hard for what you got? Good for you. Jacques Légaré also worked hard for his family, and William mutilated the body of his fifteen-year-old daughter. Fifteen-years-old, for fuck's sake. He destroyed the poor kid's face so badly she had to be in a close coffin. That, you little shit, is what I live with. Monique lives with it because we created this monster."

Tears of rage roll down the old man's cheeks.

"So if you think I'm afraid of what you might do with what you're hiding in your coat, if you think I'm afraid of dying. You're wrong. I don't give a damn. I regard you and Maurice as being as guilty as William. You supported him in his craziness. You backed him up in his Machiavellian plan despite my pleas not to. But you did it nevertheless with the result that we know. You were part of this slaughter. When you killed the lawyer in cold blood, when you disemboweled him, I understood you all gone mad. Maurice was the first to act, and you followed him like stupid zombies. I refused to do it. You called me a coward. But at least I have peace of mind. Did your actions bring back Natalie? Are you happier today? Do you sleep better at night? Are you at ease with yourself? Do you have nightmares?"

Raymond waits for an answer that will not come. He sneers curtly and nods as he sees the smile fade from Maxim's face.

"If you have a single ounce of intelligence and pride," Raymond says, "you'll pack up your smug face and go back to where you came from. William took the blame for everything. Even for Lavoie's murder instead of Maurice. Even for yours.

He took the blame for everyone. He had a big heart. Just blackened by rage and resentment. The police closed the case even though they had doubts about the confessions. You won the lottery, Maxime. For some reason, William spared you. He saw you as a brother. Be smart enough to seize the opportunity and shut the fuck up. Do you understand me?"

Maxime nods in agreement.

Raymond takes a deep breath and lowers his head.

"Good. So here's what's going to happen. I have no interest in telling the police any more than they need to know. If I had to rat you out, I would have done so already. Like I told you repeatedly, I wanted to sacrifice myself and take the blame for everything before William screwed up. Yes, even for you," he said, squeezing his index finger hard against his chest. "Not too bad for a coward, is it? There have been enough victims, enough broken families. So go back and tell Monique that you can't stay after all, that you've had an emergency call, that you're grateful and then go back to where you came from."

Maxim remains silent.

"But Maxime, look at me. Look me in the eyes," Raymond says, tearing the sunglasses off his face. "This is the last time we see each other and that you talk to my wife. Are we clear? If I see you near my house again, even once, I won't go to the police. I'll kill you with my own hands. I'll make you wish you'd never been born. How dare you threaten me here, in my backyard, when I have always treated you like a son? Consider yourself lucky to walk out of here on your own two feet. I want nothing more to do with you. If we bump into each other in a public place or anywhere else, you just nod and walk away. If anything suspicious happens to Monique, believe me, you'll have to hide for a long time. Do we understand each other?"

After a few seconds, Maxime gives a polite smile and nods.

"No, I want to hear you say it. Do we understand each other, Maxime, yes or no?"

"Yes, Raymond. We understand each other."

"Good. Now, get the fuck out and never come back here."

Raymond gives him his sunglasses back before turning on his heels and kneeling down near his plants. Maxim stands behind, motionless for a few seconds, then leaves quietly to his car parked on the street near the house. Raymond furtively sees Maxime and Monique's shadows talking through the big window at the back, and she hugs him. The sound of the car driving away is sweet to his ears. Monique sits back on the couch, her hands in front of her face.

He can hear her crying in the distance.

EPILOGUE

This is the second time in her career that Abygaelle requested time off at the end of an investigation. Each time, she isolated in a cottage in the Laurentians. The first time, it was after a scabrous case of serial rape of children by a religious community. This case haunted her for years, given her nightmares.

Sitting in a comfortable Adirondack chair on the small veranda overlooking a beautiful lake and a towering mountain, Aby recounts the entire story, from the murder of Ariane Légaré to William Primeau's suicide. She realizes that there are mysteries that aren't meant to be resolved, that she must accept not to know everything and go on her way. She will never grasp the extent of William's anger and why he sacrificed everything to focus on what was plaguing his life.

Why do people ultimately follow their destiny despite the tragedies that tarnish their lives, striving to persevere despite the horror poisoning their minds? William built a life that most people would envy, but it wasn't enough. He could not live knowing that the last survivor of his sister's assailants breathed the same air as he did, even if his involvement in the rape was negligible. Of course, he was guilty of not helping a woman in distress. On the other hand, did he deserve the death penalty? She could see in Ranger's eyes that he was having a hard time settling with his cowardice.

He's a sick, distraught soul. Aby noticed it right away. William had a destiny diametrically opposed to his; as much as Stephane was the perfect example of a troubled being, of a miserable existence, of a pitiful life. As much as William was an epitome of accomplishment, of success and of poise. That in the end, Stephane is still around despite his physical and psychological wounds, and that William chose the path of revenge and suicide, is surprising to say the least. Is it a matter of intelligence? Is it that the more lucid and brilliant one is, the more one understands that life is absurd and that one will never be fully happy? And that the less intellectually gifted people don't realize this?

The thoughtlessness of the weak-minded?

So many unanswered questions. She breathes in the distinctive smell of nature around her. The scent of fir and mud fills her nostrils as the sun's rays shine on her ivory skin.

A frugal yelp from the ground near her feet catches her attention, forcing a wide smile onto her face. The young black labrador she has just adopted is trying to tell her something. He's so cute with his floppy ears and tiny, hyperactive tail. He already loves her as if they have known each other forever. The unconditional affection of animals is reassuring and intoxicating. Far from the calculating and self-serving love of humans. Like many, she finds it easier to connect emotionally with four-legged companions than with her own kind.

She has been rebuilding herself since her teenage years, and perhaps this little ball of fur will help her in her quest to find the true Abygaelle buried deep within her soul. The one who should have prevailed over the caricature full of barriers and taboos that she has become. It made sense for protection when she was younger, but nowadays, she wonders why she lingers in the same defense mechanisms that once saved her from the darkness. If Raymond Primeau could see clearly in her, it means she doesn't hide it as well as she thought.

She named her little dog Zorro. He's black, playful and his white hair on his chest forms a kind of Z. So if another Raymond Primeau tries to break into her home without her knowledge, he will have to deal with him. Zorro restored the dignity of a home she loved before Primeau tarnished it.

She still feels a lot of anger when she thinks about the incident, but not to the same extent as before her chat with him at the café. His reaction, what he said to her afterwards, or perhaps just the fact that she expressed her rage to him, makes it manageable now. Of course, she doesn't rule out taking justice into her own hands one day. But as time goes on, the painful memory becomes less and less intense. She took advantage of her tormentor's advice and focus her energies on saving the world, not destroying it, even if she has more skills in the latter than in the former.

She spoke to Roland Michaud earlier in the day, disclosing her fading desire to get her old job back. But now she wants more than anything to make a name for herself in homicide. She belongs there, she can be as effective as in vice. And while it's a shame that her first investigation involved the most notorious serial killer in the country history, it was actually a blessing.

Whatever lies ahead for her now will never have that level of intensity again. If she can get through this one, if she can nail a smart, methodical, cunning murderer like William Primeau, then she can achieve anything. Especially with Jack and Murielle by her side. Roland Michaud told her he was glad she realized that. He told her, half-heartedly, that it saved him the trouble of turning her down. His decision to try something else was right, and her work on the William Primeau case was proof of that.

She still has this damn lump in her stomach, this unfulfilled feeling about that case. Neither Jack nor Murielle believes that William Primeau could have killed all those people. She doesn't think that Raymond Primeau is as clean as a whistle. But there's an enormous gap between what you think and what you can prove. This is something she realized a long time ago. Your beliefs don't carry any weight if you can't back them up with facts. Then, because William took it all on his shoulders before he died, it nipped in the bud any attempt to reopen the case. So if others are guilty of a murder or murders credited to Primeau, they have a tremendous chance to seize this opportunity and give back to society.

She heard through the grapevine that Raymond Primeau had finally reached out to Heather Ramsay to offer his help while she recovers from the immense shock she suffered. He's taking care of the foundation's operations, which no longer bears his son's name for obvious reasons, since people linked his image to that of a ruthless monster.

Abygaelle still cannot listen to William Primeau's recording yet. She changes the channel as soon as someone mention him. She doesn't want to hear about him no more; she wants to move on. She has not escaped unscathed despite the strength and confidence she displays to her colleagues and the media. Her guilt is still lingering, but it was also the case in Vice. Wanting to save the world is innate in her and she blames herself when she feels she didn't succeed.

She smiles fondly as she watches Zorro lay on his back to bask in the warm rays of the sun. Though she's been broken for as long as she can remember, and each investigation screws up her soul more each time, there's one thing that will keep her alive as long as it's in her.

The hope of healing.

Stephane Ranger is in his apartment, totally depleted of energy. With William Primeau's death, the pressure seems to have died down and every fiber in his body has given out on him. He ran on adrenaline for weeks; he was a key element in the capture of this lunatic. Staging his death was a genius idea by Abygaelle Jensen. At first, he didn't think it would work, but she got it right. Primeau wouldn't stop as long as he was alive. He still doesn't understand why he hated him so much.

These deranged minds rarely use logic, but the bottom line is that because of him, because he was there that fateful night, Ariane, Marc-Andre, Annie, and others died. There was one more he didn't know, and does not know why Primeau killed him. He took it with him to his grave.

He thought that tattooing the names of his mother, Ariane, Marc-André, Maryse and Annie on his chest, where his heart is, would help him get over it. But it didn't. His wound is still there, his guilt just as strong. He fell back into his bad habits. He does drugs regularly. No one cares if he's sober or not, anyway. His demons came back, they didn't have to do anything. Just wait quietly, lurking in the shadows, while his world fell apart. He didn't even try to contact his former boss to get his job back. What was the point?

Especially since the doctors could not remove the bullet from his skull. He now suffers from severe migraines several times a week.

He has nowhere to go but into the sharp claws of the evil spirit. He's trapped, he no longer has the power to go on, he has no reason to do so. He should have figured out sooner what he was dealing with and left this world long before. His death would have saved the lives of so many people if he had known.

But he didn't.

And now he has to live with survivor's guilt. And try to

understand how someone could be so resentful as to sacrifice everything he has. His wife, his children, a successful career. When he looks at William's photos, he doesn't see a sick individual; he doesn't see a madman or a sadistic killer. He doesn't see someone helpless, enraged, and out of control. He's dead now. What a mess! So many dead bodies, so many grieving families.

All for this? How soul-crushingly sad.

It's dark in his living room. He stands in the middle of the room, disillusioned. For several minutes, he kept an eye on the tree in front of the bay window of his apartment. This tree has been his anchor for ages, the symbol of a new life, of the end of his addiction. They have a fusional relationship. He looks at it, like a farewell.

He tied a rope to an anchor on the ceiling. He has shaped a noose, and slides a chair just below. He looks at his bulwark, the fir tree, but doesn't see how the conifer could save his sinking soul. He has no answer for him; it looks bland and disconcerted. Has he let him down too? He moves towards the chair, but stops. He turns around to glance at the tree again. The sun's rays pierce it and penetrate the apartment like a biblical painting. He looks at the chair, then at the tree, then at the chair again. It's too late. He has never felt so alone.

He climbs on the chair and slips his head into the knot, tightens the rope around his neck. He glances at the tree. The sun's rays have increased and now flood the apartment, like a warm, dreamy blanket. One of the sun's rays touches his foot.

He sighs and closes his eyes.

Would you like to support the author?

. . .

First of all, thank you for reading the first novel in the Abygaelle Jensen series. We hope you enjoyed it. If you did, we would really appreciate it if you could take a few minutes of your time to leave your review where you bought this novel. Reviews are really important to authors and allow other readers to discover them.

If you would like to receive two FREE short novels, introducing you to two more of the author's literary styles, sign up for Sebastyen's newsletter and download your starter library.

ABOUT THE AUTHOR

Sebastyen Dugas is an author from Montreal, Canada. He publishes in both French and English. He started his career as a journalist and then switched to a career in computer science.

Writing has always been a passion for Sebastyen for as long as he can remember. He loved to write for his own pleasure as well as contribute to blogs for other publications.

In his spare time, Sebastyen enjoys reading, photography and film. He loves to travel and has already visited more than twenty countries.

In the coming years, he wants to continue to travel the world, write more fiction and enjoy life.

You can reach Sebastyen on his website or on social media.

facebook.com/sebastyendugaswriter

twitter.com/TalkWithTheY

instagram.com/sebastyendugas

ALSO BY SEBASTYEN DUGAS

Martin Lafs Series

Epiphany From a Broken Camera

Don't Find Roger

Brevis Series

Death Ride

Stockholm

Published by Urbanum Edition

Printed in Great Britain
by Amazon

76967868R00293